How to Accidentally Fall on an Elf
The Chaos Between Us Book 1
Dionna White

DionnaWrites

Copyright © (2026 Dionna White)

All rights reserved. No part of this publication may be reproduced, distributed, or transmitted in any form or by any means, including photocopying, recording, or other electronic or mechanical methods, without the prior written permission of the publisher, except in the case of brief quotations embodied in critical reviews and certain other noncommercial uses permitted by copyright law.

This book is a work of fiction. Names, characters, businesses, organizations, places, events, and incidents are products of the author's imagination or are used fictitiously. Any resemblance to actual persons, living or dead, events or locales is entirely coincidental.

Internal book design by: Ann Bugarin

Cover design by: Ann Bugarin

Map design by: Alan Mike

ISBN Paperback: 979-8-218-86343-2

First Edition: (04/2026)

How to Accidentally Fall on an Elf

Step one: Run away from home.
Step two: Land on a handsome elf.
Step three: Fall in love.

Dionna White

DEDICATION

To Mr. Gray, who wouldn't stop walking on my laptop while I tried to write.

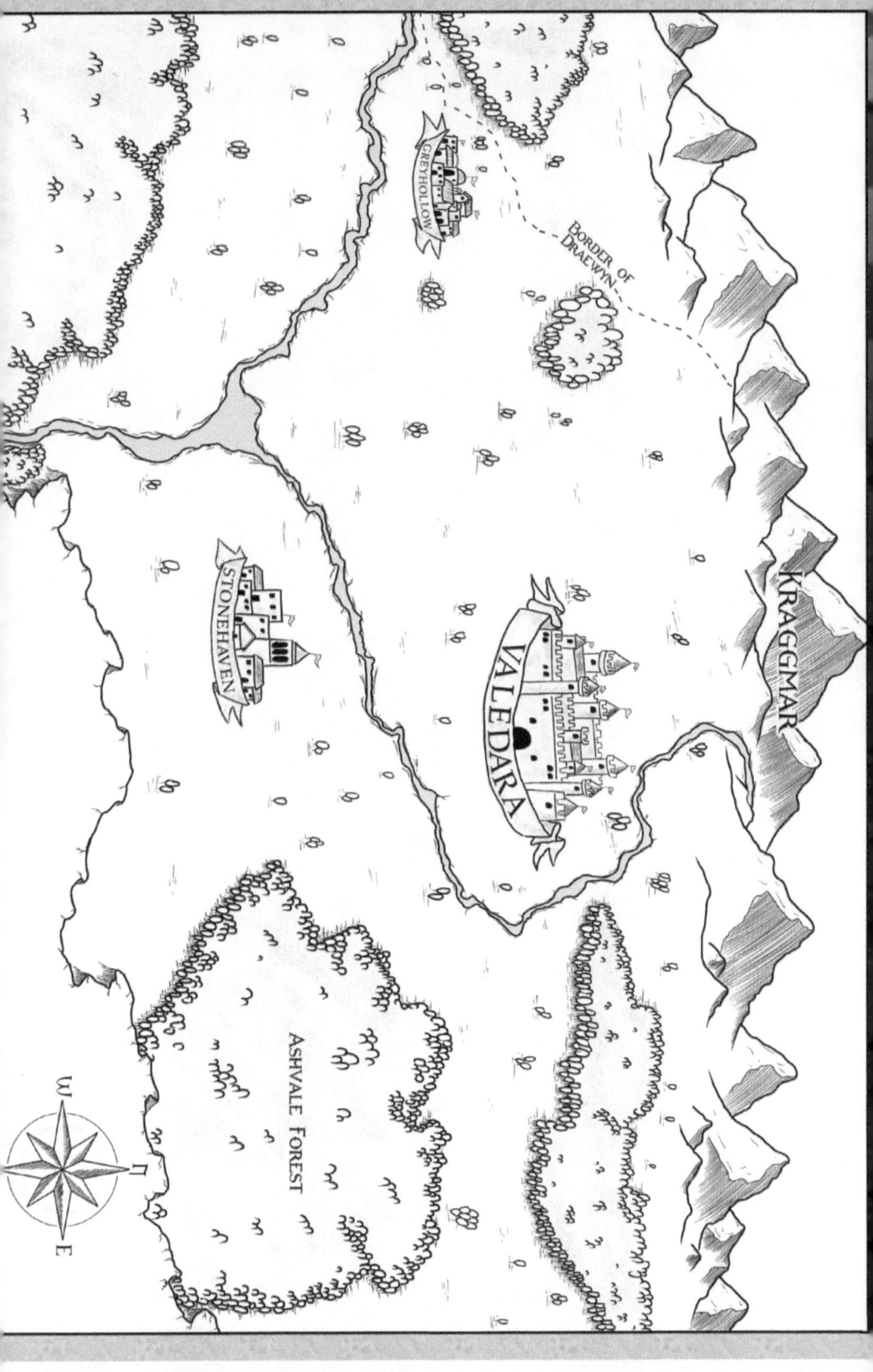

1

Esther

HOW TO SURVIVE ROYALTY: PRETEND EVERYTHING IS FINE WHILE ABSOLUTELY NOTHING IS FINE.

Princess Esther Valedara had read enough romance novels to know that no heroine ever found love between magic lessons and etiquette drills. Unfortunately for her, that *was* her entire schedule: magic, etiquette, and embroidery.

But first, she had to survive breakfast, a monumental task she was forced to endure every day. Just like her lessons, it never got any better. She took a deep breath, grounding herself, then pushed through the door. It was time for her personal hell to kick off another day.

Morning light spilled through the arched windows in soft pastels, warming the carved stone pillars and the long table set for thirty, though only three seats were ever filled anymore.

Esther slipped inside, smoothing her simple blue morning dress, trying to make her footsteps as quiet as possible. But the moment she entered, her father, King Arcturus, shot up a little too fast in his chair, like he'd been caught slouching. Lupin lurched to his feet, his chair scraping loudly against the floor.

"Good morning," King Arcturus said, his voice far too formal for a man greeting his daughter. He cleared his throat. "You, ah. Slept well?"

Esther curtsied and replied in her most practiced formal tone. "Yes, Father."

Lupin nodded sharply, almost military. "Good." Then he sat, immediately stood again, panicked, and sat once more, like a malfunctioning marionette.

Esther slowly took her seat, doing her best not to look uncomfortable.

"I noticed some military marching out earlier," Esther commented, trying to pass it off as a random, passing thought.

"Just some trouble at the borders," King Arcturus said. "Nothing to concern yourself with."

Esther nodded, biting her lip. They returned to a heavy, awkward silence that settled in her chest. No matter how long they had lived together, she had never learned how to talk to her family.

A servant poured tea. The King watched the cup with the intensity of someone observing a delicate medical procedure. Lupin stared at the fruit bowl as though it personally threatened him.

Finally, King Arcturus tried again. "Your embroidery lesson is today."

"Yes." Esther folded her hands in her lap. "It is."

"Enjoyable?" His tone sounded like an interrogation.

She shrugged. "It's fine."

King Arcturus cleared his throat.

Lupin wiped nonexistent crumbs from his plate.

Esther fiddled with her fork.

"Well," Lupin said abruptly, pushing a book across the table toward her, "I found this. I thought, maybe, you might…" He froze halfway through, eyes widening. "Not that you're childish. Or that you need distraction. Or—"

Esther looked down at the worn leather cover. He had clearly picked it with care. Something warm fluttered in her chest.

She pushed it away before it could settle.

She had long since stopped clinging to the small moments of warmth she received from her family. They never lasted.

"It's nice," she murmured, stroking the soft cover. "Thank you."

"You're welcome."

"Father," Esther cleared her throat. "The maids have been talking about a new bakery that opened on Round Rook Road. Do you think—"

"No," her father said with finality.

"But what if Lady Irene chaperoned me?" Esther pleaded. "Or you could assign a guard to me!"

"It is not wise for you to leave the castle," Lupin said, his voice stern.

"I promise I'll be careful."

"Being careful is not the issue."

"But—"

Esther's father slammed his cup down, stifling her words. The rest of the meal passed in silence.

Finally, Esther set down her fork. "I should get ready for lessons."

Both men immediately pushed their chairs back and stood. Lupin nearly knocked over his water but managed to catch it at the last second. Her father smoothed his coat, even though it hadn't shifted at all.

"Have a good day," he said, his voice formal once more.

Lupin nodded quickly. "Give Sir Basil my regards."

Esther offered a small smile that felt too thin. "I will. Thank you."

Valedara Castle had been built in three distinct eras, each visible in the walls if one knew where to look. The east wing bore the soft curves and floral motifs of Queen Elaerya's reign, warm, inviting architecture that suggested the ruler had been fond of music, art, and throwing far too many festivals. The west wing, by contrast, was sharp-edged and reinforced, built by King Thamar the Ironhearted during a century of border conflict. Thick walls. Narrow windows. Everything about it whispered: survive first, celebrate later.

Esther preferred Elaerya's wing.

Her father's council, however, had been meeting more frequently in the fortified rooms of the west wing, and the shift had not gone unnoticed. Guards stood taller. Servants whispered.

Even the air carried a tension it hadn't held during her childhood, when she remembered, perhaps imagined, the palace smelling more of lavender cakes and fresh parchment than metal polish.

The irony was that Valedara was known across the continent as "The Gentle Kingdom."

Yet inside its marble walls, the gentleness had been slowly suffocating for years.

When she was out of earshot, she let out a loud, frustrated sigh.

As she walked, her gaze drifted to the long corridor of royal portraits lining the wall. Decades of rulers stared back at her, beginning with King Lexon, founder of Valedara. The line of kings and queens continued in steady succession until it reached the final frame: her parents, painted in rich oils, frozen in a moment she barely remembered. Beside them hung a space, waiting patiently, almost expectantly, for the next monarch.

Every kingdom chose heirs differently, but in Valedara, she could have been queen. The law allowed it. Tradition welcomed it. But she had no desire to fight Lupin for the role.

He was steady, dutiful, everything a ruler should be.

And she...

She had nothing to offer.

She tore her eyes away and continued down the pristine corridor, feeling more like an intruder than a princess.

She wished she were a princess locked in a tower. Then maybe she'd be whisked away by a knight with wind-tossed hair and eyes full of adventure. But this wasn't a tower guarded by a dragon. It was a fortress guarded by men whose armor clinked like chains.

Her father called it "protection."

Esther called it "house arrest with snacks."

Even the snacks were more decorative than edible, bittersweet, cold pastries dusted with sugar she could barely taste, because Baroness Irene Levon's voice still echoed in her head: "Watch your figure, Princess."

She would never forget the lecture she received when she asked why she had to watch her figure when they were going to crush her ribcage with a corset regardless.

She was currently trudging toward the best of her least favorite lessons.

Her gown whispered around her ankles, layers of silk and satin in shades of royal blue that caught the light like water. Gold embroidery itched along her sleeves. Her jewelry clinked with every step, tiny reminders that even her beauty had weight. And the shoes, those cursed heels, pinched with every movement, each step a lesson in balance and suffering. Whoever created the blasted shoes hated women and believed the world needed more tripping hazards.

Her maid and best friend, Lucy, prattled beside her, cheerful and relentless, like someone who refused to fade into the background no matter how often the palace tried to make her.

Lucy talked like she always did—fast, bright, unfiltered—because silence in the palace had teeth. If she stopped filling the air, she disappeared. So she stayed loud.

Her ponytail swung like a pendulum, keeping time with her quick, light steps, the complete opposite of Esther's dragging gait. Esther wished she could borrow a sprinkle of her energy.

"Pretend you're a statue," Lucy said, nudging Esther's shoulders straighter. "But with more attitude."

Esther groaned. "Statues don't have to smile through magic lessons or wear corsets that make breathing optional."

She glared at Lucy's small waist, which held nothing more than an apron tied around it: no corset crushing her organs, just comfortable clothes with pockets. The scent of cinnamon still lingered faintly on Lucy's sleeves. Warm, sweet, and cruelly tempting.

The guards stood rigid as Esther passed, their armor polished to a mirror shine. They didn't smile at her anymore. No one in the palace really did. Ever since rumors of border skirmishes began creeping into council meetings, the entire castle had tightened like a clenched jaw. Servants walked more quietly. Ministers whispered behind stacks of maps. Even the air felt heavier, as if the walls themselves were bracing for bad news.

Valedara demanded perfection from its royals, composure, control, and elegance. A flawless façade for a kingdom beginning to fracture at the edges. Sometimes Esther wondered if the palace was so pristine because everyone inside was afraid to leave a trace, fearful that any imperfection might crack the illusion of stability.

Her eyes drifted back to the nearest portrait, the one she always lingered on without meaning to.

Her mother.

Queen Estella's likeness glowed softly beneath the chandeliers, painted in warm golds and rose hues. People still spoke of her as if she had been carved from sunlight, radiant, beloved, the kind of queen who could warm even the coldest marble hall. Esther tried to remember her voice, her face, anything real... but all she ever grasped were feelings. Warmth. Safety. A sense of being held.

Some servants still left white blossoms beneath her mother's portrait. Quiet offerings. Unspoken grief. Queen Estella had been the kind of ruler people told stories about long after the storytellers themselves had died, graceful, empathetic, powerful without ever being cruel. The kingdom flourished under her reign. People said gardens bloomed brighter when she walked through them, that children stopped crying when she bent down to their height.

Esther had no memories sharp enough to confirm any of it.

Just warmth.

And the soft shape of a smile she wasn't sure she hadn't invented.

The older nobles still compared Esther to her mother, though never in ways meant to comfort.

"Estella had perfect posture."

"Estella mastered fire theory by age fourteen."

"Estella would never set a tutor on fire, dear."

Esther desperately wanted to resemble her mother, yet every time her magic flared uncontrollably, or panic choked her, she felt further from that ideal, as if she were a rough sketch of a masterpiece she could never replicate.

Sometimes she thought the palace missed her mother more than it loved *her*.

"Posture," Lucy said, tapping her elbow. "Shoulders back. Chin up. Look expensive." She mimicked the Baroness, throwing her shoulders back, hands on her hips, nose turned up. "You'll be in for one hell of a lecture if Baroness Levon sees you."

"She's already here?" Esther groaned. She looked out the window at the pink sky. The sun had barely risen, and her etiquette lesson wasn't until half past noon.

"For a while now. I had the joy of serving her tea in the guest lounge."

"Why is she so early?" Esther exhaled, already anticipating Lucy's response. She was surprised the Baroness hadn't insisted on having a room in the palace, there was plenty to spare after her father cut the number of servants.

"Because she's a cuckoo bird. Your lessons should've ended years ago, but she's clinging to the hope that your father will notice her one day as long as she sticks around. You're just a victim of her cause." Lucy sighed dramatically.

Esther wasn't sold on Lucy's theory about the Baroness. She had worked with Esther since she could barely walk and was said to be her mother's close friend. Yes, Esther was twenty-one and should have finished her lessons years ago. And the Baroness was at the castle every day, all day. But she never went out of her way to be in the king's presence. It was all very suspicious. Not cuckoo-bird suspicious, just weirdly suspicious.

They stopped at the door to the practice chamber. The wooden surface was carved with glowing runes, pulsing faintly like a heartbeat. They had been put there the first time Esther set a tutor on fire. The tutor quit the same day they started. It was hard to get a teacher after that.

Lucy handed her a biscuit wrapped in cloth, its buttery scent instantly grounding her. "Here, I snatched this from the kitchen. Sugar helps your spells behave."

Esther took it, warmth seeping into her fingers. "If you weren't my maid, I'd knight you."

Lucy grinned. "If I were a knight, wait, am I a guy or a girl knight?"

"Why does it matter?"

"I need to know what equipment I'm working with!" she said, crossing her arms. "Anyway, semantics later. Try not to set any chairs loose this time. Basil can't afford any more grays in his hair."

Esther cringed at the memory. In the last lesson, she had accidentally brought an innocent chair to life while trying to heat some tea. The chair ran away on all four of its animated legs, Basil still atop it. It scurried like a weird spider and was eventually found in the barn, where the sheep ate it. Such a tragedy: to bring life into something only for it to be immediately consumed by farm life. Since then, Basil had been hunting for a rune sigil that could be added to the room to contain anything like that.

"No promises," Esther muttered.

Lucy gave her a final, reassuring pat on the back before sprinting down the hall, her comfortable-looking shoes squeaking on the floor.

Esther exhaled and stepped inside the room, wishing she had the same luxury of comfortable shoes to help her endure the lessons.

The chamber smelled faintly of smoke and wet stone. Scorch marks decorated the floor like souvenirs from past disasters.

Magic hummed faintly beneath the tiles, like a heartbeat beneath stone. Esther had grown up surrounded by it, woven into the architecture, embroidered into banners, but understanding magic and controlling it were very different things.

Every mage was taught the same fundamentals:

Magic comes from emotion.

Runes give it shape.

Runespires keep it safe.

The first two rules Esther understood well enough; the third she found deeply insulting. A runespire was meant to focus a mage's power, jewelry inscribed with microscopic sigils capable of containing unruly spellwork: necklaces, earrings, bracelets, even anklets, if one lacked dignity. The palace owned hundreds. And while they worked flawlessly on most people...

...Esther's magic tended to ignore them.

Or melt them.

Or occasionally fling them across the room with enough force to crack a window.

Lucy once joked that Esther's magic wasn't fire, lightning, or heat, it was pure spite. Basil refused to confirm or deny.

Other kingdoms categorized magic differently. In Kraggmar, it was considered a sign of ancestral blessing. In elven lands, it was treated like a craft, something to refine as patiently as glassblowing.

But here in Valedara?

Magic was treated like a tool. And sometimes a weapon. And in Esther's case, a liability.

Golden magic was rare. Revered. Feared.

But no one could explain why hers behaved like it had opinions.

Sir Basil was already there, looking as nervous as he always did before a lesson. His hair was brown, streaked with gray, and he dressed as if he'd been personally wronged by fashion. He had been with her since she was sixteen, and the exhaustion showed in the deep lines of his brow.

"Greetings, Sir Basil." Esther curtsied.

"Enough with the formalities, Princess. Ready for another lesson in control?"

"That depends," Esther said, dragging herself to the center of the room, slouching again now that Lucy was gone. Basil cared less about her posture than about surviving the lesson. "Are we measuring success by the number of fires or the size of the explosion?"

The faint charred scent from last week's disaster still clung to the walls. Those pea-green curtains were ugly anyway, so Esther decided her magic had done everyone a favor by burning them.

He sighed. "Neither. Today we practice patience. Remember: magic mirrors your heart. Control that, and you'll control your power."

"Right, right. Control my heart. Easy. I'll just bottle up twenty-one years of emotions. Problem solved."

Esther twirled a strand of her too-perfect honey-blonde hair. Her maids had put it in a half-up style, adorned with ruby hairpins that they claimed made her amber eyes 'pop.' She didn't know what that meant. She just sat there, as always, while the maids prattled on about their clothing choices to each other, excluding her. They never spoke to her directly.

"Let's begin," Basil said, pretending not to hear her. "We'll start with drying this towel. Fire is just concentrated heat. So. Calm thoughts. Gentle heat. No explosions."

He handed her the damp towel, which dripped faintly onto the rune circle she stood in, a precaution her first tutor had insisted upon when she was ten, though it had flooded the entire second wing of the castle. It took weeks to fix all the water damage.

Now, this room had so many runes encrusted in it that almost any disastrous lesson could be contained.

Almost. Their previous lesson had proven that no matter how protected a room was, there was always a way for Esther to dismantle it.

Esther carefully picked up the damp towel with two fingers, as if it were a deadly weapon. "Okay. Calm thoughts. Gentle heat. Minimal explosions." She closed her eyes and pictured serenity: a still pond, a clear sky, a woman who didn't want to scream into a pillow.

The towel twitched. Gold static sizzled. Steam curled up from the corners. Basil's left eye started to twitch in sync.

"Steady," he cautioned, taking a significant step back.

"I'm perfectly steady," Esther lied.

The towel hissed.

Then, *whoosh!*

A jet of water shot forward, splattering Basil full in the chest. Luckily, it didn't look boiling.

"Princess!" he sputtered, dripping, his robes clinging to him in a way that made him look like a drowned terrier. Not all men were attractive when wet, it seemed.

"In my defense, the towel is dry now," Esther said sheepishly, holding it out to her mentor. She tried, and failed, to hide the twitch at the corners of her lips.

If only it had ended there, but no. The towel flopped from her hands and, of course, came to life.

"Bad towel! Stop that!"

It didn't stop.

It slithered across the floor like a deformed snake and wrapped around Basil's leg like an affectionate pet.

Basil pinched the bridge of his nose and muttered something about early retirement. Esther could have sworn she saw more hairs turning gray right before her eyes.

The door burst open. "I heard a splash!"

"And the loud one returns," Basil groaned. "This isn't good for my blood pressure."

Lucy surveyed the chaos: the towel, the puddles, Basil's soaked robes, and his twitching eye. "You drowned your tutor again, didn't you?"

"It was an accident," Esther said, her face flushed from holding back laughter.

Basil wiped his glasses. "Princess, please. I beg you, breathe before you bring something to life. How do you even manage to do such high-level magic by accident?"

Lucy grinned, leaning against the doorframe. "Progress! Last week we lost a chair."

"Is that why you have a net prepared?" Basil asked, his voice full of exasperation.

"I'm always prepared!" Lucy puffed out her chest, proud of her vigilance. "Speaking of which, I brought the new book you wanted." She pulled the rectangular, brown paper-wrapped item out of her apron pocket.

Esther's eyes lit up. "You found it?"

Lucy smirked. "Straight from the underground steamy book club: Proper Etiquette for Improper Thoughts."

Basil grimaced. "Lucy, no—"

"Lucy, yes," she said, handing the book to Esther. "Don't worry, Basil. It's just about... dancing."

Esther unwrapped the brown paper as if it were treasure. "Dancing sounds nice."

Lucy winked. "Especially the horizontal kind."

Basil choked. "Lucy!"

"What? It's educational."

Esther bit back a laugh. "Lucy, one day you're going to get us both exiled."

"Maybe," Lucy said with a grin. "But first, it's time for embroidery."

Esther muttered curses as Lucy ushered her out. The smell of smoke and sugar trailed behind them.

Maybe, Esther thought, as she glanced back at the chaos, she could find a tower to hide in after all. She might even hire a dragon to burn it down.

2

Esther

How to stay composed: first panic, then panic harder, then make a terrible decision with confidence.

"You only stabbed your finger three times today," Lucy praised with a sympathetic smile. "But what exactly is this supposed to be?"

"A dragon," Esther said, massaging her aching fingers.

"Looks like a slug," Lucy hummed. Esther snatched the handkerchief from her judgmental friend with a huff. If she squinted really hard, it was obviously a dragon! Slugs didn't have horns or breathe fire. The orange thread was obviously fire. Lucy was too blind to see the masterpiece before her.

"Dragons are strong and powerful—"

"And majestic, unlike this slug."

"And offer protection! Which I will give to my brother." Esther anxiously rubbed the fabric between her fingers, feeling the loose, scratchy thread.

"May this valiant slug offer its slimy protection."

"Just for that, you'll be joining me for tea," Esther said, sticking her tongue out.

Lucy froze mid-step. She turned slowly, eyes wide with dramatic horror. "Esther, please. I beg your forgiveness!"

"You are coming to tea," Esther said, taking her by the arm.

Lucy placed a hand on her heart. "This is a cruel punishment for your faithful maid, who only told you the truth!"

"It's just tea," Esther insisted.

"With the Baroness," Lucy hissed, while Esther dragged her by the elbow.

They walked into the sunlit sitting room. The Baroness stood waiting, tall and immaculate in dove-gray silk, her expression carved from authority. The table between them was arranged as flawlessly as a military presentation.

She surveyed them with the efficiency of someone taking inventory.

"There you are," the Baroness said. "Late."

Esther checked the clock again. "We are early."

"You are late," the Baroness repeated, pointing at the chairs. "Sit."

Lucy muttered under her breath as she sat.

"More importantly," the Baroness said, sipping her tea, "I heard the news that Lupin is preparing to travel to Kraggmar. Took your father and brother long enough to finally agree to the political marriage."

"Marriage?" Esther sputtered, her fingers tightening in her lap. "To the orc kingdom surrounded by jagged peaks?"

Kraggmar.

The name alone summoned half-remembered images from her childhood lessons, jagged volcanic mountains clawing into stormy skies, and fortresses carved directly from obsidian cliffs. Orc culture valued strength, honor, and endurance. Esther valued... embroidery and crying quietly in hallways. Not exactly a promising cultural fit.

Somewhere in Basil's endless scrolls, she had seen maps of Kraggmar's northern valleys, howling with winter winds even in summer. Their king, stern, seasoned, rumored to have united the fractured clans decades ago, was respected across continents.

But to Esther, this didn't feel like an alliance at all.

It felt like exile wrapped in ceremonial brocade.

"Oh, it appears I spoke out of turn. Act as if I said nothing."

"You can't just pretend you didn't say anything!" Lucy shouted, slamming the table.

"Manners!"

"You can't just pretend you didn't say anything," Lucy repeated, this time in a far more appropriate tone.

"But I didn't say anything."

"Did you—did she—oh, she's a demon. A vile demon," Lucy seethed.

"Well, look at the time. It's getting late. Let us meet again tomorrow, after you talk with your father."

Esther didn't wait for another word. She raced down the hall, leaving Lucy to deal with the sputtering Baroness.

She imagined jagged peaks clawing at storm clouds, and the sharp, iron scent of the forges that crafted orcish armor, the complete opposite of Valedara, with its lush forests and clear rivers streaming through valleys.

She stood outside her father's study, gathering the courage to knock. She wanted answers.

The council meetings had been changing lately. Esther could feel it in the way advisors bowed more quickly, spoke more quietly, and glanced at her for longer. Something had shifted in Valedara, something her father refused to name.

Lupin, despite his awkwardness, had begun to carry himself differently, too. Straighter posture. Sharper eyes. As if he knew more than he wished he did, as if he bore secrets heavier than armor.

Her father... he had always been distant, but lately, he looked exhausted. Not physically, but in the way people look when they are losing battles no one else can see.

Esther pressed closer to the door.

She didn't want to be a pawn.

She just wanted to know.

Just as she was about to knock, her father's deep voice penetrated the thick door. "This is the only secure way to establish our alliance with Kraggmar."

Esther froze. She could barely make out the muffled voices beyond the door and seized the opportunity. She pressed her ear against the wall, straining to focus on the conversation.

"Isn't this marriage a bit too sudden?" Lupin asked in a hushed tone.

"We're out of time. Our borders won't last much longer," her father said, his words cold and final. "We need this union. Now."

The air crackled around her, magic biting at her fingertips. This was a conversation she was not meant to hear. Just like always, it was about her, with no room for her voice.

Her stomach twisted. Kraggmar. The orc kingdom. The one with a fifty-year-old king.

Her mind spiraled. She tried to imagine her future husband, who probably had warts. And now, apparently, an arranged marriage to her.

She pressed closer to the door, her heart pounding so loudly it drowned out their hushed voices. Eavesdropping was wrong, but it was the only way Esther could gather information. Her father would always say something like, "This doesn't concern you," or some other version of 'stop asking questions' when she tried to learn things directly.

She tried to get as close to the cracked door as possible, her heart thumping when the floorboard creaked beneath her. She stopped breathing, afraid she had given away her presence. But after a silence that stretched over several agonizing heartbeats, the conversation continued.

Her father sighed, his voice tired. "It's the only way to secure peace. She will adapt. We'll announce the engagement at the Harvest Ball."

For a moment, she stood frozen, her heartbeat lodged in her throat.

It wasn't just fear twisting inside her. It was betrayal.

They hadn't warned her.

Hadn't spoken to her.

Hadn't even considered her voice.

A memory surfaced, her father laughing as he hoisted her onto his shoulders during the Harvest Festival. Lupin handed her candied apples. A time when she believed she could earn their affection simply by being good, quiet, perfect.

Somewhere along the way, she had slipped from daughter to duty.

Esther, useless princess of Valedara, was about to be married off to an old orc king with a wart. They'd finally found a use for her, a sacrifice for a treaty wrapped in silk—a stain scrubbed from their perfect view.

Her ears rang. The room tilted. Her already too-tight corset seemed to shrink two sizes.

She spun on her heel and bolted down the hall, skirts whispering furiously. Her shoes clicked on the marble floors that caught the orange light of the dying sun. The chilled air grew hot and suffocating and candles flared as she rushed by.

She cursed the architects who had designed the halls absurdly long. It felt like an eternity until she finally arrived at her personal chambers.

She slammed her door. Then, remembering her etiquette training, she opened it again to close it more gently.

She fell to her knees with ragged breath. She tried to catch her breath, but the air, heavy with polish and wax, refused to satisfy her lungs.

"Calm thoughts, gentle heat," she muttered, quoting Basil. "No explosions."

Maybe she had misheard. She had caused many explosions lately; perhaps it had taken a toll on her hearing.

A nearby candle flickered nervously.

"Calm thoughts, no explosions," she repeated over and over in a trembling voice.

The candle responded by doing the exact opposite, and exploded. She wondered why there were so many candles in the palace and decided she wasn't the problem. The problem was the unnecessary number of candles that could blow up.

Smoke curled up the walls. Esther groaned. "Of course. My life's burning down before the wedding even starts."

For a moment, she considered letting everything burn, letting her magic consume her until nothing remained that could be sold. Maybe then, she could be free.

Crack!

Esther glanced over and met her eyes in a mirror that cracked like a spiderweb.

Her reflection stared back: singed hair, red eyes, and a less-than-perfect posture—the disgraced princess of the Valedara royal family.

"Oh, fantastic," she sobbed. "Even the mirror's judging me."

The pieces of glass tinked against the overly polished floor, almost like a sad melody, scratching the pristine surface Esther hated so much.

Basil's favorite catchphrase surfaced as she looked at the previously flawless mirror. The beautiful golden frame remained perfect, as if to mock her, stunning on the outside, empty and broken on the inside.

She had never seen such a perfect symbol. Seeing it ignited something inside her.

Ambition.

She didn't want to sit around and accept everything as she always had. She wanted to taste freedom, even if just for a moment.

She glared at the glistening shards of glass and made up her mind.

She recited a quote she had read at least a million times. "She'd never been allowed to choose a single thing in her life," she whispered to the shards. "Tonight, she'll choose freedom... even if it kills her."

It was from chapter ten of Love, Lust, and a Locked Tower, the first forbidden book Lucy had ever smuggled to her when they were teenagers. It had been Esther's first taste of secret rebellion, reading books unfit for a royal lady.

It felt symbolic to use a quote from her first rebellion to start her next one. She repeated the words, savoring how right they felt on her tongue. Dramatic, yet perfect.

She wanted to erase everything that made her look royal. First, she kicked off her heels, which had blistered her feet. Then she loosened her corset and let her heavy silks tumble to the floor. She stripped away everything else until only her undergarments remained.

Even then, she still felt too royal. There was nothing more she could change. She twirled her hair, brainstorming what else she could do to alter her appearance, to remove more of the shackles holding her.

Then it dawned on her. There was one more thing she could change.

Esther grabbed the small embroidery scissors her instructor had insisted she keep in her room. She had argued that she would never need them in the sanctuary of her personal chambers. Now, finally, she did.

Her hands shook with a mixture of fear and excitement. She lifted the cold metal to her shoulder and took a deep breath.

Snip.

She froze. She looked at the lock of hair pooling at her feet. Her whole body trembled, panic and exhilaration mingling through her. She inhaled deeply, then snipped another lock, the panic ebbing as more hair fell softly to the ground.

She picked up the largest shard of the mirror to inspect her work. She looked horrible. Her face was a splotchy red, her eyes swollen, and her uneven hair fell just above her shoulders in jagged strands. Despite the mess staring back at her, for the first time, she actually recognized the girl in the reflection.

"Hi," she said softly to the new *her*. "You look like bad decisions and freedom." The bad decision was not checking the mirror before hacking at her hair like a frenzied lumberjack.

Then came the supplies. For the first time, she had to pack, not her servants, *her*. And she had absolutely no clue what a runaway princess should take on an adventure toward freedom.

Was she excited? Scared? She didn't know. What she did know was that she was about to do something crazy and think about the consequences afterward, not before. Because if she had thought ahead, she might have stopped and avoided attempting magic she had only glanced at in a spellbook.

She was confident she could draw the simple six-pointed star inside a circle. The spell itself wasn't the problem, but she had never been allowed even to attempt it. Her father and brother strictly forbade it, fearing she might do something absurd, like create a black hole.

She gulped, imagining all the ways the spell could go wrong. Her lips trembled into a grin. Maybe she laughed. Maybe she cried. Hard to tell with her heartbeat thundering in her ears.

She steeled herself because there was no turning back. She had already chopped off her hair. So if she didn't disappear, she risked turning to dust before the Baroness's lecture was over. She did not want to be sentenced to death by lecture.

She threw on her softest travel dress (the one she technically wasn't allowed to wear), wrapped a cloak around herself, and grabbed a satchel. Inside went: eight romance novels (for reference), a hair ribbon (for emergencies), and the now slightly smushed pastry (for sugary support).

"That should do it. Who needs bread when you have smut?"

She stood in the middle of her room, taking in everything one last time—the book her brother had given her. The stack of embroidery mishaps was shoved under her bed. The portrait of her mother at Esther's age. Lastly, her eyes landed on her desk. The quill pen her father had given her on her sixteenth birthday sat pristinely beside decorative paper.

Esther slowly walked over, thinking of all the things she should say before she left. But she didn't have time.

She settled on two short letters:

Father,
I love you. But I am not a treaty. Please don't send anyone after me who isn't
  fireproof. Better yet, don't send anyone.
—Esther
P.S. Tell Basil I dried the towel.

And another:

Lucy,

If I die, burn my extra secret books. You know where they are. Love you forever.
—Esther

P.S. You'd be a male knight, to gloat about having the biggest sword. Very important.

If she had more time, she would have written letters to Basil and the Baroness as well, but she didn't know what would be appropriate. She wanted to thank them for never giving up on her and to apologize for not being a good princess.

She sniffed and blinked hard, willing herself not to cry. She gave herself a moment to collect herself before making either the best or the worst decision of her life.

"What happened to your hair?" Lucy's shout split the quiet, immediately muffled by Esther's palm over her mouth. Esther both loved and hated her friend's uncanny timing. At that moment, it leaned more toward hate.

"What happened to knocking?" Esther whispered, releasing her hand from Lucy's mouth.

"I haven't knocked on your door since my first day as your personal maid. Now tell me why you look like that." Lucy spread her arms wide, gesturing at Esther's entire being. She didn't know where to begin. The mismatched, untied boots, wrinkled cloak, and wrongly buttoned dress all painted a picture of a woman who didn't know how to dress herself. Because she didn't, and it couldn't have been more painfully obvious.

"Long story. Short version: arranged marriage. Warted orc king. I'm leaving."

Lucy peeked into Esther's satchel as she straightened her buttons and cloak. "You packed eight books and no food?"

"I have a cinnamon roll!"

"You can't even start a fire," she grumbled, kneeling to swap Esther's boots to match.

"Actually, I always start fires," Esther said, pointing at the puddle of what used to be a candle and the slightly singed curtains.

"Why is it always the curtains?" Lucy shoved two meat pies into Esther's satchel. "Here. Try not to die stupid."

"I'll try my best."

"Good girl." Lucy squeezed her tightly with trembling arms. "Go before I cry and think better of not stopping you."

"I love you." Esther hugged her back hard, holding back her own tears, then ran. She was grateful for the embrace before she disappeared. She might have regretted it otherwise if they had never seen each other again.

"Yeah," Lucy's voice cracked. "I'll buy you as much time as I can. Now go."

Esther ran without looking back. If she did, she couldn't trust herself to keep going. She just wanted to see one more place before she left, the only place she could ever breathe and feel alive.

The garden her mother had loved so dearly.

She couldn't remember her face anymore, aside from portraits. But she still faintly remembered having scones and milk with her mother during afternoon tea in this garden.

"Mother," she said softly into the wind, "if you can hear me, please don't let me die stupid. Or messy."

She took a deep breath. She had never used a teleportation spell before; her father had strictly forbidden it. But she had read about it. She decided not to think about how it could go wrong. She would deal with whatever happened after.

She drew the rune sigil she vaguely remembered into the ground.

The wind whipped her cloak. Golden static tickled her skin, warming the cool air around her.

She closed her eyes and let go. Mind blank. Emotions as empty as she could muster.

The world bent, light flared, and then she vanished into a golden fog.

Lucy's voice echoed in the background.

"Don't die stupid!"

3

Esther

How to make an unforgettable entrance: like a sparkly duck.

Lucy jinxed Esther with her parting shouts.

She screamed as she fell, the sound tearing from her throat and scattering into the wind. The air whipped past her ears in a roar, stinging her cheeks and tangling her chopped hair. Static exploded off her skin like a shower of shooting stars, streaking through the sky and fading into the orange glow of sunset.

Esther really hated the color gold.

Her magic shimmered gold, the chains on her jewels glinted gold, and even the cursed crown that marked her as the palace's property was gold.

Every reminder of her cage gleamed in that same too-bright hue—the color of rules, of expectations, of things that pretended to be beautiful.

She could go the rest of her life never seeing it again, which wouldn't last much longer at the rate she was falling.

Valedara's tutors had tried to teach her about topography, ley lines, and magical interference zones. But Esther had spent most of those lessons sneak-reading romance novels behind atlases. She vaguely remembered Basil saying something about teleportation being "dangerously unstable without a designated anchor point," followed by, "Princess, please stop doodling hearts around assassin characters."

She should have asked where teleport spells normally landed.

Flat ground?

Soft moss?

Preferably a mattress?

Certainly not plummeting through the sky like a dramatic shooting star whose life choices were questionable at best.

There had long been old legends about teleportation mishaps, noble mages reappearing halfway through barn walls, or emerging inside fountains wearing nothing but embarrassment. Basil once told her, "Emotional instability will scramble coordinates."

Well. She was the poster child for emotional instability. So this? This was deserved.

She mentally prepared herself to become flatter than the cinnamon bun she'd packed. And knowing her luck, the bun would probably survive.

She thought of those most dear to her as she plummeted toward her demise. In order:

Dear Mother, your daughter indeed died stupidly.
Dear Lucy, please, please, please burn those books.
Dear Basil, I didn't blow anything up this time.

She decided not to send any thoughts or prayers to her father and brother, who were going to marry her off to an orc who already had children and probably lovers.

As if to rub salt in the wound, her satchel ripped open, releasing all its contents to the wind. The cinnamon bun that she would soon match slapped her in the face. The sugary glaze clung to her bangs, filling her nose with the scent of cinnamon and humiliation.

She could only imagine what the newspapers would say:

Disgraced Princess of Valedara: A Pile of Goop Surrounded by Smut.

Maybe she should have accepted her fate and married the orc king, but she quickly decided death was better.

She had acted rashly. But if they had invited the orc king to a dinner or afternoon tea instead of plotting behind her back, then she would have reacted more calmly.

Probably not, but it was the principle of it.

"What the hell?" a deep voice shouted, cut off by Esther's landing.

The impact drove the air from her lungs in a violent oof. Her vision spun, her head throbbed, and for a long second, she could only register warmth.

She hit something solid yet soft, like a mattress that needed breaking in.

The ground smelled of moss and mint: a clean, sharp, faintly sweet aroma that made her brain feel fuzzy. A scent she could melt into.

If this were death, it was surprisingly comfortable.

"Did she just fall from the sky?" a woman asked, rough and incredulous.

"Like a meteor," a gravelly voice responded.

"A meteor with legs that needs to get off me."

The "warmth" beneath her shifted.

Oh no.

She wasn't splattered on the ground, dead.

She was very much alive.

And on top of someone.

She didn't know if this was good news or if she should have gone with death. All she knew was that the Baroness must never find out.

Esther groaned and lifted her head, reluctant to acknowledge reality.

Her hair stuck to her face in sticky strands of cinnamon glaze and sweat. Her vision steadied enough to see the person she'd landed on, and her brain promptly short-circuited.

He was the most unfairly handsome man she'd ever seen. Pale skin dusted with soot. Long, dark hair tied in a loose braid that gleamed red at the edges in the setting sun.

Elves were known for their ethereal beauty; this one looked like the kind that ruined lives. His attire, a dark, close-fitted tunic stitched with thin silver thread, marked him as an adventurer. She recognized the pattern from a dusty volume titled *A Beginner's Guide to Handsome Men and Their Homelands*... or something similar.

So, what was he?

Beautiful.

Annoyed.

And currently pinned beneath her.

She had accidentally fallen on an elf.

"I can explain," she said quickly. "This isn't... whatever it looks like."

"It looks like you fell on me," the elf said flatly. His voice was smooth and calm in a way that made her stomach queasy.

This was definitely not how the heroines in the novels started their journeys.

"Right. So exactly what it looks like." She laughed weakly, pushing at her tangled hair. Bits of pastry clung to her scalp. One boot was missing entirely.

Baroness Levon's lectures screamed in her memory. In a single misstep, she'd undone years of etiquette, posture, and self-control.

"Up you get."

A dark, tawny-skinned half-elf lifted her effortlessly by the arms. Esther's feet dangled as if she weighed less than a feather. The woman's grip was firm but careful, her palms warm and calloused.

"Huh? You look familiar... have we met before?" she said as she gently set Esther down.

Esther shook her head, unable to recall a maid as tall as the woman in front of her.

The half-elf stood nearly six feet tall, muscles coiled like rope beneath her fitted shirt. Tight pants hugged her generous hips, accented by a long sheathed sword. Her skin carried a faint scent of vanilla and citrus, a softer fragrance than any perfume in the palace.

"She's glowing."

Esther turned toward the voice, deep and grumpy. The speaker was an orc with massive, mountain-like shoulders and rust-colored hair that clashed with his green skin, like an inverted carrot.

She noted the absence of warts and the rather attractive face beneath his tusks.

"I'm Vorrik."

"Now's not the time for introductions."

"I'm Nythir." The handsome elf stood and dusted dirt from his tunic, ignoring his companion completely. "So, are you with the bandits? Or just in the wrong place at the wrong time?"

"Bandits?" Esther asked.

As if summoned by the word, an arrow flew past her face. She would have been skewered if the half-elf hadn't yanked her aside like she weighed nothing.

It was then that Esther realized they were surrounded by ten, no, fifteen, men. They were an assortment of races: orcs, humans, dwarves, and beastkin. Covered in scars and filth, she doubted they'd be recognizable if they bathed. Grime clung to their clothes, and it looked as if they hadn't showered in months.

One of the bandits stepped forward, dragging the edge of his rusted blade along a tree trunk until bark peeled away in curls. Another spat at her feet, grinning with blackened teeth. Two more circled to the left, blocking any escape path.

Esther swallowed hard as the half-elf woman shifted protectively in front of her, but even she looked tense now. The men were closing in. Their weapons weren't raised yet, but their predatory smiles said everything.

Esther's skin prickled; the air tightened around her lungs. This wasn't like the palace, where threats were whispers. These men wanted to hurt her.

"That pretty little thing might fetch a good price," one of the grimy men leered at her. Esther's stomach flipped.

She was indeed in the wrong place at the wrong time.

Cold sweat broke out across her skin, her breath hitching, her vision blurring.

She had been so protected in the castle, sheltered from the world's darker side. She didn't know what to do, and her magic decided panic was the best plan of action.

"Can we break her in before we sell her?" another bandit laughed creepily.

Vorrik stepped between her and the bandits, positioning himself protectively. Nythir flanked her other side, throwing up a barrier to shield them from the onslaught of arrows.

Esther's vision blurred. She was terrified. She had never been outside the palace gates before. She didn't know what to expect. Her novels always had a knight saving a princess, not a princess landing in front of a band of vagrants.

Outnumbered.

Without guards.

"Why is the ground shaking?" Vorrik asked, his hand on his axe.

"Oh, for moon's sake. She's lit up like a firefly. Look at her hands."

Esther's fingers trembled. Gold sparks danced along her skin, crackling like embers. The air around her pulsed with heat, warping under the surge of magic. Her throat tightened. She could taste the fear, bitter and metallic.

The castle had not prepared her for this.

Her magic didn't obey logic.

It obeyed emotion.

And right now, terror was pouring through her veins like molten metal.

Her fingertips tingled, then burned, then blazed, light swelling faster than she could breathe. Her fingers went numb under the force of her frenzied magic.

"Everyone, move!"

A thunderous boom drowned out Nythir's voice.

Sparks flew. Trees splintered. Men screamed.

Golden light engulfed them.

Esther blinked through the settling dust—a few charred trees smoked in the distance. The air smelled of copper, smoke, and something burnt.

Her ears rang. Vorrik and the half-elf lay on the ground, blinking in disbelief. Nythir was covered in soot, his hair singed at the ends.

And all around them...

Pieces of what might once have been bandits littered the clearing.

"Oh no," she whispered. "Oh no, no, no..."

Her whisper turned into a shriek. The wind carried it through the trees, scattering birds into the darkening sky. Her throat burned from the smoke, her eyes stung, and her heart hammered.

"I don't think she's with the bandits," Vorrik said, helping his half-elf companion up.

"Well, that was effective." Nythir chuckled and patted her on the back. "Good job."

Esther straightened at the words.

She was being praised.

For the first time, her chaotic, uncontrolled magic was being praised.

Then it hit her.

She was being praised for killing several men.

They had attacked her first, but blowing them up went beyond self-defense. Not that she knew anything about self-defense.

Esther had dreamed of adventure once, of freedom, open skies, and daring rescues. But novels hadn't prepared her for the smell of burning flesh or the weight of unintended violence. She wanted to be brave, not dangerous.

Something wet and heavy slapped against her shoulder, interrupting her morbid thoughts. She turned to see a severed arm slide into the dirt beside her boot.

"I think I'm going to be sick," Esther whimpered, falling to her knees.

She wanted to be someone her mother could be proud of, not someone whose magic lashed out like a wounded animal.

She didn't want this power.

She didn't want to hurt people.

In a matter of minutes, she had gone from princess to runaway to murderer.

"I think I'm concussed," the other woman groaned. "I'm Lyssara."

"About time you told us who you are, girl."

"I'm Es— "

Whack.

Something hard, possibly karma disguised as debris, hit her head. The world tilted sideways, the smoke softening to silver around the edges.

Esther's last coherent thought before darkness swallowed her was that at least she had finally managed to leave the palace.

Though her next stop might be the dungeon.

4

Nythir

HOW TO CARE FOR A SKYBORN CATASTROPHE: IGNORE ALL THE RED FLAGS.

Nythir crouched beside the unconscious girl who had just been knocked out by a book—Proper Etiquette for Improper Thoughts.

He burst into startled laughter that echoed through the trees. It cracked through the forest so sharply that a flock of dusk-feathered finches shot from the canopy. His companions stared at him as if he had finally lost whatever remained of his sanity, and maybe he had. Most people would be terrified of a mage capable of obliterating a camp with a single emotional impulse. But he felt... curious. Intrigued. Alive in a way he hadn't in years.

She had fallen from the sky straight into his life. This wasn't a sign from fate; it was a gut punch.

She smelled faintly of embers and roses, with a surprising hint of cinnamon, likely from the pastry mashed into her hair. Her dress was scorched, her cloak half-burned, and the phoenix sigil still pulsed with a faint gold, as if refusing to acknowledge that its wearer was unconscious.

A catastrophe, wrapped in silk and cinnamon.

He brushed a lock of soot-stained hair from her face.

He knew power like that didn't come from training; it came from heritage.

Or destiny.

He wasn't sure which was worse.

"She's either royalty," he said, "or an explosion disguised as a woman."

Lyssara groaned. "Are we sure she isn't cursed?"

Vorrik poked Esther's cheek and shrugged. "If she's cursed, it's a fun curse. Can we keep her?"

Lyssara scowled. "She's wearing royal silk, idiot. We can't just keep her."

"Not just royal silk," Nythir added, pointing to the unmistakable symbol of a phoenix in flight embroidered on her cloak. "Royal silk with the imperial insignia."

The orange stitching stood out like a beacon, ready to attract every thief and scoundrel in sight. She was lucky she'd landed on him and not the bandits. There was no way she would have survived on her own, even in the safest city in the world, yet she had dropped straight into the middle of a deadly forest where bandits were hiding.

Vorrik gasped. "She's a symbol?"

"She's a problem," Lyssara muttered.

"She's interesting," Nythir said.

That was enough for him.

He heard a soft rustle behind him and turned to find a small forest creature, barely bigger than a squirrel, peering out from a burnt shrub. Its body was smoke-gray, its eyes pale gold, mirroring the glow pulsing beneath the girl's skin. A dusk-fawn, half-magic, half-mammal, drawn only to intense arcane signatures.

It approached cautiously, sniffing the air.

Nythir lifted a hand. "Easy."

The creature stepped closer, not to him, but toward Esther, as if her magic were a hearth in an endless winter.

It touched its small nose to the hem of her cloak, then gave a tiny, chiming bleat.

Vorrik clapped. "It likes her!"

Vorrik tried to pet the dusk-fawn. It bit him hard, tearing his skin with jagged teeth before scampering back into the brush.

Lyssara hissed, "That thing never comes near humans. What kind of magic is she carrying?"

Nythir didn't answer.

Because he already knew.

Dangerous magic.

Lonely magic.

Magic that would one day demand a price.

And stars help him, he wanted to be there when the bill came due.

"Can you two at least help me search the bodies—well, body parts—I guess, for proof of job completion while we figure out what to do with the girl?" Lyssara grumbled, tossing a scorched leg to the side.

The Adventurer's Guild wasn't a single organization; it was dozens of independent groups operating under the same code. Most took odd jobs: escort missions, monster culling, courier work. Nythir's trio specialized in dismantling bandit rings and recovering stolen goods, mostly because Lyssara liked punching thieves and Vorrik liked lifting heavy things.

Proof of completion varied: guild rings, insignia fragments, enchanted seals. Burning bandits to ash complicated matters significantly.

"She looks like trouble," Nythir said, smiling down at the unconscious woman. She looked so helpless. Dainty.

His instincts told him to protect her, and he had learned a long time ago to always follow his instincts.

"Good," Vorrik said. "You love trouble."

"You could say I'm passionate about it," Nythir said, smirking. "It's how I ended up with you two."

Lyssara rolled her eyes. "Wonderful. He's imprinted."

"Like a duck," Vorrik added.

Nythir raised an eyebrow. "A very dangerous, very flammable duck."

"Which of you is the duck?" Lyssara demanded.

"Unclear," Nythir said. "Check back later."

The forest clearing crackled with residual magic. Burnt earth glowed faintly, and the trees, scorched and bowing inward, still hummed with the aftershock of her uncontrolled power. Every guild he had ever worked for would kill to get their hands on someone like her.

Or kill her out of fear.

He felt neither impulse.

Something in her magic tugged at him like an unspoken promise, or a warning.

He wasn't sure he cared which.

"Found something!" Vorrik shouted, holding up a severed finger with a ring. "Proof!"

Lyssara tripped over a torso, Vorrik caught her, they flirted horribly, and Nythir gagged into his sleeve.

He lifted the girl into his arms, adjusting her carefully so her head rested against his shoulder. She weighed almost nothing.

But her fate, whatever it was, felt heavy enough to crack a kingdom.

He had met runaways before. Many. Some fled debts. Others, enemies. A few, fates they were too afraid to face.

But this girl wasn't running from anything.

Her magic felt like she had been running toward something, and had landed horribly off-target.

"So, we're keeping her?" Vorrik asked again as they began to walk.

Lyssara muttered about liability and paperwork, but even she stole a glance at Esther with interest.

They passed the still-smoking ruins of the bandit camp. The bodies were little more than silhouettes etched into the soil. Magic had done that. Her magic.

The dusk-fawn followed for a few steps, then turned and darted back into the trees, leaving a tiny trail of gold sparks behind it.

Nythir exhaled through his nose, slow and steady.

He knew danger.

He knew power.

He knew the sharp edge of fate when it brushed against his skin.

He looked down at the unconscious woman in his arms.

And he knew, with absolute clarity, that nothing in his life would ever be gray again.

"Welcome to the mess," he murmured. "Let's see what color you paint it."

Nythir adjusted his hold on the unconscious girl as they headed back toward camp. A faint curl of smoke still trailed from her dress, and the pastry crumb in her hair stubbornly refused to fall out. Her magic twitched against him now and then, like a sleeping cat swatting at dreams, reminding him she was capable of blowing up a small village before breakfast.

He should have been terrified.

Instead, he felt... energized. Curious. Irrationally protective.

Behind them, the clearing still glowed like a recently offended volcano.

Ahead, Vorrik was already trying to brainstorm what to feed her when she woke.

Nythir exhaled a slow laugh.

"Stars above," he muttered, "I really did adopt a disaster, didn't I?"

But he didn't put her down.

Not even for a moment.

5

Esther

How to sort out feelings: panic quietly, loudly, or somewhere in between.

The ground was cold and unyielding beneath her, damp seeping through her sleeves.

But her face...

Her face rested on something warm, smelling of vanilla and moss.

She wondered if Lucy had crawled into her bed again, unbecoming of a maid, but they never acted like master and servant when no extra eyes were around.

"You're so warm. I love it," Esther murmured, wrapping her arms around her friend.

"Finally awake, Princess?"

That was not Lucy's voice. It was deep and smooth, like silk.

She bolted upright, her head colliding with something firm.

"Ow!" She clutched the back of her head.

"Holy, you broke my nose," the elf, Nythir, grumbled, holding his bloodied face.

It was then she realized she was on top of the overly attractive elf.

Again.

She couldn't believe it. She, esteemed princess of Valedara, had straddled a man who was not her husband.

Twice.

She squeaked and skittered backward. The fire snapped in alarm beside her. Sparks leapt upward, too high, too bright.

Her magic flinched awake.

Pebbles near her feet rattled. A tiny flame on the log twisted upward, growing taller, as if trying to console her.

"Oh no," she whispered. "Not again, stop, stop!"

The world blurred.

Burnt meat.

Ash on the wind.

A scream. Her's. Theirs'. She couldn't tell.

And then came the worst truth of all:

"I'm a murderer," she choked out. "I killed them. I killed them, and it wasn't even on purpose."

In the palace, danger had always been hypothetical, something spoken of in council rooms or tediously annotated in her tutors' scrolls. Heroes in her novels defeated enemies with elegant swordplay or morally convenient unconsciousness. They didn't... explode people.

In the garden, she used to imagine adventures, freedom, daring rescues. Not *this*. Not scorched earth, severed limbs, and the metallic taste of power she never wanted. She felt the bile rise in her throat.

Her mother had been graceful with magic, gentle even at her fiercest. Esther had inherited none of that control, only the raw, wild force of a golden flame that answered her fear with violence.

She wrapped her arms around herself.

What if this was all she was?

A disaster in royal silk, now without even the silk.

A memory flashed: Lucy tugging her into a closet to gossip, Lucy stealing pastries for her, Lucy promising she'd never let Esther be alone.

Lucy would never forgive her for this.

She bit her lip until it hurt.

"Hey," Nythir said gently. His voice felt strange in the quiet, too loud, too human. "Breathe. You're all right."

He approached slowly, like she was a trapped animal.

Every tutor Esther had ever had warned her that uncontrolled magic could corrupt the heart. But none had explained how to handle guilt. No one told her how to breathe after the first time magic didn't save, it destroyed.

There was no etiquette lesson for this.

No elegant script for apologizing to the dead.

Her gaze flicked to him, unfocused and wet. "I didn't mean to," she whispered.

"I know."

He knelt but didn't touch her. Even at arm's length, he could feel the poison of her guilt.

"Are you upset about turning the bandits into… confetti?" Lyssara asked. "You shouldn't be."

"Confetti?" Esther echoed weakly.

"They had a warrant." Lyssara held a crumpled parchment inches from Esther's face.

WANTED
Dead or Alive
Multiple murders, theft, extortion...

"Wanted posters actually exist?"

"Did you seriously just ask that?" Lyssara gaped. "These were posted in every tavern and inn for fifty miles!"

"That is so cool," Esther whispered in awe. "So... they were really bad?"

"The worst," Nythir chuckled.

"So I'm basically a hero?" Esther popped up.

"Something like that." Lyssara ruffled her hair. "You did good, kid."

Esther gawked at them, eyes wide like an owl. She didn't feel right taking lives so easily. But as she read their misdeeds on the wanted poster... she felt strangely at ease with what she had done.

"She really did a number on your nose," Vorrik laughed.

"Your commentary is not required," Nythir grumbled.

"Oh my stars, I should have healed you!" Esther panicked, tossing the parchment aside.

"No—" He raised a hand.

Too late.

Golden light washed over him.

"Nythir!" Vorrik screamed.

"Hold," Lyssara commanded.

"Still in one piece," Nythir said as gold slid off his body like glitter. He tapped his perfectly straight nose.

"And not confetti," Lyssara added.

"I told you I could fix it," Esther said smugly.

Rustle. Rustle.

A half-decayed squirrel burst from the leaves.

Esther screamed.

Vorrik stomped it.

The eyeball landed on Lyssara's shoulder.

Then Lyssara puked. Then Esther. Then both again.

"She murders, heals, necromances, and sets things on fire," Nythir wheezed.

"And we need you to light the fire again," Lyssara wiped her mouth and gestured toward the fire pit.

"Absolutely not," Esther said through heaves.

Vorrik leaned in close. "When Nythir stands near you, the fire flares."

"That's because I'm handsome," Nythir murmured, leaning in a little too close.

The fire popped. Esther stared at the group in confused contempt. They had used Nythir's face against her as a fire starter.

Later, she sat on a log beside the flames, wrapped in a borrowed cloak and a blanket of exhaustion. The forest buzzed with night magic, small flame-moths flickered through the air, drawn toward her, mistaking her golden sparks for a broodmother.

A tiny creature with ember-tipped ears approached her boot, sniffed, then bowed.

"Why, why is it doing that?" she whispered.

"It thinks you're a fire deity," Nythir said casually.

Esther made a noise somewhere between a sob and a groan.

Lyssara crossed her arms. "Right. Rules. If you're traveling with us, you follow the Adventurer Code."

"The what?"

Vorrik unrolled a scroll. "Rule one: don't die."

"Rule two," Lyssara added, "don't kill us."

"Rule three: if you have to explode something, give notice," Vorrik said.

Nythir hummed thoughtfully. "Rule four: maybe don't straddle strangers."

Esther turned scarlet. "That was, AN ACCIDENT!"

"And finally," Lyssara said, "who are you?"

"Essie," she whispered, thinking of her mother's voice calling her that on warm afternoons.

"And the symbol on your cloak?"

Esther froze.

She slowly lifted the cloak from her lap and stared at the phoenix sigil.

Her heart cracked.

In one motion, she tore it off and hurled it into the fire.

"What cloak?" she said, maintaining perfect royal composure.

The orange thread curled and dissolved like a dying sun.

"Do you even know how much that was worth?" Vorrik whispered.

Esther swallowed the hollow ache in her chest.

"No," she said.

And she didn't care.

The flames reflected in Nythir's eyes as he watched her, amused, impressed, and far too handsome for someone who could so thoroughly shatter her emotional stability.

When he smiled at her like trouble incarnate, she wondered, just faintly, if Lucy would consider it stupid to die, if the cause was a devilish smile.

6

Nythir

How to camp: trust no twig, leaf, or suspicious nighttime breeze.

Nythir enjoyed the quiet softness of the night under a full moon. Crickets hummed in the dark, steady as a heartbeat. The forest breathed in a slow, even rhythm. Smoke from the dying fire curled through the air, sweet with the warm scent of Essie's magic.

Nythir kept watch from the edge of the camp, one knee drawn up, his knife resting lazily in his fingers. The firelight reached him in flickers—just enough to glint off the steel.

Behind him, Esther slept.

She had drifted off mid-sentence, halfway through explaining why cinnamon buns were superior to diplomacy. Now she lay bundled in Nythir's far-too-large cloak, hair a tangle of gold and soot. She looked serene—like she wasn't in a dangerous forest at all. She truly had nothing to fear with him watching over her, but she could have afforded a bit more caution.

The ground was still scattered with faint traces of her magic, tiny shining specks that pulsed with each exhale. It was an enchanting sight that lured dragonflies to dance through it, weaving patterns until Nythir couldn't tell which glimmer belonged to magic and which to nature.

"Never seen anything like it," Vorrik rumbled from across the fire. He poked the embers with a stick. "You sure she's not some kind of demigod?"

"She's definitely something," Lyssara said, leaning back against a log. Her onyx braid glowed faintly orange in the firelight. "You don't blow up fifteen men and half a forest by accident. Or wear the royal insignia on your cloak."

"Maybe she's cursed," Vorrik offered. "Or possessed. Or both."

Nythir didn't answer. He watched the rise and fall of Esther's shoulders. Even asleep, her fingers twitched—as if the magic in her veins refused to rest.

Lyssara followed his gaze. "She's too clean, even with the soot," she murmured. "Look at those hands. No calluses, no scars. And her accent's polished as a palace floor."

Vorrik squinted at Esther. "You're saying she's—" he paused dramatically, waiting for someone else to finish.

"A noble mage," Lyssara concluded. "One that works close to the king. It's the only theory that makes sense."

Nythir finally spoke, voice low. "Close... but not quite."

Both of them looked at him.

He didn't take his eyes off Essie. "Her terrible lying skills, the royal insignia, the golden magic... Old scriptures said the golden bloodline died with the queen. Clearly, someone lied."

He let out a slow breath. "I'd wager the power was hidden—and we just rescued the Princess of Valedara."

"That explains why she looked familiar," Lyssara muttered. She began drawing idle lines in the dirt with a stick, as if her hands needed something to do. "Vorrik, do you remember when that really pretty lady visited the orphanage and gave a huge donation?"

Vorrik frowned in concentration. "The one who brought all the meat? The meat that fed us for a whole week!"

Lyssara groaned. "I said donation, not food."

"It was a food donation."

"It was expired meat from the butcher's wife! Half the orphanage got sick! I'm talking about the other one—the woman who looked just like Essie, only taller."

Her gaze drifted to Essie, who was now snoring with a thin string of drool slipping from her mouth.

"And more refined," Lyssara added under her breath.

"Oh yeah," Vorrik said far too quickly.

He definitely did not remember.

Lyssara sighed. "I heard the head of the orphanage speaking to her. She called her *Queen Estella*."

Nythir's expression sharpened. "Are you certain?"

"Positive. I wasn't supposed to hear, but I've always had a natural talent for spying." She lifted her chin, as though it were a skill worth putting on a résumé. "She used to visit often. And on her last visit... she promised she'd come back for my birthday."

Her voice wavered—just enough for Nythir to notice.

"But she never did," Lyssara finished quietly. "A few weeks later, news of the queen's death spread. That's when I stopped doubting who she really was."

Vorrik scratched his beard. "But why would the princess teleport into Ashvale and... y'know...dramatically annihilate bandits?"

Lyssara shrugged, lips curling into a smirk. "Who knows? Maybe she's running from an arranged marriage. Or her etiquette lessons. She kept mumbling something about that in her sleep."

Queen Estella's golden magic had been legendary—gentle yet fierce, warm enough to heal frostbite, bright enough to light entire caverns. It was said she never raised her voice, only her will, and the world bent around her like metal to flame.

Some even claimed her death shattered Valedara's equilibrium.

The years after her loss grew colder.

Darker.

More hollow.

Nythir wondered what the queen would think of her daughter—falling from the sky, blowing up criminals, crying into cinnamon pastry glaze.

Probably: *"Yes, that is exactly my child."*

Nythir's mouth quirked. "You two can gossip later. For now, she's just another runaway with a dangerous temper."

Lyssara stretched, cracking her knuckles. "So we're not telling her we know?"

"No. There's more to her than a sheltered girl."

"So we do get to keep her!" Vorrik boomed—earning a rock to the forehead, courtesy of Nythir's impeccable aim.

Silence settled over them. Only the fire spoke, snapping softly as it devoured the last of the wood.

Lyssara tilted her head, studying him. "You're curious about her."

He didn't deny it. His eyes drifted back to Essie—her hand tucked near her face, soot streaking her jaw, that faint golden warmth still hovering in the air around her. "She's... interesting."

Lyssara smirked. "That's what men always say before they end up hexed or heartbroken."

Nythir stood, stretching out stiff muscles. He had learned quickly that reacting to Lyssara's taunts only encouraged her.

He stepped closer to the fire and adjusted a loose blanket over Esther's shoulder. The glow beneath her skin softened under the fabric, her magic humming quietly, as if soothed.

"She can keep her secret," he said. "At least until she's ready to use her real name again."

Lyssara's grin softened. Vorrik snorted, tossing another branch into the fire. "This is going to be fun."

Nythir didn't disagree.

The fire cracked, scattering sparks into the dark. They rose like tiny fragments of gold, drifting upward before fading into the trees—just like her magic.

"It's settled then," Nythir said, positioning himself between Essie and the open forest. "We should rest before the forest becomes too active."

7

Lucy

How to avoid consequences: cry strategically and weaponize eyeliner.

"Try not to die stupid!" she had shouted—and then the world had erupted in gold.

The sky above the palace still glowed faintly, the aftershocks of Esther's magic flickering across the clouds like fading veins of lightning. Lucy watched the last ripple disappear behind the mountains, her stomach dropping with it.

Boom!

A golden lightning strike flashed in the distance, shaking the castle walls. She winced. That definitely wasn't subtle.

Heavy footsteps thundered toward Esther's chambers.

Lucy slapped her cheeks, inhaled sharply, and prepared herself.

It was her time to shine.

She straightened her apron, lifted her chin, arranged her expression into something perfectly balanced between tired and annoyed, then stepped directly into their path.

"What's all the racket?" she demanded, voice sharp with perfectly executed confusion.

The tallest guard lifted his lantern, the light spilling across the hall. "We were tasked with investigating this wing. Including the Princess's chambers."

"She is already asleep," Lucy said immediately. "Her magic lesson today was very draining."

The shorter guard puffed out his chest. He always looked like a toad trying very hard to pretend he wasn't a toad. "We must see her with our own eyes for the report."

Lucy blinked slowly. Then, with the kind of icy calm that could curdle milk, she repeated: "You mean to tell me… you wish to enter the Princess's chambers. While she is asleep."

The firelight caught her eyes just right, and both guards instinctively stepped back.

"It is a matter of security!" the short one insisted, voice cracking straight through bravado.

"No," Lucy hissed, stepping into his space so forcefully he nearly tripped over his own boots. "It is a matter of respect. I watch her day in and day out. I greet her in the morning and send her off to slumber. I guard her more fiercely than any knight in this entire glittering prison. And you think you can stroll into Princess Esther's bedroom after I have told you she is asleep?"

Her voice rose—not theatrically, not intentionally, but with real emotion. Real fear. Real fury. She didn't need to pretend anymore; her heart had already broken open.

"I wonder," she said softly, dangerously, "what punishment *his majesty* will give you when I inform him that low-ranking guards attempted to violate the sleeping Princess's privacy."

The taller guard paled. "F-f-forgive us. It is as you say. We will report she is safe in her chambers. Please—please do not speak of this."

Cowards, she thought. These men, these guards who could stare down armed orcs, trembled at the idea of upsetting a maid. Their armor was nothing more than decoration. They weren't worthy of serving Esther.

They whimpered before scampering down the hall, boots squeaking on polished marble.

Pathetic. Lucy wanted to spit on the floor after them, but the maid in her wouldn't allow it. She settled on something better: sneaking into their quarters later to rub peppers into their undergarments during training.

Her knees nearly buckled once they turned the corner. The lantern light from their retreating steps dimmed, leaving the corridor cold and empty. Her breath rushed out in a shaky gust.

She had bought Esther minutes. Maybe hours. No more.

Lucy slipped back into Esther's room and collapsed onto the enormous bed. The blankets—soft as rose petals, warm as summer—wrapped around her like a memory. Here, there were no roles, no duty, no palace politics. They were simply best friends in the rawest sense.

What was she supposed to do now?

Esther had always been stubborn, sarcastic, quick-witted... but never defiant. Never reckless enough to flee the palace. From the outside, she looked like a porcelain doll on display—quiet, graceful, demure. The perfect curated princess.

But Lucy knew the truth.

Esther was a butterfly encased in amber. Beautiful. Unbreathing.

Dying slowly in stillness.

Watching her live like that ate away at Lucy, and she hated herself for not having enough power to save her.

The guards compared her to a canary in a gilded cage. They were wrong. A canary could at least sing.

Lucy remembered the first time she saw Esther cry—not the polite, quiet tears of a princess, but a full, terrified sob when she accidentally singed her own eyebrows during a lesson. Lucy had marched right up, stolen a pastry off a silver tray, and shoved it into Esther's hands.

"Eat. Sadness burns calories," she'd said.

Esther laughed through her tears.

Lucy had been loyal ever since.

Lucy's gaze drifted to the note on the vanity — the ink barely dry. Esther's handwriting was messy where the strokes had trembled.

Lucy,

If I die, burn my extra secret books — you know where they are. If I live, I'm bringing back a man. Love you forever.

— Esther

P.S. You'd be a male knight, just to gloat about having the biggest sword. Very important.

Lucy's throat tightened. She didn't know whether to laugh or cry. Probably both. Esther always wrote like her emotions were on fire.

If Esther lived, she promised to bring home a man.

If she died... she asked Lucy to burn the smut library.

Lucy chuckled weakly through her tears. It was such an Esther specific worry to have when running away without a plan. Lucy clutched the letter to her chest, tears prickling her eyes again. She had introduced Esther to smut in the first place. *The Forbidden Forest* had been their downfall. There was no going back after that. They had since become obsessed with books. It was the perfect getaway for their loneliest moments.

She curled deeper into the bed. The scent of jasmine oil still clung to the pillows, soft and soothing—a ghost of the girl who had lain here hours ago.

Bang.

The door slammed open.

Lucy jolted, her heart clawing at her ribs. She yanked the blankets over her head, willing herself into the shadows. Moonlight flickered faintly across the floor, too dim to give away her hiding spot.

Heavy, deliberate footsteps creaked closer.

She forced a moan, half-princess, half-actress, hoping to sound like a disgruntled royal rudely awakened.

The steps stopped.

Her breath caught.

"I know it's you, Lucy."

The voice cut through the darkness like a blade.

So much for buying Esther more time, Lucy thought.

8

Esther

HOW TO SURVIVE THE FOREST: ACCEPT THAT THE TREES MIGHT HATE YOU PERSONALLY.

At dawn, Ashvale woke up angry.

Esther had barely managed a few hours of blissful, soot-scented sleep before the forest itself decided to come alive. One moment, sunlight was only beginning to brush the treetops; the next, the entire forest stirred like a giant creature stretching after a long night.

Leaves unfurled with a whispering sigh. Moss brightened from gray to vivid green. Vines rippled and lifted like lazy serpents waking from a nap. Roots shuddered beneath the soil, cracking like knuckles.

She had never seen anything like it.

In twenty-one years, Esther had never expected to become a weapon. She also never expected to be used like one so early in the morning.

The group ran at full sprint through the living forest. Lyssara led the charge, her blade slicing through vines that swung down like hungry ropes. Nythir stayed just behind her, parrying roots that erupted from the ground like spears.

Once the sun rose fully above the canopy, Ashvale came alive with a vengeance—and absolutely none of it was Esther's fault. If the trees could have glared at her, she was certain they would've.

She might've appreciated the breathtaking morning sun peeking through trees, the dew sparkling on sentient leaves, the soft groaning of awakening branches... if she weren't draped over Vorrik's shoulder like an oversized magic lantern.

"Fire!" Vorrik bellowed, as though she were a trained weapon.

He angled her downward.

"Wait—no—Vorrik!" Esther sputtered, but her hands flared gold, eager traitors.

Flames shot from her palms, blasting a rotting stump barreling after them. The stump burst into shrapnel, scattering charred bark across the forest floor.

"Hell yeah!" Nythir whooped, sounding far too delighted about her apparent combat usefulness.

Much like the bandits did, she thought. Which immediately made her stomach flip. Whether it was guilt or the fact that Vorrik's shoulder bounced like an unsteady horse, she couldn't tell.

"Try not to set the whole forest on fire!" Lyssara shouted, ducking a vine that snapped like a whip.

Vorrik ignored her entirely. He stomped through a curtain of moss that slapped Esther in the face, leaving her coughing up green fuzz. The world was a blur of emerald light and golden sparks.

"Left! Left!" Nythir barked.

"I am going left!" Vorrik roared.

"No, my left!"

A branch smacked into the side of Vorrik's head, leaving maple sap smeared across his cropped hair. Esther burst into hysterical laughter.

She extended both hands. Fire roared free, incinerating the offending limb in a whoosh that filled the air with burning sugar and woodsmoke.

"Are you enjoying this?" Nythir panted.

She was.

Despite the fear and chaos, a wild exhilaration thrummed through her. She'd started the morning terrified—but somewhere between dodging killer vines and blasting rogue shrubbery, exhilaration had taken over. She felt alive. Freer than she had ever been within polished palace walls that smelled of roses, lemons, and expectations.

Then—light. Actual sunlight.

The oppressive trees parted, spilling them into a wide clearing. The air hit her sharply—cool, crisp, smelling of wet earth and something sweet, like flowering clover. Rolling green hills dipped away from the forest edge. Down in the valley, rooftops glittered as morning sun reflected off the river.

"Out," Lyssara wheezed, bending over her knees. "Oh gods... we're out."

Vorrik slowed to a stop and finally—blessedly—lowered Esther to the ground. Her legs were jelly. She dropped to a knee, lungs burning, eyes watering from smoke and adrenaline.

Behind them, the sentient vines recoiled into the shadows, rustling like scolded pets. One leaf slapped irritably against a trunk.

"I think it's mad at us," Esther said.

"Good," Vorrik grumbled, smacking dirt off his armor. "It started it."

Nythir clapped her on the shoulder, grinning. "Look alive. Town ahead. And I smell bread. And beer."

His braid was stuffed with twigs. His face was flushed. His hair a disaster. And somehow, he had the audacity to look even more attractive like that. Esther tore her gaze away quickly before her magic betrayed her.

Vorrik stretched. "Anyone else hungry?"

Lyssara nodded. "I could eat an entire chicken."

Nythir smirked at Esther. "And you? Lost any pastries lately?"

She glared. "It was a strategic bun deployment."

He tilted his head. "Is that what we're calling catastrophic gravitational failure now?"

"Shut up," she muttered, cheeks warm.

Down below, a small town nestled against a silver river, smoke curling lazily from chimneys. The faint sound of laughter and music floated up the hill.

No walls trapping her. No guards watching her. No carefully orchestrated lessons or suffocating expectations.

This was nothing like Valedara's marble symmetry.

It was messy.

Lived in.

Human.

She loved it instantly.

Her heart hiccuped.

Then, she bolted.

"What the—Essie!" Nythir shouted, his voice lost to her laughter. Her hair whipped behind her as she tore downhill, bare soles pounding the dew-kissed grass. Every scent, every sound, every color rushed at her—bread baking, dogs barking, children shrieking with morning joy.

Freedom.

Real, actual freedom.

She kicked off her last remaining shoe, savoring the cool tickle of grass between her toes. Nythir caught up faster than she expected and grabbed her arm. Momentum toppled them both, sending them tumbling downhill. They rolled through mud and morning mist until they landed in a heap, Nythir half-sprawled over her.

He gasped. "What— what was that?"

"Running," she giggled, breathless.

"Running from what? We're out of the forest."

"Exactly!" she beamed up at him. "Look at it! It just looks so fun!"

"At least wait for us before you blindly run to someplace unknown," he sighed, still pinning her gently to the earth. "Again."

"She didn't run before," Lyssara called, hands on her hips as she stood over them. "She teleported. Now kiss and make up. I need a bath."

Esther's magic flared with embarrassment—and promptly set the ends of Nythir's hair on fire.

9

NYTHIR

How to avoid attention: fail spectacularly and loudly.

"Running," she'd said, as if that explained anything.

As if sprinting half-dressed, half-dead, and entirely insane down a hill made sense to *anyone*.

And yet, when she laughed as they rolled through the grass…when sunlight hit her face, and she looked—moons help him—*happy*.

It made perfect sense.

By the time they trudged through Stonehaven's main gate, they looked like a traveling collection of curses in humanoid form. That being said, no one batted an eye at their state; Stonehaven had seen worse. The scent of woodsmoke, frying batter, and river wind filled the air, masking the sulfur and burnt sap clinging to them from Ashvale. No one going into their local forest came out unscathed. Some never came out.

Nythir knew he looked half feral. His hair was a frizzy, singed disaster, coated in ash and streaked with grass. Mud smeared one entire side of his face. His tunic smelled like burnt moss and regret.

Essie matched him perfectly. Except she was still barefoot, having lost her remaining boot when it *burst into flames* during their tumble. He was happy it was the boot, not him. He knew he was playing with fire, and getting burned was worth the risk, but he'd prefer to avoid it if he could.

Her silk dress, once pristine and elegant, was now splattered with dirt, torn at the hem, and decorated with little flecks of crispy vine remains. A phoenix among ducks, reduced to a soot-covered, barefoot whirlwind.

They needed to fix her appearance soon.

Not because she didn't look lovely, stars, she could wear a potato sack and still dazzle a room. But because her noble quality was starting to show in a way that drew attention.

No sane commoner carried themselves with her grace, spoke with her diction, or blasted animated shrubbery with royal-level magic.

He'd never met anyone so dangerous to his peace of mind.

Lyssara trudged ahead of them, muttering about needing a real bath, clean clothes, and possibly divine intervention.

Vorrik followed behind her, shoulders drooping, looking like someone who'd been personally insulted by nature itself.

The marketplace hit him like a wave—bright fabrics flapping in the breeze, hawkers shouting, children running underfoot, and above all, *the smells.*

Essie froze at the aroma of fresh bread, frying batter, caramelizing sugar, and sizzling meat. Dawn hunger and last night's skipped breakfast stirred the air into a tormenting feast.

Her stomach growled loud enough that a passing dog glanced at her.

"We should... maybe feed her," Nythir muttered.

"Feed us all," Lyssara corrected.

Before they could move on, Essie drifted toward a vendor with a glowing clay oven and stacks of blistered sweet potatoes, nestled in their skins and steaming in the cool morning air. Smoke curled around them like warm hands.

Nythir didn't even ask her if she wanted any. He silently paid the vendor immediately while she drooled.

The vendor wrapped a sweet potato in parchment and handed it to Essie with a knowing nod.

She held it reverently, inhaling. The warmth seeped into her fingers, turning her cheeks pink.

Nythir felt something in his chest tighten. He watched her entire soul leave her body on her first bite.

"This is..." she whispered. "This is the most delicious thing I've ever tasted."

"It's just a sweet potato," he said, amused.

"No," she insisted. "It's freedom flavored."

He nearly choked.

They ate it together as they walked, Essie's steps bouncing.

Her hair caught the sunlight in wild gold tangles while her laughter drifted between the vendors like a bell.

"I've never eaten while walking before," she admitted quietly. "I wasn't allowed."

He stopped mid-step.

No breakfast.

No walking.

No boots.

No choices.

He exhaled slowly.

"You're allowed now," he said.

Her smile was small but bright.

"I know."

Something warm flickered in his chest.

"Oh, Helga," Lyssara called out to a young dwarf whose pointed hat added two feet to her. It was a bright pink triangle that really stood out in the crowded streets. Gaudy but practical. "I need some clothes delivered to our room at Moonpetal."

Lyssara flicked a gold coin—picked from the bodies in Ashvale—with flawless aim. Helga snatched it out of the air and bit it.

Nythir would never understand how mangled corpses didn't bother Lyssara at all, but a zombie squirrel had traumatized her for life.

"What would you like, Mrs. Lyssara?" Helga said, biting the gold coin to check its authenticity. "I've got a few new leathers and furs delivered just today!"

"It's not for me. It's for the missy back there." She pointed over her shoulder.

"I can pay for it myself," Essie said too loudly, fumbling through her satchel, before remembering it had a massive hole in it.

All that remained was lint and shame.

Her face reddened.

"You played a key part in our job," Nythir said gently. "The least we can do is replace your clothes. Add a new satchel and cloak to the order. I'll pay when it's delivered."

"Green," Vorrik said immediately. "Make her a green dress. It's my favorite color."

Helga turned to Essie expectantly.

"Well what would you like, Miss...?"

Essie froze.

Nythir leaned down. "Introduce yourself."

"I'm... Essie," she said, curtsying.

Helga clapped with glee. "Oh she's refined! She'll clean up beautifully. Now, are you looking for a dress or something more in Mrs. Lyssara's style?"

"A dress," Essie said. "Please."

"And color?"

Nythir leaned in again, voice low. "Green would suit you."

Her cheeks flushed pink.

"I-I... I'll go with green."

Before her sparks could give her away, Nythir took her hand, covering the glow.

Her hand was warm.

His chest felt warmer.

When he asked her to hide her magic, she went utterly still.

Her hands turned cold.

He frowned—but Helga interrupted, bustling between them with measuring tape and questions Essie could never answer.

Not style.

Not fabric.

Not color.

Not even footwear preference.

She looked at others for permission with every question. Like a girl raised to never choose anything for herself.

Lyssara eventually answered for her.

When Helga asked about footwear, he saw the exact moment Essie realized she was still barefoot. She wiggled her toes and looked around, awestruck that there was no one reprimanding her over it.

They found plain brown leather boots, sturdy and worn-in. Perfect for travel. And most importantly, ready for her size.

Her dress would take a bit longer.

"See you at Moonpetal," Lyssara said, shooing them toward the inn.

"What's wrong?" Nythir asked as they walked, noticing how Essie's spark had dimmed. Her steps were slower.

"Nothing."

"You look glum," Vorrik said.

"Leave her alone," Lyssara snapped. She looped an arm through Essie's and pulled her close. "Girl talk. Come along. The men can go... do men things."

Somehow, this resulted in Essie disappearing upstairs with Lyssara, leaving Nythir and Vorrik standing in the hall like abandoned puppies.

"How did I get booted from my room?" Vorrik muttered, tossing his bag into a corner.

"The same way I got stuck with a smelly orc in mine."

"I do not smell," Vorrik snapped. Then sniffed his armpit and grimaced. "That's not me. That's the forest."

Nythir sat heavily on the nearest bed.

"What even is girl talk?"

"Probably things we're not supposed to hear."

Vorrik frowned deeply. "Do you think if I wore a dress—"

"No."

"We'll see them at dinner," Nythir said, rubbing his temples. "For now... apparently we do... 'men stuff.'"

"What is 'men stuff?'"

Nythir sighed. "Moping until our women come for us."

10

Esther

How to unwind: try relaxing while your brain does the opposite.

The bathhouse's steam and lavender soap still clung to Esther's skin as she and Lyssara stepped back into the small inn room. Through the open window drifted the echo of vendors shouting prices, carried on river wind and tangled with the mouthwatering scent of roasted nuts and fresh pastries from the town square below.

Her sense of freedom and rigid etiquette training immediately went to war over the temptation to lean out the window and buy everything in sight.

Nythir and Vorrik had been sent away under strict orders—*no loitering, no hovering, no arguing*—and Esther's hair was still damp, curling in short, messy waves around her face. No pins. No stiff braids. No maid tugging at loose strands and tutting in disapproval.

She felt uncomfortable. Unstructured.

And yet, oddly lighter for it.

She couldn't stop smiling.

Her first communal bath.

Her first morning in a town.

Her first sweet potato was eaten while walking.

Everything felt strange and new. She was having fun for the first time in over a decade. This was nothing like reading about freedom in a book—and the realization stung. She regretted not reaching for it sooner.

"Was it really your first time in a communal bath?" Lyssara asked, scrunching something that smelled like warm coconut and citrus into her coils.

"Yes," Esther admitted. "It was very… unique. I wouldn't mind doing it again."

She had expected to feel awkward—exposed, even—but instead the warm water, gentle chatter, and lingering woodsmoke from the bathhouse hearth had soothed her in a way palace baths never had. No maids were hovering behind her. No heavy silence. No rigid expectations pressing down on her shoulders.

Just warmth. Steam. Running water. Women laughing.

The bathhouse itself felt like a living thing, its stone worn smooth by generations of bodies. Low lanterns glowed amber, stained by years of steam, and wooden pegs were carved with tiny sigils meant to ward against slipping and sickness alike. Esther noticed how everyone brought something different. Mismatched towels. Shared soaps. Chipped bowls of oil passed freely from hand to hand. No one watched her closely. No one cared who she was. In the palace, baths had been private affairs of perfection and silence. Here, they were maintenance. Of bodies. Of community. Of survival.

Children had splashed at the edges of the pool, earning scoldings from their mothers and giggles from each other. The sight had stirred a brief ache in Esther's chest—memories of her own mother, lost too early—but the sound of their laughter chased the sadness away.

"Well that's odd," Lyssara said. "Being a maid and all. I thought palace staff shared living and bathing quarters."

Esther froze, her breath catching painfully in her throat. She had forgotten the lie she frantically told in the bath, when Lyssara pressed the issue.

In the palace, her world had been routine and rigid:

Lessons → tea → silence at meals → more lessons → embroidery → evenings locked away with smuggled books.

She had never asked Lucy where she slept.

She'd never even thought to.

The realization sat heavy and wrong in her chest. Lucy hadn't just chosen to stay. Lucy had never been given the space to leave.

"I—my hours were different," Esther said finally, her stomach tightening. "As a personal maid, I had more private accommodations."

She winced inwardly. The lie scratched her throat on the way out. Lucy had always been there—at meals, during lessons, through every waking hour, always beside her.

Esther realized, with a slight and painful pang, how little she truly knew about Lucy's life outside of her own shadow.

"That seems lonely," Lyssara said softly.

The words hit like a stone.

Her own loneliness.

Lucy's loneliness.

How Esther had clung to Lucy like a lifeline—and how Lucy had quietly accepted the weight of it. Guilt settled thick and sticky against her ribs.

"It was," Esther whispered. "For both of us, I think."

Knock-knock.

"Delivery for a Miss Esther," Helga called from outside.

Steam still drifted off Esther's skin as Lyssara tied her robe tighter and flung the door open.

"Perfect timing!" Lyssara cheered. "Nythir! Come pay for this!"

A sleepy grumble echoed from the adjoining room.

"That was fast," Nythir yawned. "How much?"

"Five marks and three petals," Helga replied, dropping a surprisingly heavy box into Lyssara's arms. A faint scent of pine and wool drifted from it.

Esther blinked at the unfamiliar mix of currency. Marks she knew, the standard coin stamped and regulated by the crown. Petals were something else entirely. Pressed bits of lacquered wood, traded in river towns where business moved faster than royal oversight ever could. They were favors and promises, debts remembered long after the coin had changed hands.

"That much? After the crown she gave you?"

"That was for priority service," Helga said without shame, holding out her calloused palms.

"Swindler," Nythir muttered—but he paid anyway. His voice was irritated; his mouth, however, betrayed him with a slight upward twitch.

Vorrik barreled past a moment later. "Food and beer?"

"After we get ready," Lyssara said firmly. "We'll meet you at Luna's Tavern. Out!"

The door slammed.

Then Lyssara smiled wickedly.

"Sit, cinnamon bun."

"Cinnamon bun?" Esther repeated, confused.

"You know—the one we washed out of your hair." Lyssara patted the bed. "Now sit. Your hair is a battlefield."

Esther obeyed, cheeks warming. The inn mattress was thin and stiff, nothing like the plush featherbed she'd grown up in. But she liked it—its simplicity, its honest creak, its realness.

Lyssara combed through gently, coaxing out tangles. The scent of coconut filled the air. Each careful stroke felt grounding.

Lucy used to brush her hair the same way, quick and efficient, fingers practiced from years of untangling silk and stubborn knots alike. There had never been room for gentleness then. Only necessity. Esther wondered when care had turned into obligation, and whether Lucy had ever noticed the shift before Esther had. The thought settled uncomfortably in her chest, warm and volatile, stirring beneath her skin like embers beginning to wake.

"You remind me of my friend," Esther murmured. "Lucy. She always helped me. Took care of me."

Lyssara hummed thoughtfully. "And do you want people to take care of you?"

Esther hesitated. "I want to know people better. Not just be taken care of."

Lyssara's grin sharpened. "Especially a certain dark-haired elf?"

Before Esther could deny it, one of the candles on the table flared violently.

The flame leapt an inch higher, casting jittery shadows across the walls.

"I'm sorry!" Esther squeaked. "I—I didn't mean—"

"Don't apologize," Lyssara said calmly, lowering the flame with a wave of her hand. "Magic mirrors emotion. Nothing shameful about that."

Esther groaned at hearing Basil's favorite phrase when lecturing her. He started every lesson with that quote.

Lyssara finished brushing, then stepped back with a low whistle. "We need to trim this later. You look like you fought sentient scissors and lost."

Esther laughed because that exact scenario had happened once. She had been seven. The scissors had won.

Lyssara flicked her wrist and promptly tossed all three candles out the broken window.

"You don't have to do that!" Esther cried.

"Essie," Lyssara said gently, pulling out the green dress, "everyone has things they can't control. Vorrik snores like an earthquake. Your magic is just louder."

Esther swallowed. Louder, yes, but also deeper. Her magic had never felt neat or singular. It moved in layers, sometimes steady and sometimes raw, as though it carried strength without the structure to hold it. Compared to the careful magic she had been taught about, hers always seemed to burn a little too bright, reaching before she was ready.

The dress shimmered softly in the light filtering through the window—dark forest green, simple, knee-length, belted at the waist. No lace. No jewels. No heavy embroidery.

Esther slipped into it. The fabric scratched faintly against her skin—unfamiliar, but not unpleasant.

The skirt swished when she twirled, light as wind chimes. It hugged her waist gently instead of cinching sharply.

"How do you like it?" Lyssara asked.

"I love it." Esther's voice was barely audible. She had never worn a dress made for movement instead of painful beauty. Even her travel dress had been too tight, too rigid.

"Good. Next time we'll pick something even better. Now that you're learning to choose."

Next time.

As if Esther belonged here.

As if she deserved to stay.

If she could choose how she dressed, where she stood, how she moved... what else had she been allowed to choose without realizing it?

"I like the belt," Esther added shyly.

Lyssara beamed. "Next order: more belts."

Then Lyssara launched into an exaggerated stage performance.

"Behold—our mighty party! Lyssara the Fearless! Vorrik the Brawn-Heavy! Nythir the Occasionally Useful Healer! And Essie the Magnificent! Torcher of plants *and* humans alike!"

Esther's laughter filled the room, bright and uncontained.

For a moment, they sounded like something out of one of Esther's old storybooks. Heroes with silly titles, shared meals, and laughter bright enough to scare away shadows. She held onto the sound, tucking it carefully into her chest, already aware of how fragile moments like this could be. Storybooks never spent much time on what happened after the adventure ended.

"Now," Lyssara said, grabbing Esther's boots and tossing them into her hands, "let's get you to dinner. Boots on, Cinnamon Bun. The boys are lost without us."

11

Nythir

How to enter a tavern: hope your traveling companions behave (they won't).

The girls had kicked them out.

"Privacy," Lyssara had said, physically herding Nythir and Vorrik into the hallway with a towel and a glare. "Go to Luna's. We'll find you when we're done."

Whatever *girl time* meant apparently involved a lot of steam, hair-related rituals, and Essie trying not to die of embarrassment. Nythir told himself he wasn't thinking about that. Or about how the last time he'd seen her, she'd been barefoot and grinning, hair wild from their downhill run and sweet potato sugar dusting her lips.

Which was precisely why he was now in Luna's Tavern, nursing a beer he didn't want.

The unease settled deeper than simple boredom. Nythir was used to the quiet hum of his own magic, steady and contained, but tonight something felt off balance, like a chord left unresolved. Esther's presence had a way of brushing against his senses, not loud or invasive, just warm and strangely familiar. Being apart from her made the absence noticeable. A hollow space where something had begun to resonate and now did not.

"Why am I stuck here with you?" he grumbled, lifting the mug anyway.

The beer was lukewarm and slightly sour, foam clinging stubbornly to the chipped rim. The heavy oak bar beneath his elbow felt sticky from a hundred spilled drinks. The whole place smelled like roasted meat, stale ale, hearth-smoke, and the tang of too many bodies crammed into one room.

"Because we're waiting for girl time to end, I think," Vorrik said cheerfully, already halfway through his second orc-sized mug. He wiped foam from his tusks with the back of his hand. "Luna! Another beer!"

"Nope," Luna said, snapping a towel over her shoulder as she slid past. Her silver hair was tied back, the rest falling in soft curls that brushed the low neckline of her dress. She flashed him a practiced, dazzling smile that didn't reach her eyes. "I refuse to deal with an inebriated Vorrik without his wife around ever again. I made that mistake once."

"That's not fair! I'm a paying customer!" Vorrik protested.

"You're an *annoying* customer," Luna shot back, snatching his empty mug. "Especially without Lyssara to wrangle you. No wife, no beer."

Someone hollered from across the room, "Bar wench! More shots at table three!"

The loudest table in the tavern roared with laughter—the seven men in gaudy, jewel-toned vests and far too many rings. Their clothes looked expensive if you didn't know what real noble fabrics looked like. Nythir did. Which meant he knew these men were the kind of rich that came from bad decisions and worse morals.

Every guild worth its salt had rules that mattered more than contracts, and one of them was simple. You did not endanger an informant. Tavern owners, brokers, and bartenders like Luna were the lifeblood of cities like Stonehaven. They heard everything. Names, routes, rumors, and mistakes whispered after too much drink. Anyone who treated an informant as disposable quickly found themselves without work, allies, or warning when trouble came knocking.

Karl's type eventually showed up in every trade hub. Men who followed caravans and festivals, flashing coins just real enough to pass casual inspection. They borrowed influence, borrowed names, and borrowed patience from people who could not afford to lose either. Stonehaven tolerated a lot, but it remembered everything. Karl had already crossed the invisible line. He just did not know it yet.

Nythir already knew how this would end. Karl would not be thrown out tonight. That would be messy and public. Instead, the problem would be handled quietly, with witnesses forgetting details and debts being settled through the proper channels. Jobs like this rarely came with formal postings. They came with looks, favors, and sunrise meetings.

He took a slow sip of his drink, letting the bitter taste linger on his tongue as he watched them.

"It's not unusual to see new faces in Stonehaven," he said, mostly to himself.

Essie would fit in perfectly in a town built at the center of a popular crossroads. New faces came and went as often as the rising and setting sun—and Luna would remember every single one of them, no matter how brief their stay.

Vorrik followed his gaze and winced. "They're dressed like a peacock with no sense of color."

Luna sashayed over to the rowdy table, hips swaying in a way that made half the tavern turn their heads.

"Oh my," she purred, leaning forward just enough for the men's gazes to drop exactly where she wanted them. "More shots already? Karl, might I interest you in one of my more *exclusive* drinks? On the house, of course."

The man in the center—Karl, apparently—laughed and slapped her on the backside. "If you insist, sweetheart."

Luna's professional smile didn't falter, but a muscle jumped in her jaw.

Nythir's grip tightened around his mug.

It was not the slap alone that sealed Karl's fate. It was the confidence in it. The assumption that nothing would happen. Nythir had seen that look before, usually right before someone learned how badly they had misjudged the room. Karl was no longer just a nuisance. He was a problem.

Problems like Karl rarely needed killing. That was crude. Inefficient. Most were dealt with through pressure, exposure, or removal from profitable routes. A broken reputation lasted longer than a broken bone. By morning, Karl would either be gone from Stonehaven or valuable to someone else. Either way, Luna would be compensated.

"Barkeep," Nythir called.

In guild circles, titles mattered. "Barkeep" was not an insult or a role. It was a signal. It meant business could be discussed without drawing attention, and that the speaker understood the rules of discretion. It told the listener that whatever followed would be handled professionally, with debts remembered and favors repaid.

"I'll be right there," she sang back, setting the tray of shots down in front of Karl and his companions. She laughed at something one of them said, head tilted, fingers resting lightly on his arm. To anyone else, she looked entirely charmed.

To Nythir, she looked like a woman cataloguing her enemies.

She glided back to the bar, grabbed Vorrik's mug, and turned the tap. Froth bubbled up—but the scent hit Nythir first.

Water.

No bitterness. No amber hue. Just Stonehaven well water.

"This is wa—" Vorrik began.

Luna stabbed a fork into the bar an inch from his hand, never losing her smile.

"If Sable does not get here soon," she said through gritted teeth, her voice pitched low enough that only they could hear over the din, "I am going to cut off that gremlin's hands and feed them to him."

Her eyes flicked toward Karl's table.

"Which gremlin?" Vorrik asked, yanking his hand back and visibly reconsidering his life choices.

"The one who thinks my ass is public property," she said brightly—then louder, seamlessly cheerful, "Here you are, sir!" as she slid the fake beer back to him.

Nythir almost pitied Karl.

Almost.

"Exclusive drinks, huh?" Nythir said lightly, setting his mug on the bar. "Think you can find one for me?"

Luna's gaze sharpened.

"Of course, sir," she said in her customer voice. "I'll get that for you right away."

"Why does *he* get beer?" Vorrik muttered.

"Because I'm not an idiot," Nythir said under his breath, "and I can read a room."

"Something's happening?" Vorrik asked, genuinely baffled.

Nythir tipped his head toward Karl's table. "Luna is siphoning information from the men dressed like a traveling circus."

Vorrik's expression shifted from confusion to sympathy. "Oh."

He glanced back at the table.

"They don't know what's about to hit them."

Vorrik handled problems that required presence. Nythir dealt with the ones that required patience. Together, they ensured jobs never escalated beyond necessary. Stonehaven preferred its violence contained, its deals clean, and its informants alive.

"Exactly."

Luna returned with a fresh mug for him, the foam thick and proper this time. He didn't want it, but he took a sip anyway and leaned across the counter, slipping on his best lazy half-smile.

"If Nythir is flirting with Luna," the regulars liked to say, "shut up and don't interrupt."

So no one listened too closely when they whispered.

Nythir slid a copper coin into her cleavage. "Payment for the beer."

The more inappropriate the gesture, the more invisible it became. To strangers, he was just another drunk, and she was just another bartender playing along for tips.

"Oh my, how generous," Luna said brightly. She flashed the flower-etched side of the coin toward Vorrik and the others. "You make me as happy as a caged bird who's learned to sing."

"Birds shouldn't be caged," Nythir murmured. "Maybe I should set you free."

"How about tomorrow at sunrise?" she replied smoothly. "I hear the view is lovely just past the bend."

Sunrise meetings were never romantic. They were neutral ground. Early enough that tempers had cooled and witnesses were scarce. Whatever Luna brought tomorrow would determine the scope of the favor, and whatever Nythir offered in return would set the terms. Information for action. Protection for cooperation. That was how guild relations stayed profitable and bloodless.

"I'll look forward to it."

"Bar wench! What's keeping you?" Karl shouted.

If being an outsider in Stonehaven hadn't already been obvious, that sealed it.

Luna leaned closer to Nythir, her smile never slipping, teeth grinding behind it. "The bird is going to get killed if Sable doesn't arrive soon."

Nythir pitied her.

He wouldn't have been able to keep up the act while getting groped. If the guild master didn't arrive soon, Luna was going to find the most painful poison and make them suffer.

She grabbed a blue bottle and poured out amber liquid. Nythir rarely saw her pull that drink. The men were about to get very honest, very fast. Luna usually preferred subtler methods—something about savoring the euphoria of information—but even she had her breaking points.

"What does the birdcage mean again?" Vorrik asked.

"Why have codes if you're not going to remember them?"

"I don't need to remember them when I have you to tell me."

"Seriously," Nythir sighed. "Do you at least remember what the coin means?"

"Engraved side up means help, right?"

"Oh, look. He can remember stuff. Lyssara's going to be upset when she finds out drinking is cancelled."

"No more drinking?" Vorrik grumbled. "That is so unfair."

"Life's unfair. Drink your water."

12

Esther

How to hide feelings: stare intensely and pretend it's normal.

They looked like a pair straight out of one of her novels.

Nythir stood at the bar, smiling at a woman whose silver hair caught the lantern light like spun starlight — the kind of woman romance books described as effortlessly stunning. The type who didn't accidentally summon explosions when nervous.

Esther tugged at the uneven ends of her own hair, wishing she hadn't hacked it off like a sleep-deprived lumberjack. If she'd known her teleportation spell would drop her into a band of adventurers—and in front of an unfairly attractive elf—she would have:

Not cut her hair.

Packed makeup.

Reinforced her satchel so her guidebooks wouldn't be lost to a murderous forest.

"Looks like he's got some business with Luna," Lyssara said. "Best not to interrupt them. Let's take a seat."

Best not to interrupt them?

Nythir did not look out of place behind the bar. That unsettled her more than it should have. He spoke easily, held himself like someone used to being listened to, not because of rank but because of competence. It dawned on her that this was not his first negotiation disguised as conversation.

Esther shoved her hands deep inside her cloak so no one would notice the faint gold flickering under her skin. Her eyes darted around the tavern, scanning for her natural predator—candles.

None.

Instead, lanterns glowed with floating light orbs—expensive rune devices she'd only seen during palace balls. They were finicky, high-maintenance, and required regular magical absorption.

Rune lanterns like these weren't decorative indulgences. They marked places of importance. They were meant to keep magic stable in crowded rooms and to quietly record disturbances. Esther realized, a little belatedly, that this tavern was not simply a place to drink. It was a place where things were watched, remembered, and acted upon.

She sank into the corner table beside Lyssara. It provided the perfect vantage point to keep an eye on the bar while remaining invisible.

Invisible.

In her previous life, she had never been invisible.

But here. *With friends.* Her chest fluttered at the thought.

Something tugged at her awareness, faint but persistent. Not fear. Not excitement. Something steadier. Esther frowned, pressing her fingers together as her magic shifted in response. When she glanced toward the bar and met Nythir's eyes, the sensation settled immediately, as if a string pulled too tight had finally gone slack.

Then reality crashed back in.

Her lips trembled, butterflies thrumming violently in her stomach.

"Stop looking over there like he's a fish at the campfire," Lyssara muttered.

"I have no idea what you mean."

"And stop sitting like a princess."

"P-Princess?" Esther squeaked. Her bloodstream felt like boiling water, static crackling down her arms. Outside, a splash was followed by a string of curses.

"What makes you say that?" she whispered sharply.

"Oh, moons." Lyssara winced as the entire window beside them splintered with a loud crack. "I meant the posture. The way you're sitting on your cloak like it's a throne."

Esther swallowed hard.

"Maybe a drink will relax you. What do you like?" Lyssara asked.

"I've never had alcohol."

"What," Lyssara gasped dramatically. "You're twenty-one?"

"Almost twenty-two."

"You poor, sheltered child! We're fixing that tonight." Lyssara flagged down Luna—just as Nythir leaned in to slip a coin between the woman's breasts.

Crack!

Esther wanted Lucy's arms to cry into. She should've kept her interactions with men strictly to reading novels.

There was an undercurrent in the room that had nothing to do with flirtation. Voices pitched just low enough. Laughter timed too carefully.

Esther felt it prickle along her spine, as magic warnings did, the sense that something was being decided nearby without her consent or understanding.

"Well," Lyssara groaned, dragging a hand down her face, "she's definitely going to notice that now."

"Good thing there aren't candles," Esther muttered, staring at the ruined window.

"Good thing indeed. Oh—they're finishing up. Come on." Lyssara moved to join the others.

Esther didn't.

She stayed tucked in the shadows, staring through the cracked window.

Sunset stretched endlessly, unblocked by palace walls. Rolling paths, distant mountains, even the edge of Ashvale—everything lay open before her.

It was beautiful.

It hurt.

"That's a very big crack," Nythir chuckled, sliding into the seat across from her.

His voice—she hated how much she loved the sound of it.

"Is it true you've never had alcohol?"

"It's true," she murmured, avoiding his gaze. Her stomach twisted. For the first time in her life, she worried about the damage she could cause.

"Try this one." He nudged his mug toward her. His fingers brushed the rim—the same fingers that had just touched Luna.

She pushed it back. "I don't want to."

"Just a sip?"

Stars, she wanted to. But—

"I can't even control my magic sober," she whispered. "If I drink—"

"Why not?"

"Did you not hear what I just said?" She clenched her hands under the table to hide the faint glow. Shame prickled down her spine.

The cracked window. Her uneven hair. Her entire existence.

She was the runaway Princess of Valedara. And he had smiled at Luna like... She bit her tongue.

Without touching her, without even looking at her hands, Nythir shifted. His magic brushed against hers like a steadying breath. The glow dulled, then softened, responding to him in a way it had never done before, either to discipline or command. Esther swallowed, shaken by how easily her power listened.

"I heard you," Nythir said softly. "I just don't see the problem."

"My magic—"

"Is fine," he said gently. "I'll take care of you and your magic. Just like at the campfire."

Her breath hitched.

"But you told me to hide my sparks," she whispered.

"What—oh." His expression shifted as understanding dawned. "Essie... you misunderstood."

Her heart stopped. "I don't understand."

He reached across the table and took her hand—warm, steady, unafraid of the glow beneath her skin.

"Your sparks," he murmured, "are identifiable. Beautiful. Alluring. They shine too bright. I wasn't telling you to hide because I don't like them." His thumb brushed her knuckles. "I like them too much."

Her breath left her in a trembling rush.

"You're running from something," he continued quietly. "A girl in silk dresses doesn't just teleport into a dangerous forest. I don't need the details yet. But until you're ready..." His gaze softened. "You're ours now. And we can help."

Her throat tightened as something warm and terrifying bloomed in her chest.

No one had ever said that to her without strings attached. Not tutors. Not nobles. Not even well-meaning allies. The words did not cage her. They made space. Esther realized with quiet terror that this was what safety felt like, and that made it far more dangerous than fear.

"Is this the lil' mage Lyssara told me about?" Luna appeared with a drink, glowing pink and purple. The sweet scent wafted up instantly. "Essie, right? Or should I call you Cinabun?"

"Cinabun?" Esther squeaked. "Uh... sure?"

"You're adorable. Waste of a good evening to sit in a dark corner with grumpy here." Luna plopped down beside Esther, looping her arm through hers. She was soft, warm, and very close.

This felt familiar, Esther realized.

Like a rival love interest trying to stake a claim on the male lead. She really wished she had her guidebooks to navigate this situation.

"I mind," Nythir grumbled.

"Oh? Why?" Luna purred, pressing closer.

"Because you're interrupting."

"You're in my tavern."

Esther looked between the two, confused by the tension. It was completely different from their earlier flirting. Before, they had looked like a perfect painting hung on palace walls. Now, they resembled two dogs about to fight over the last bone.

Luna leaned in. "Lyssara said Cinabun here wasn't spoken for. Or is she?"

Two sets of eyes fixed on Esther.

Her mind went blank. "Maybe?"

Nythir's sky-blue eyes darkened into a storm, jaw ticking.

Luna laughed. "Coy. I like it."

"What do you mean, maybe?" Nythir growled.

Esther panicked. "I didn't agree to anything, but the arrangement—well—I ran away—so maybe—"

"So that's what you're running from," Nythir said, smirking as if it weighed nothing.

She had said too much.

Esther grabbed the sweet drink Luna had set before her and chugged it.

"Woah!" Luna cheered. "Look at her go! Chug! Chug!"

Soon, Esther was several drinks deep, laughter spilling from her like sunlight.

Then she and Luna were dancing in the center of the tavern, spinning wildly as a cheering crowd gathered.

Strong hands caught her by the waist, pulling her close.

"Are you having fun?" Nythir asked, his voice warm against her ear.

"So much fun!" she shouted, breathless.

Maybe her father had been wrong. Maybe alcohol didn't make her magic worse.

Maybe... freedom did.

Or maybe—it was being allowed to be herself. But she didn't yet know what that truly meant.

"Dance with me," Esther twirled, throwing her arms around Nythir's neck.

His calm persona cracked, and she glimpsed a momentary look of shock on his face.

"Your wish is my command," he chuckled. The slight sound sent warmth rushing through her. "But not here."

Nythir guided her gently through the overcrowded tavern and into the crisp night air. The chill caressed her flushed cheeks.

She didn't know if she felt so warm from the alcohol or from the way Nythir's long fingers clasped hers.

She settled on both—but mostly Nythir. She did not want him to notice how much he affected her.

As always, her magic betrayed her. Sparks flickered along her fingers. She tried to pull away, but he held tighter.

Instead of scattering, the sparks settled into a slower rhythm, matching the calm cadence of Nythir's magic. Where her power usually surged and recoiled, it now moved with purpose. Not restrained. Not silenced. Simply guided. The realization left her breathless.

"I don't know how," Esther muttered, eyes on their moving feet.

"What don't you know?"

"Heart and mirrors."

"What about them?"

"How to... heart my mirror."

"I have no clue what you're talking about," Nythir chuckled, "but I'll do my best to heart your mirror."

"Really?" Esther squeezed his hand.

"Really." He squeezed back. "We're here."

They arrived in a small garden, the scent of roses thick in the night air. A fountain trickled in the center, moonlight reflecting off the water. It looked neglected—small cracks and chips in the once-beautiful structure—but Esther sympathized with it.

The rose bushes were wild and unruly, leaves sprouting in all directions, overpowering the small red buds. They weren't the perfectly tended blooms of her childhood, but somehow their fragrance was more potent, more alive. They were still beautiful without the strict control a gardener would have imposed.

She loved her mother's roses, but these wild ones... they resonated with her.

Wild things did not lack beauty. They lacked permission. Standing there, surrounded by roses that had grown without approval or pruning, Esther wondered for the first time if her magic had been waiting for the same freedom.

"It's dirty and dark here," Nythir said, lighting a lantern in the corner. "But we can dance without a crowd." He gave a slight bow and held out his hand.

"I've never danced with a man before," Esther admitted, placing her hand in his. The lantern flickered with her heartbeat, but she wasn't worried. Somehow, she knew her flames wouldn't betray her—not this moment.

"I'm proud to be your first," he whispered, barely louder than the flicker of the lamp. He guided her into a gentle waltz. It was the first dance she had ever learned, years ago, tucked away in lessons long forgotten—and now, finally, she could use it.

The moon hung low over Stonehaven by the time Nythir walked Esther back to the inn. Their fingers—warm, faintly sparking—reluctantly parted at the door.

The moment their hands separated, her magic stirred uneasily, like something woken too soon. The glow beneath her skin dimmed but did not fade, lingering in quiet protest. Esther pressed her palm to her chest, unsettled by how wrong the distance felt after only a few hours.

She swayed slightly, drunk on sugar, alcohol, and freedom. Golden light still clung to her skin like the last embers of a dying fire.

"Sleep," he murmured, brushing a soft curl from her cheek.

"Only... if you do too," she mumbled, eyes half-lidded.

He almost laughed, almost leaned in, nearly let reason slip away—but the inn door creaked behind them, and the moment vanished like smoke.

Essie blinked up at him once more, soft and drowsy, then disappeared inside. The scent of roses and cinnamon lingered long after she was gone.

13

Lucy

How to perform a spectacular breakdown: hydrate for optimal tears.

The next morning, Lucy straightened her uniform and muttered, "You ready?" She was preparing herself for her best performance yet.

"No," Basil grumbled. "I'll be at my station. Please, don't be too dramatic. It needs to look authentic."

"I am never dramatic. If anything, you are—with how you slammed the door open with a 'I know it's you, Lucy.' I swear, my soul left my body. I briefly saw my grandmother. May she rest in peace."

"See? Dramatic. Stop it." Basil rolled his eyes. Lucy stuck her tongue out. She hadn't expected any allies—especially not Esther's magic tutor.

The previous night had been a disaster of confessions and hastily-made plans.

"Please, explain to me why the Princess's magic erupted in the rose garden. Along with your compliance in the matter," Basil said, ripping the quilt off Lucy.

"I need a minute to get my story straight," Lucy muttered. "And how did you know it was me?"

"I don't need a story. I need the truth. Also, your aura is different from Princess Esther's."

"Marriage. Orc with Warts. Runaway Princess." Lucy rattled off what she knew. "I thought only the highest-class aura knights and mages could sense aura."

She looked Basil over from head to toe—he couldn't be in either category.

"I was once the head of Queen Estella's personal guard, thank you very much. That said, I know for a fact that was Princess Esther's magic—and her aura disappeared from the castle. And you sent the palace guards away. What is this about orcs with warts?"

Lucy had been told not to judge a book by its cover. She always did, though. She only looked at books if the cover caught her eye. Basil's book did not match his cover, though it explained why everyone in the palace called him 'Sir Basil.'

"I told you everything I know."

"Lucy, we're on the same side."

"What side?"

"The princess's side. I am loyal to her."

"You're telling me, if you caught Esther in the act of running away like I did, you would've let her go?"

"I would have followed her."

"What?" Lucy laughed in disbelief, but stopped when she met his eyes. "You're serious?"

"I promised the late Queen that I would keep the princess safe."

"Even more reason you would have stopped her."

"Keeping her safe doesn't end at her physical well-being."

"What are you saying?"

"You read so much, yet you're so dense," he sighed, rubbing the bridge of his nose. "When the Queen gave her life for her daughter, the King lost his courage. You know the saying, 'if you love something, set it free?'"

"You're calling the King a coward?" Lucy asked, awestruck.

"Yes. King Arcturus became too afraid to let his daughter have freedom. Not after she died once—"

"Died?" Lucy cut him off.

"Tale for another time. Moral of the story: the King's love became suffocating due to fear. He thought he was protecting his daughter, but he was breaking her. I don't think it could ever be fixed if she stayed in that environment."

"What? No! Story now! What do you mean died?" Lucy threw a pillow at him. It hit his chest and thudded to the floor louder than expected.

"You need to tell me your story now. We need a plan for when they realize she's missing. Did you think of that?"

She had not. Which, in hindsight, was probably a problem.

Lucy burst from Esther's chambers with a shriek that could rival a howler monkey in a turf war. She had gargled salt water beforehand—purely for optimal shriek range.

"The princess is missing!" she cried, lifting her skirts and sprinting down the halls. Falling wasn't in her plan, but scraped knees added authenticity to the scene.

She skidded to a halt and slammed open the double doors to the King's study. She'd always wanted to do that. The echo alone was worth at least a six out of ten on the dramatic scale.

"What is the meaning of this?" Prince Lupin demanded, dark circles shadowing his amber eyes. He and the King were poring over documents in the overly decorated study. Did they really need a stuffed lion head staring at them like that?

"Princess Esther is missing!" Lucy dropped to her knees and let the tears flow. She made sure to apply extra mascara and eyeliner for dramatic effect.

"What?" King Arcturus thundered. "She was confirmed in her quarters by none other than you!" He slammed his fist onto the table, sending ink spilling across hopefully unimportant documents.

"It is as you say," Lucy's voice cracked. She didn't have to fake that part—she hadn't accounted for just how terrifying the king could be. "She was exhausted after her magic lesson—where she successfully dried a towel—and so she turned in for bed after a relaxing rose bath."

"Yet now she's missing?" Prince Lupin grabbed her chin, forcing her gaze upward.

"As you say, my lord!" she cried, smudging the black makeup under her eyes for added effect. Lupin looked so much like Esther that Lucy almost got comfortable and considered saying something very obscene—but no. She was there on a mission. The prince and king were uptight. Esther was fun. Lucy would have run away, too.

"Is there any knight in the castle who could track down Est—Princess Esther?"

Cue Basil.

"We haven't had anyone in the castle with such a skill in over a decade," Prince Lupin growled, dropping Lucy's chin like it was a trivial thing.

Basil missed his cue.

"We must send out a search party," the king said. "Call a guard to take this maid to the dungeon. We will extract answers from her."

"If only," Lucy tapped into her inner howler monkey, "there was an old man in the castle who could sense aura!"

She had no one to write to burn her super secret stash of books. Could she trust Basil to burn both Esther's and hers?

"What is all this ruckus?" Basil entered.

"Sir Basil?" King Arcturus said. "Perfect timing. I am in need of your help. But first, summon guards to take this maid to the dungeons."

Basil did not arrive exactly on cue.

"I am innocent, your majesty! Please take pity on this loyal, hard-working maid!" Lucy flailed dramatically.

"Let's not be hasty. Why is Princess Esther's personal maid being thrown in the dungeon?"

"Esther is missing," Prince Lupin said, jaw ticking. Lucy appreciated his low voice. Her head was starting to ache from the king's shouting. "This maid was the last to see her, supposedly. Now my sister is gone, and it must be tied to her magic lightning strike in the rose garden."

Basil nodded thoughtfully. "I just reported to Captain Aldric that the magical residue in the garden does not match Princess Esther's, nor anyone else in the castle. May I investigate her personal chambers?"

"Of course," King Arcturus said calmly. Lucy felt a pang of guilt at the king's somber expression but quickly flicked it away. It was his fault she ran away. How could he keep her locked up just to marry her off to an orc?

"The maid will accompany us. You can determine the validity of her story after my verdict."

"My savior!" Lucy clasped her hands together and looked up at Basil adoringly. He returned a glare of pure disgust. Rude.

"Her aura is still strong in her chambers," Basil said, standing in the center of the room. A broken mirror and messy bed added drama to the scene. It went against every fiber of Lucy's sense of order not to tidy up—but Basil insisted it helped set the stage. She did smooth out the hair, though.

"Which means?" the king's voice cracked.

"She was in her bed no more than three hours ago. I must conclude this maid is innocent."

"My daughter..." The king's eyes glistened, but he quickly composed himself. A heavy silence passed before he continued. "Do you have any insight as to her whereabouts, Sir Basil?"

"I can deduce she left of her own volition. There is a teleportation sigil drawn on the floor, by the mirror." Basil had planted it the previous night. Not exactly a lie. They had only shifted the time and location, so Lucy couldn't be blamed.

"Enough!" King Arcturus's voice boomed, shocking Basil and Lucy straight. "I've patiently waited to see what ploy you were horribly acting out, but this is just laughable."

"That is true," Basil said flatly.

"You can't admit it that easily," Lucy hissed.

"I know my daughter's magic. I assumed her maid was hiding one of Esther's disasters again, so I left it be. But for her to have run away... never would I have thought."

"It's your fault," Lucy interjected, irritation winning over respect. She shoved Esther's letter at him.

She expected the King to get mad at her defiance, but instead, he looked stricken. Silence fell over the room, broken only by the sound of rapid heartbeats.

"Father, I will send an order to the most esteemed guilds and lead the search with the royal guard."

"You can't. I need you in Kraggmar. We need this alliance."

"My sister is more important than an alliance," Prince Lupin seethed.

If that were true, they wouldn't have sold her off, Lucy thought.

"I have heard whispers of an alliance. At risk of being impertinent, may I ask the details?" Basil asked.

"No point in hiding anything now," the King sighed. "Lupin will be traveling to Kraggmar to bond with Princess Arietta before their marriage after the Harvest Ball."

Lucy and Basil didn't need telepathy to know they were thinking the same thing. Their princess had jumped to conclusions and run away from a marriage that was not hers. If the room weren't so tense, she would have laughed. That misunderstanding and rash reaction were on brand for Esther.

"The King is right. The wedding must proceed to solidify our alliances. It would also be too dangerous to reveal the princess is out there without protection to anyone outside her close circle. I will take on the responsibility of searching for the princess."

"You?" Lupin asked incredulously. "You're the one who collaborated in a lie about her escape."

Lucy did not like the way the prince looked at Basil. The only ones who could disrespect him were Esther and herself—no one else. Not even the prince.

"He has the power to sense her magic and past experience leading the royal guard. And he cares about Esther. In fact, I'd wager he knows more about her than you," she bit out.

"Finally decided to stop talking weird?" Basil whispered. She stomped on his toe, earning a pained grunt.

"It's impossible with only one retired guard," the King said. "I... don't know what to do."

Lucy's heart panged. For once, the King simply looked human. At this moment, he was nothing more than a lost, worried father hoping his daughter was safe.

"I will request help from The Brass Sparrow," Basil said, emphasizing the guild name.

"The Brass Sparrow? The most elite guild that doesn't bow to anyone, even royal power? How will you get their help?" Lucy asked theatrically, despite no longer needing to act.

"I have personal relations with the guild master. He's my brother-in-law. We've remained close even after my wife's death."

"And I'll go with! I've spent from dawn to dusk with the princess every day for the past... how many years? If anyone can recognize her from afar, it's me."

"I will put my trust in you, Sir Basil. Please, bring my daughter back."

When Lucy left, she was sure she had seen the intimidating King of Valedara crying into a letter.

14

Nythir

How to recover: regret everything, then do it again tomorrow.

The sun rose far too early.

Stonehaven's morning light pressed harshly against his eyelids, dragging Nythir awake to the muffled sound of retching in the adjoining room, the crackle of a dying hearth, and Vorrik's rattling snores. The crisp bite of cold air poured through the window, carrying scents of baking bread, wet earth, and river wind.

Instead, he found himself dragged into a morning full of consequences and regret. Allowing Lyssara and Vorrik to drink unsupervised topped the list.

The air was sharp with early frost, every breath puffing white clouds as he exhaled. Stonehaven's streets were barely waking—lanterns flickering low, shutters creaking open, and the distant clang of a blacksmith beginning the day echoing faintly across the river.

Stonehaven pretended to be quiet in the mornings, but it was never asleep. Stonehaven did this every morning—played at innocence while sharpening its teeth. The city was built on old stone and older secrets, layered atop each other like sediment. If you listened long enough, you could hear the past whispering through cracked walls and sewer grates.

People said the Information Guild merely listened. Nythir knew better. Listening was only the first step. Recording came next. Then deciding who lived long enough to regret what they'd said. Information flowed here the way water did through cracked stone—slow, steady, and impossible to fully dam.

Merchants traded rumors with their bread. Dockhands listened better than priests. And the Information Guild thrived because this city sat between too many borders, too many grudges, and too many roads that led somewhere dangerous.

Nythir trusted Stonehaven the way one trusted a blade: functional, familiar, and fully capable of cutting you if you grew careless.

Blades were honest things. They did not pretend to be anything other than what they were. Essie moved through the world like a candle in a draft—bright, earnest, and blissfully unaware of how many hands wanted to cup her flame. Stonehaven would notice her eventually. Cities always saw things that didn't belong.

"I told you not to drink," Nythir grumbled, pulling his cloak tighter. "I leave you alone for one minute and you both drown yourselves in beer."

"It was more than a minute," Vorrik groaned. He pressed a cold slab of raw steak to his swollen black eye. The meat dripped onto his tunic, adding a bloody, metallic tang to the morning air.

"You're being too loud…" Lyssara moaned, her voice thick with misery. She was still in her nightgown and slippers, a satin bonnet hiding the hair disaster beneath. She moved like a wounded animal, each shuffle punctuated by another pitiful groan.

Birds sang in the background—their happy chirps aggravating Nythir further. He should've still been in bed, under a blanket, where he could hear Essie breathing in the adjoining room.

Essie remained at The Moonpetal Inn—soft, warm, unmoving. An innocent boulder suffering the consequences of her first night of freedom. Technically second, but she was knocked out by a book her first night, so she needed a redo.

A vendor called in the background, announcing a newly released coffee flavor.

"Orchard-spice nut caramel brew! Perfect to take the chill from these brisk mornings!"

Essie would have laughed at the name. She would have asked if "orchard-spice nut caramel brew" was three drinks pretending to be one. He could already hear it—gentle teasing, eyes bright despite the headache, warmth bleeding into a place that had felt hollow longer than he cared to admit.

He hated how easily she occupied his thoughts now. Hated even more that he didn't want her to leave them.

Nythir made a mental note to deliver her breakfast: eggs, oranges, maybe honey water. Something gentle. He wished he could give it to her as soon as she awoke, but he couldn't be so lucky.

He cursed the brightly colored men from the previous night. They quickly rose to the top of his enemies list for being the catalyst of his miserable morning. He was the number one enemy on the top of that list for offering help to Luna in the first place. But he needed to stay in the informant's good graces to get the top jobs.

Informants were not friends. They were not allies. They were forces of nature that demanded respect. You did not threaten them, and you did not cross them unless you were prepared to vanish—or be made an example of.

Luna was worse than most. She didn't collect information to sell—it collected *her*. People came to her willingly, smiling, grateful for the privilege of being useful. And when she smiled back, it was never clear whether you'd just been helped or marked.

Nythir had seen what happened to people who realized too late which one they were. Luna, especially, operated on favors like currency. One good turn bought you silence. Two bought you protection. Three bought you survival.

Nythir had intended to cash in exactly one favor. He had not planned on owing her anything.

They waited at the outskirts of town for Sable, shivering in the bite of early morning.

The world around them slowly awoke. Chimneys puffed. Carts rumbled over cobblestone streets. Children ran around while mothers called after them. The frost on the leaves dripped, drinking in the warmth of the rising sun.

The road hummed beneath his boots, a low vibration he felt more than heard. Restless trade routes. Messages delayed. Coin changing hands too fast or not at all. When systems that relied on routine began to stutter, it meant someone somewhere was pulling threads they didn't fully understand—or didn't care what unraveled.

Empires didn't collapse all at once. They frayed first.

Travelers whispered of stalled caravans and missing couriers. Of guild contracts being pulled without explanation. Of borders tightening where they had once been loose.

Something was shifting. Slowly. Quietly.

And Stonehaven, ever the listener, was already adjusting its grip.

It all contrasted horribly with the two hungover disasters standing in the dirt.

"Where is she?" Lyssara complained, flopping dramatically to the cold ground. "I'm dying. Can you please heal me?"

"No." Nythir didn't even look at her. "I told you not to drink. I am not using my magic for a hangover."

"I bet you'll do it for Essie," she muttered.

"Of course," he said instantly.

Lyssara groaned louder in a mixture of pain, amusement, and accusation. "Favoritism. Obvious favoritism."

Favoritism implied choice. This didn't feel like one. It felt like gravity—inevitable, inconvenient, and impossible to negotiate with. He hadn't decided to care. He had simply woken up one morning and realized the world was sharper whenever Essie wasn't within reach.

That frightened him more than any informant ever could.

Nythir ignored her, gaze drifting to the memory of the previous night.

The way Essie's sparks glowed in the moonlight, painting her skin in molten gold.

The soft hush of roses in the garden breeze.

The whisper of her laugh brushed his collarbone as she leaned closer. Her breath was warm on his neck.

He never had a favorite color before. Now he did. *Gold*.

And he cursed his companions and all their future descendants for taking him away from that color so early in the morning. He hated mornings. He especially hated this morning above all other mornings.

Sable finally arrived—boisterous and unbothered. She stretched languidly, like she'd woken from a peaceful nap instead of a brawl. At least she had enough delicacy to not slap a meat slab on her black eye. She wore it proudly, like a trophy.

His magic stirred again, subtle but insistent, coiling tighter instead of loosening as the sun climbed higher. He had learned to trust that feeling long before he learned to trust people. Magic didn't lie. It reacted to pressure, to intent, to threats not yet visible.

Whatever was coming had already taken its first step.

"Good morning!" she bellowed.

Lyssara clutched her head and retched into a bush. Birds scattered from nearby branches at the sheer volume of her misery.

"You're late," Nythir said flatly. He wasn't even angry anymore. He was just dead inside.

"Only by a few minutes." Sable yawned, rubbing her non-swollen eye. Her short silver hair stood in every direction like a startled hedgehog. Her leather armor smelled faintly of ale, smoke, and poor decisions. "So what business do you have with me?"

"You mean a few hours," Lyssara hissed, wiping her mouth with the back of her hand. She kicked Vorrik's boot. "Wake up. She's here."

"An attack?" Vorrik shot upright, then immediately wavered and collapsed in a heap of limbs and pain.

"You're not under attack, you giant oaf," Sable laughed.

"You're the one with business," Lyssara grumbled. "Not us."

Sable blinked. "Luna said you had a job for me."

Silence. A slow, dawning, shared one. An uneasy tingle crept down Nythir's spine.

Lyssara's face drained of color. "We got played?"

"It seems so," Sable sighed. A crow called in the background, almost mockingly.

"Why?" Nythir asked, voice sharpening. Something cold and heavy settled in his stomach. "Where is Luna?"

"I think she said she was going to Moonpetal—"

Nythir's breath hitched once—sharp and involuntary—before instinct took over. If Luna was moving openly, it meant she wasn't worried about being seen. And that meant whatever game she was playing, she was already several moves ahead.

Nythir didn't hear the rest.

He was already gone.

The sound of his boots blended into the bustling city. He narrowly dodged carts. He didn't have time to think.

He only knew one thing: *something was wrong.*

15

Esther

How to trust breakfast: with extreme caution and mild paranoia.

The morning sun pried through the curtains like an overly eager intruder, landing directly across Esther's eyelids. The light felt too bright, too sharp. Like someone had carved it with a knife and angled it right at her face.

The room felt different in the daylight.

Not dangerous. Not hostile. Just... alert. As if the walls were listening instead of resting, the way the palace halls always had.

Daylight had always been the most dangerous time in the palace. Shadows hid intentions, but light exposed expectation. Morning meant lessons. Corrections. Smiles that did not reach the eyes. She had learned early that being watched did not always mean being protected.

Esther had grown up learning the subtle difference between safety and supervision, and this felt uncomfortably close to the latter.

Freedom, Esther was learning, did not arrive quietly. It arrived jangling nerves and setting off alarms she hadn't known were still wired into her body. The palace had trained her to anticipate harm before it happened. Even now, safety felt like something she had borrowed and would be asked to return.

She groaned and burrowed deeper into the pillow. The lingering scent of spilled ale clung to her hair, sour and stubborn. Her head throbbed in sync with the tavern's distant morning bustle below. Each clatter of dishes bounced around her skull like a personal punch to her brain.

Her legs felt heavy, as if phantom vines still wrapped around them from yesterday's sprint through a tantrum-throwing forest. Her back ached with the memory of dancing far too enthusiastically while tipsy. And her dignity...her dignity was hurt from existing anywhere near Nythir with alcohol involved.

Dignity had been one of the first things she'd learned to guard. Not because it mattered to her—but because it mattered to everyone else. A princess who embarrassed herself was a liability. A princess who laughed too loudly was undisciplined. A princess who wanted anything at all was dangerous.

She had murky memories of dancing in the tavern with Luna and others she didn't know. She had a feeling that she had made a complete fool of herself.

Yesterday had been... a lot.

And she never wanted to move, speak, or be perceived again.

Wanting to disappear was familiar. She had mastered stillness long ago—how to breathe quietly, how to make herself smaller without shrinking, how to exist without leaving marks. What unsettled her was not the exhaustion, but the absence of regret. She did not regret laughing. She did not regret dancing. She did not regret wanting more.

A floorboard creaked by the doorway.

Then a warm smell of fresh cinnamon, toasted sugar, and roasted coffee beans drifted toward her. The air thickened with it, cozy and nostalgic. For a heartbeat, she could almost feel Lucy brushing her bangs back, placing a smuggled sweet roll under her nose while whispering gently, "Wake up before your father realizes you're not in bed."

It had only been a few days. But it felt like she hadn't seen her closest friend in years.

"Wakey wakey, Cinabun," a cheerful, sing-song voice chimed.

Esther groaned and yanked the thin blanket over her head. The fabric was cool against her overheated cheeks.

"Come on," the voice laughed. "I even brought you coffee."

The bed dipped beside her, light enough not to jostle her but deliberate enough that the mattress gave a little sigh beneath the weight. Esther peeked out from the blanket.

Luna sat poised on the mattress like an artist's muse, legs tucked gracefully beneath her. Her silver hair now gleamed violet in the sunlight. Not a single strand out of place. Not a trace of hangover. Not an ounce of shame.

Esther blinked. "Do you... also work for the inn?"

Luna smirked and offered the steaming mug. A swirl of cream spiraled across the surface like delicate artwork.

"Nice guess, but nope."

Luna moved like someone who knew exactly how much space to take up. Not too close. Not too far. She settled beside Esther with practiced ease, like she had done this a hundred times before—for different people, in other rooms.

It was oddly comforting.

And that, Esther realized distantly, was what made it unsettling.

Esther pushed herself upright with the enthusiasm of a corpse rising from the dead—fitting, really. The motion sent a lightning bolt of pain through her skull. The room tilted, then settled. Her stomach sloshed unpleasantly.

And the memories of last night, after she left the tavern, trickled in. Completely clear despite the inebriated state she had been in. The boldness. The dancing. The almost kissing someone under a moonlit sky.

She was never drinking again. Probably.

But maybe she would. When she needed some liquid courage.

To maybe almost kiss a handsome elf again.

"Then why are you delivering breakfast?" she whispered, embarrassed by how dry and cracked her voice sounded.

"Because I was curious." Luna's tone danced between mischief and sincerity. "And I like watching people wake up. Here, try it. I guessed the cream and sugar."

Esther accepted the mug as if it were a sacred relic. The ceramic was warm beneath her palms, grounding her. She inhaled the scent. It smelled rich and sweet, with too much sugar but exactly the right amount of relief.

She took a sip. Warmth spread down her throat and blossomed in her chest. She took another.

Her magic stirred before her thoughts caught up. It never waited for permission. It responded to fear faster than reason, to emotion faster than logic. That was why they had called her unstable. That was why she had been trained to suppress instead of understand. Feeling too much had always been the problem.

When she was calm, it stayed warm and quiet, like sunlight behind closed eyes. When she was afraid, it prickled and sparked, demanding release. Her tutors had called it instability. Her father had called it dangerous.

Esther had learned to call it a warning.

"Have you ever been told you're too trusting, Cinabun?" Luna leaned in, her breath brushing Esther's cheek like a teasing breeze.

"A few times," Esther admitted quietly.

"You shouldn't drink things from strangers."

Esther froze.

The words hit something old and buried. A rule etched into her bones long before she understood why it existed. Her stomach turned, not from the coffee, but from memory—thick and bitter and wrong, clinging to the back of her throat like a warning she'd failed to heed once before.

Her heart lurched so hard she felt it echo in her ribs. Her hands trembled, the mug rattling faintly against the saucer. Her magic prickled awake under her skin like static lightning.

Luna lunged.

In one swift motion, Esther's wrists slammed into the mattress, pinned by deceptively delicate hands. Coffee splashed across the sheets, dark droplets soaking into the linen and dripping to the wooden floor with soft, rhythmic patters.

Esther gasped—no, choked—as Luna's weight settled across her hips.

She kicked her legs, struggling to break free, but Luna's grip was fierce and unyielding. Esther couldn't escape with her measly strength alone.

She couldn't move. She couldn't breathe. Her legs went numb at the edges, tingling.

This wasn't how danger was supposed to feel.

There were no raised voices. No drawn blades. Just warmth turned sharp, and familiarity was misused. Her magic flared too late, confused by the sudden shift, scrambling to protect her from something it hadn't recognized as a threat soon enough.

She had mistaken kindness for safety.

The palace specialized in that mistake. Kindness was easier to accept than control. Easier to obey. Easier to forgive. Esther had never learned how to recognize danger that smiled.

The realization hurt worse than the fear.

Magic flared up—instinctive, wild—begging to defend her, but she forced it down with sheer, terrified will. She knew what happened when she lost control.

A whisper curled through her mind like smoke: *"Don't die."*

"No," Esther's voice cracked. "No, please—"

Her vision blurred at the edges. The scent of cinnamon turned suffocatingly sweet. A cold tear slid down her cheek, trailing into her hairline. She wasn't in the inn anymore. She was in a small bed with worn sheets and winter-chilled air, unable to breathe, unable to cry, unable to—

Her heart hammered painfully.

Luna leaned down until their noses almost touched.

"I am very skilled at making potions and poisons," she purred.

"Poison?" Esther squeaked. The word detonated inside her like a memory-shard. Her pulse stuttered—too fast, then too slow.

Her body remembered before her mind allowed it. Heat. Then cold. A pressure in her chest that made breathing feel optional. Someone crying. Someone begging her to stay awake. The memory fractured before it could take shape, but the fear remained—raw and immediate.

Her body remembered something her mind refused to name: something cold, yet burning, that ended in darkness.

A woman's trembling voice whispered, *"Please—stay with me."*

Heat pressed against her chest. Too hot.

Magic ripped through her veins like molten lava.

A heartbeat stops, then starts again.

Not again. Not again. Not again—

Luna startled, then guiltily said, "No—no, not poison."

She released Esther's wrists so quickly that it left a ghost of pressure behind. Luna cupped her cheeks gently, thumbs brushing away tears with light, apologetic strokes.

"I'm not going to hurt you," she said softly. "Stars, I misjudged that horribly."

Esther hid her face in her hands. Her breaths came shaky and uneven. "Then... what was that for?"

"Truth potion," Luna winced. "Well...fake truth potion. It wasn't real. I was...messing with you."

Esther looked up, wet, blotchy cheeks glistening. "Truth... potion?"

"I know, I know." Luna flopped backward dramatically on the mattress, limbs strewn like an exhausted cat.
"You're too scared and too adorable, and now I feel like a villain."

Esther sniffed, trying and failing to regain composure. "Then why? Why do it?"

Luna stared at the ceiling, then sighed. "Because I know who you are."

Esther's blood turned to ice. Her typically reactive magic went eerily still.

Esther had lived her entire life under the assumption that anonymity was protection. That if she could just pass as ordinary, she could survive. The idea that someone had seen through her anyway—had known and waited—sent a tremor through her bones.

"What?" she whispered.

"I know you're the princess. And that you've run away from home."

The title felt heavier than it ever had in the palace. There, it had been armor. Here, it was exposure. A spotlight she had not consented to step into.

Luna said it like it was small talk at a tea party—as if it were a simple, inconsequential matter.

"What do you mean?" Esther rasped.

"I didn't drug you!" Luna sat up, raising her hands in surrender. "I just lied about the truth potion to see if you'd confess."

"The other part."

Luna hesitated only a second. "You ran away from home?"

"The *princess* part!" Esther exploded, practically levitating upright. She nearly headbutted Luna in the process. Her heart roared in her ears like the stomping march of guards.

"Shh!" Luna slapped a hand gently over her mouth. "Do you want the whole town to hear?"

"The princess part," Esther repeated through the muffling hand, determined.

Luna sighed. "Princess Esther Valedara."

Esther stared, wide-eyed, waiting for Luna to elaborate. But she did not. Esther got the sense that Luna liked watching people squirm—like Lucy did. She loved Lucy, but she really didn't need a second one in her life.

"How do you know?" Esther squeaked after Luna removed her hand.

"Simple." Luna shrugged. "I co-own the Information Guild. I have contacts everywhere."

"Even in the castle?"

"Especially in the castle."

Esther's stomach twisted. The castle—the cold palace where servants spoke in whispers, where her father's paranoia hollowed the halls—had spies.

She felt violated. And also... impressed? She wasn't sure.

Esther had always trusted first and questioned later.

Trust had been the only rebellion available to her as a child. If she could not choose her life, she could at least choose to believe people meant well. It had kept her gentle. It had also made her vulnerable.

It was the opposite of how guards and soldiers survived. The opposite of how Nythir moved through the world, all sharp edges and quiet calculations. She wondered, not for the first time, if that was why she felt safer around him.

He noticed danger before it touched her.

She noticed it only once it had already settled into her bones.

"When will the guards arrive?" she asked, wiping away tears. She hoped she could at least say goodbye to her traveling companions she was already deeply attached to.

She should have known that freedom and love could not last. She couldn't escape her fate.

"Never, as long as I'm around." Luna preened, then leaned in and kissed Esther's forehead like a proud aunt.

Her magic didn't calm completely.

Something else stirred beneath the fear—an unfamiliar ache that felt like being seen and almost lost at the same time. Her magic hovered, restless, waiting for a familiar presence to anchor it.

It hovered beneath her skin, restless and searching, like it was waiting for something familiar to answer it. Esther wiped her eyes, breath unsteady, and wondered why the fear hadn't fully retaken hold.

Then the door exploded inward.

"You damn succubus!"

Nythir's voice hit first. Then his entire body tackled Luna off the bed. They crashed to the wooden floor with a thud that rattled the windowpanes.

Luna yanked his hair. "Don't be speciest! I'm only a quarter succubus!"

"I don't care what you are!" He headbutted her, and Esther cringed at the echo it made.

"Hasn't your mother ever told you not to hit a lady?" Luna kneed him in the stomach.

He wheezed. "You're not a lady. You're a bitch."

Esther sat frozen on the bed, clutching her stained blanket like a lifeline.

The painting-perfect duo from before now rolled around like two alley cats fighting over a fish bone. Their hair was wild, noses bloodied, and insults flew like arrows.

Most importantly... they were definitely not flirting.

Relief bubbled up in her chest, warm and unexpected. She found herself smiling. Luna wasn't a rival. She was... something else. Complicated, dangerous, unpredictable—but not competition. Still, maybe an enemy. That part remained up for debate.

Nythir finally pinned Luna's wrists to the floor, face flushed, breathing hard.

"Explain yourself!" he snarled.

Luna smirked up at him. "You're bleeding. It's a good color on you."

"Oh my saints," Esther blurted. "Both of you stop! You are bleeding on my clean floor!"

Both froze.

Both looked at her.

Both immediately resumed arguing about whose fault the blood was.

Esther dropped her face into her pillow and groaned. This was her life now. And unfortunately, the pillow muffled, but did not hide her final, exasperated scream:

"I wasn't even awake for fifteen minutes!"

16

NYTHIR

How to keep your princess alive when the universe clearly wants her dead.

Nythir burst through the doorway so hard the hinges screamed. Luna barely had time to blink before he threw himself at her, knocking both of them to the floor.

She fought like a feral kitten, all claws and cheap tricks.

He fought like someone who'd been awake for five seconds and already regretted everything.

By the time they'd rolled halfway across the room and back, Essie's voice cut through the chaos like a dagger:

"You are bleeding on my clean floor!"

Nythir froze mid-headlock.

Luna froze with her teeth an inch from his wrist.

They both slowly turned toward Essie.

She looked... small. Shaken. Eyes pink with fading tears. And that made something inside Nythir snap clean in half.

The pressure behind his eyes did not fade when he saw her. It intensified. Sharp and focused, like a lens snapping into place. His magic did not surge outward—it drew inward, tightening its hold as if preparing to shield something fragile. That reaction bothered him. Healing magic responded to injury, not proximity. There were no injuries...yet.

His magic stirred low and insistent, humming beneath his skin like it wanted to surge forward and shield her from everything at once—the room, the people in it, the very air she had breathed moments before. He forced it down, breathing carefully. Healing magic responded best to control, not fury.

But stars—he was furious.

Luna noticed it too. She eased up, sliding out from under him like a cat deciding it was bored with the fight.

That didn't stop Nythir from glowering. "What did you do to her?"

He had asked that question before—over different bodies, in other rooms, with various blood on his hands. It had never sounded like this. There was too much restraint in his voice, too much effort not to tear the room apart.

Luna dusted herself off, smug despite the bruises. "Oh relax, mutt. If I wanted your princess romantically, I'd have flirted with her, not straddled her for a prank. She's cute, but not my type. I like women who bite back."

Nythir blinked. "I'm a purebred elf, you're the mutt. Also, Essie literally punched a vine demon yesterday."

"Yes," Luna sighed dreamily, "but she didn't do it on purpose." Then she added flatly, casually: "Congratulations, she is very safe from me. Vorrik should worry, though."

"Good," Nythir muttered, then frowned. "Wait—why congratulate—never mind." He did not like the knowing look on her face.

"And look," Luna said brightly, "I only fake-poisoned her!"

"Luna!" Essie squeaked.

"Okay, okay," Luna waved her hands. "Bad prank. Terrible prank. Possibly war-crime-adjacent prank. I'll fix it. Come to the tavern later, Cinabun. We'll talk privately. Just us girls."

Nythir snapped, "No."

Essie straightened, chest puffed out. "Yes."

"No."

"Yes."

"No—"

"I'm not being controlled anymore, Nythir." Her voice trembled, but her chin lifted. "Not by my father, not by my kingdom, not by anyone."

That shut him up. He swallowed his instinct to argue. He also swallowed the urge to point out she'd slipped up, mentioning the kingdom. He was going to have to train her to be more sly.

Luna did not feel like a threat in the traditional sense.

That was what unsettled him most.

His instincts screamed loudest around blades and ambushes—clear dangers, honest ones. Luna felt like pressure without impact. Like standing too close to a cliff edge with nothing visibly pushing you forward.

He hated that his magic could not decide what she was.

Luna beamed like a rewarded cat. "Perfect! I'll meet you there." She twirled toward the door, her exit interrupted by it slamming open again. Nythir knew it would soon become his job to repair the hinges.

Lyssara strode in first, still in a robe and bonnet, eyes scanning the room like she expected bodies. Vorrik ducked under the frame behind her, his shoulders nearly brushing the sides. Last came Sable, Luna's half-sister, expression flat as stone. Nobody would guess that the delicate flower and bulldog, as Stonehaven residents fondly labeled them, were siblings.

"What happened?" Lyssara demanded.

"Why does it look like a tornado attacked?" Vorrik added.

Sable's voice was quiet and exhausted. "Luna, did you terrify another civilian?"

"Civilian?" Luna gasped. "That's my new best friend! Treat her with respect!"

Essie's jaw fell open, eyes as wide and glossy as a barn owl. Luna winked at her. Nythir did not like whatever secret the two shared. Essie's quivering lip had him contemplating murder.

He gently placed his thumb over her wrist. Her pulse raced too fast.

"You're shaking," he murmured.

"I'm fine," Esther whispered, unconvincingly.

He guided her to sit, kneeling in front of her. "Give me your hands."

The moment his fingers closed around hers, the pressure eased.

Relief flooded him so abruptly that it almost staggered him. Not just emotional—physical. As if something inside his chest had finally aligned. His magic settled into her like it recognized the shape of her fear and knew how to cradle it without smothering.

Not completely. But enough that his breath came easier. His magic flowed instinctively, silver light threading outward in careful lines, answering the frantic hum beneath her skin.

He had healed dozens of people before. Cuts. Burns. Broken bones.

This felt different. Like his magic recognized her before his mind did.

Her magic vibrated against his senses—bright, erratic, compressed too tightly beneath her skin, like a storm trapped behind glass.

No wonder she feared losing control. Anyone would, carrying that much power without understanding how to let it breathe.

Nythir inhaled and let his own magic glow warm around his fingers. A soft silver shimmer from his runespire trailed out, easing the tremor and loosening the tightness in her breath.

Slowly, the hum synchronized.

Her frantic energy softened, matching the steady rhythm of his own. The pressure that had coiled in his chest unwound, leaving behind something warmer. Quieter.

Nythir froze.

Magic did not do that by accident.

He had spent years studying spell response, mana exhaustion, and sympathetic resonance. This fit none of the known models. Bonds like this were discussed in theoretical texts and dismissed as metaphors. He had denied them, too.

Esther sagged with relief. "Thank you."

The word landed deeper than it should have. Gratitude implied choice. Trust implied risk. Both sat heavy in his chest, unwanted and undeniable.

Luna plopped herself beside her. "My turn!"

"No," the entire room said in unison.

Sable arched a brow. "I could use healing. Vorrik and I took blows in training."

Nythir scoffed. Apparently bar fights now counted as training.

Esther perked up. "I can help."

Nythir nearly choked. "Essie, you're exhausted." He wasn't prepared for any more necromancer mishaps.

"But I can," she insisted, worry pooling in her eyes. "They're hurt."

Before he could stop her, she slid off the bed and reached for them. She was unnaturally quick when she wanted to be.

Lyssara extended her arm first, unafraid. Esther brushed her fingers over a cut along Lyssara's bicep. Warm gold light rippled out. The wound vanished.

Vorrik stepped forward next. He grinned sheepishly as Esther's hand grazed his bruised shoulder. She inhaled deeply before letting her light engulf him, washing away all his wounds.

Then came Sable. She stepped forward silently, waiting. Esther laid her fingers gently on her shoulder. Light pulsed—and this time, something else flickered.

Sable inhaled sharply. "What was—" Her voice shifted mid-sentence, higher, softer, as if she hadn't smoked like a chimney all winter.

They all stared as Sable's face subtly reshaped itself. Fine lines smoothed. Her jaw softened. Her eyes brightened as if shedding years of exhaustion. Even her hair grew, wavy locks reaching her shoulders.

"Oh," Esther whispered. "Oops."

Sable touched her now-smooth cheek in stunned silence. Jowls gone, no longer resembling a bulldog.

"You... reversed my age?"

Esther panicked. "I'm sorry!"

Luna shot up like an alert prairie dog. "Esther. Sweetheart. Cinsbun. Precious flower. *Do me next.*"

"No," Nythir barked.

"I'm serious! Tighten my jawline! Give me back my twenty-year-old thighs!"

"No."

"What about fifteen? I was adorable at fifteen."

"Absolutely not."

Sable added, "I wouldn't object to a second round—"

"Out." Nythir grabbed Luna by the elbow. Vorrik took Sable by the hand. Together, they herded both sisters into the hallway like misbehaving goats.

Luna shrieked like a goat, too. "Let the girl express her art!"

"You're banned," Nythir said.

"You can't ban me!"

"Watch me."

The door slammed. Silence returned.

Lyssara looked between Essie and Nythir. "Explain why Luna was here."

Vorrik cleared his throat. "In simple words."

Esther wrapped her arms around herself. "I... can't."

Lyssara stepped closer. "Essie—"

"No." Essie backed up. "Please stop asking."

Vorrik raised his hands in surrender. Lyssara exhaled hard, frustrated but understanding.

Nythir stepped to Essie's side. "She'll speak when she's ready."

He held her gaze. Those amber eyes of hers were going to be the end of him.

He had spent his life trading in secrets. Guarding them. Selling them. Burying them when necessary.

This one, he decided, would never be currency.

Whatever Essie carried—past, power, or crown—was hers to reveal. And anyone who tried to take it from her before she was ready would answer to him.

Until then, he would be the space between her and the world. He did not frame it as devotion or destiny. He framed it as a necessity. And necessities were things he did not abandon.

He'd fight off every goddess-blessed, chaos-infused, boundary-obliterating information broker in the country to protect her.

Even if that was Luna. Especially if it was Luna.

He shared a knowing look with Lyssara.

Lyssara had noticed it too. The way his attention never entirely left Essie. The way his stance shifted to block lines of approach without conscious thought. She didn't comment. Warriors rarely did when they recognized something dangerous forming.

Luna—the information queen—knew Essie's identity. Vorrik... they would explain it to him later.

The room felt sour. They all wanted Essie to confide in them. But they would wait until she was ready.

For now, their goal was simple: keep Essie safe. She was theirs after all. And they would always protect their own, no matter the past—or whatever enemies followed.

17

Lucy

How to begin a journey: pack lightly, panic heavily.

Lucy and Basil had barely three hours before departure. It was a whirlwind of frantic packing, hushed planning, and dodging overly curious guards. Luckily, they had anticipated the king's panic and prepared most of their belongings the night before.

The palace had always made Lucy itchy.

Not literally—though the laundry starch certainly didn't help—but the kind of itch that settled beneath the skin when something was wrong and no one was fixing it. The walls watched. The guards listened. And the silence pressed in like it expected obedience in return.

Esther had gone quiet here. Smaller.

Lucy had noticed it years ago. The way Esther's shoulders drew inward after lessons. The way her laughter thinned when specific halls swallowed sound. Lucy hadn't known how to fix it then. She only knew she would never let it happen without witnesses again.

If the palace wanted obedience, it would get resistance instead. Lucy had never been noble enough to be protected by reputation. She survived by being inconvenient to remove.

Lucy had one last critical task before she set out on her princess-chasing journey.

The sun hung bright and merciless overhead, painting the white palace stones in blinding gold. It made her miss seeing her own gold.

Most guards were either stationed or clattering around the training yard, their shouts echoing through the corridors. Perfect.

Lucy slipped into the servants' quarters, the air thick with the scent of unwashed linens, starch, and old soap. Her pockets bulged with peppers she'd ground into a vicious paste that burned even through cloth. She inhaled. The sharp, vinegary sting pricked her nose like fire. *Excellent.*

Lucy preferred deterrents to weapons. Weapons escalated. Deterrents humiliated. A guard who couldn't sit, walk, or breathe comfortably would think twice before overstepping again. Pain taught faster than lectures.

Guards liked to pretend they were neutral. Lucy knew better. They protected titles, not people. They followed orders, not instincts.

Neutrality was a luxury afforded to those who never suffered the consequences of inaction. Lucy had seen guards look the other way while Esther cried herself hoarse behind closed doors. Pretending not to see was still a choice.

Esther had learned to smile at them.

Lucy had learned exactly how much pepper it took to ruin a man's dignity without leaving permanent damage.

She smeared pepper juice generously into all the garments she could find: drawers dangling from lines, stacks of folded shirts, even the captain's prized woolen socks. Nothing was safe from her wrath. The fabric absorbed the spicy oil instantly, releasing an aroma so potent that her eyes watered.

"May your next shift be lively," Lucy whispered as she rubbed the final smear into sweat-stained underwear.

Then came step two. She tiptoed between bunk beds, the air growing mustier. One by one, she gently tucked slivers of poison ivy into pillows, careful not to touch the oils.

A faint, earthy, bitter scent rose from the leaves. "It's what you deserve," she muttered. "For ignoring her. For letting her be lonely."

A flash of heartache pricked her. Esther had deserved so much better than these cold hallways and colder people.

Even Baroness Levon—the Cuckoo Bird—was better than them.

At least the Baroness had hovered. Hovering meant noticing. Lucy would take awkward concern over polished neglect any day.

Satisfied, Lucy wiped her hands on a vinegar-soaked cloth to neutralize the oils, then skipped out of the room, the echo of her footsteps bouncing down the hall like a gleeful little war drum.

She changed quickly in the women's quarters. The scent of lavender soap and old cedar drifted from the wardrobes, slipping into practical travel clothes—not too different from her maid uniform, just without the apron or extra pockets.

Her bag sat ready: neatly folded clothes, toiletries, her beloved mascara, and a tiny vial of concentrated tears-of-onion for emergency dramatics. She was proud of being early. Punctuality was practically her religion.

But she was prouder of being Esther's best friend. Princess or maid meant nothing to her. Esther was her sister. Lucy would walk through hell barefoot to protect her. She might even burn the castle down if it came to that. Not that she wanted to. Cleaning was her specialty, not espionage—but she would absolutely do it.

She stopped in the kitchen on her way out, the air warm and buttery from fresh rolls.

"Good afternoon," she called.

"Good afternoon, Lucy," Greta, the head cook, replied without looking up. That was the full extent of their relationship.

The other servants avoided her eyes as she passed, not out of fear, but out of caution. Caring too loudly about a princess who cried at night was a good way to lose your position. Or worse, be transferred somewhere quiet and forgotten.

Lucy didn't blame them.

She just refused to be them.

Lucy grabbed six small, round, steaming rolls.

Esther never ate enough when she was anxious. Lucy had compensated quietly for years—extra bread, sugared fruit, honey stirred into tea. Small rebellions were still rebellions if they kept someone alive.

The scent of yeast and toasted crust clung to her fingers as she left. She rarely interacted with staff unless necessary. They talked behind her back. They resented how quickly Esther had taken to her. They muttered words like "pet" and "undeserving."

Lucy had memorized who said which words. Who sneered. Who stayed silent. People thought maids were invisible. Lucy collected faces like receipts.

They didn't realize the most significant difference between her and the other staff: *courage*. She hadn't used tricks to become Esther's personal maid; she simply treated her as a living, breathing person.

The palace didn't need chains to keep people in line. It ran on softer cruelties—whispers, favors withheld, doors that stopped opening when you approached. Servants learned quickly which halls to avoid and which nobles liked their tea just wrong enough to justify a punishment.

Lucy had survived by being useful. Esther had survived by being obedient.

Neither of those things was safe.

She brushed past two guards in the hall. They straightened, puffing up like peacocks.

"Afternoon, Lucy," one said with a wink.

She smiled sweetly, then stabbed him directly in the ego: "Not interested. Try again when you grow a spine."

Insults were another deterrent. Men hated being dismissed more than they hated being refused. Lucy wielded that knowledge like a blade.

He sputtered as she wheeled her luggage toward the gates. The worn wheels clacked over uneven stone, jerking with each crack.

Basil was already waiting. Lucy's jaw dropped.

He leaned casually against the carriage, puffing a cigar that smelled warm and woodsy, smoke curling around him like he'd stepped out of a portrait of a dignified rake. The scent suited him disgustingly well.

Basil wore authority like a borrowed coat—heavy, uncomfortable, and clearly not his. To the court, he was dependable. Predictable. Safe.

Lucy knew better.

Men like Basil didn't stay loyal to crowns. They stayed faithful to people. Basil had the look of a man who knew precisely how wrong things were and had chosen to proceed anyway. Lucy trusted people like that because she was the same breed.

"You're early," she accused, affronted.

He raised a brow. "You're late to being first."

She stomped toward him, offended. "Since when do you smoke?"

"Only on rare occasions." He exhaled a swirl of fragrant smoke, then snuffed the cigar with precision. "Are you ready? Your luggage appears light."

"I have money bags with me," she jabbed a thumb toward him. "So I didn't need much."

He grumbled, which delighted her.

They boarded the carriage. The padded bench was soft, faintly scented of old perfume. They settled in while the coachman checked the reins.

Lucy hated that Esther wasn't there to argue with her. To tell her she was overreacting. To ask if she really needed six rolls and three vials of onion tears.

The silence felt wrong.

Esther was always the quiet one—but she was never absent.

Absence was louder than silence. Lucy had spent years orbiting Esther's presence—adjusting, compensating, protecting. Without her, the world felt poorly balanced.

Lucy had just begun imagining her future greatness as a traveling hero when a shrill screech split the air. Both she and Basil flinched. Lucy recognized the voice instantly and prayed she was wrong.

She stared in horror as Baroness Irene Levon sprinted toward them across the courtyard. She moved fast despite her heels, corset, two giant bags, and elaborate skirts swishing violently. Sunlight glinted off every jewel pinned to her bodice, making her look like a bedazzled runaway chandelier.

She looked ridiculous.

Ridiculous people rarely ran toward danger. Lucy clocked the bags. The speed. The refusal to stop. Something tightened in her chest despite herself.

Nobles didn't move unless it benefited them. Which meant either Irene Levon was a fool—or she had decided Esther mattered more than decorum. Lucy quietly revised her mental ledger.

However, that did not mean Lucy wanted to get trapped with the Baroness on a wild princess hunt.

"Coachman, *go*!" She started hitting the carriage like her life depended on it. Because it did.

The coachman ignored her, dutifully finishing his inspection of the mare's bridle.

The Baroness reached them in record time. Lucy cursed loudly, earning a disappointed look from Basil.

"Add these to the luggage," she thrust her bags at the poor coachman.

"Absolutely *not*!" Lucy threw herself across the carriage door like a rabid ferret, cursing colorfully as she almost fell out. "What are you doing?"

"Language!" Irene scolded, horrified. "I am joining you, of course."

"You must be confused. You are not joining us."

"King Arcturus informed me of the ordeal," Irene said primly, glancing at the coachman so she wouldn't reveal too much. "I am coming with you."

"We don't need a cuckoo bird!" Lucy hissed. What Lucy meant was: *we don't need another cage pretending to be protection.*

"Cuckoo? You ungrateful child, move aside."

"No."

"Yes."

"No."

"Lucy!" Basil's voice cracked like a whip. She stiffened. He didn't yell often, so when he did, she knew to listen. She sat down reluctantly, arms crossed, glaring murderously.

Basil offered the Baroness a hand into the carriage like a gentleman, which Lucy did not approve of in any way.

"This carriage is cheap," Irene said the moment her skirts swamped half the interior. "If I had known, I would have prepared a different one."

"A bigger one, too," Lucy muttered.

"Yes, well, we'll fix that at the next inn—oh!" Irene suddenly brightened. She rummaged through her bag. "I brought something for you."

Lucy blinked, eyes full of distrust.

The small cloth bundle smelled of vanilla and brown sugar. She opened it slowly.

Gingersnap cookies.

"Esther told me they were your favorite," Irene said simply.

Lucy stared at them like they might bite. Esther remembered things like that. The realization hurt worse than any insult.

Lucy's outrage cracked just a fraction. After a silent moment, she muttered, "Fine. You can sit near me, but don't touch my bags."

The Baroness smiled knowingly. She knew exactly how to handle disgruntled youths.

Basil hid his amusement poorly. Lucy mouthed some very choice words at him and shoved a gingersnap into her mouth.

And so the carriage rolled forward, carrying the three most unlikely allies the kingdom had ever seen.

Esther ran toward freedom, unaware of what awaited her.

Lucy ran the other direction—to gather answers, allies, and enough leverage to tear down anyone who tried to cage her again.

Someone had to do the unglamorous part of saving a princess.

Lucy planned to be very good at it.

Saving a princess didn't require a sword. It required memory, spite, and a willingness to be underestimated. Lucy had all three.

18

Esther

How to listen carefully: pretend you understand everything while understanding nothing.

Dusk settled over the street in muted lavender, lantern light catching on the cobblestones as Esther and her companions approached Luna's tavern. The warm glow did little to calm the nerves coiling in her stomach.

They walked like a unit, whether they meant to or not. And yet, she had never felt more singular. Everyone around her had a role they understood—scout, shield, blade. Esther carried something heavier than a weapon and less defined than a crown. No one had trained her for *this* kind of walking.

Lyssara scanned for threats. Vorrik stayed close enough to block a blow meant for her. Nythir hovered at her side like a drawn blade pretending to be a person.

No one told her what to do. The absence of instruction should have felt freeing. Instead, it left her unmoored. The palace had taught her how to obey, not how to choose. Choice felt like standing at the edge of a high place without rails.

"You could at least consider letting me accompany you inside," he said for the seventh time, voice low and edged with frustration. "You don't know what Luna wants."

Esther kept her gaze forward. "I do. She wants answers. And I'm not giving them while everyone watches me squirm."

He scoffed softly. "Essie—"

"No." Her tone left little room for argument. Nythir recognized it instantly, though he still looked ready to argue on principle alone. His shoulders tightened in a sulky sort of way that was absolutely not subtle.

The others walked behind them, unusually quiet. It wasn't too quiet. It was heavy, uncomfortable, silent—the kind that made the air hard to breathe.

When they reached the tavern door, Vorrik stepped forward, clearing his throat.

"We know Luna knows something about you," he said gently. It was much different than his usual gruffness.

Gentle Vorrik made Essie feel more anxious. It felt strange—like when a teacher scolded you, afraid to be too harsh on royalty. She hated that feeling.

Lyssara crossed her arms, her expression somewhere between vexed and protective. "And we know you're not ready to tell us. So we're not pushing." She sighed. "Doesn't mean we're not worried, though."

Nythir nodded, though his scowl remained firmly in place. Esther worried his face would get stuck like that.

Sable opened the door from inside, her smile bright—until she caught the tension in the group. Her expression softened, quickly replaced by a frown.

"What the hell did Luna do now? You all look ready to burn a castle down."

"Careful. You just had your jowls magically removed," Vorrik said, back to his usual tone.

Nythir glanced at Esther, brushing his hand lightly against hers. "We respect your privacy. We'll wait for you to tell us in your own time."

The words hit her harder than expected—soft and warm and a little painful.

Wait. She wasn't going to be able to lie forever. She knew this, but didn't know when to reveal her secret.

"Thank you," she murmured, anxiety spiraling. She felt that when she told them, it would be the end of this chapter of their journey. She didn't want it to end.

She regretted lying. The web was spun, and she was a bug stuck in it, waiting for its demise.

Lying had never been part of her lessons. Silence, yes. Deflection, certainly. But this—carrying truth alone while people stood close enough to catch her if she fell—made her chest ache. Secrets were easier when no one cared.

Luna appeared behind Sable, gorgeous as ever. "Essie. Upstairs. Now."

The entire group stiffened as if someone had just threatened their collective mother. Luna had a lot of practice ordering adults around, and for a moment, Esther felt as if she were back in her etiquette lessons.

Silently, she followed Luna up the narrow staircase, heart thudding and head hung.

Upstairs, the room was small and warm, filled with the smell of spiced tea and candles. Esther scowled at her worst enemy. Luna shut the door with a quiet finality that made Esther's heart skip a beat.

"You've grown," Luna said softly, her voice tinged with memories Esther couldn't quite place.

The words landed strangely.

Luna looked young—unfairly so—but her eyes carried a depth Esther had only seen in people who had lived through things they never spoke about. For the first time, Esther wondered if Luna had known her mother not as a queen... but as a woman.

The thought tightened something in her chest.

Before Esther could ask what she meant, Luna moved to a desk and opened a drawer. She pulled out a thin gold bracelet etched with delicate vine-like lines. At first glance, it looked like a runespire, but something about it felt different. It radiated a soft, warm hum.

"Your mother left this with me when you were just a baby," Luna said, stepping close. "She said I'd know when to give it to you."

Esther's breath hitched. "My mother?"

Luna gently took Esther's wrist and fastened the bracelet around it. The metal hummed faintly, warm against her skin. It pulsed softly, in rhythm with her heartbeat.

Controlling her emotional sparks.

The steadiness was comforting—and unsettling. Control had always been imposed on her, not offered *with* her consent. Esther couldn't tell yet whether this was protection or another kind of cage.

"It will help steady your magic," Luna explained. "Not suppress it. Just control the overflow when your emotions run too hot."

Esther swallowed hard. "She knew I'd need this?"

Luna nodded. "Your mother had foresight magic. No grand prophecies—nothing like that. She saw fragments of others' futures, never her own."

Esther's chest tightened. "So she knew she wouldn't—"

"Be with you as long as she wished?" Luna finished softly. "Yes. She knew her time was short. And she knew you'd have a journey she couldn't guide you through."

Esther had been told foresight was a gift. Luna said it like a burden. Seeing fragments of other people's futures meant living surrounded by endings you could never soften—only prepare for. Esther wondered how many of her mother's smiles had been shaped by knowledge she wasn't allowed to share.

Her mother had always been spoken of as gentle. Wise. Beloved. No one ever spoke of her as deliberate. This—leaving artifacts behind, planting people like seeds—felt intentional in a way that made Esther's breath hitch.

Esther stared down at the bracelet, vision blurring at the edges.

"Your mother used what time she had to set things in motion," Luna continued. "Quiet protections. Allies in unexpected places."

Esther had grown up believing loyalty was loud—oaths, banners, visible devotion.

Her mother's loyalty had been quieter. Distributed. Hidden in ordinary people who smiled politely and waited decades to matter.

It was terrifying.

And brilliant.

Esther's life unfolded in a new pattern—not a line, but a web. Each person who had stepped forward, each kindness she had mistaken for coincidence, had been placed with care. Her mother had not trusted one safeguard. She had trusted *many*.

Sable, leaning in the doorway, added, "We owe the Queen everything. Her charity kept our families alive when no one else cared."

The words landed heavier than praise. Gratitude implied debt. And debts, Esther knew, were never collected gently.

Luna's eyes softened. "People like Sir Basil. Baroness Levon. Myself. Sable. All given small tasks meant to guide or protect you when the time came. There are others, loyal to the queen, who saved us all. We know of each other, but we are not to involve ourselves until our time."

The names rang like bells, loud and demanding. Pieces Esther hadn't known were missing began clicking into place—softly, painfully, inevitably.

The Baroness's refusal to end lessons and her daily visits to the palace. Basil's return to guide her after his early retirement due to injury. And why hadn't he abandoned her even after all the grueling lessons that grayed his hair?

None of it had been random. Esther felt foolish for never questioning it—and small for realizing how protected she had been without knowing it.

Luna squeezed her shoulder. "You're not alone, Esther. Not now. Not ever. Your mother made sure of it."

Something warm and fragile bloomed in Esther's chest at hearing her name. Even her magic seemed to understand the moment; the candles didn't flare, her fingers didn't spark. Only the bracelet shone gold.

"Thank you," she whispered. "But I've never heard of such a runespire. Why didn't my father or teachers ever try to use it?"

"This is the only one ever made, by your mother. As you know, mages are rare. Powerful ones? Even rarer. And one strong enough to make this?" Luna grazed her finger across Esther's wrist. "There was only one who could make it."

"Then why didn't she leave it with—"

"It wasn't time," Luna interrupted. "Your mother left a letter as well."

She held out a small, yellowed envelope. Dust clung to it, and it smelled faintly of roses.

Esther hesitated. Letters carried finality. Once read, they could not be unread. She had survived so long on unanswered questions that the idea of clarity frightened her more than ignorance.

Esther slowly reached for it, fingers shaking. She carefully peeled off the red wax seal stamped with the royal phoenix. Tears sprang to her eyes at the familiar, elegant letters:

My beloved Essie,
You must remember: Magic mirrors your heart. A mirror cannot reflect a broken heart. One day, when your heart is no longer caged, your mirror will reflect with great beauty. When that time comes, you will no longer need this runespire. It is merely a stepping stone. Learn to be free. To love and despair without constraints or fear. To be all that you are.
I love you so much, my darling child.

Tears dampened the paper in Esther's trembling hands.

Her mother had not written instructions. She had written permission. To feel. To fail. To love without containment. Esther pressed the letter to her chest like a promise she didn't yet know how to keep.

She didn't know how much her mother had seen in her prophecies—or that such magic existed beyond myth. But she knew one thing: her mother had given her a blessing for the unroyal adventuring she was now undertaking, and it warmed her chest.

"Thank you," she whispered, wiping her tears. For the first time, she felt she was truly on the path to something extraordinary—a path she would pave, master, and follow with her mother's unseen guidance.

The bracelet was warm. Steady.

Esther realized, distantly, that this wasn't just protection. It was an expectation. Her mother hadn't only prepared the world for Esther—she had prepared Esther for the world.

Expectation did not ask whether she was ready. It simply waited. Esther had spent her life being prepared *for* things. This was the first time something had been prepared *for her*.

Luna opened the door, smiling knowingly. "Come. Before that brooding shadow you travel with decides to break my door down."

Sable huffed. "He absolutely would."

Esther sighed. Yes, he absolutely would. She followed them down the stairs, bracelet warm against her skin, toward her worried companions, toward the path her mother had foreseen long before her first step.

Esther followed into the future, layered with expectation, watched by people who remembered her mother's choices. Whatever came next would not be simple. Her mother had never prepared her for simplicity.

She had so many questions—about her mother, everyone involved, and even the woman guiding her now. Exactly how old was Luna?

Esther winced at the phantom pain from etiquette lessons. No matter how curious, some questions were forbidden.

19

Nythir

How to protect a secret princess: distract everyone, lie convincingly, and pretend you're not jealous of idiots with dimples.

Nythir had learned three truths since Essie fell out of the sky and added chaos to his life, which he had previously thought was impossible:

First: she attracted chaos like lanternlight coaxed moths into its glow.

Second: her chaos had a tendency to explode.

Third: he apparently had no self-preservation instincts, because he kept following her anyway—like a professional moth.

Lanterns didn't choose the moths that found them. They simply burned. The responsibility always fell to whoever stood close enough to keep the flame from becoming a signal fire.

Morning light slanted through the inn's warped glass windows, washing the room in warm pastels that made Stonehaven look softer than it really was. Almost serene. Down in the street, carts rattled over cobblestones, and someone shouted about fresh bread. A typical, boring morning.

He used to hate mornings, but over the past few days, he'd found them less horrible. He still hated them—but just a little less with Essie nearby.

Nythir leaned against the window frame, watching Essie through the warped reflection. She stood near the bed, frowning at the thin gold bracelet etched with vines. It hummed faintly, and the air around her felt... different. Less agitated. Less chaotic. Her magic, which had always shimmered against his senses like a barely contained storm, now flowed like a tranquil stream in neat little channels.

The bracelet did its job too well.

Tools that worked perfectly were the most dangerous kind. They discouraged vigilance. He didn't trust anything that removed risk without teaching the cost.

From a tactical standpoint, it was brilliant—no stray flares, no obvious tells, nothing that screamed *royal mage with catastrophic potential*. From a healer's perspective, it stabilized her better than any grounding spell he'd ever learned.

From a personal one?

It felt like watching someone dim their own light to survive.

Survival demanded adaptation, not erasure. He had seen what happened to people who learned to shrink instead of sharpen. They lasted longer. They lived less.

"I still don't like that it came from Luna," he muttered.

Knowledge was leveraged. And Luna collected leverage like other people collected jewelry—openly, proudly, and with intent. The idea that Essie had been vulnerable in someone else's hands gnawed at him.

Essie startled. "I thought you were watching the street."

"I am," he said. "And you. And the door. I'm very efficient."

She rolled her eyes, but the corners of her mouth twitched. "You're sulking. Again."

"I'm not sulking," he lied. "I'm assessing risk."

"You're sulking," she repeated, fastening the bracelet. The metal pulsed once in time with her heartbeat. No sparks. No lanterns flared. "And risk has already been assessed. Luna said my mother left it with her."

"That's the part I don't like," he muttered.

So far, that was the only truth he had heard from Essie. Luna knew her mother, and the bracelet was made by her. But she still refused to give any information about herself. Actions made it obvious, but he wanted to hear it from her lips.

He didn't like that Luna knew more about Essie's past than he did. He didn't like that Essie had cried in another person's arms. And he definitely didn't like that Luna had been the one to give her a gift that made her feel safer in her own skin.

Essie flexed her fingers experimentally. Gold light glowed beneath her skin, then smoothed out—as if the bracelet itself was smoothing it.

"It works," she whispered, awe softening her features. "I can... breathe. Inside."

"You're perfect with or without it," Nythir said.

"You mean it?" Her eyes were wide with confusion, hope, and something he couldn't quite name.

"Come on," Lyssara called from the door, interrupting the moment. Nythir cursed. She was already dressed in travel leathers, her braid looped into a crown to keep it off her neck, a recently sharpened sword at her hip. "Job board opens in ten. If we're late, Sable will give our caravan to someone boring."

Vorrik lumbered in behind her, strapping an axe across his back. "And we can't let that happen. I'm emotionally attached to that route."

"You're emotionally attached to food," Lyssara said. "The caravan happens to go through our hometown."

"Attached regardless," he said proudly.

Essie perked up, bracelet forgotten. "We're really taking the escort job?"

"Yes," Nythir said, pushing off the window. "You wanted to see more of the world. This is the safest way—doesn't involve teleporting into a bandit nest."

He had wanted to show her the world gently. Slowly. Not like this—through threat assessment and kill zones. But the world rarely waited for permission.

"I told you, that was only once."

"Once is enough," he said. "Let's not add to your explosive death count."

Her smile faltered. Guilt flickered in her gaze. He regretted the words immediately.

"That's not what I—"

"It's fine," she said too quickly. "You're right. Caravan. Job. No more accidental killing."

He wanted to hold her. Whisper apologies into her ears. Take away all the pain his idiotic words caused. He had never cared if his words hurt someone. But not Essie. Never her.

Lyssara's gaze lingered on him longer than necessary.

She had fought beside him long enough to recognize the signs—jaw too tight, magic held too carefully, attention split in ways that got people killed.

"You're compromised," she said quietly.

He didn't bristle. Lyssara never used that word lightly. Compromise meant altered priorities. Altered priorities got people killed. He just disagreed about who was at risk.

"Feelings later," Lyssara clapped dramatically. "Coin now. Move it, ducklings."

Nythir cursed again.

Luna's tavern was quieter in the daylight. Last night's chaos had boiled down to sticky tables and the faint smell of ale clinging to the beams. The lantern orbs dimmed for morning, bathing everything in soft amber.

The window Essie had cracked was boarded up, leaving the corner dark and sullen. Vorrik had conveniently been tossed through it during their tavern brawl, so they weren't responsible for repairs. He was useful sometimes—but never when he meant to be.

Sable stood by the job board, arms crossed, now looking twenty years younger and twice as annoyed.

"Stop staring," she growled as they approached.

"I'm not staring," Nythir lied. "I'm observing the outcome of irresponsible healing."

"Tell your mage duckling she owes me ten years of back pain," Sable said. "But my knees haven't felt this good since I was twenty."

"You're welcome," Essie said shyly. "Actually, I have a tiny, little, unimportant question."

Sable's stony expression cracked into a quick, fond grin before she could stop it. "Yeah, yeah. What do you need, Cinabun?"

Nythir hated them calling her that.

Essie leaned in close and whispered, "How old is Luna?" She needed to work on her whispering skills.

Sable barked out a laugh as Luna ran over frantically before anything could be revealed. She jabbed a thumb at the board, changing the topic. "Caravan to Greyhollow. Three wagons. Paying well above average. Leaving in an hour. Their usual escort fell sick. I told them we'd take it."

"Greyhollow," Vorrik said happily. "Home sweet miserable home."

Lyssara elbowed him. "It's not miserable. It just smells like wet sheep."

"And sweat," he added.

Essie leaned closer to the parchment, distracted from her previous question. "How far is Greyhollow?"

"Four days at caravan speed," Nythir said. "A little longer if the road's bad."

Her eyes widened in awe. "Four days," she said, voice hushed. Four days of open road. Four days away from the palace. Four days where anything could happen. She looked like an adorable barn owl about to take its first flight.

Sable cleared her throat. "Caravan master's waiting in the yard. Try not to terrify him."

"Who, me?" Nythir asked innocently.

"Yes," Sable and Lyssara said in unison.

The caravan master was a compact dwarf with a beard so carefully braided it could have been used as a measuring tool. It nearly reached the ground, covering the entire front of his body. He checked them over as if buying horses: weighing armor, scars, the set of Nythir's shoulders, the gleam of Lyssara's sword.

Then his gaze landed on Essie. Nythir saw the exact moment the man decided she was too soft for the road.

"This one," the caravan master said, pointing. "What does she do?"

"She's with me," Nythir said smoothly. Essie's brows shot up, but he ignored it.

"She's a mage," Lyssara added. "Very efficient at... crowd control."

The man's eyes flicked to the faint scorch marks on Nythir's sleeve, then to the way his cloak had been neatly burned shorter on one side.

"I see," he said slowly. "Does she behave?"

"No," Vorrik said.

"Yes," Nythir said at the exact same time.

The caravan master squinted.

Nythir felt the calculation settle in his bones.

Essie was a liability. Too soft-spoken. Too honest. Too visibly unused to the road. Anyone with eyes would underestimate her—and anyone with sense would exploit that.

Underestimation was only helpful if you knew when it was happening. Essie did not. That made her powerful—and exposed.

He chose her anyway.

The decision surprised him less than it should have.

"We'll keep her in check," Lyssara sighed. "She's more useful than she looks. Discount if she accidentally explodes bandits."

The man hesitated, then shrugged. "As long as she explodes the right people. Payment on arrival." He jerked his head toward the wagons. "We leave in thirty."

Nythir guided Essie away before she could apologize to anyone for existing. He made a silent vow: she would never apologize for that again. As far as he was concerned, she never had to apologize—even if she was at fault.

"You don't have to speak," he said under his breath. "Let Lyssara and me handle the talking when coin is involved."

"That feels rude," she whispered back.

"That," he said, "is why we handle the talking."

Caravan escorts were supposed to be easy coin. Predictable routes. Boring threats. Bandits who scattered once steel flashed, and numbers turned against them.

Lately, none of that had been true.

Guild boards were full of "last-minute replacements" and "unexpected losses." Too many caravans limped in, missing guards. Too many never arrived at all. Something was tightening along the roads—and it wasn't hunger alone.

Roads reflected politics faster than courts ever did. When caravans stopped arriving intact, it meant borders were tightening somewhere upstream. Hunger followed. Then desperation. Then, violence was presented as an opportunity.

It looked like the type of day where nothing could possibly go wrong. They set off under a bright, deceptive sky. The wind whispered through the trees, leaves starting to turn shades of red and orange. Everything was beautiful, quiet, and tranquil.

Until one of his companions inevitably caused a disturbance, ruining it all.

The caravan consisted of three covered wagons, two open carts, and a couple of merchants riding alongside, eyes darting to every bush as if it were a bandit in disguise.

Essie rode in the middle of the formation on a clay-colored mare. Nythir rode beside her.

"You can ride closer to Lyssara if you want," she offered after an hour of riding silently, surrounded by the banter of the travel party.

"I'm fine here."

"You keep looking around."

"Yes."

"As if you're expecting something to jump out and kill us."

"That's because I am." He scanned the tree line. "It usually does."

She pursed her lips. "Optimistic."

"Experienced," he corrected.

She fell quiet, watching the road. Nythir studied her posture. From the way she sat straight, shoulders back, to her loose grip on the reins—all of it screamed noble-trained rider.

"Slouch," he murmured.

"What?"

"Slouch. You're riding like you're leading a parade."

"I don't know how to slouch on a horse," she hissed, muttering something about etiquette lessons. Nythir wasn't worried about her magic exploding someone—he couldn't care less about that. He worried about her talking to anyone and revealing her not-so-hidden secret.

Nobility lived in posture long before it lived in titles. You could take the crown away and still spot a ruler by the way they occupied space.

He reached over, nudged her shoulder until she crooked forward a bit. "Like this. Think 'mild back pain,' not 'royal portrait.'" After saying it, he realized there must have been portraits of her. He hoped one day she'd let him see them.

She tried to follow his instructions and somehow made it look like she was being tortured.

He sighed. "We'll work on it."

A laugh drifted back along the line. One of the younger merchants, a lanky boy with sun-browned skin and annoyingly bright green eyes, twisted around in his saddle to grin at her.

Nythir catalogued the boy automatically.

Friendly posture. Loose confidence. No visible weapons. The kind of man who relied on charm instead of caution. Dangerous in a different way.

Charm unsettled him more than blades. Steel announced its intent. Smiles waited for an opportunity.

The irritation that followed was sharp, immediate, and inconvenient. There it was. Unwanted. Unhelpful. He filed it away under *distractions to be dealt with later.*

He told himself it was vigilance. He was very good at lying to himself.

"First time on the road?" the boy asked. "You look like a festival banner."

Nythir did not grind his teeth.

"Yes," Essie said, polite as ever. "First time outside the city, actually."

"Seriously?" The boy whistled. "You're in for a treat then, miss. Name's Teren." He flashed a smile that probably worked on tavern girls. "If you need someone to show you around camp tonight, I know all the good spots to sit. Less rocks."

Nythir's magic prickled under his skin so faintly he could almost see it.

Essie brightened. "That's very kind. I—"

"She'll be with us," Nythir cut in. "Training."

Teren glanced at him, then back at Essie.

"Right," he said slowly. "Didn't mean any offense."

"None taken," Essie said quickly, shooting a look at Nythir.

Teren winked at her before turning back around.

Nythir kept his gaze on the road, imagining the boy tripping over his own feet into a puddle.

"You didn't have to do that," Essie said after a long moment.

"Do what?"

"Answer for me."

"Yes, I did," he said. "Because you would have said 'yes' to anything that sounds even vaguely friendly."

He had crossed a line there. He knew it. The trouble was, the alternative felt worse.

Her mouth opened, then closed. "That's not true."

"It is," he said. "You're starved for warmth and acceptance. It makes you too trusting."

He cursed at himself for reprimanding her, but he couldn't stop the agitation boiling out. Her fingers tightened on the reins. The bracelet glowed faintly, restraining her sparks, aggravating him further.

"I'm not helpless, Nythir."

He believed her. That wasn't the issue. The world didn't care whether someone was helpless—it cared whether they were protected.

"I never said you were helpless," he replied. "I said you're trusting. Those are different."

She looked away, jaw tight. Guilt slid cold through his chest. He wasn't angry at her—he was furious at the world that had left her so desperate for ordinary kindness.

"I just want you to be careful," he added quietly.

"I am careful."

"You teleported into Ashvale," he said.

She glared at him. "Are you ever going to let that go?"

"No. Just make sure to teleport me with you next time."

She sighed, and some of the tension eased from her shoulders.

They rode until the sky shifted from blue to lavender. The caravan master called for a halt on a flat stretch between two low hills. The carts were rolled into a loose circle to block the wind, and a fire was built in the center.

The smells of cooking meat and woodsmoke filled the air. Conversations rose and fell. Lyssara shared stories. Vorrik ate loudly. Merchants laughed. The day had been surprisingly calm, leaving Nythir on edge.

Essie perched on a log near the fire, boots dangling above the dirt. Her green dress was streaked with dust along the hem, a smudge of road grime on her cheekbone. She looked... happy. Tired, but happy. For the first time since she joined them, she looked at ease in her surroundings.

"That one's Orion," Vorrik said, pointing at a constellation with a strip of dried meat hanging out of his mouth. "Hunter of wild sheep. Lyssara told me if I misbehaved, he'd come down and take my tusks."

Lyssara snorted. "I said I would take your tusks."

Essie laughed, head tipped back, gold sparks barely visible where the firelight reflected in her eyes. Nythir pretended not to watch, though the warmth her laughter brought made him want to.

Teren drifted closer, two tin mugs in hand, far too confident for someone who had known them less than a day.

"Brought extra," he said, offering one to Essie. "Just watered wine. Helps with saddle ache."

Nythir stepped between them before he could stop himself.

"I told you," he said pleasantly, "she's training with us tonight."

Teren blinked, then shifted his gaze over Nythir's shoulder. "Well, what does she say?"

Nythir hated him a little.

Essie peeked around him, eyes flicking between the two. "I can do both," she said cautiously. "A little training, then sit somewhere that doesn't smell like fish and orc feet."

Vorrik looked offended. "My feet smell like triumph."

"You can barely walk," Lyssara said. "Triumph lost."

Teren grinned. "See? She's got good taste. I'll only steal her for a bit. Just to show her where the stream is. Quieter there."

Essie perked up. "A stream? With real running water?"

"Not imaginary running water," Teren said. "Figure we can go when most folks turn in."

"Perfect," she said.

Nythir swallowed a curse. He could tell her no. He could pull rank as healer, as the least hungover member of the party, as the one with the most sense of caution.

But he saw the way her fingers curled around the mug, knuckles white. The flicker of panic beneath the excitement. The way she clearly expected someone to make the decision away from her.

She didn't want to be controlled anymore. "Not by my father. Not by my kingdom. Not by anyone." That's what she had said.

"Fine," he said. "After training."

Teren clapped him on the shoulder like they were friends. "Didn't know you were her father," he said, eyes glinting.

Nythir ground his teeth. If he had strong attack magic like Essie, Teren would have been in several more pieces. Cooked. On purpose.

But he could only harness healing and defensive magic. Most mages could only control one or two types. Essie was the exception.

He had always hated the types he had. They didn't suit him like combat magic didn't suit her. That was why he had gone on a journey to strengthen his fighting skills. Yet he still became the "healer" of a group. He simply used his skills to his advantage.

"I'm her healer," he said. "Which means if she gets hurt, I fix it."

"Then I'll make sure she doesn't," Teren said easily. "Scout's honor."

Nythir doubted the boy had ever been a scout.

Essie exhaled, shoulders lowering. "Thank you," she said—to him, not Teren. For the compromise? For not locking her in a wagon? He wasn't sure.

He just nodded and moved away before she could see the war on his face. He still had time to lock her in a wagon.

Lyssara sidled up next to him as he began setting up practice wards around the fire.

"You hate this."

"Yes."

"You can't stop her."

"I know."

"She'll be careful," Lyssara said. "She's not completely oblivious."

"She thought wanted posters were a novelty," he reminded her.

Lyssara sighed. "Fair point."

They worked in silence for a moment. Nythir drew faint silver sigils in the dirt while Lyssara sharpened her sword.

"Going to keep watch?" she finally asked.

"Yes."

"All night?"

"Yes."

Lyssara hummed. "You could also just admit you're jealous."

"I'm not jealous," he said.

"Oh?" Her mouth curved. "Then you're okay with them canoodling in the starlight?"

He glared at her. She laughed, clapped him on the back, and went to harass Vorrik instead.

Night deepened. Stars bled into the sky. The fire crackled down to coals. Nythir watched Essie practice minor spells. She created and extinguished a tiny ball of gold in her palms. The bracelet glowed with each pulse, smoothing the energy before it could surge out of control.

He enjoyed the comfort the bracelet brought her, but hated how it hid her. He also hated Teren looking at her.

So he layered his own precautions instead. Silent. Invisible. Bound to her spark. If she stepped too far into danger, the wards would sing. If someone else did, they would scream.

Eventually, the caravan quieted. People crawled under wagons or into bedrolls. Someone finished a song on a lute with a last, wobbly chord.

Essie stood, brushing dust from her dress. Teren mirrored her motion. Nythir's jaw clenched.

"I'll be back," Essie said, oblivious to the tension. "We're just going to see the stream."

"Stay within the wards," Nythir said. "If you step beyond them, I'll know."

She shivered at the warning—or the promise—cheeks pink. "Understood," she whispered, and followed Teren into the darkness. Their laughter drifted back as they disappeared beyond the wagons.

Nythir sat perfectly still.

The fire popped. Night pressed close.

Letting her go felt like stepping back from a ledge he had been guarding with his entire body.

He could stop it. Could forbid it. Could justify it with a dozen practical reasons.

Instead, he loosened the reins.

The pressure didn't leave. It simply waited.

His magic whispered against the wards. A silver net stretched around camp, specially tuned to Essie's spark like a wire tuned to a note.

He could feel her moving, just at the edges of his senses. He settled in, every muscle tight. Jaw aching.

If anything went wrong, if her magic spiked, if that boy so much as breathed wrong, he wouldn't need magic to destroy him.

After all, he thought grimly, when it came to trouble, Essie never did anything halfway. It was his self-appointed job to handle all her problems.

He had crossed a line somewhere between Stonehaven and the open road.

He was no longer guarding a contract. Or a mage. Or even a secret.

He was guarding *her*.

That realization settled with unsettling ease. Contracts ended. Jobs concluded. This did not feel temporary. And Nythir had never been careless with things that could change the shape of his life.

20

Esther

How to tell if someone is flirting: ask a friend. Not yourself. Definitely not yourself.

Esther had never walked through a camp at night before. Her nightly strolls in palace gardens with stiff, silent servants were nothing like this. She drank in the lanterns' soft glow, the low murmur of whispering fires, the sky stretching wide above her like a lake of stars. It felt like stepping into someone else's dream.

The palace after sunset had always belonged to guards and ghosts. Daughters did not wander. They were escorted, observed, and corrected. The simple act of walking freely at night made her chest ache with happiness, edged with disbelief.

Or maybe she was dreaming—and she never wanted to wake.

She wasn't used to being allowed anywhere this late. Palaces locked their daughters in long before midnight. All she could do was read by candlelight, staring out her window and wishing for adventure.

"Careful there," Teren said as she stepped over a wagon wheel. "Ground dips close to the water."

She smiled politely. "Thank you."

The bracelet on her wrist pulsed gently, almost as soothing as a hot bath. Her magic stayed tucked neatly under her skin, like a sleeping cat. For once, her heartbeat didn't conjure sparks or trembling light.

Calm felt unfamiliar. She had grown accustomed to her magic reacting first—announcing fear before she recognized it. Now her body was quiet, and she didn't yet know how to listen without the warning bells.

She felt... strange. She liked not creating havoc, but the absence of sparks felt wrong in a way she couldn't place. For the first time, she wished for a magic lesson with Basil.

Teren led her between two leaning pines, then down a narrow slope where moonlight pooled over a stream. Water burbled softly over smooth stones, catching silver across the ripples.

"Oh," Esther breathed. "It's beautiful."

She had imagined this scene countless times, yet it was more breathtaking than she'd imagined. She wanted to bring Nythir here.

"Greyhollow streams usually are," Teren said proudly. "Come sit."

He gestured toward a fallen tree, smooth from years of weather. She perched carefully, smoothing her green dress, trying to sit like a proper person. Her etiquette tutors had never prepared her for log seating.

"We're already in Greyhollow?" she asked. Nythir had said four days or more. It had barely been a full day.

"Just the outskirts. Greyhollow is a large city, great for merchants. A few days till the market square," Teren said.

"Oh. That makes sense," she nodded.

"You're not from around here," Teren said, sitting too close. "I could tell from the way you ride... and talk."

Esther blinked. "Do I talk wrong?"

"No," he laughed. "You talk like someone kept indoors a lot."

It wasn't said cruelly. That made it harder to place. Esther searched for the correct response, the way she had been taught—polite, neutral, non-provoking. No lesson covered what to do when kindness felt tilted.

"That's accurate," she admitted softly. She had been trapped, not merely kept.

"First real road trip, then?" he asked.

"Yes," she whispered. "First... everything."

Teren's gaze lingered. "We don't meet many like you on the road."

"What kind?" she asked, genuinely curious.

"Soft and sweet," he said.

Esther froze. The words were wrong. Soft had always meant manageable. Sweet had always meant pliable. Compliments like that had followed her through palace halls, usually right before someone decided what was best for her.

She regretted not listening to Nythir. He noticed danger before it touched her. He catalogued tone, posture, and proximity. Esther noticed danger only when it pressed too close to ignore. She hated that difference—and relied on it all the same.

"Thank you," she said politely, though her smile didn't reach her eyes.

"I meant it," he murmured, leaning closer.

Her stomach fluttered unpleasantly. Not like when Nythir was near—this was wrong.

The breeze shifted.

Silver brushed the edge of her senses—thin and familiar. Nythir's ward. Watching without watching. The realization steadied her in a way she did not yet have language for. Even from afar, he could see past her fake smile. She focused on the warmth of his magic and relaxed a little.

"You're quiet," Teren said. "Am I making you nervous?"

Esther shook her head. "No. Just thinking."

"About?"

"Horse slouching," she said, unwilling to reveal her thoughts. "Apparently I ride like a parade."

Teren laughed, amused but not cruel. "He seems protective."

"Who?" she feigned ignorance.

"Tall one. Stern face. Handsome—but no competition for me."

Esther smiled helplessly. "That describes eight people in our party." Except for the handsome part. Nythir was the most attractive.

"Fair," he said. "But he watches you."

Her face heated. "He watches everything."

"He watches you more."

That did strange things to her chest. Her magic hummed beneath the bracelet.

"I don't know what you mean," she muttered.

Teren's fingers brushed her arm—lightly, too lightly.

Esther stiffened. His touch made her skin crawl.

"You know," he murmured, "you don't have to stick with them all night. We could—"

He moved closer. Close enough, she felt his breath.

Physical danger announced itself. Raised voices. Drawn blades. Panic that burned hot and obvious.

This felt quieter.

A look held too long. A smile that lingered past politeness. Words that sounded kind but pressed too close to something fragile inside her. Esther had never been taught how to defend against *this*.

Resistance had never been framed as an option—only endurance. She knew how to survive discomfort. She did not yet know how to refuse it.

"N–no, thank you," she said quickly, jumping off the log. "I enjoyed seeing the stream. I should get back to—"

"Hey," he said, grabbing her wrist.

Her magic flared.

A single spark burst from her fingers and fizzled away like a dying ember.

The bracelet hummed softly, steady and obedient.

It kept her magic in check. It did not keep her safe. Esther realized the distinction with a chill that had nothing to do with the night air. Control over her magic did not mean control over her life.

The words slammed into her chest.

"No," she gasped, pushing away from him. "Let go—"

"I'm just trying to—"

She couldn't hear him anymore. The world blurred. Her vision tunneled. The bracelet throbbed with her pulse, trying to keep her magic contained. She didn't want it included. It made her feel silenced in a whole new way, but she had to rely on it for everyone else.

Esther had wanted freedom more than anything.

She was beginning to understand the price of it.

Freedom meant choosing when to say no—and accepting that some people would hear no as a challenge instead of an answer. "Teren, please—"

A twig snapped.

A voice, cold and edged with steel, cut through the darkness.

"Take your hands off her."

Esther didn't have to turn. Didn't have to breathe. She knew that voice. The words didn't rescue her. They *ended* the moment. That mattered more.

Teren released her immediately. "It's not what it—"

Silver magic rippled like a warning.

And Esther calmed, knowing Nythir had arrived. She hated that relief came so easily—and loved it just the same. One day, she would learn how to protect herself without needing someone else to step between her and the world. Tonight was not that day.

21

NYTHIR

HOW TO INTERRUPT A BAD SITUATION: BRING A ROCK, A BAD ATTITUDE, AND ABSOLUTELY NO PATIENCE.

Nythir had been sitting on a wagon axle, pretending to sharpen a knife and absolutely not watching the ward-thread that tracked Essie's magic.

Until it spiked.

Not dangerously—just wrong. Fear compressed instead of flaring. A tight, jagged note in the ward-thread that didn't belong to surprise or excitement. Nythir was already moving before he finished identifying it.

The forest swallowed him in long shadows.

He found a rock along the way. It fit nicely in his palm. He chose it deliberately. Heavy enough to end the situation. Light enough to stop short of something permanent. Violence was a tool, not an impulse—and tonight, it needed limits.

Probably.

All he knew was he couldn't stab the guy without consequences—despite how much he wanted to.

He moved silently between the pines, silver magic weaving around his steps, until he reached the stream clearing.

He saw them instantly.

Her breath uneven, her eyes wide with fear. Teren was too close, forcibly holding her to him.

Something inside Nythir went very, very quiet.

Then very, very loud.

"Take your hands off her," he said evenly. Calmly. Menacingly.

Teren spun, letting go as if burned. Lucky for him, that damned bracelet kept him singe-free. "I wasn't doing anything—"

Nythir didn't break stride. He walked calmly and confidently, like a trained assassin, with the aim of one, too.

The rock that had previously been in his palm cracked Teren cleanly on the forehead with masterful precision.

Sadly. Just enough to drop him. Not enough to kill him.

Teren let out a startled rooster's cry and collapsed into the dirt.

The danger had passed.

Safety did not arrive with the absence of a threat. It came slowly, in increments—through breath returning, tension loosening, space being reclaimed. Nythir stayed alert, counting those seconds instead of assuming them.

Nythir did not relax.

Experience had taught him that the aftermath was where most mistakes happened—when people assumed safety instead of confirming it.

Essie bolted to him, eyes gleaming. "Nythir!" She all but tackled him with her embrace.

"You alright?" he asked, slipping his arms loosely around her.

Essie nodded, but the tremble in her hands and arms said otherwise.

"He grabbed you?" Nythir asked, stroking her hair. He wasn't sure what to do with his hands; he'd never cared to comfort someone before.

"Yes," she whispered weakly, her voice breaking.

"Are you hurt?"

"No. I just—he was too close. I was scared."

Nythir exhaled harshly, anger flickering beneath his ribs. "You said yes to walking with him."

Her breath hitched. "I didn't know he meant—anything."

"You never do," he said, gentler than he felt.

She sniffled, chipping away at his heart. He was not good at the whole comforting thing.

"Essie. Look at me."

She did.

He took her wrist—the one Teren had grasped—and turned it over gently. No bruises. But her pulse raced like frightened hummingbird wings beneath her skin.

"I'm not angry at you," he said softly.

Her shoulders loosened a fraction. "You sound angry."

"I'm angry on your behalf."

She blinked. Hard. "I don't know the difference."

Of course, she didn't.

He swallowed, carefully brushing his thumb over her knuckles. "Then I'll teach you."

It wasn't a promise of protection. It was a promise of knowledge. Those mattered more in the long run.

She stared at him like he'd handed her a spellbook full of answers.

A groan rose from the ground behind them. Teren attempted to sit up, clutching his forehead. "What... hit me?"

"A falling rock," Nythir said flatly. "Nature is dangerous."

Essie elbowed him weakly. "Nythir."

He ignored her. "You're done for tonight. And if you go near her again, the next rock won't stop at falling."

Nythir had guarded secrets, caravans, and contracts.

This was different.

This was a boundary—and once crossed, it did not reset.

Teren wisely lay back down.

Nythir guided Essie away from the stream, keeping close but not crowding her. "We're going back to camp."

"I'm sorry," she murmured.

He stopped walking.

Her apology hit harder than the situation itself. Not because it was unwarranted—but because it was automatic. As if fear alone constituted guilt.

Something old and vicious stirred in his chest. That reflex had been taught to her. Carefully. Repeatedly.

"What are you apologizing for?" He needed her to hear this part. Not later. Not softened. Now, while the moment was raw enough to rewrite.

"For... not understanding. For trusting too easily. For making you worry."

He turned toward her fully, moonlight brushing pale gold over her features.

"You didn't do anything wrong."

Her breath caught. "But—"

"You trusted someone because you want to see the good in people." His voice softened despite himself. "That's not a weakness."

"It feels like one."

"It's not." He hesitated, then added, "And I'd rather spend the rest of my life throwing rocks at idiots than see you lose that."

He had always believed vows mattered more than blood.

Perhaps that was why he had been so careful with them.

"Nythir," she whispered, her voice small but full of something warm, something scared, something hopeful. "Why are you always—always—"

He reached up, brushing a loose strand of hair from her face.

"Because you deserve people who protect you," he said. "Not people who make you afraid."

Her eyes glistened. The bracelet pulsed gold. And for the first time since they'd arrived at the stream, Essie exhaled without shaking.

"Can we go back now?" she asked.

"Yes," he said. "But can I ask to do something first?"

"Of course. I owe you for saving me."

"I don't want it out of obligation," he said, gently taking her hand. "I want to do what that filth tried—*but correctly.*"

"What was he even trying to do?" Essie asked.

Nythir couldn't help but laugh. She wasn't playing coy—she was just that clueless.

"Why are you laughing?" she pouted. "I freaked out when he grabbed me. Oh no! Was he trying to kidnap me? You want to kidnap me?"

The question chilled him. Kidnapping was violence with structure. This had been something quieter—and far more common. That difference mattered. He would not let her misname it. "Essie, he was trying to kiss you."

"K-k-kiss?" she shouted, turning redder than a tomato. "You want to kiss me?" Her voice pitched as some of his favorite sparks escaped the confines of the bracelet. He basked in the knowledge that the runespire Luna gave her couldn't stand a chance against his connection with Essie.

"Yes." He traced a finger along her warm cheek and bent down a little closer. "Push me away if you don't want to. I won't be mad."

He waited because waiting was the point. Power meant nothing without restraint. Desire meant nothing without choice.

He waited a beat. Then another.

Then he kissed her, and sparks ignited.

Nothing cracked or went up in flames. Her magic responded differently—not as defense, but recognition. Gold scattered gently, unafraid. Nythir catalogued that too. Magic, like people, behaved differently when it was not being cornered.

Even the bracelet she wore couldn't keep her magic from reacting to him. And he revealed that.

She didn't push him away or pull back. She pulled closer. Her hands trembled, clutching his tunic.

She more than welcomed the kiss. She reciprocated it.

It was then that Nythir realized he had been jealous. The realization did not shame him. It clarified him. Jealousy was not possession—it was awareness sharpened by risk.

He hadn't known what that emotion was before, but what he did know was that he would never admit it to Lyssara.

Some protections were written in ink. Others were written in intent—and enforced without hesitation. Intent, once set, demanded follow-through. And Nythir had never abandoned something he chose to guard.

22

Esther

HOW TO MAKE CAMP MORNINGS INTERESTING: ADD ONE BOLD ELF, ONE CONFUSED MAGE, AND AT LEAST ONE PERSON INSISTING ON BRINGING A GOAT.

Esther woke the next morning with warm sunlight across her face, a faint ache in her lips and an aching back from sleeping on hard ground all night. She regretted her past decision to pack only eight books, which had been lost to the universe moments after teleporting.

Sleeping under the stars felt like something out of a fairy tale.

Fairy tales never mentioned how hard the ground was or how exposed everything felt without walls. She should have packed a pillow. It would have softened her landing and improved her sleep quality.

Still, she had slept better than she ever had in silk sheets. Safety, she was learning, was not the same as luxury.

The camp was awake. People talked. Horses snorted. Someone was already burning breakfast. It was Vorrik. For someone who loved food so much, he was a terrible cook.

Essie sat up and stretched her aching muscles. The skin on the back of her neck tickled. She felt intent eyes on her and instinctively knew she shouldn't look—but did anyway.

Nythir was staring at her from across the fire like a man who wanted to say good morning and possibly commit arson.

Her instinctive response was to hide. Instead, she froze. Hiding had been her first reflex for years. Standing still—being seen—felt like a new skill she had not practiced enough to trust.

He stood and walked over like a wolf stalking something inevitable.

Esther, for some reason, felt her survival instincts activate. Her non-existent ones, because she didn't fight or flee.

No—she hastily stood and greeted him. It was easier when moments were private. Public acknowledgment—daylight, witnesses, familiarity—was much harder. Esther did not yet know how to hold something precious without trying to fold it away.

"Good morning," she said quickly, biting her tongue. She brushed her fingers through her knotted hair. She didn't know if it was a blessing or a curse not to have a mirror, because her hair felt like a tangled disaster created by a caffeinated squirrel.

"Essie," Nythir said, his voice firm, as if he were about to ruin several lives before breakfast, "we need to inform the group."

"About what?" she asked, fingers stuck in a particularly stubborn knot.

He didn't answer. He took her free hand—her other still trapped in her hair—and gently guided her toward the group. Esther appeared to have been the last to wake.

Lyssara wandered over, chewing dried fruit, her hair also a mess, and her sword strapped on like she was ready to fight someone purely for fun.

Esther felt better about her own appearance.

Vorrik followed with his usual sunshine energy and a piece of bread in his mouth. His earlier attempt at breakfast had turned to dust while he cooked it. It was impressive how bad he was. His cooking skills were possible worse than Esther's magic control—and that was saying something.

Teren was sitting on a log, pretending to be invisible. He avoided eye contact with everyone, which made Esther feel a little guilty. She decided to check on his rock-shaped injury later, when Nythir wasn't paying attention.

Which could take a while, because he seemed alarmingly good at paying attention to her.

Nythir cleared his throat and loudly declared, "Essie and I are married now."

The universe paused.

A spoon clattered.

Someone choked on their tea.

Esther stared at him while everyone stared at her.

"What?" She had intended to whisper, but shouted instead.

Lyssara squinted. "Married as in… legally? Emotionally? Socially? Accidentally?"

"Yes," Nythir said confidently.

"No," Esther squeaked. The absurdity grounded her. If the world was going to tilt, at least it was tilting with witnesses.

"Explain," Lyssara said, pulling up a chair that absolutely had not existed one second ago.

Nythir nodded solemnly. "Essie and I kissed."

Lyssara and Vorrik stared blankly.

Esther stared at them, staring blankly at her. And everyone stared at them, staring at each other. It was like one of those weird nightmares that weren't necessarily scary, but made a socially anxious person's skin crawl.

And Esther was the portrait-perfect example of a socially anxious person.

At that moment, if she hadn't been wearing her mother's bracelet, she would have combusted into a pile of human goop just to escape. Death by fire was better than whatever she was experiencing currently.

"And," Nythir continued, "I vowed years ago I would only ever kiss one person. Therefore—"

"No," Esther repeated, louder this time. "Wait. No."

"—we are married."

Lyssara made the sound of a cat choking on a lemon.

Vorrik clapped his hands once like a proud father. "Well! That escalated!"

Teren stood up so fast he tripped over a bucket.

Nythir ignored all of them. "It's simple," he concluded with all the confidence he should not have had.

"It is not simple!" Esther yelped. "People don't get married for kissing!" Her objection surprised even her. She wasn't afraid—she was startled. There was a difference, and noticing it felt like progress.

"You absolutely aren't," Lyssara said. "You need witnesses. A ceremony. A signed document. A cake. Possibly a goat, if the priest is dramatic enough."

Vorrik nodded sagely. "Ours required a goat. It stared directly into my soul."

Esther was trying to breathe normally, but her lungs had recently decided to be decorative instead of functional.

"Nythir," she whispered, "we are not married."

"Legally, not yet. But in spirit, yes we are."

Then he did something that shocked everyone. He leaned down and kissed her on the cheek.

Esther saw her life pass before her eyes. She was not built for this level of cardiac violence before breakfast.

Vorrik cheered.

Nythir smiled, looking far too handsome and smug after almost killing her via a direct heart attack.

Lyssara put her hands on her hips. "You two need to have an actual conversation about actual marriage, not whatever... whatever *this* is."

"It's fate," Vorrik said with profound, unearned wisdom.

"No it isn't," Esther squeaked. "You can't just... jump all the steps! You need things! Like dates! And presents! And cake! And—and—paperwork!"

"And a goat," Vorrik added.

"I don't want a goat at the wedding!" Esther shrieked in an octave that would put the wedding goat to shame.

Nythir slid his hand into hers again, causing Esther to squeak like a distressed mouse.

"Essie," he said softly, "if you're already married, you can't be forced into an arranged marriage. And I want to marry you."

Esther's mouth fell open. Her heart stuttered. Her magic fluttered like a startled butterfly under her skin.

The logic landed harder than the declaration. Protection framed as a partnership instead of confinement. It frightened her and relieved her in equal measure.

"You want to marry me?" She asked with a shaky voice.

"Yes," he said simply.

Lyssara threw a blanket over her own head like she needed sensory deprivation to cope.

Vorrik began humming the wedding march under his breath, adding a few goat sounds for realism.

Teren hid behind a barrel. The poor guy had probably woken up and chosen fear.

Esther stared at Nythir. Then at his hand. Then into his eyes.

Her voice was tiny. "O-okay. Maybe the idea... isn't terrible." The words were small, but they were hers. Not a duty. Not a concession. A choice made in daylight, with witnesses, and the option to change her mind.

Nythir's expression brightened with the warmth of a sunrise.

Lyssara yanked the blanket off her head. "Wait—no—that's *not* how logical discussions work!"

Vorrik gasped dramatically and grabbed the nearest merchant. "Where is the nearest goat?"

"No goats!" Esther cried.

But she was smiling. Smiling like an idiot in love.

Because she was an idiot in love. She waited for guilt to follow. For shame. For the instinctive urge to apologize for taking up space. None of it came.

Then it hit her.

Oh no. Oh no no no.

She was in love.

With an elf who committed to marriage like it was an invitation to afternoon tea. She had absolutely no idea how to navigate this new emotional development. But for once, not knowing felt like a possibility rather than a failure.

Nythir squeezed her hand gently.

"Good," he murmured.

Lyssara covered her eyes. "You two are going to kill me."

Vorrik patted her head. "I'll look for a goat."

"No goats!" Lyssara snapped, remembering the horrible bleating menace at her wedding. "This is why adults shouldn't be left unsupervised."

23

Lucy

How to survive travel with nobles: don't.

"Finally!" Lucy shouted, her voice echoing through the empty streets, likely disturbing some poor resident's sleep.

Lucy had tried. Truly. She had prepared snacks, rehearsed patience, and even entertained the thought that maybe—just maybe—this trip would not make her consider a life of crime. She had been wrong on all counts.

"Mind your manners, child," the Baroness hissed. "Even the roosters have yet to crow."

Lucy didn't care. She had been stuck in a carriage with the two most stagnant people she had ever had the dismay of traveling with for five days.

Five whole agonizing days. It might as well have been a newly discovered torture technique, tested on her firsthand.

Basil had attempted a conversation on day two. By day three, he had stopped speaking unless spoken to. By day four, Lucy was sure the Baroness was doing it on purpose.

Lucy had a newfound sympathy for Esther. Sympathy, and something sharper beneath it. Lucy didn't like how easily people decided what was best for Esther. She liked even less that Esther had been trained to accept it.

When they returned to the castle, she vowed to do her best to sabotage all of her horrid lessons, consequences be damned.

They would have arrived before sunset if the carriage wheel hadn't broken off—thanks to a sentient pinecone of all things.

The driver had gotten too close to Ashvale, insisting it was a shortcut to Stonehaven. Story had it that a very antisocial mage once lived in the forest and had cast a spell to keep others from disturbing them. Apparently, even riding along a side road near it was too much of a disturbance.

Lucy made a mental note never to return. Places that enforced boundaries aggressively, either protected privacy or hid something worth protecting.

Lucy turned around and flipped off the forest in the distance. The Baroness gasped at the rude gesture.

The sun had started to rise behind the trees, casting the forest in a dusty rose hue that made it look like a famous painting.

But Lucy knew better. The more attractive something looked, the higher the risk. Lucy considered this one of her more reliable survival rules. It had yet to fail her. Including where she herself was concerned. She felt that law in her bones—since she herself was one of the most attractive people she knew. And she was very dangerous in quiet ways.

A rooster crowed in the background, signaling that life was soon to awaken. Lucy pointed toward the sound.

"Happy now? The roosters are awake."

The Baroness made a sound that reminded Lucy of an asthmatic pug. Lucy had once met a pug with more fortitude. And better breathing.

Lucy smiled cheekily before twirling around and entering Moonpetal Inn, leaving Basil and the idiotic coachman to unload the cargo. She was not made for heavy lifting.

"Greetings," a compact elderly woman said. "Are you in need of a room today?"

"Good morning," Lucy replied. "Actually, I need three."

"Oh dear. I'm sad to say we only have one available. We're currently repairing two of our rooms after some rowdy guests."

And just like that, Lucy's torture continued. She briefly considered arson. Decided against it. Too early in the morning, and she hadn't had breakfast yet.

She cursed the travelers who had destroyed the rooms. "May everything they eat turn to ash," she whispered to whatever deity would hear her prayers—good or evil, she did not care.

Suddenly, the strict castle walls and regulations about coming and going didn't seem so bad. After this journey, she would never travel again.

"Fine," Lucy groaned. "But you'll have to inform the overly dressed pug out there." She jerked her thumb toward the window, where the edge of the Baroness's enormous hat was visible. Lucy would never understand the point of such large, gaudy hats nobles loved so much.

Lucy barely had time to enjoy the old woman's horrified expression before the inn door jingled again and the Baroness stormed in, hat feathers first.

"Lucy," she squawked, "why does the innkeeper claim there is only one room? Surely she can relocate the peasants."

"Sure," Lucy said brightly. "If you want to go outside and physically drag a family of six out of their beds at dawn, be my guest."

The Baroness paled. "Absolutely not. Commoners bite."

Lucy opened her mouth, closed it, then opened it again. Some arguments were not worth winning aloud.

"Exactly." Lucy clapped her hands together. "Great news, Basil. We're about to experience horrors no man has ever walked through before."

Basil—poor, sweet Basil—already had the look of a man questioning all of his life decisions. Lucy liked Basil. He was competent, tired, and did not mistake authority for intelligence. It was a rare combination.

"We haven't slept in two days…"

"Perfect," Lucy chirped. "Then you'll be too tired to complain."

Lucy led the group down the creaky hall toward a door labeled BATH-HOUSE in peeling paint. The Baroness recoiled as if the wood itself were contagious.

"Communal," she whispered, trembling. "As in… people… bathe… together?"

"Relax," Lucy said. "It's early. We'll be alone."

She pushed open the door.

Steam drifted lazily through the air, glimmering faintly in the morning light. Large stone tubs, full and heated, waited. Empty.

Lucy inhaled deeply. Hot water solved more problems than diplomacy ever had.

"See?" Lucy gestured. "Fresh hot water, no other humans. Your worst nightmare defeated."

The Baroness minced inside like her shoes were allergic to public flooring. "I suppose… it could be worse."

Lucy bit her tongue to avoid saying *It usually is.*

The Baroness tested the water with one gloved finger, then recoiled. "It's so hot I may perish."

"Good," Lucy muttered. "Boil off the attitude."

"What was that?"

"I said bold of you to test the water yourself."

They bathed quickly. Lucy fully immersed herself, sighing dramatically with relief, while the Baroness clung to the edge of her tub like it might swallow her whole.

When they finished, the Baroness sniffed, "I miss the lemon scent of my bath."

Lucy shrugged. "I miss my will to live."

Back in their room, Lucy grabbed the stack of blankets and pillows she'd charmed from the innkeeper and plopped them in the far corner.

"What," the Baroness demanded, "are you doing?"

"Building a nest."

Lucy had never slept well in a bed that wasn't hers. Too soft meant vulnerable. Too big meant watched. Floors, corners, and piles of blankets were honest.

"A... nest?"

"Yes. I don't fight my enemies on an empty stomach, and I don't sleep in the only bed in the room when the elderly need it more."

The Baroness's eye twitched. "Absolutely not. You will take the bed."

Lucy snorted. "No. You need it more. Your bones sound like branches breaking in a weak breeze."

"How dare—my bones are youthful and sturdy!"

"I think the only youthful and sturdy thing in the room right now is me."

"Enough of your sass, child! You will take the bed, and that is final!"

"Make me—"

Basil dropped his pack with a thud that rattled the window.

"Enough!"

Both Lucy and the Baroness froze mid-glare. Lucy respected raised voices only when they were earned. Basil's was.

Basil pointed at the bed. "Both of you. Bed. Now."

"We are not—" the Baroness began.

"I am not—" Lucy tried.

"It is big enough for two," he said, somehow whispering and yelling at the same time. "I have slept in trenches and snowstorms, with a dislocated shoulder and a goblin chewing my boots. But I cannot sleep through you two bickering like alley cats. Get in the bed, and be quiet."

Lucy and the Baroness exchanged a long, horrified look.

"Fine," they muttered in unison, climbing onto opposite sides of the bed like cats forced to share a sunbeam.

Lucy stared at the ceiling and considered all the choices that had led her here. She regretted none of them. That felt suspicious.

Lucy wrapped the blanket around herself like a burrito of suffering. The Baroness lay stiffly, hands folded atop her chest, as if preparing for her own burial.

Basil blew out the candle and took a seat on the rickety chair across the room.

They slept.

Lucy awoke to the delightful sensation of being crushed. She accepted this as penance for some unspecified sin.

The Baroness had, at some point, rolled over and latched onto Lucy like an emotional barnacle. Basil snored softly in the chair, tilted at a forty-five-degree angle that suggested spinal betrayal.

Lucy pried herself free and sat up.

"Right," she announced, stretching. "Time to meet the Brass Sparrow." Lucy had heard enough about the guild to know two things: they respected results, and they despised hesitation. She had plenty of the first and none of the second.

Basil jolted awake with a gasp. "Are we under attack?"

"No," Lucy said, wondering why men always assumed they were under attack. "Worse. We have to socialize."

The Baroness adjusted her hat. "Lead the way, child," she said, even though Lucy was not the one with connections.

And together, one stubborn maid, one cranky knight, and one perpetually disgruntled noblewoman set off toward the most notorious guild in Valedara.

Lucy felt eyes on her back as they walked—familiar, steady, and deliberately distant. She didn't turn around. Whoever it was didn't close the space either. The awareness lingered anyway, quiet and unclaimed, like something patient enough to wait.

24

Lucy

How to handle a bleating noblewoman: pretend she is background noise.

Lucy skipped behind Basil as he led them through a dirty, narrow alleyway that smelled of mold and moss. The air clung to her skin, damp and sticky, as if the alley had not breathed fresh wind in years. Somewhere behind them, water dripped in an uneven rhythm that echoed off the walls.

The Baroness sounded like a dying rat as she trailed behind. Lucy did not know humans could make such high-pitched squeaks. She was almost impressed. Almost.

"Are you sure this is the correct way?" she squawked, tripping on her dress, which was much too wide for the route they took.

"I'm positive," Basil groaned for what felt like the hundredth time.

Lucy, on the other hand, enjoyed their stroll. She was used to tuning out shrill noble voices. Selective hearing was a survival skill. Lucy had learned it young—what to listen to, what to let dissolve into static. Panic screamed. Danger whispered.

The smell of farm animals and sweat hit her first. They stepped out onto a dilapidated farm, where chickens scratched the dirt, goats bleated in complaint, and cows grazed lazily in the warm sunlight. Damp hay and goat musk mixed in the air, earthy and sour. A cow let out a long, mournful low that sounded like it objected to their presence.

"There is no possible way," the Baroness whispered harshly, covering her mouth with her handkerchief.

"Yes, this is the Brass Sparrow," Basil said.

Lucy liked places that lied about what they were. They usually meant business.

She did not know whether the sound that came next was the Baroness or a goat, but she laughed so hard she nearly doubled over. Her laughter carried all the way to the sagging barn door.

She clutched her stomach, fighting for breath, and made a special place in her memory to store the Baroness's horrified expression. It would be perfect to pull out whenever she needed a good laugh. Lucy treasured moments like this. Joy weaponized was still joy.

"That is enough, Lucy," Basil reprimanded, using the same voice he used during Esther's lessons.

The barn door creaked when he pulled it open. It sounded like the hinges were screaming for mercy, which worried Lucy that it might fall off right then. Somehow, it survived. Sometimes the things that made the most noise were the ones that outlasted everyone.

Meaning the Baroness might be immortal. Lucy would put money on it. Spite fueled many long lives.

Inside, Lucy was about to stuff a dirty rag into the Baroness's mouth if she did not stop her constant bleating.

She complained about everything: the crooked door, the rickety stairs, the funky smell, the cold draft from a cracked window. Dust floated in slow spirals through beams of pale sunlight. The floorboards groaned under every step, brittle and splintery.

"Brom, I am here on official business," Basil called out.

To whom he was speaking, Lucy could not tell. The square room had no doors aside from the entrance, no stairs, nothing but cracked windows and old, mismatched crates. It looked more like a storage room that had given up on storing things—or a backup chicken coop that never received chickens. Currently, it housed only a spider, which was crafting an intricate web.

Lucy really hoped he was not talking to the spider. She wondered if the lack of sleep and traveling had taken such a toll on him that he was imagining things. He was no longer in his prime, after all.

Just as she opened her mouth to question Basil, she heard footsteps beneath them.

Creak.

A trapdoor snapped open in the corner. Metal hinges screeched, sharp enough to make her teeth ache.

Lucy shifted her weight automatically, ready to bolt or strike. Old instincts didn't retire just because you were tired.

A flash of bright red hair appeared before the rest of the man's head popped up.

"Basil. My dear brother and his companions. Come in, come in," he said, cheerful and far too loud for such a room. Cool air rushed up from the dark opening, smelling of stone, old parchment, and something faintly metallic.

"Let us go," Basil sighed, descending the hidden stairs.

"Go where?" the Baroness shrieked, but Basil was already gone.

Lucy had read about stranger entrances in adventure books, and she was too tired to question weird holes in barns. Heck, even the palace guards had secret passages to get intimate with the maids. She had seen some really creative routes taken there.

Stone steps led them down into a long hallway lit by glowing orbs. Every step echoed sharply, bouncing off the walls in hollow rings. The air grew colder the deeper they walked, until her breath fogged faintly in front of her face. Dust mixed with the scent of leather, ink, and old stone. The walls were slightly damp when her fingers brushed them, grit clinging to her skin.

Sadly, the Baroness also followed, her heels clicking angrily behind them as she muttered nonstop.

"Who are your friends? Oh wait, where are my manners. I am Brom, pleased to meet you."

"This is—" Basil began.

"I'm Lucy," she rushed forward. "I can introduce myself, thank you very much."

"Wow. She is a spicy one. I like her," Brom whistled and winked. His hair shimmered like copper wire in the orb light. "How about the well-dressed madam back there?"

"I am Baroness Irene Levon," she said, executing a perfect curtsy despite the cramped stone tunnel.

Lucy rolled her eyes. They were in a creepy tunnel where there was no reason to maintain etiquette. She was beginning to see why Esther never graduated from her lessons with the Baroness—her standards were unreachable.

"Lovely to meet you, madam." Brom took her hand and kissed the back of it. The Baroness turned pink. "No ring, I see. How is such a beautiful woman still single?"

Her eyes darted to Basil. Lucy nudged him hard in the side, silently screaming for him to save them all. Lucy had perfected the art of redirection. Unfortunately, Brom appeared immune.

"That is enough, Brom," Basil sighed. "Stop evaluating my companions."

"Spoil sport," Brom chuckled, continuing to lead the way.

"So, who exactly are you?" Lucy jogged beside him. "You called Basil your brother."

"Exactly as you heard, young miss."

"Brother-in-law," Basil clarified. "He is the guild leader of the Brass Sparrow."

"This guy?" Lucy blurted, scowling. "He does not look like it."

The Baroness scolded her for her manners while Brom laughed. Lucy still could not believe this stringy, flirtatious man was the infamous guild leader.

"Oh, we are here," Brom announced in the middle of the hallway.

He pulled a small piece of paper from his sleeve and dropped it onto the floor.

Lucy froze as the stones beneath them shuddered. A low rumble vibrated up her boots and into her bones. The air tingled sharply, like the aftermath of a lightning strike. One by one, stone steps unfolded from the floor, clicking into place like pieces of a puzzle.

Lucy's humor evaporated. This was not parlor magic. This was infrastructure.

She had never seen a key rune used in person. She knew the basics—they looked simple—but their execution required the precision of a master. One wrong placement, even a hair off, and the mechanism could collapse.

Which meant every wall and every section of this hallway had been built with runes. If Brom had misaligned even one of them while activating the passage, the ceiling could have crushed them all. Precision like that wasn't luck. It was preparation layered on obsession.

A cold sweat prickled down her spine. Lucy quietly rescinded every internal insult she had made about Brom in the past five minutes. She respected people who earned fear honestly.

Brom was terrifying.

25

Lucy

How to find joy: treasure noble discomfort like it is fine art.

The Brass Sparrow headquarters was not a decrepit goat farm. Well, technically, it was above ground. Below, it was bigger than the palace library. At least, it was larger than the palace library in her imagination.

Lucy had never been allowed inside the palace library because maids didn't need access to "delicate literature." Esther had tried to sneak her in when they were young, but the princess did not have enough power to get a 'mere maid' past the guards.

Lucy remembered Esther's furious whispering, the way she'd tried to argue rules into changing. It hadn't worked. Rules are rarely bent for the people they hurt.

The moment Brom pushed the door open, Lucy's jaw nearly hit the floor.

A chandelier hung from the ceiling. Having lived in the castle for nearly a decade, Lucy could spot expensive decorations from a mile away—and that chandelier was expensive. The kind nobles pretended to be "simple" and "tasteful" while secretly bragging about it.

The entire space opened into a lavish hall: plush carpets, tall bookshelves, polished marble floors, and tapestries that looked handwoven by someone who didn't hate their life.

"Wha—?" Lucy croaked. "Where did the goats go?"

The Baroness pressed a trembling hand to her chest, looking personally offended by the change in scenery. Lucy catalogued the reaction carefully. Shock. Disorientation. Loss of footing. She savored it like a well-executed painting.

"I am confused. And I dislike being confused. Someone explain this immediately."

Lucy never thought there would be a day she agreed with the Baroness, but here she was. She'd never admit it, though.

Basil cleared his throat. "The Brass Sparrow prefers… discretion."

Lucy ran to the front door and poked her head out. "It's a shack on the outside," she said. The scent of farm animals gave way to the smell of ale and something metallic. Exactly what one might expect a back alley to smell like.

"More like a crime on the outside," the Baroness grumbled, shutting the door.

"And apparently a palace on the inside," Lucy muttered.

Brom waved them over to the lounge area, his demeanor far too chipper for someone who lived in a crypt-like tunnel system.

"So," he said, slapping a stack of papers onto a glossy table, "tell me what kind of mess you're knee-deep in. If it's royal, political, or involves improbable property destruction, that's my specialty."

Lucy and Basil exchanged a look—it was definitely the first two. The property damage was yet to be determined, but it was highly likely, given Esther's involvement.

Basil gave Brom the short version: Princess missing, teleportation spell, Lucy's flawless improvisation skills, and finally, the King assigned Basil to track Esther down.

Brom listened with a slow-building grin. Then leaned back in his chair. Then groaned into his hands.

"Oh, that's a disaster," he said cheerfully. "You're going to need Sylva."

Basil froze. Lucy wondered why Basil froze—and why Brom seemed so excited. Even the Baroness stopped judging the decor long enough to squint at the strange interaction unfolding.

Lucy trusted Basil's instincts more than his temper. If he didn't want Sylva involved, there was a reason—and Lucy filed that reason under *important*.

"Sylva?" Basil repeated, voice tight.

"Yes, Sylva." Brom drummed his fingers on the chair. "He's our expert in wild goose chases."

"We are not chasing geese," Lucy muttered.

"You are," Brom said. "You just don't know it yet."

Lucy disliked people who spoke as if inevitability were a favor.

Basil drew a slow, deep breath—the kind usually reserved for his magic lessons with Esther. "We don't need Sylva," he said.

"Oh, you really do," Brom corrected. "And to get Sylva, you'll need to talk to Rhea."

Basil's eyelid twitched. Lucy had never seen anyone besides Esther—or herself—make his eye twitch.

The Baroness gasped. "Rhea?"

"Wait." Lucy blinked. "You know her?"

"Of course I know her," the Baroness hissed. "She is—"

But she didn't finish.

Because the door at the far end of the hall flew open, and a woman with warm brown skin and a smile bright enough to light all of Stonehaven crashed in like a summer storm.

"Basil!"

The room tilted. Not magically—emotionally. Lucy had learned to recognize the sound of history entering a space.

Lucy had never seen Basil look startled. Annoyed? Yes. Irritated? Always. But startled? Never. Yet there it was—the exact expression when Rhea barreled into him, wrapping him in a hug that sounded like it cracked at least one of his ribs.

"Oh," Lucy whispered. "She's pretty."

"And familiar..." the Baroness hissed sharply.

Rhea released Basil and turned, beaming at the group with the warmth of a hearth.

"Come in, come in! Basil, you should have written ahead. I would've made tea."

Lucy blinked. She talked like she knew him well. Suspiciously well.

"Explain," the Baroness demanded, poking Basil with her fan as if trying to provoke a confession.

Basil inhaled. Rhea beat him to it.

"Oh! You must be Irene. It's been so long!"

The Baroness went sheet-white. Lucy nearly dropped her satchel.

"You know—" Lucy pointed at the Baroness, "—her?"

"Oh, yes." Rhea laughed lightly. "She used to frequent the same social circles as me before the Queen helped me choose my real path." She waved a hand vaguely.

Lucy did not miss the Baroness's rigidity. That kind of stillness only came from old choices and older debts.

"Helped you?" Lucy and the Baroness said in unison. Lucy did not like how in sync the two of them had been in the last hour.

Rhea gestured toward the interior rooms. "Please, we should sit. This story requires tea. Possibly alcohol."

"Definitely alcohol," Basil groaned, causing Lucy's jaw to drop yet again. Basil drinking was unheard of—she felt like she was watching sin unfold firsthand.

They moved through another door, etched with a key rune. Lucy held her breath as they passed through.

Inside, a cozy parlor awaited: cushions everywhere, fox-shaped carvings, and even porcelain teacups decorated with foxes. Lucy guessed Rhea really liked foxes.

Or foxes liked her. Lucy had noticed that décor often reflected more than taste.

Rhea poured tea and settled gracefully. "Basil and I were arranged to marry," she began.

Lucy choked on air. Her thoughts jumped immediately to Esther. Funny how often "arranged" translates to "endured."

"Yes, Lucy, it's true," Basil muttered before she could ask.

"You had a wife?" Lucy hissed. "A whole secret wife?"

"Former wife," he corrected.

Rhea gave him a fond look. "He was a good husband. Just not the right one."

"And whose idea was the... separation?" the Baroness asked.

Rhea smiled softly. "Basil's. He knew I was in love with someone else and granted me a route to freedom." Granted. Lucy chewed on the word. Freedom that needed permission always came with strings.

"With whom?" Lucy asked quietly.

Rhea's eyes sparkled. "With someone I wasn't supposed to."

As if on cue, footsteps padded from the hallway, nails clicking on the floor. Lucy turned, expecting a pet fox.

A tall man with pale skin and silver hair entered. Fox ears flicked atop his head while his pale eyes studied them with quiet caution. He was elegant, dangerous, and handsome enough to make Lucy rethink every life choice she'd ever made. Dangerous didn't always mean cruel. Lucy respected the distinction.

"That," Rhea said with pride, "is Asher."

Asher bowed slightly, voice smooth as velvet. "Welcome."

Lucy tried to bow back and nearly knocked over the tea tray.

Behind him was a more petite figure: a younger beast-kin with silver hair curling at the ends, warm brown skin, and a tail flicking lazily behind him. He wasn't much taller than Lucy herself, which she noted with quiet scheming: if she ever had to intimidate him, she could manage.

His gaze lingered a fraction too long—then snapped away like he'd caught himself touching something hot. Lucy felt it anyway. Not attraction. Awareness.

"Is this the group?" the boy asked, voice like warm honey. "The trouble hunters?"

Lucy bristled. "We are not trouble hunters."

He smirked. "You smell like trouble."

"I smell like lavender," she snapped.

"Sure," he said, unconvinced and grinning.

Rhea beamed. "Lucy, Basil, Irene—this is my son. Sylva."

Sylva flicked his ear. "And you're the ones dragging me into a goose chase."

Lucy stared. Sylva stared back, unreadable. Then his tail swished, and she tried not to stare at the very warm, huggable fluff. The movement wasn't idle. Lucy had grown up around enough animals to recognize restraint masquerading as calm.

"Don't worry," he said. "I'm good at chasing things that don't want to be found."

Lucy swallowed. That did not bode well for Esther, who absolutely did not want to be found. She was not prepared for the extra—arguably adorable—chaos joining their hunt.

26

ESTHER

HOW TO HANDLE CONFLICT: LET YOUR FRIENDS FIGHT WHILE YOU QUESTION YOUR LIFE CHOICES.

The caravan rattled along the dirt road like rusted bells tied behind a running horse. It was loud, shaky, and one unfortunate bump away from disaster.

Esther clutched her satchel tighter. She did not have enough emotional stability for disaster—not today, not with Nythir looking at her like he wanted to say good morning in *that* tone. The tone that made her want to bury herself under the nearest rock until her soul evaporated.

"Essie," Lyssara called from atop her horse, "you look like a disgruntled shrub. Sit up."

"I like being a shrub," Esther muttered. Shrubs didn't call attention to themselves—they thrived quietly in the background. That was her. She aspired to be just like the shrubs they rode past.

The caravan stretched ahead: six wagons, two dozen merchants, and several goats Vorrik insisted were emotional support animals. They were obviously not. The air smelled of hay, wood, spices, and impending doom.

Esther had learned to recognize that feeling—the quiet stretch before something went wrong. It lived low in her chest, like a held breath she hadn't chosen to take.

As if summoned, doom arrived.

Thunk.

An arrow embedded itself in the road, inches from Esther's horse.

Sound vanished for a heartbeat. The world narrowed to distance and direction and the certainty that she had been almost—but not quite—too slow.

The riders shouted. The goats screamed.

Nythir drew his dagger, shielding her before her mind could process the near miss.

She didn't protest. She registered it instead—how quickly he moved, how carefully he positioned himself without forcing her backward. Protection without displacement. It mattered.

"Ambush," he barked.

More arrows rained from the trees. Merchants ducked behind crates. One man dove off his wagon, rolling in the dirt like he had trained his entire life for this moment.

Esther's hands flared with gold, her panic igniting her magic. Sparks shimmered under her skin, eager and wild.

Her thoughts spiraled. She clenched her eyes shut, bracing for *Bandit Explosion ACT II*.

Panic always felt the same: heat, pressure, and the sense that something terrible was about to escape her, no matter how tightly she held on.

The bracelet pulsed once, like a warm, anchoring hug. Her magic softened and coiled inward instead of bursting outward. Nothing exploded. Nothing caught fire.

The calm didn't erase the fear. It redirected it—channeling the surge into something survivable. Esther wondered, distantly, how often her mother had needed the same interruption.

Steel clashed ahead. Lyssara leapt from her horse, slicing an arrow mid-flight as if she had trained since birth to argue with projectiles.

Vorrik charged with all the grace of a drunken avalanche.

Teren immediately hid behind a barrel, pants stained with pee.

Nythir glanced toward her. "Essie. With me."

Her stomach flipped—not romantically. Well, a little romantically. Mostly from terror.

Two bandits bolted toward a wagon where a merchant couple cowered. Esther lifted her hands, trusting her mother's gift.

The bracelet pulsed again. Magic streamed from her fingertips in a controlled burst of golden light. A bright wave shot across the path, sending the nearest attackers flying backwards, squawking like disgruntled pigeons.

The magic felt different when it listened to her. Heavier. Older. Like a language she had once known and was slowly relearning.

Nythir grinned smugly. "Perfect."

The word warmed and terrified her in equal measure. Perfection had never been a compliment in the palace. It had been a demand.

Esther blinked at her own hands. "I meant to do that. I think."

"Good," he said. He parried a blade with effortless precision. "You'll need to do it again."

A dozen shadowy figures emerged from the treeline. Some wore mismatched armor; others brandished rusty blades and crossbows. Even she could see the holes in their sloppy formation.

"Seriously," Lyssara groaned. "Why does everything try to kill us?"

"It's our faces," Vorrik said, swinging his axe. "We have very killable faces."

"Speak for yourselves. I have a very kissable face, right Essie?"

Esther inhaled deeply, pretending not to hear Nythir's comment. She focused. Her magic was hot and lingering, waiting for her command.

The chaotic rush in her chest calmed into focus. She lifted her hands, sending golden whirlwinds outward. They swirled around the nearest attackers, lifting them gently off their feet and depositing them into a ditch.

"Oh," she gasped. "I did it. I did not blow anyone up."

She waited for guilt to follow. It didn't. That startled her more than the magic.

Lyssara cheered. Vorrik whooped. Teren peeked from behind his barrel.

Nythir stepped closer, eyes bright with approval. "You are incredible."

Esther's brain promptly melted. She blushed and stumbled, a bumbling mess.

The last surviving bandits turned and ran. Merchants peeked from their wagons, trembling but unharmed.

A bearded merchant approached, wiping sweat from his brow. "Bless the moons," he said. "Thank you. Bandits have grown bold these past months. The roads are no longer safe. The tension between Valedara and Draewyn has every desperate fool trying his luck."

Esther stiffened. She heard more than fear in his voice. She heard preparation. People only talked like this when they expected things to get worse.

Lyssara crossed her arms. "I thought the alliance with Kraggmar was supposed to make travel safer."

"Alliance," the merchant repeated with a bitter laugh. "There's been no update on this supposed alliance in months. Folks are scared war will break out from the east before any alliance can be solidified."

"What war?" Vorrik asked.

The merchant blinked. "The sixteen-year conflict with the Draewyn Dominion. You've truly not heard? Their king has raided Valedara's border villages for decades, and King Arcturus just watches as his people suffer."

A chill crawled up Esther's spine. Draewyn. War.

Her vision blurred. Her breath vanished. Suddenly, she was small again, barely six years old. Cold stone pressed into her knees. The sharp, bitter taste of poison numbed her tongue.

It had never gone away entirely. She had simply learned to live around it.

Her mother's voice whispered frantically: "Essie. Do not fall asleep. Stay with me."

The world dissolved into ringing. Gold flickered violently down her arms while her bracelet hummed, straining to contain itself. Containment hurt. Not physically—existentially. Like being told to breathe shallower when you were already drowning.

"Essie," Nythir grabbed her shoulders. "Essie, look at me."

Her knees buckled. Nythir caught her and gently lowered her to the ground. She couldn't see what was in front of her anymore.

"Hey. You're alright." Lyssara knelt, shielding Esther from the merchant's eyes. That mattered more than the magic. Being hidden was different from being restrained. "Nythir, calm her."

"I am trying," he growled.

The bracelet pulsed hard. Nythir poured his steadily flowing silver magic into her, coaxing the frantic energy to stabilize. Slowly, the sparks faded, and Esther remembered how to breathe.

"I am fine," she lied with the confidence of someone who was absolutely not fine.

Lying felt safer than explaining. Explanation led to questions. Questions led to choices she wasn't ready to make.

Nythir glared at her like he wanted to set the world on fire for daring to tremble.

Lyssara looked at her like she knew better.

Vorrik looked at her like she needed a goat.

The merchant, blissfully unaware of the chaos he'd caused, continued in a thoughtful tone.

"King Maelrik presses harder every season, putting pressure on Valedara to come to terms with their beliefs or go to war. The assassination attempt over a decade ago was just a warning." Esther's heart stuttered. Warnings were meant for survivors.

"Rumor has it, there has been talk of a royal marriage with Kraggmar to solidify borders."

Esther froze. So that was it. Not just power. Not just legacy. Leverage.

"We've heard enough," Nythir barked.

The merchant blinked, confused, then backed away.

Once he was out of earshot, Lyssara whispered, "Essie, are you alright?"

She pasted on the weakest, most suspicious smile imaginable.

"Just a little tired," she lied. There was no way she could tell them she was one of the royals who might stop a war she knew nothing about.

Nythir didn't believe her. Lyssara didn't believe her. The goats probably didn't believe her.

But no one pressed. And she loved them all for that. Silence, she was learning, could be mercy instead of neglect.

The caravan resumed its slow journey. Wagon wheels creaked over the dirt, continuing as if no battle had ever happened.

Esther breathed shakily. Her past was clawing its way into her present, and she wasn't sure she was ready to remember what happened all those years ago.

She stared ahead at the long road stretching between the trees. For the first time since leaving the palace, Esther wondered: *Am I running from the right danger?*

For the first time, Esther wondered if the danger she feared most wasn't behind her—or ahead—but waiting for her to stop running long enough to choose.

27

Esther

How to remain composed: have a panic attack quietly where no one can see you.

Greyhollow appeared over the hill like a colorful splash of life against the forest. Bright awnings covered busy stalls. Merchants called out prices with theatrical flair. The smell of roasted chestnuts, fresh bread, and spiced tea drifted through the air. Horses snorted, wagons rattled, and at least five people shouted about discounts simultaneously.

It should have felt cheerful. Cheer had always felt fragile to Esther. Something painted on the surface was meant to distract from what lay beneath.

But behind the bright fabrics and loud voices, Esther saw a another truth.

Dozens of tired travelers lingered near the outer gates. Children slept curled against satchels. A few families camped near the well with nothing but threadbare blankets.

Lyssara surveyed the crowded square with a scowl. "Refugees?"

"They're from the most recent attack on Ryzik. I heard the whole town was turned to shambles," Teren said from a safe distance, behind a wagon.

Esther's heart squeezed.

She had grown up learning the names of flowers and formal dances while her people learned how to run. The imbalance sat heavily in her chest.

She knew her father had kept her sheltered, blind to political strife, but she couldn't believe she'd been so ignorant of her people's suffering.

She watched a young mother hush a crying toddler as she stirred thin porridge over a small fire. Another man frantically bartered with a vendor, holding out a cracked toy in exchange for bread.

Esther looked away too late. The image lodged itself behind her eyes, unwelcome and permanent.

The caravan rolled into the central square. Merchants approached immediately, greeted their hired protectors, and handed over payment. The guild ledger was signed. A few people clapped. Others bowed gratefully.

One of the goats tried to eat the ledger. Nythir stopped it just in time, but the goat glared at him like it was personal. Esther almost laughed. Almost. The sound never made it out.

Payment done, Lyssara stretched and said, "We should head to the orphanage to rest."

"Rest sounds nice," Vorrik yawned. "But what about food?"

"We'll have food at the house," Lyssara replied, her tone sharp like a mother scolding a child. "Now, let's go."

Nythir held out his hand to Esther, and she took it. She didn't overthink it—she needed the grounding, even if the touch made her heart trip over itself. Grounding had become a skill she borrowed from others when she couldn't find it herself.

The orphanage stood at the far end of town, nestled between a tailor's shop and a candle maker. Its pale stone walls and bright blue shutters gave it a sturdy, welcoming look. Someone had painted stars along the sign: *Stardrop Orphanage.*

Despite its size, the building seemed far too small for the number of children who poured from every corner—chasing each other through narrow paths, playing with carved toys, or sitting quietly with bowls of soup. Older teens carried wood or tended to the little ones.

Everywhere Esther looked, she saw too many children for one home. Her throat tightened. Numbers blurred together. Faces did not.

Nythir opened the front door. Voices and warmth spilled out. Long tables stretched wall to wall, bowls of stew simmered on a counter, and a few cots were tucked into corners.

A woman stood near the hearth, stirring a large pot. Her hair was streaked with silver, her skin sun-worn, her expression a careful balance of kindness and exhaustion.

She turned to greet them—and froze. Her ladle slipped from her hand as she stumbled a step forward.

"Estella," she whispered, though the name sounded far too loud to Esther.

The name struck like a physical blow. Esther had spent years hearing it spoken carefully, reverently, never like this—raw and accidental.

The woman approached slowly, wonder in her eyes, reaching as if to touch a memory.

"No," she murmured. "Your hair is shorter. Your eyes are younger. Forgive me... for a moment I thought..." She pressed a trembling hand to her mouth. "I thought the Queen had walked through my door again."

Esther stepped back, her breath hitching.

The woman blinked away tears and looked at her anew. "You are her daughter," she said, voice firm and final.

Esther's heart froze. She had never expected anyone to recognize her this far from the palace—and yet she was recognized because she looked like her mother. Recognition had always been her greatest fear. It meant expectation.

"I have waited for you," the woman breathed. "For years. Estella said the princess would come here when the time was right. She described you. She told me to watch the travelers. She told me to look for golden light."

Esther's magic prickled in response, traitorous and bright, as if it wanted to confirm the truth she was denying.

Several children nearby turned, wide-eyed, staring at Esther. Children believed things adults had learned to doubt. That made their faith far more dangerous.

One little boy whispered, awestruck, "Princess?"

Esther's breath shattered in her chest.

"I am not," she said, but her voice was paper-thin.

The woman smiled sadly. "You do not need to say it aloud. Your face tells the story she left behind."

Nythir stepped forward, creating a protective barrier between Esther and the woman. The instinctive relief that followed terrified her. She did not want to need a shield—especially not when the threat was truth.

"This is adult business, out you go, out you go," Lyssara said, ushering the children out the back door. Vorrik blinked, bewildered, as she dragged him along.

Esther forgot how to breathe. She felt cornered. Seen. Exposed. Her heart pounded, her magic flickered. Too many eyes. Too many whispers.

Panic didn't roar. It compressed—squeezing her thoughts into something sharp and unmanageable.

She turned and ran. Running had always worked before. Distance softened things. Time dulled edges. She prayed it would work again.

She thought she heard Nythir calling after her, but she was too afraid to look. She would break if she saw the betrayal—or the concern—in his eyes.

She shoved through the doorway and burst into the bright town square. Her boots slapped against the stone as she ran past merchant stalls and startled goats. She didn't stop until the world blurred into streaks of color.

Only when she reached the quiet edge of the forest did she slow. She leaned against a tree, hands shaking violently.

Trees didn't ask questions. They didn't expect answers. Esther clung to that silence like a lifeline.

Her mother had been here. Her mother had spoken of her. Her mother had prepared for her arrival.

Preparation implied certainty. Esther had none.

Ever since receiving her mother's letter, Esther had become entangled in a grand scheme that moved too fast. People were waiting for her—people who needed a royal voice she didn't know how to give.

She pressed her trembling hands to her forehead. Her mother had left her more than memories. She had left the responsibility. Responsibility didn't ask if you were ready. It simply arrived and waited.

And Esther had run from it.

Sliding down the tree trunk until she sat on the forest floor, the bracelet pulsed gently against her wrist—a constant reminder of her mother's will.

It felt heavier than gold. Heavier than magic. Like a hand reminding her she could no longer pretend ignorance.

She whispered into her palms, "I am not ready."

But deep down, she feared the truth: the world might not wait for her to be.

And for the first time, Esther wondered if waiting had ever been an option at all.

28

NYTHIR

How to find someone who runs: follow the place your heart refuses to leave behind.

Nythir ran.

He ignored the shouting merchants and bleating goats. A cart rattled as its driver yanked the reins, swerving just enough for Nythir to slip past. Greyhollow's colors smeared together around him—bright fabrics, hanging charms, crates of fruit flashing by as he cut through the square.

Somewhere behind him, Lyssara barked orders while Vorrik crashed into something that sounded expensive.

None of it mattered.

Essie had run. And all he could think, as he sprinted past the last row of stalls, was how she moved that fast on those short legs of hers.

He caught the faint imprint of her footsteps in the trampled dirt, leading toward the trees. The noise of the marketplace thinned behind him, replaced by the hush of the forest at Greyhollow's edge. Sunlight filtered through the leaves in dappled patches. The air smelled of earth and crushed grass instead of sweat and spices.

He spotted her at the base of an old elm, tucked into its roots as if she wanted the ground to swallow her. Her hands shook so hard he could see it from a few paces away.

She did not hear him. Not until he carefully knelt beside her.

"Essie," he said softly.

She flinched and folded in on herself, chin sinking to her knees.

He did not touch her. He sat next to her instead, close enough to be there, far enough that she could breathe. The bark pressed into his back. A bird hopped somewhere above them, scratching against the branches.

"I am here," he said. "Not to crowd you. Just to sit with you."

For a long time, the only sound was her ragged breathing and the distant murmur of the square. A breeze stirred the leaves, brushing cool fingers over the back of his neck.

When she finally lifted her head, her eyes were red and shining, full of something that looked like despair.

"I am a mess," she whispered. "I cannot do this."

"You do not have to talk yet," Nythir said gently.

But she did. Once the first crack appeared, everything spilled through.

"I know nothing about her," Essie said, voice trembling. "Everyone else does. Everyone knows more about my mother than I ever did."

Her fingers found the fabric of her sleeves and twisted, wringing the cloth like she was afraid it might vanish if she let go. She took a shaky breath, staring at the dirt between her boots.

"In the palace, no one talked about her," she said. "It was forbidden. If I asked, the King changed the subject. The servants went quiet. They said her name was sacred. They said it was painful to speak about her. They said it was better to let her rest."

Nythir shifted a little closer, letting his shoulder brush hers. A small, steady point of warmth. He stayed silent, afraid that any word from him would shatter the fragile strength it took for her to speak.

Essie swallowed hard. For a moment, the air felt heavier, like the forest itself had paused to listen.

"All I truly knew," she said, "was that she was warm. That she was kind. That she was a good queen. That people loved her. That she had magic." Her voice cracked. "Sometimes, it felt like her magic never left. Like the palace remembered her even if no one spoke her name."

She pressed a shaking hand to her forehead, fingers digging into her hair.

"I did not even know she was one of the strongest mages in Valedara's history until Luna told me the truth," she said. "Everyone else knew. Everyone spoke of her like she was a legend, a miracle, a light the kingdom lost."

Tears spilled over again, tracking down her cheeks. One dropped to her knee, darkening the fabric.

"And I know almost nothing," she whispered. "I do not know her stories. I do not know her magic. I do not know her spells or her strengths or her past. I only know that she is everything I am not."

Nythir hesitated. There were moments when Esther's magic felt too precise, too familiar—like something remembering itself rather than being born.

Essie hugged her knees closer, shoulders trembling.

"How am I supposed to live up to a woman I barely remember?" she asked, words breaking. "How am I supposed to be the daughter of someone I never truly knew? I am lost. I am scared. And I feel like I am failing a mother who deserved better."

Her voice fell to almost nothing.

"I cannot be her," she said. "I cannot even begin to understand her."

Nythir exhaled slowly. He had seen her furious, stubborn, terrified, brave. He had never seen her this undone, crushed beneath a weight no one had ever taught her how to carry.

He reached toward her and paused halfway, giving her time to pull away. She did not.

Very gently, he brushed a tear from her cheek with the back of his knuckles. Her skin was cool from the shade of the tree.

"Essie," he said softly. "You do not have to be her."

She blinked at him, eyes blurry and confused.

"You are not failing her," he went on. "Those who failed are those who kept her memory locked away from you. You grew up with silence instead of stories. With rules instead of guidance. With expectations instead of truth."

Essie's gaze dropped to the ground again. A beetle crawled across the toe of her boot, and she did not seem to notice.

"Your mother was not meant to be a legend you must compete with," Nythir said. "She was your mother. And the grief others carry is not yours to shape into duty."

Her throat bobbed as she swallowed.

"You think you are failing because you do not know enough," he said quietly. "But you are here. You are trying. You care. That alone would have made her proud."

Essie shook her head, slow and miserable.

"I do not feel strong," she said.

"Strength is not a feeling," Nythir replied. "It is something you discover when you refuse to stay broken."

He hesitated, words gathering like stones he had avoided lifting for years.

"You asked how I stay calm," he said. "How I know who I am. The truth is, I did not."

Essie sniffed, dragging her sleeve over her nose without much dignity. "What do you mean?"

"My life used to feel gray," Nythir said. "I was born in a town so small it never made it onto any map. We had one road, one tavern, and one old man who shouted at the clouds for changing too fast. Every day was the same. Quiet. Predictable. Empty."

A wry smile tugged at his mouth.

"I worked in a tannery for a while," he said. "All day, every day, it was the same dull leather and the same smell that clung to my clothes no matter how often I washed them. I was surviving, not living. I felt like I had no purpose. Nothing that felt like color."

Essie watched him with wide, wet eyes, as if it had never occurred to her that his world could ever have been anything but bright.

"Then I met Lyssara and Vorrik," he said. His smile softened. "Two nightmares who walked on two legs and laughed around a campfire. They dragged me out of that gray world and tossed me into chaos. Loud, annoying, wonderful chaos. The kind that makes your blood move again."

Essie's lips twitched, the faintest ghost of a smile.

"But even with them," Nythir continued, "something was missing. There were fears I did not understand. Emptiness I could not name."

His voice lowered. He slid his hand along the grass until his pinky brushed against hers.

"Then I met you," he said, his heart hammering far too fast for someone only sitting. "You brought more color into my life than anything before."

He stared at their hands, fingers barely touching.

"You confuse me," he admitted. "You surprise me. You terrify me. And you make every day feel like something new."

Essie's breath caught. Her fingers curled, just a little, against his.

"I do not know who I am without you anymore," he said quietly. "And I do not want to."

Her eyes filled again, but the tears were softer now, like rain after a storm instead of the storm itself.

"I do not know who I am either," she whispered.

"That is all right," he said. "We can find out together."

He did not say that some paths find you whether you seek them or not.

A fragile silence settled over them. The leaves whispered overhead. Somewhere in the distance, a merchant shouted about a sale on turnips, faint and far away, like another world entirely.

Very carefully, Essie leaned into him, resting her weight against his side. He wrapped an arm around her, steady and warm, holding her like something both precious and strong.

She let out a long, shuddering breath, the kind that feels like finally settling down a burden no one else could see.

"Nythir," she whispered, "I do not know if I can be anything like my mother."

"You do not need to be," he said. "Just be Essie. That is enough."

This time, he felt it when her body loosened under his arm. She did not say she believed him, but something in her posture shifted, just a little, as if a tight knot had eased.

They stayed like that for a while, listening to the rustle of branches and the distant clatter of the town reassembling itself after their dramatic exit.

"Come," he murmured at last. "The others are worried."

Essie hesitated, then nodded. When she unfolded herself and pushed to her feet, her legs wobbled.

Nythir rose with her, ready to catch her if she swayed.

Her hand found his without thought, fingers threading between his like it had always been meant to fit there.

He took it.

And this time, when they walked back toward Greyhollow, he did not let go.

29

Lucy

How to travel with a grumpy man: ignore all pleas for silence.

Lucy hurried to catch up to Basil, who walked like he was fleeing the big bad but couldn't be bothered to actually break into a run.

"You can't just drop your lore like you're commenting on cloud patterns!"

"My lore?" Basil asked, speeding up.

Sadly for him, Lucy had spent years chasing a princess who speed-walked out of her problems. She was built for this.

"Yes, your lore! 'My brother-in-law runs the most notorious guild.' 'My dead wife is not dead.' 'I have a beastkin step-son.' What else are you hiding? Are you even human, or is that a secret too?"

"How do you talk so fast?" Basil groaned. "And he is not my step-son."

"He kind of is. You never divorced her. Just faked a death."

"She has a point," Sylva said, tail flicking.

The agreement landed oddly. Sylva didn't side with people casually. Lucy clocked it as a coincidence and moved on, even as something quiet in her chest stayed alert.

Basil slowed, defeated in the way only a man haunted by past decisions could be. "Why are you so interested in my past?"

"I'm not! I'm just… concerned. I need to know who I'm traveling with. I absolutely do not care about your incredibly suspicious and definitely uninteresting history."

Sylva's lips curled. "She's interested."

"That settles it then," Basil muttered.

"How does that settle anything?" Lucy demanded.

"I can sense lies," Sylva said. His voice stayed neutral, almost careful—like he was choosing each word with restraint instead of pride. Lucy had expected smugness. She got consideration instead, and it unsettled her. "More accurately—hear them."

Lucy stopped short. Slowly, deliberately, she turned to stare at him.

"You mean to tell me," she said carefully, "that I have been emotionally naked this entire time?"

Sylva tilted his head. "Yes."

"How intriguing," the Baroness said between gasps. "How does it work?"

"My ears can hear a distortion when someone lies," Sylva explained. "It's like a wrong note in a song. Beastkin often develop abilities tied to survival. Hearing lies keeps you alive."

Lucy stared at his ears in horror. "Can we return him to sender?"

"No," Basil said flatly.

Lucy crossed her arms dramatically. "Fine. Then I refuse to speak ever again."

Sylva's gaze flicked to her mouth and away again immediately.

"Blessed silence," Basil grumbled.

She gasped. "I can still hear, you know!"

"I was counting on it."

Before Lucy could deliver a monologue about betrayal and the fragile nature of trust, Sylva's ears twitched.

"You already lied again."

"I didn't even say anything!"

"You said you wouldn't speak." His tail swished smugly. "Lie."

Lucy stomped the ground. "I hope a squirrel drops a pinecone on you."

"That is oddly specific," the Baroness whispered, still recovering from oxygen deprivation.

They continued down the merchant road, carts and caravans rumbling past. Sylva stayed close enough to notice changes in the crowd and far enough not to touch her. Lucy had spent her life learning the difference between hovering and guarding. This was neither.

Refugees, traders, wandering mercs—everyone seemed to be heading in or out of Stonehaven. It was bustling enough that Lucy could almost pretend Basil's personal storyline wasn't unraveling beside her in real time.

Stonehaven was busy—but not relaxed.

Lucy noticed the way people glanced at Basil and then quickly looked away. Not recognition exactly. More like instinct. The kind people developed when they lived under too many guild shadows.

"So," Lucy said, hands clasped behind her back, trying to look casual despite radiating curiosity like a dying star, "if Sylva isn't technically your step-son, what is he?"

Basil exhaled, as if this were the worst question she had ever asked. "A complication."

"A complication with ears," Sylva added.

"And sharp teeth," Lucy said. "And the kind of overly dramatic eyeliner nature gives you."

"Lucy," Basil warned.

She blinked innocently. "What? I'm simply gathering facts."

"You're interrogating me."

"I'm conversationally investigating," she corrected.

The Baroness had recovered enough to chime in again. "I personally think this Sylva sounds quite charming. A tragic backstory? A hidden bloodline? A complicated family tree? Very romantic."

"It is not romantic," Basil snapped.

Lucy elbowed him lightly. "It's a little romantic."

Basil stopped walking and looked to the heavens, as if asking some higher power to take him now. "Can we please stay focused? We are going to see the information guild's leader. The less said, the better."

"Why?" Lucy asked, narrowing her eyes. "Is he scary? Dangerous? A criminal mastermind? Does he also have secret children?"

"No."

"Sylva?" Lucy hissed. "Did he lie?"

Sylva paused, listening. "...No."

"Ha!" Lucy pointed triumphantly at Basil. "Your son is on my side now."

They turned down a narrower lane, merchant stalls thinning as stone buildings pressed closer together. The air smelled of smoke, old wood, and something bitter beneath it. Lucy recognized the scent of the wards as if it were home. They were littered around the palace—especially near Esther's wing.

A wooden sign swung overhead.

Luna's Tavern.

"We're here," Basil said.

"At a tavern?" the Baroness asked, affronted.

"Yes," Basil said tightly. "Keep your voice down. And don't mention my wife. Or Sylva. Or anything at all, really."

"Yes, sir!" Lucy nodded enthusiastically. She had never been in a tavern before.

Sylva whispered, "She's lying."

Lucy inhaled sharply. "I am not—okay, fine, I am a little lying, but only because you're impossible to resist messing with."

"Lucy," Basil said, pinching the bridge of his nose for the fifteenth time in the past hour, "I need you to behave."

She saluted. "I will be the picture of maturity."

"She's lying again," Sylva added.

Lucy turned and smacked his arm. "Stop listening to things!"

He startled—not from the hit, but from the contact. Then relaxed, as if filing it under allowed.

"That is my entire purpose," Sylva said, unimpressed.

Basil groaned. "I regret everything."

"Good!" Lucy chirped as they stepped toward the door of Luna's Tavern. "Because I'm absolutely positive this will go perfectly fine and not at all explode in our faces."

"She's lying again." Sylva's ears flicked, sharper than before—then settled. He glanced at Lucy like he was measuring distance, timing, and patience all at once.

Lucy froze.

"...Okay, maybe a little explosion."

Basil sighed. "Wonderful."

He pushed open the door.
And all hell promptly began preparing itself.

30

Lucy

How to Spot Trouble: look for pink hair.

The tavern door creaked open, and instead of the smoky, ale-stained chaos Lucy expected, the inside of Luna's Tavern was unnervingly clean.

It shouldn't have been. The sign said tavern.

But the floors gleamed like polished bone, lanternlight pooled warmly across spotless tables, and a faint scent of lavender-and-mischief drifted through the air. It smelled less like spilled ale and more like a crime scene waiting to happen.

Lucy had read enough mystery books to know what a potential crime scene looked like.

The first indication: nothing was that clean without having something to hide.

The second indication: the air itself felt... arranged. Not enchanted exactly—Lucy didn't have the vocabulary for magic—but managed. Like the room had rules it expected everyone to follow.

Even the sound was wrong. The tavern should have been loud—laughing, clattering mugs, someone yelling about a card game gone tragic. Instead, the noise was a careful murmur, as though each patron had been trained to speak in indoor voices and plausible deniability. Conversations didn't spill. They stayed neatly within the circles of the people who had them.

Lucy's gaze flicked to the corners. Lanterns hung in just the right places to eliminate deep shadow.

Tables were spaced far enough apart that no one could "accidentally" brush shoulders. The bar top had faint rings carved into the wood—old stains. She leaned closer.

They were too precise to be stains. If she looked closely enough, she could see a pattern forming.

Basil noticed her noticing and subtly tugged her sleeve. She could read his thoughts as clear as day. *Don't touch anything, you menace.*
Lucy's mouth twitched. She was going to touch everything.

Sylva noticed, but he didn't stop her. Just shifted closer, like he trusted her judgment enough to prepare for the consequences instead of preventing them.

The third indication arrived before her fingertips could betray her.

A woman sat on the bar counter as if it belonged to her and also like gravity was a polite suggestion.

Beside her was a pile of scrolls, ledgers, and spy reports so blatant they might as well have been labeled "Definitely Spies."

Her hair was cotton-candy pink, tied up in a high, glossy, dramatic ponytail that swished like it had an ego of its own.

Any hair that bright meant trouble. Lucy felt it in her gut.

"Good day, Luna," Basil said, shutting the door gently behind them.

"Says the liar," Sylva whispered, just loud enough to be heard and just quiet enough to pretend he hadn't.

Basil shot him a practiced glare. The kind Lucy suspected had been honed through years of putting out magical fires started by people who were technically family.

Luna smiled like a cat presented with entertainment. "Oh," she purred. "The rest of the circus arrived."

"Another circus," came a voice from the stairs. "I just got rid of Karl. He was so filthy, even the hellhounds didn't want a bite of him."

"Sable?" Basil's eyes widened. "What happened to your face?"

"Rude," Sable said, instead of answering.

Lucy squinted. Sable did, in fact, look like someone had tried to rearrange his face using only their fists and a strong sense of spite. One cheekbone was bruised, her lip split. She carried herself like it didn't hurt.

Which meant it probably hurt a lot.

"And you," Basil continued, pointing accusingly at Luna's hair. "Why is it pink today?"

"Why not?" Luna twirled the end of her ponytail around her finger. "It brightens the room."

"That is not an answer. You change it every week—purple, blue, teal, chartreuse. Do you use potions? Why is your hair a seasonal wardrobe?"

Luna gasped dramatically. "You remembered all my colors. How touching."

"I remembered because they were distracting," Basil grumbled. "And chemically questionable."

Lucy leaned in, delighted. "So it is potions?" Her newest life goal was to change her hair to scream trouble.

"Oh, sweetheart." Luna winked. "Everything's potions if you're creative enough."

That sounded like either life advice or a threat. Lucy wasn't sure which, and somehow that made her like Luna immediately. She was bright, sharp, and too comfortable in a room full of people who clearly knew better than to annoy her.

Before Lucy could demand instructions for hot-pink hair, Basil straightened, the way he always did right before doing something he didn't want to do. He gestured stiffly.

"Luna, this is Baroness Irene Levon."

The Baroness stepped forward as if approaching a wild animal she intended to domesticate through sheer social status. "Good afternoon."

"And this is Lucy," Basil finished. "Princess Esther's maid."

Lucy gave a little wave, because this entire situation was so absurdly not within her job description that manners felt like a weapon. "Hello. I promise I only bite when provoked."

Sylva's ears twitched, then deliberately settled. Lucy got the distinct sense he was choosing not to listen to something.

Lucy added quickly, "That was a joke. Mostly."

Luna's mischief-filled eyes flicked over Lucy like she was reading an invoice. Then she beamed.

"Oh, I like you already. Come sit. The actual tavern won't open for a while, so we can talk freely."

The Baroness hovered as if the barstool might be contagious. She chose a stool anyway, with the grim acceptance of a woman performing charity work.

Lucy hopped up without hesitation.

Luna poured water into mismatched glasses, and Lucy noticed the way she poured: not into the center of the cup, but slightly off to the side, as if avoiding a mark carved at the bottom. Basil noticed too. His jaw tightened.

"Haven't seen you in a while, Sylva," Luna said, not looking up.

"You know each other?" Lucy asked, eyes narrowing.

"Sparrow business," Sylva said simply. "Sometimes Luna requests aid."

"Mostly via bribery," Luna added cheerfully.

"Your bribes are awful," Sylva replied. "And expired."

"It builds immunity."

Basil wasn't listening anymore.

His gaze was fixed on a boarded-up window to the left. Thick planks were nailed crookedly over shattered glass. A few splinters jutted out like teeth. Whoever had boarded it up had done it quickly and not gently.

Basil inhaled sharply. Then the entire mood of his body shifted from annoyed to alert in the space of a heartbeat.

"Esther was here," he said. "Recently."

Lucy's head whipped around so fast her neck cracked. "I knew it was too clean! Wait—how do you know?"

"I can see the trace of her magic," Basil said, voice low.

Lucy squinted at the boards. Squinted harder. "Oh, yes. I see it."

Sylva snorted. "No, she doesn't."

Lucy elbowed him and kept squinting anyway, because she refused to be defeated by a piece of wood and her lack of magical education.

Basil stepped closer to the window, stopping just short of touching the planks. He didn't have to touch them to know. His eyes tracked along the edges like he could read the air.

Lucy felt it then. Not the magic itself, but the way the room responded to Basil noticing it. The careful murmur of conversations in the tavern dipped. Not silent, but cautious. A few patrons shifted. One man in the corner suddenly became very interested in his drink.

This place was clean because it was controlled.

Basil's voice tightened. "Her magic clings. It always has. Most spells dissipate like heat after a flame. Hers...lingers."

"What does that mean?" Lucy asked, quieter than she intended.

"It means her emotions were high," Basil said. "Often due to anger or fear."

The Baroness made a sound that might have been a gasp or might have been the beginning of a faint. "My princess broke a—a window? In a tavern?" She clutched the edge of her seat. "I need water. Or smelling salts. Or both."

Luna slid a glass to her with the ease of someone handing a knife to a person who didn't know what to do with it. "She's fine," she said lazily. "Mostly."

"Mostly?" Basil barked, spinning on her.

"Oh, calm down," Luna drawled. "I gave her coffee and asked her a few friendly questions—"

"You interrogated her," Sylva corrected.

"Semantics," Luna said sweetly.

"Princesses do not get interrogated in taverns," the Baroness declared, voice trembling with aristocratic offense.

"She wasn't a princess," Luna said, her smile softening in a way that somehow made Lucy more nervous. "She was simply Essie."

Lucy's vision sharpened like a knife. "Where is she?"

Luna hopped off the counter with a satisfied sigh, like she'd been waiting for that line. "Ah. That's the part where I help."

Lucy did not like her tone. Help from people like Luna usually came with fine print.

"She left a few days ago," Luna said. "Took the Larkspire Road south. Flower fields. Very scenic. Very safe. Probably."

Basil stiffened. "She went south?"

"Yes," Luna said, blinking slowly. "Very south."

Sylva's ears flicked. His gaze turned distant for a heartbeat—the way it did when he was listening past words.

Lucy pointed at Luna like her finger was a deadly weapon. "She's lying."

Luna gasped, scandalized. "Excuse me?"

"Your left eyebrow twitched," Lucy said triumphantly. "Everyone has a tell."

"It did not—"

"It just did," Sylva added helpfully.

Luna slapped her hand over her eyebrow.

Lucy stood, slamming her palm on the bar. "If you wanted to mislead us, why pick the prettiest, most postcard road? That's just sloppy."

"Sable," Basil said slowly, eyes narrowed, "why is she misleading us?"

Sable leaned against the stair rail, expression bored in a way that felt practiced. "Because if she tells you the truth outright, you'll walk straight into it. If you think you outsmarted her, you'll run."

Lucy blinked. That was... annoyingly clever.

Luna smiled wider, clearly pleased with herself. "I do like a motivated customer."

"Customer?" the Baroness choked.

Luna waved a hand. "Metaphor. Mostly."

Lucy narrowed her eyes, stomach twisting. "So Essie didn't go south."

"No," Basil said, frowning. "The opposite of south is—"

"North," Sylva said. "Caravans. Travelers. Trouble." The way he said it wasn't fear. It was familiarity. Lucy wondered how often he followed paths like this—and who he usually followed them for.

He tilted his head, listening again, and Lucy watched as his ears twitched. Whatever the distortion was, he was tuned to it like a predator.

"She went toward Greyhollow," Sylva said. "I can smell it on Basil's reaction too. Not a lie. Fear."

Lucy's stomach dropped and steadied with equal force.

Greyhollow.

The place Esther had run off to. The place she'd somehow ended up in, even without trying.

The Baroness squeaked, fan snapping open with military aggression. "Greyhollow? That dreadful, sheep-infested—"

"Yes," Lucy said, already moving. "Greyhollow."

Basil cursed under his breath, the kind of curse that had experience behind it.

Lucy paused at the door long enough to look back at Luna. "Why didn't you just tell us?"

Luna leaned against the bar as if the entire kingdom was her stage. "Because you needed to decide to chase her. Not because Basil asked. Not because I told you. Because you chose it."

Lucy hated that it worked. She hated it so much.

"Tell Cinnabun I miss her already!" Luna called, cheerful as a bell.

Lucy stuck her tongue out and slammed the door behind them.

Outside, the air felt colder. Or maybe Lucy was only noticing it now. Stonehaven's streets were busy, but the bustle no longer felt comforting. It felt like motion for motion's sake. The people were moving so they didn't have to think about what chased them.

"She must not be that smart if she tried lying in front of Sylva," the Baroness said, fanning harder as if she could blow away danger through etiquette.

"You're right," Lucy said. "And she did say they work together."

"That's because I told her I could only detect lies when I'm touching someone," Sylva said casually.

Lucy stopped mid-step so abruptly that Basil almost ran into her.

She turned slowly. "The lie detector... lied?"

Sylva shrugged, tail flicking. "It's better if fewer know how it works."

Lucy stared at him, mind racing. "But you told us."

Sylva's ears angled back, strangely shy for someone who looked like he could bite through a lock.

"Well... you're Uncle Basil's friends."

Basil made a small sound that might have been a cough or a suppressed emotion. "Don't call me that."

Sylva blinked. "Lie."

Lucy barked a laugh before she could stop it. The laugh tasted of relief and panic mixed.

The Baroness snapped her fan closed with finality. "Enough chatter! We must leave immediately!"

She stormed ahead with the determination of a woman marching to war.

Lucy watched her for two full seconds.

Then she sighed and jogged after, falling into step beside Basil.

"I'm leaving the explaining to you," she told him. "You can break it to her that we can't travel north tonight without collapsing, dying, and becoming cautionary tales told to children."

Basil pinched the bridge of his nose. "Perfect. My favorite job."

Lucy grinned, heart pounding with determination and something sharper beneath it.

Esther was running toward freedom, or maybe running toward something she didn't understand.

Regardless, Lucy refused to let her do it alone.

Lucy had chased princesses her entire life. She knew their patterns. She knew their stubbornness.

She knew how they ran when they were terrified.

And she knew, with sick certainty, that Esther had never been running away.

She'd been running toward the first place that might tell her the truth.

Lucy tightened her grip on the strap of her bag and picked up her pace.

Maid, menace, and professional princess-chaser, she survived another day of traveling.

31

LUCY

How to Survive Social Chaos: pretend you understand the plot while everyone else falls in love.

Rhea's house sat tucked between a quiet bakery and a cobbler's workshop, its chimney puffing out warm-smelling smoke carrying hints of bread and herbs.

A carved wooden sign was nailed above the door: The Sparrow's Crumb.

Lucy wanted to kiss it.

Not because she loved bread, but because it represented the one thing she craved most in the world.

A separate room.

A room not shared with Basil's dramatic sighing or the Baroness's sleep-whimpering.

She could almost cry, but her tears were precious tactical tools and needed to be deployed sparingly.

Rhea opened the front door before they could knock. "Welcome. I set up rooms for all of you."

"Bless the moon, the sun, the old gods, the new gods, the questionable ones in Basil's herb drawers—I don't care which one—thank someone."

Rhea blinked. "That's... a lot of deities."

"Why do you know what is in my herb drawer?" Basil demanded.

"I'm leaving my gratitude options open," Lucy said reverently, sweeping past him.

They stepped inside. The home was small and cozy in a way that felt earned, not curated. It smelled like warm dough, cracked pepper, and the citrus oil Rhea used to polish the counters. A little fireplace crackled quietly in the corner, and Lucy clocked the absence of wards immediately.

Not unprotected. Just... trusted.

Sylva relaxed the moment they stepped inside. Not visibly. Just... in the small ways Lucy was beginning to recognize. Like his body had decided this place didn't require him to be on high alert.

Dinner consisted of hearty bread, a thin vegetable stew, and a single roasted chicken, clearly stretched to feed too many people.

Frugal. Careful. Kind.

Lucy devoured it like it was a royal feast.

"So," she said, leaning forward over her bowl with predatory intent, "tell me more about Basil's lore."

Basil groaned on instinct. "No."

Rhea chuckled into her cup. "He was always like this. Grumpy. Hard-working. Fussy about his boots."

"I am not fussy."

"He once returned an entire set of military boots because the stitching was wrong," Asher added from the kitchen doorway.

"It was wrong," Basil snapped.

Lucy slapped the table with delight. "This is gold."

The Baroness cleared her throat delicately. "Rhea, dear, if you don't mind me asking..." She folded her hands. "Why did you give up being a countess? And Basil? It seems... quite the sacrifice."

Rhea's smile softened. Not sad, but resolved.

"For love," she said simply. "I wanted Asher. Basil made sure I could leave without harming my family's reputation."

Asher moved behind her, brushing a quick kiss to her temple as he set down more bread.

Lucy's eyes sparkled. She clasped her cheeks. "This is the most romantic thing I've ever witnessed. Basil, you're a tragic backstory."

"I reject that title."

Lucy wasn't listening. She was too busy cataloguing everything for Esther later: the way Rhea leaned into Asher without thinking, the way Basil watched the door even while sitting, the way Sylva listened more than he spoke.

Then Rhea turned toward the Baroness with casual, lethal accuracy.

"And what about you and Basil?" she asked lightly. "I always felt bad when our marriage was arranged. You were absolutely head over heels for him during our girlhood days."

The room froze.

The Baroness sputtered. Basil choked.

Lucy leaned forward like she was watching a puppet show.

"What—absolutely not—I never—why would—"

"She's lying," Sylva said calmly, sipping his drink.

The Baroness slapped a hand to her chest. "Sylva!"

Basil stared at her, color rising in his neck. "You—you? With me?"

"No!"

"Lie," Sylva added again.

They both flushed scarlet.

Lucy clasped her hands under her chin.

Oh no.

They're idiots. They're in love, and they're idiots.

Basil cleared his throat loudly. "We should rest."

"Yes!" the Baroness squeaked. "Rest. Separate rooms. Far apart."

They stood simultaneously, looked at each other, looked away, and promptly nearly walked into the same wall.

Lucy watched them go, deeply unsettled. Traveling had officially become an active threat to her will to live.

Lucy awoke to raised voices.

She rolled out of bed and followed the sound of the Baroness actively fighting with clothing.

"I cannot dress like a commoner!" the Baroness cried. "People will stare!"

"That's the point," Lucy said, tying her hair up. "They stare because you look like you're about to attend a palace ball. We're heading north. Mud exists. Dirt exists. People exist."

"That is not a reassuring list!"

Lucy crossed her arms. "Drop the noble act. Drop the title. Don't you want Basil to call you Irene?"

The Baroness froze.

"That is…" she whispered, face pink, "irrelevant."

"It's very relevant," Sylva's voice called from downstairs.

Lucy grinned. "Victory."

Sylva's quiet amusement brushed against her like a warm touch. Lucy pretended not to notice. It was becoming a full-time job.

Rhea entered with folded clothes. "These should fit you. They're simple, but warm."

The Baroness took them like sacred artifacts.

When she returned, Rhea clapped softly. "You look lovely."

Basil paused mid-step. "Oh," he said quietly. "You look… very pretty."

Lucy gagged.

Before she could retort, Sylva entered the lounge, and Lucy's soul aggressively evicted her body. Her body reacted before her pride could intervene. Heat rose to her face. Her pulse skipped. It was wildly inconvenient.

He wore a pale-blue warrior's outfit adorned with silver accents, crossed belts, and layered armor plates. His tail flicked lazily, ears perked forward. Tan skin and sharp pale eyes contrasted beautifully with the cool tones of the outfit.

Lucy stared. Her mouth may have dropped open—just a little.

Sylva frowned. "Why are you looking at me like that?"

His voice was neutral. His ears weren't. They angled forward a fraction, attentive in a way that made Lucy feel seen without being cornered.

Lucy frantically fumbled in her satchel, ripped out a notebook, and scribbled at lightning speed: *You look weird dressed like that.*

Sylva snorted. Loudly.

"You wrote it down to avoid the lie detection?" he said. "That means you're lying."

Lucy slammed the notebook shut and slapped it to her chest.

Before she could recover, voices drifted in from outside—familiar ones.

"Rhea?" a man called. "You home?"

Rhea stiffened just a fraction. Lucy noticed.

The door opened, and a dark-haired man stepped inside. Something about him felt... off. Not dangerous. Not magical. Just wrong, like a painting with a skewed perspective.

"Brother," Rhea said, smiling. "You're early."

Lucy blinked.

Brother?

"Do you have a second brother-in-law?" Lucy asked, practically drooling at the man who sauntered into the room.

The man smiled back — polite, pleasant, absurdly handsome—the exact opposite of Brom, who looked forgettable.

His gaze flicked over the room, cataloguing everyone in it in the space of a breath.

"Theo," Rhea said warmly. "These are friends."

Lucy stared harder now.

Theo was the most handsome man she had ever seen. Navy-blue waves caressed his slim, tan face. Dark blue eyes looked far too welcoming. A cream dress shirt and vest barely hid a toned body.

Lucy did not trust that.

Her eyes narrowed.

"Stop staring," Sylva said, jabbing her side gently. It was a question disguised as contact. Lucy didn't flinch. Sylva relaxed at her acceptance of his touch.

Theo's gaze flicked to them for just a moment. Lucy sensed calculations happening at the speed of light before he settled on a casual smile.

Lucy's stomach flipped.

Rhea chattered cheerfully, completely oblivious. "He helps with the Sparrow. Logistics, mostly."

"Sparrow," Lucy repeated slowly.

Theo smiled. "Among other things."

Lucy's brain screamed. Something about him felt familiar, but she would never forget a face like his. It could have been because he looked very similar to Rhea... but that didn't seem right.

She watched Theo move as if he were playing a role that required him to take up as little space as possible. People like that were never small by accident.

"Well," Lucy said brightly, "you're quite attractive."

Theo laughed easily. Too easily.

"I know. This face comes in handy from time to time."

Sylva's tail twitched.

Lucy grinned.

Oh.

Oh, she was going to enjoy this.

Traveling, it turned out, wasn't just dangerous.

It was full of men wearing faces that weren't theirs.

And Lucy had a very particular talent for noticing when the story didn't add up.

32

ESTHER

How to Survive a Reunion: prepare for bone-crushing hugs.

Vorrik hit her like a runaway boulder.

One moment, Esther was standing, trying to breathe normally after the emotional avalanche under the elm. Next, her feet were off the ground, her torso trapped in a bear hug, and her ribs screaming in protest.

"Essie!" Vorrik roared, spinning her once like she was a particularly beloved sack of flour.

"Vorrik—Vorrik—lungs—" she wheezed.

He froze mid-spin. "Oh! Sorry!"

He set her down so fast her knees wobbled. Nythir's hands immediately steadied her shoulders, warm and grounding.

Lyssara slapped Vorrik's arm. "You absolute mountain! You can't just break the princess!"

Then, ignoring her own words, she did the exact same thing Vorrik did. "Essie! I'm so sorry!"

"What?" Esther croaked, her face buried in Lyssara's chest.

"I—" Lyssara nuzzled her. "I was so used to you being... you, I forgot who you are. You look exactly like her. The Queen. Except shorter. And without the dignity."

"Lyssara," Nythir warned.

"She knows I love her," Lyssara said, releasing Esther so she could breathe once more. "But Charon saw it too. Of course she did. I should've realized she'd recognize the resemblance. But I didn't know the Queen left a message. For you." Her voice cracked, eyes full of tears.

"Hey—hey—don't—" Esther reached out, only for Lyssara to grab her hand and squeeze it so tightly Esther thought the bones might fuse together.

"You were just this tiny runaway girl with terrible balance and worse survival instincts," Lyssara said, voice wobbling. "I didn't want to scare you away. But I was also selfish. I wanted to be a protector to the daughter of the woman who saved our entire town. The Queen who helped me walk again. The reason half the people in Greyhollow survived the plague."

Vorrik nodded, tears falling freely. "When I saw Lyssara running at me on two legs with the biggest smile I've ever seen... I thought I was dreaming. It was like a goddess appeared just to protect us orphans. Give us a chance to not just survive, but to live."

"We couldn't offer her anything in return." Lyssara's arms trembled, but she still held firm against Esther. "But she didn't care. She made sure to visit often. Not just the orphanage. She visited everyone in need. Healed them. Listened to them. She was Greyhollow's saint."

Esther's heart twisted sharply. "I didn't know any of that." She paused, voice small. "Do you only see me as her shadow?"

Lyssara sniffed loudly. "She was the best. And you—gods, Essie—" She pulled her into a crushing hug that made Essie squeak. "You're not her, but you're you. And that's just as good."

"The way you argued with a man twice your size this morning was amazing," Vorrik added. Earlier that morning, she had confronted a drunken man harassing a younger woman. It had escalated quickly—yelling, shoving, and finally a kick to the shin—until Vorrik intervened.

"I never knew the Queen," Nythir said softly, "but I do know you have the makings to be your own goddess. Not just the shadow of one."

Esther didn't know how to respond except to melt into them, hands gripping their shirts, eyes stinging.

Vorrik wrapped his arms around both of them, making a Lyssara–Esther sandwich and sobbing into Lyssara's shoulder.

Nythir stood at her side, expression soft and warm in a way that made Esther's chest fold in on itself. She leaned into him without thinking. His hand slid to her back, anchoring her.

Then, in classic Vorrik fashion, he ruined the moment.

"So... does this mean Nythir's gonna be king now?"

Lyssara choked on her own spit. "Oh fuck—"

Vorrik gasped. "We'll have all the power!"

Lyssara covered her face. "No. No power. No crowns. No—whatever the hell kings do. Absolutely not. We are not responsible enough."

Nythir blinked slowly. "I do not want a crown."

"Good," Lyssara snapped. "Because you'd lose it within a week."

Vorrik nodded enthusiastically. "Or Essie's magic would explode it!"

Esther groaned into her hands. "Please. Stop talking."

They did not.

But they closed in around her again—a chaotic, loud, tear-soaked knot of arms, warmth, and affection—until her throat ached from holding back more tears. Nythir gently placed his arm around her shoulder and guided her back toward the orphanage.

The orphanage quieted once the children fell asleep in a tangle of limbs, patched blankets, and stuffed animals that were well past their years. Vorrik and Lyssara snored in opposite corners of the tiny guest room, one on a pile of quilts, the other on the floor with a borrowed pillow.

Nythir sat at the end of the hallway, keeping watch. He was always keeping watch.

Esther found Charon in the front room, sipping tea while the last lantern flickered low. She looked tired—not from the lateness of the night, but from having too many mouths to feed, too many children to care for, too much stress for a single woman to bear.

"You wanted to know about her," Charon said. "Your mother."

Esther sat across from her, hands tightening in her lap. "Yes. Please."

Charon nodded once, motion slow with memory.

"She wasn't born noble," she began. "She was born in this very town. She garnered attention for being exceptionally gifted. Her magic healed where others failed. It soothed storms. It calmed children."

She smiled faintly. "She became queen not through politics, but through kindness."

Esther swallowed. "I never knew."

"Of course you didn't," Charon said softly. "The court liked rewriting her story. But we remember her. The poor. The sick. The orphans. The forgotten."

She gestured toward the sleeping children. "Many of them live because she cared. But when she died, so did those in power who cared."

A tear slipped down Esther's cheek before she could stop it.

"She left something for you," Charon said gently, reaching into a small wooden box. "She told me that when her daughter found her way to me, to give it to her."

She handed her a folded letter, sealed with wax imprinted with a tiny sun.

Esther's breath hitched. Her mother's seal. Her mother's handwriting. A letter in the hands of someone she had just met—yet again.

Her fingertips trembled as she broke the wax and unfolded the paper. The ink had faded, but the words glowed in her eyes like gold:

My dearest Essie,
If you are reading this, then fate has guided you farther than fear could ever hold you. I cannot know the life you grew into beside this one path I saw, but I know your heart.
Lead like a queen, my love—Not with the crown, but with compassion, not with power, but with purpose.
Never forget your heart. It is your most extraordinary magic.
My love is always with you.

Esther pressed the paper to her chest. Her fingers sparked, as if they were responding to the trace of magic left in her mother's words.

"I didn't know her," she whispered. "Not really."

"But she knew you," Charon said. "Before you were born, she spoke about you like you were the sunrise."

Esther covered her mouth to keep from breaking. Footsteps moved quietly behind her. Nythir's hand landed softly on her shoulder, kissing the top of her head. She didn't turn around—not yet. She just let herself feel it:

The love she had lost.

The love she had found.

And the love she didn't fully understand yet, warming her from where he stood.

33

Esther

How to help others: sweat, cry, haul buckets, and try not to traumatize any orphans.

Esther had always believed she understood what work looked like. She had watched it, after all—servants moving silently through palace halls, guards drilling in the courtyard, seamstresses hunched over embroidery frames until their fingers ached. She had thanked them. She had been kind. She had noticed.

She had never lifted anything heavier than expectation.

The first bucket of water sloshed against her boots and soaked the hem of her borrowed skirt within seconds.

"Oh," Esther said faintly.

Lyssara snorted from beside her. "Careful. That one bites."

Esther tightened her grip and tried again, bracing herself the way she had seen others do. The bucket still dragged, her arms trembling as she hauled it across the orphanage yard. Her shoulders burned almost immediately, muscles protesting a life of disuse.

She told herself not to complain. Not even internally.

Around her, the children moved like a practiced unit. One passed her a cloth without being asked. Another took the bucket from her when it tilted too far, sloshing water onto the dirt. No one laughed.

No one scolded her.

They simply adjusted.

A girl no older than ten wrung out a rag beside her, hands moving quickly and efficiently. "You've got to tilt it first," she said kindly. "Otherwise it fights you."

"I see," Esther said, swallowing hard. She tried again, copying the motion.

The bucket obeyed.

That felt worse, somehow.

By the time the sun climbed higher, Esther's palms were raw. Soap stung tiny cuts she hadn't known were there. Sweat trickled down her spine beneath borrowed clothes that smelled faintly of smoke and old linen. Her magic stirred restlessly under her skin, reacting to exhaustion the way it always did—flaring, then pulling back, uncertain.

She kept working anyway.

She scrubbed floors until her knees ached. She stirred soup thick enough to feed too many mouths with too few ingredients. She hauled sacks of grain and stacked them carefully, apologizing every time she dropped one—until Lyssara gently took her wrist.

"You don't have to say sorry," Lyssara said. "You're helping."

"I know," Esther admitted. "I just... I slow you down."

Lyssara smiled, soft but tired. "Everyone does, at first."

That didn't help.

At the soup kitchen, the line never seemed to shorten. Bowls were passed down, worn wooden counters. Children carried them carefully, hands wrapped around chipped rims for warmth. Esther ladled until her arm shook, steam fogging her vision.

Voices drifted around her.

"They say Kraggmar won't join the alliance."

"They say Valedara's hoarding grain."

"They say Queen Estella would've fixed this."

Esther's ladle paused.

No one noticed.

"She would've," an older man said firmly. "She always did."

"She's dead," someone muttered.

"So they say."

Esther swallowed and kept serving.

No one looked at her like she was royalty. No one bowed. A few thanked her. Most didn't. They were too tired, too hungry, too busy surviving to care who she was.

That hurt.

It also felt... honest.

By the time they returned to the orphanage, Esther's limbs felt like they belonged to someone else. She sat heavily on the steps, breathing hard, fingers trembling as she flexed them. Her bracelet weighed heavily against her wrist—a familiar anchor, a familiar cage.

She slid it off.

The relief was immediate. Her magic loosened its grip, the constant pressure easing like a held breath finally released. For a moment, the world sharpened—colors deeper, sounds clearer.

Too clear.

The ground beneath her feet vibrated faintly. Just once.

Esther stiffened, heart pounding.

"Essie?" Nythir asked quietly.

"I'm fine," she said quickly, forcing the magic down, shoving the bracelet back on. The pressure returned, comforting and suffocating all at once.

She stood too fast.

The shout came a heartbeat later.

"Korin!"

A boy stumbled, clutching his arm. Blood welled bright against dirt. Esther's breath caught painfully in her chest.

"No," she whispered.

She was there before anyone else, hands glowing instinctively as she knelt. Her magic surged—too much, too fast—fear feeding it like fuel. The air crackled. A nearby squirrel twitched.

The ground beside them stirred, and Esther got a horrible feeling in her gut that this had happened once before.

A squirrel corpse, long dead and stiff, jerked upright as if yanked by invisible strings.

Lyssara screamed. Again.

Korin gasped in horror.

The zombie squirrel chattered.

Esther swore.

Vorrik stomped it flat without hesitation, leaving only fur, dust, and the faint sound of traumatized silence behind.

Korin stared at the flattened spot on the ground like it might bite him again.

"I'm so sorry—" Esther began.

"For the love of the stars," Lyssara groaned, rubbing her face, "that is the second undead squirrel this month—! Why is it always squirrels?!"

Esther wished the earth would swallow her whole.

Charon approached then, calm despite the lingering horror in the air. She looked at Esther with a strange tenderness.

"You really are just like your mother."

Esther blinked. "What... what do you mean? My mother didn't reanimate rodents."

Charon laughed softly, eyes filled with nostalgia. "Oh, she absolutely did. Squirrels, frogs, an entire flock of birds once. Estella's magic was... unpredictable back then. Wild. Just like yours."

Esther stared.

"She caused chaos wherever she tried to help," Charon continued fondly. "But that's how the Council noticed her. They took her in, trained her. Even then, she could barely keep her power from spilling out."

Esther swallowed hard. "And the foresight? That wasn't something she learned?"

"No," Charon said quietly, eyes softening as memories swam behind them. "She didn't see the future until she carried you. That magic had never appeared before—and hasn't since."

A strange warmth spread through Esther. Pride, fear, grief, awe, and confusion all tangled together.

"I miss her," Esther whispered.

"I know," Charon murmured. "But she would be proud. You're beginning to see the world she tried to protect. When her visions first began, she tried to change the future. But along the way, she changed. She decided to lay the groundwork instead."

Esther's chest ached.

"So I'm following her path."

Charon shook her head. "No. You're walking beside it."

Nythir found her later, sitting alone under the stars.

"I don't know how to do this," she admitted, voice barely audible. "I want to help, but everything I touch feels like it could break."

Nythir sat beside her without speaking for a long moment. Then he said, "You stayed."

She looked at him.

"You could've left," he continued. "You didn't."

That was all.

Esther looked down at the bracelet in her hands. The younger children were sleeping inside. In the shadows of a war she'd been sheltered from.

Esther exhaled slowly, the weight of the day settling into something steadier. Not certainty. Not confidence.

Resolve.

Tomorrow, she would wake sore and tired and unsure again.

But she would wake here.

And that, she realized, was the beginning.

34

LUCY

How to Travel: don't. You will regret it immediately.

Lucy had thought that the Baroness joining their travels was the worst that could happen.

She was very, very wrong.

If Lucy didn't need to remain visible enough to function as a decoy for Esther's escape, she would have abandoned the group by day two and lived feral in the woods, possibly with squirrels. Maybe she'd score a cool wolf companion and become ruler of the woods.

They had barely left Rhea and Asher's cozy little home when chaos began its morning calisthenics.

The road was narrow and rutted, framed by low hedges and skeletal trees stripped bare by early cold. Fog clung low to the ground, the kind that promised unpleasant surprises and damp socks. Lucy was still mid-complaint about breakfast portions when two men burst from the brush, shouting something vague and coin-related.

Lucy opened her mouth to scream—purely for dramatic effect—but Sylva was already moving.

One blink, he was beside her; the next, he was everywhere. Blue fabric flashed, silver buckles caught the light, and his dagger moved like it had opinions about where it belonged. The thieves went down fast, one tripping over his own ambition, the other groaning into the dirt like he'd reconsidered all his life choices at once.

Lucy stared.

Her pulse hadn't slowed. That annoyed her more than the blood.

"What?" Sylva asked, flicking blood off his blade with practiced ease.

"I—I'm..." She snapped her mouth shut so she didn't accidentally say *deeply attracted*.

"...observing." It was the safest word she could grab in a moment where her brain offered far worse options.

He gave her a look. A very knowing look.

She threw a pebble at him.

He dodged.

Lucy had the irrational thought that he hadn't been watching the pebble at all—that he'd been watching her.

Sylva fought three more thieves by midday, one of whom had been hiding behind Basil's horse for a full minute before deciding that attempting robbery "right now" was a good idea.

It wasn't.

Lucy found herself impressed. And then irritated at being impressed. And then impressed again.

Sylva walked ahead of her with the quiet confidence of someone who had never known fear in his life. He stayed just far enough ahead to clear danger without blocking her path. Lucy hated that she recognized the intention.

Meanwhile, Lucy tripped over a root.

Twice.

"I meant to do that," she muttered.

Sylva glanced back. "Lie."

Lucy scowled. "I hate your ears."

"You love my ears."

"Lie," she shot back.

He smirked.

By the time the sun dipped low, they reached a roadside inn called *The Roasted Trout*, which smelled like burnt onions, damp straw, desperation, and something that might once have been meat. The sign looked like someone had painted a fish while blindfolded and in emotional distress. It was almost as bad as Esther's dragon embroidery.

Inside, the air was smoky and stale. A bard played a single tune on repeat—three chords, none correct.

Sylva positioned himself without thinking—between her and the loudest pockets of movement. Lucy clocked it the way she clocked exits: subconsciously, gratefully, and without permission.

The Baroness took one step in, inhaled, and gagged.

"Oh heavens," she croaked. "It smells like someone cooked misery."

Lucy clapped her hands before wiggling her fingers dramatically like a magician. "Welcome to travel!"

Basil rubbed his eyes hard enough to erase his vision. "I'll be in the tavern. Listening for rumors. Avoid trouble."

He looked directly at Lucy when he said it.

Lucy saluted. "Trouble? I've never even met her."

"You are trouble," Basil muttered, walking away.

As soon as he disappeared, the Baroness whispered, "Is it truly safe? Will he be all right?"

Lucy shrugged. "He's fine." Then, because the universe rewarded chaos, she added, "He does look good from behind."

The Baroness turned pink and stared very hard at the wall.

Later, Basil returned smelling like a tavern and poor decisions. Every time the Baroness looked at him, she made a small, distressed *oh!* sound and pretended to cough.

Then Basil dropped a spoon.

Both dove for it at the same time, smacked foreheads, and nearly fell over.

Lucy gagged loudly.

"Can you two not flirt in my line of sight? I'm eating."

"We are not—" the Baroness sputtered.

"I am extremely uninterested in—" Basil began.

"Lie," Sylva interjected helpfully, without looking up from sharpening his dagger.

They both froze.

Lucy nearly died of secondhand embarrassment.

Lucy escaped outside the inn for fresh air. The night was cool, the moon bright and round, and for a fleeting moment, everything felt quiet.

Which is precisely why the universe ruined it.

Two men stumbled from the shadows, ale on their breath. "Hey, sweetheart," one slurred. "Pretty girl like you shouldn't be alone."

Lucy sighed. "Listen. I've had a long day. I really don't—"

The second man grabbed her wrist. For half a heartbeat, Lucy went still—not weak, just calculating. That pause terrified her more than the grip.

"Oh," Lucy said flatly. "Absolutely not."

Before she could decide whether to kick, stab, or scream, a shriek pierced the night.

"Unhand her, you barbaric vermin!"

The Baroness descended like divine judgment, handbag raised above her head.

The first man blinked. "What—"

Whack!

Coins exploded from the bag like metallic fireworks. She continued her frantic assault until the two men dropped like sacks of wet flour.

Lucy stared.

The shaking didn't start until it was over.

The Baroness stood panting, hair wild, eyes blazing with aristocratic wrath. "No one touches my—my—my Lucy."

Lucy blinked. "Your... Lucy?"

"My responsibility," the Baroness corrected, voice wobbling. "Obviously."

Lucy's lips curled into a slow grin. "Uh-huh."

The Baroness quickly composed herself. "Are you harmed?"

"No." Lucy swallowed, her chest unexpectedly warm. "Thank you."

The Baroness lifted her chin with a huff. "Good. Handbags are expensive."

The two walked back in, the Baroness looking like she'd survived a windstorm and Lucy smiling despite herself.

Sylva glanced up from the table. "What happened to you two?"

Lucy dropped into a chair. "The Baroness just wiped the forest floor with two men using a purse."

Sylva's eyes widened. "Respect."

Basil rushed over. "Are you hurt?"

"No," Lucy said. "But my worldview has shifted."

The Baroness folded her hands primly. "Nothing happened."

"Lie," Sylva said.

Lucy snorted so hard she choked.

Basil and the Baroness locked eyes for a second too long, both blushing, both instantly looking away.

Lucy groaned. "I swear, if you two fall in love in front of me, I *will* eat rocks."

Basil: "We're not—"

Baroness: "We would never—"

Sylva: "Both lies."

Lucy slapped her forehead. "I hate traveling."

Sylva smirked. "No, you don't."

Lucy glared at the table. Maybe she didn't hate it entirely, but it was definitely trying to kill her.

The inn eventually settled into something resembling sleep.

The bard stopped playing. Someone extinguished a lantern. The smell of burned onions faded just enough to be replaced by wet wood and old smoke.

Lucy lay on her back atop a lumpy mattress, staring at the ceiling beams. One of them had a crack shaped vaguely like a bird. Or a sword. Or possibly a poorly drawn map. She decided not to think too hard about it.

Her wrist still ached faintly where the man had grabbed her. She flexed her fingers, grounding herself in the knowledge that she hadn't been alone when it mattered.

She rolled onto her side and pressed it against the mattress, annoyed that the sensation hadn't vanished with the danger and annoyed that she'd frozen for half a second before the Baroness appeared like a wrathful ghost armed with a purse.

Lucy wasn't used to being rescued.

Footsteps creaked softly outside the door.

"Lucy?" the Baroness whispered, as if afraid of waking the entire building. "Are you awake?"

Lucy hesitated. Then, "Unfortunately."

The door opened just enough for the Baroness to slip inside. She looked smaller without her posture sharpened for battle—hair loosened, sleeves rolled down. She held her handbag clutched to her chest like a shield.

"I wished to ensure you were truly unharmed," she said stiffly.

Lucy propped herself up on one elbow. "You saved me with loose change."

The Baroness winced. "I lost three buttons."

"I will carve their names into history."

That earned a small, shaky laugh.

They stood there awkwardly for a moment, neither quite knowing what to do with the silence.

"You did not scream," the Baroness said quietly.

Lucy blinked. "I... what?"

"When the man grabbed you," she continued. "You didn't scream. You assessed. You prepared to act."

Lucy hadn't realized that was what she'd been doing.

"I don't like feeling helpless," she said finally. "I usually talk my way out of things. Or make myself a problem."

The Baroness nodded slowly. "So do I."

That surprised her.

"I am not brave," the Baroness added. "But I am... tired of being afraid."

Lucy swallowed, something warm and strange settling in her chest.

"Well," she said lightly, "for what it's worth, you were terrifying."

The Baroness straightened a fraction. "Good."

She hesitated at the door. "Sleep well, Lucy."

Lucy watched her leave, the door clicking softly shut behind her.

She lay back down, hands folded on her stomach, listening to the muffled sounds of the inn.

Basil's quiet footsteps pacing. Sylva's steady breathing somewhere nearby. A world that did not pause just because she was overwhelmed.

For the first time since leaving the palace, Lucy felt something shift.

Not safety.

Not certainty.

But... being counted.

She didn't know what tomorrow would bring. More thieves. More arguments. More chaos.

But she knew this: she would not be invisible.

And somehow, she smiled at the thought.

35

Esther

How to Choose Between Love and Duty: cry a little, pretend you're fine, repeat.

Esther woke to the sound of gentle breathing beside her.

For a moment, she didn't move. She didn't breathe any deeper than necessary. She lay still and let the world exist without her, balanced delicately on the rise and fall of the chest beside her.

The fear, the memories, the weight of her mother's legacy were all washed away for the barest of moments as she drank in the morning sight of Nythir.

Nythir slept on his back, one arm flung above his head, the other resting where she had tucked herself closer sometime in the night. His hair had come loose from its braid and spilled across the pillow in dark waves. A faint scar crossed his collarbone. It was old and half-hidden. Something she had noticed once and never asked about.

Esther shifted slightly, testing the space between them. Nythir stirred but didn't wake, only turning his head toward her as if he could sense her pulling away. His fingers tightened unconsciously in the blanket.

For a few precious seconds, the world felt small. Manageable. Like all that mattered existed within the quiet space between their breaths.

She even found herself smiling faintly at the familiar background noises—Vorrik's horrendous snoring rattling the walls, Lyssara muttering something about squirrels in contempt during her sleep.

Then the rest of the world crept back in.

The orphanage.

The hungry families.

The whispers of war were tightening around Greyhollow like a closing fist.

Her mother's letter pressed heavily in her pocket, the folded parchment a constant reminder that she had been left something more than grief. She had been left with responsibility.

For one reckless heartbeat, she imagined letting the world sort itself out and letting councils argue, and kingdoms fall into whatever shape they chose. Letting Lucy scold her, Basil sighs dramatically, and everyone survives without her intervention.

She imagined choosing him.

The image was fragile. Beautiful. Impossible.

Esther slipped carefully from the bed, gathering her cloak with practiced quiet. She paused at the door, looking back once more.

"I don't know how to do both," she whispered, though he couldn't hear her. "But I'm trying."

She swallowed hard.

Love felt so small next to all of that.

Not unimportant… just fragile.

She slipped from the bed before anyone else woke, careful not to disturb Nythir. She paused only long enough to press a quiet kiss to his forehead and whisper a promise she wasn't sure she could keep.

"I'll be back soon."

Greyhollow was already awake.

Carts rattled, merchants shouted, and the scent of baked bread and smoke mixed in the air. Esther wrapped her cloak tighter around herself and bought fresh rolls, small wheels of cheese, and whatever vegetables she could afford from the orphanage's meager fund—supported mainly through Lyssara and other kind souls—not those wealthy enough to make change.

A farmer gave her a discount simply because she smiled—an action she had taken for granted just days before.

Esther pulled her hood low and walked.

She carefully spent the orphanage's coins, making sure to stretch it as far as possible to feed the children. Bread still warm from the oven. The cheese was cut unevenly because the seller's hands shook. Vegetables bruised but usable, sold cheaply by a woman who smiled like she hadn't done so in days.

"You've got kind eyes," the woman said, pressing an extra carrot into Esther's basket. "Your mother had eyes like that."

Esther's breath caught.

"Thank you," she managed.

She moved on quickly after that, heart pounding too hard in her chest. Everywhere she looked, the strain showed itself in small, unignorable ways.

A man with a bandaged shoulder trying—and failing—to lift a sack of grain on his own. A mother carefully breaking a loaf into pieces so small that Esther wondered how they could possibly be enough. An elderly craftsman staring at a half-rebuilt stall, fingers hovering uselessly over tools he could no longer afford to replace.

some recognized her.

That was worse than she expected.

This was Valedara. Her kingdom. Her responsibility. And yet she walked among them unnoticed—another cloaked woman with a basket and too much concern in her eyes.

This is what Mother saw, she thought—*every day*.

The realization settled heavy and cold in her stomach.

Esther slowed near the edge of the square, resting her basket against a low stone wall. She pressed her palm flat against the cool surface and breathed.

You can stay, a treacherous voice whispered. *Just a little longer. You're helping. You're here.*

Another, quieter yet sharper voice answered back.

You're hiding.

She closed her eyes.

Love pulled at her relentlessly, warm and persuasive. Duty pulled differently—not louder, not kinder, but with the weight of inevitability. The knowledge that if she turned away now, she would never stop turning.

She straightened.

I need to be better, she thought.

I need to fight for them.

I need to—

"Esther!"

A blur of blond curls slammed into her, knocking the breath from her lungs.

"Lucy?" Esther squeaked, arms full of an aggressively hugging maid. Her ribs were one attack-hug away from collapsing.

Lucy pulled back just long enough to grab Esther's face between her hands. "Oh my stars, I've finally found you! Do you have any idea how hard it is to track a missing princess who is actively avoiding being found?"

Esther blinked. "What—? How—? Why are you here?"

"No time!" Lucy hissed, yanking her into a narrow alley between two buildings. "Listen carefully. I can't stay long. And you especially can't be seen with me. Basil has the eyes of a hawk and the patience of a graveyard."

"What are you talking about?" Esther whispered frantically.

"We have a search party," Lucy said, glancing around like a spy in a children's book. "Basil. Baroness Levon. Sylva—Basil's secret fox child."

Esther's heart flipped. "A search party? For me? And Basil has *what*?"

"Focus!" Lucy snapped. "You vanished from a castle. I performed a masterful act of concern. Basil nearly combusted from stress. The Baroness is absolutely in love with him and keeps pretending she isn't. It's unbearable."

"Lucy, you are saying too many things too fast."

"No time for pacing!" Lucy grabbed her shoulders. "Meet me tonight. Late. By the north gate. Alone."

"Lucy, wait—why—"

"No questions!" Lucy hissed. "I have to distract Basil and the Baroness before they wander this way. We'll discuss whether you're coming back to the palace or continuing your grand rebellion later. My sanity depends on this."

Esther stared at her. "...Lucy, why is there a search party? What are you even doing here?"

Lucy backed away, finger pressed to her lips. "Tonight. North gate. Be sneaky."

"Lucy, wait—why tonight? Why alone?"

Lucy hesitated, just for a heartbeat.

"Because," she said lightly, already stepping back, "I don't trust your timing—and I definitely don't trust mine."

"Lucy!"

But she was already gone, sprinting off with her cloak flapping wildly, muttering about cover stories and lying creatively.

Esther stood frozen in the alley, arms full of food, heart racing.

Her life had unraveled in ways she never could have predicted. And apparently Lucy—her constant, her anchor—had become a covert operative.

Esther pressed her fingers to her forehead and exhaled slowly.

Tonight.

North gate.

She looked toward the orphanage, then back the way Lucy had gone.

She could tell someone.

She could warn Nythir.

She could explain.

Esther closed her eyes.

And chose not to.

Tonight, then.

She turned back toward the orphanage, her steps steady even as her thoughts raced. Duty pulled her forward. Love tugged behind her.

And somewhere between the two, Esther realized, was the moment everything would change.

36

Esther

HOW TO MAKE A NOBLE SACRIFICE: WEEP INTERNALLY WHILE BEING AWKWARD EXTERNALLY.

The orphanage was quieter than usual when Esther returned

Children napped in uneven bundles across cots and benches, limbs tangled together for warmth.

The older ones swept the courtyard in lazy, circular patterns that suggested both routine and exhaustion. Lentil porridge lingered in the air, its scent clinging to the stone like a memory that refused to fade.

Everything looked the same.

Esther felt wrong inside her own body.

Each step echoed too loudly in her ears, as though the ground itself were aware of what she intended to do. Her fingers trembled when she closed the gate behind her, the metal latch colder than it had any right to be.

Nythir knelt by the wall, carefully repairing a splintered chair leg. His sleeves were rolled up, forearms dusted with sawdust and faint, old scars. His hair was tied back loosely, a smudge of charcoal darkening one cheek where he'd forgotten to wipe his hands.

When he looked up and saw her expression, his smile faltered immediately.

"Essie? Are you hurt?"

"No," she whispered. "Just... thinking."

He didn't press. Nythir never did. He waited, steady and present, as if he trusted her to find her way to the truth on her own.

She hated how much that made her love him.

Esther folded her hands together so he wouldn't see them shaking.

"I want to go out for a bit," she said softly. "With you. Just us."

"A stroll?" His brows knit together. "Now?"

"Yes." She forced a brittle smile. "A stroll."

His hesitation lasted only a heartbeat before he nodded. "Of course."

They walked through the outer plaza as evening began to settle, the city shifting into its second life.

Lanterns were being lit one by one, their glow uneven where oil was scarce. Merchants argued quietly over closing prices. Somewhere, a child laughed too loudly, the sound sharp against the backdrop of fatigue.

Usually, Esther could lose herself in Nythir's presence—in the warmth of his shoulder near hers, in the way their steps fell into unconscious rhythm. Tonight, her attention snagged on everything else.

Two women argued over a loaf of bread that was clearly too small to satisfy either of them. A man slept on the curb, ribs visible even beneath his coat. A little girl held out a cracked bowl, eyes too old for her face.

Each sight reopened the same wound.

Nythir noticed the way her gaze lingered. "We can turn back," he offered gently. "The market can be… a lot."

"It's not the noise," Esther murmured. "It's everything."

She wanted to remember him. The way he drifted closer when the crowd pressed in. The protective angle of his body. The glances he kept sneaking at her like she was something fragile and precious.

But instead, all she saw was what her people lacked.

What they needed.

What she had the power to help, if she gave up everything else.

She swallowed hard. "Nythir… would you—could we—"

He looked down at her, eyes soft. "Anything."

"Could we rent a room tonight?" she blurted.

He blinked.

Once.

Twice.

A faint, bright red flush crept up his neck.

"Rent a—" He choked. "A room? For… sleeping?"

Esther felt her own face ignite. "Not for sleeping."

"Oh." Nythir froze completely, ears rigid, eyes wide like a startled animal. "Oh!"

She covered her face with both hands. "You don't have to! I just—I want—I mean—" She dropped her hands helplessly. "I want to choose something for myself. Just once. And I choose you."

He stared at her like she'd just said the moon had been carved for him personally.

"Essie," he breathed, "are you sure?"

Her throat tightened. "Yes."

He swallowed so hard she saw it move. "Then... yes. Of course. We can. I mean. Yes. Absolutely. Tonight. A room. Together."

He paused. "Not for sleeping."

She groaned and buried her face in his cloak while he laughed nervously, hands hovering awkwardly, unsure where he was allowed to touch.

The inn they chose sat on the edge of the district, tucked between shuttered shops and quiet alleys.

It smelled of clean linens and old wood. The lanterns burned low and warm.

The innkeeper's knowing smile nearly undid them both.

Upstairs, behind the closed door of their room, the world narrowed.

The bed was neatly made. The lantern cast a golden glow. The space felt too small and far too intimate.

"If you want to change your mind," Nythir said quietly, closing the door, "I'll still be here. I'll still want you."

Esther crossed the room and took his face in her hands. "I don't want to change my mind."

As soon as her eyes met his, he pulled her against him. His mouth met hers hungrily. His calm demeanor fell away as he frantically, clumsily deepened their kiss.

Esther moaned, arching her body into him. His tongue slid against her lips, begging for entrance.

She obeyed.

Nythir's hand slid up her back, thumb brushing over the place where her pulse fluttered wildly beneath her skin. Esther gasped softly into his mouth, the sound unguarded, and felt his control waver in response.

"Essie," he murmured, barely more than breath.

The way he said her name with such need made her knees weaken.

She pressed her forehead to his, breathing him in. The room felt impossibly quiet, as though the world itself had paused out of respect.

"I want this," she said. "I want you."

"I need you," he breathed, tightening his hold on her.

Esther laughed awkwardly. She wasn't sure what to do next or how to continue.

Then Nythir lifted her. Unlike his usual calm and calculated movements, this was an ungraceful effort that made her grin as she hooked her legs around him and met his lips again. She rocked into the heat she felt, moaning into his mouth.

Nythir misjudged the distance to the mattress in his frenzied need for her, toppling them onto the rough mattress. Nythir caught himself with a soft, helpless laugh that vanished the moment Esther kissed him again.

Esther's hands slid under his collar, over warm skin, drawing him down until there was barely space for breath between them.

Nythir licked along the curve of her throat with reverent attention, lingering where her pulse fluttered, while her legs tightened instinctively around his hips. He moved without quite realizing it at first, a slow, instinctive rock that drew a soft sound from them both as his hands began to explore, gentle and sure all at once.

"Are you ready?" he asked, his hand already traveling under her dress, up her thigh.

"Yes," she answered with a shaky voice.

She squeaked when his teasing fingers finished their journey up her thigh and rubbed against her.

"It's okay," he soothed, kissing her mouth again. "Just touching." He let his fingers explore the soft, swollen folds, finding a slick, startling wetness. She was ready for him. The knowledge made him dizzy with desire. He found a little nub, hard as a pearl, and circled it with a tentative finger.

Esther cried out, her whole body tensing. "What is that?"

"Something good," he rasped, watching her face. Her eyes were squeezed shut, her lips parted. He kept up the gentle, circular motion, learning what made her gasp, what made her legs fall open wider.

He slid a finger lower, into her heat. She was so tight, so unbelievably hot. He pushed in slowly, up to his knuckle.

"You feel... incredible," he gritted out, his own need a throbbing ache. He added a second finger, stretching her gently, preparing her. She was panting now, little cries escaping with each exhale.

Her breaths became short, frantic pants. Her hands clawed at the sheets. He watched, mesmerized, as pleasure overtook her, as her muscles tightened and a flush spread across her chest. With a sharp, broken cry, she came apart around his fingers, her body bowing, then melting into the mattress in a series of shuddering waves.

She lay boneless, her chest heaving. Slowly, she opened her eyes, dazed and glowing.

"That's not fair," Esther sighed.

"Oh?" Nythir teased, playing oblivious.

She huffed a quiet laugh, breathless and fed up, fingers tightening in his shirt as if she'd finally had enough of his restraint.

"You're doing that on purpose," she murmured.

Then, before he could deny it, she shifted her weight and rolled them both with surprising ease.

He went willingly, laughter breaking from him as he landed on his back, eyes bright and utterly unbothered as Esther settled astride him.

"Impatient," he teased softly, hands sliding to her hips. She smiled down at him, all heat and triumph, very clearly done waiting.

"This time, I'm not straddling you by accident," Esther smiled.

"It would be a problem if you were," he huffed.

Nythir grabbed her hips and rocked against her. She may have been on top of him, but he was the one in control.

"I want to see you," he groaned, tugging at the buttons on her dress. Esther caught his fumbling fingers before he could reveal her to him. "You first," she huffed.

He laughed softly, breathless, and let his hands fall away as Esther shifted her weight and reached for him instead, fingers quick and decisive. She made short work of his clothes, tugging and pushing until fabric was forgotten somewhere at the edge of the bed, his attention fixed entirely on her.

When she returned to her own dress, it was slower now, deliberate, the slide of fabric and the shared intake of breath saying far more than bare skin ever could. By the time they met again, knees braced and hands roaming, there was nothing left between them but the shared need.

"Ready?" he asked, pushing his cock against her entrance.

She nodded and rocked into him. It burned as he pushed into her, spreading her open. But it was mixed with pleasure. And above all else, they were connected.

She was connected with the man she loved, for the first and last time. She was soaking in all his sounds and touches. Committing everything about him to memory.

They came together beneath the lantern's glow, the world narrowing to heat and breath and the steady press of his body against hers. Esther clutched at his shoulders as sensation overwhelmed her, grounding herself in the solid truth of him.

When the light dimmed and the night closed around them, Esther let go. Just for a little while.

Later, wrapped in warmth and quiet, she lay with her cheek pressed to his chest, listening to the steady rhythm of his heart. His arm was draped over her waist, possessive without meaning to be, protective in the way only someone deeply asleep could be.

Esther traced idle patterns against his skin, memorizing this too.

She did not cry.

But the ache in her chest told her she would remember this for the rest of her life.

She should have been happy. Sated. Safe.

Instead, guilt gnawed at her ribs.

She reached out, brushing her fingertips across Nythir's forearm. He didn't stir.

"I'm sorry," she whispered so softly the lantern couldn't hear it.

"I love you. But they need me more."

She closed her eyes.

Tonight, she would return to the castle.

Tomorrow, she would accept her arranged marriage.

Carefully, she removed her bracelet and set it beside him, a small token of her fleeting time together. She hoped, selfishly, that he might remember her sometimes, just as she would never forget these moments.

Esther lingered at the door, taking one last look.

Then, with a deep, steadying breath, she stepped into the night.

37

Esther

How to keep a secret talk private: step one—don't be Esther.

The streets were empty at this hour, the frost-slick stones gleaming under the full moon's sharp light. Greyhollow felt as if it had paused, as if the city itself were holding its breath. Even the wind seemed still.

Esther's boots echoed too loudly against the stone as she walked. Each step carried the weight of a choice already made. The cold sharpened everything. She counted her steps without meaning to—stone, stone, crack, uneven patch—focusing on the rhythm to keep her thoughts from unraveling.

Somewhere behind her, Nythir slept. The thought slipped in uninvited, vivid and dangerous. She imagined the weight of his presence where she had left it behind. If she stopped now—if she even slowed—she was sure she would fold inward on herself and run back.

Don't look back, she told herself.

Her magic stirred restlessly beneath her skin, sensitive without the bracelet's steady pressure. Not flaring. Not yet. Just aware—as if it knew something she didn't.

The city felt wrong in its stillness. Too quiet.

Esther drew her cloak tighter and forced her feet to keep going. Tonight was about duty. Tomorrow could deal with regret.

She rubbed at the bare skin where her bracelet used to sit, fingers circling the faint indentation it had left behind. Without it, her magic lay closer to the surface—raw, responsive, and humming softly beneath her pulse. Exposed.

This is my decision, she reminded herself—*no one else's*.

Lucy waited near the north gate, arms wrapped tightly around herself against the cold. Her colorful hair was pulled back messily, curls escaping their tie. Her breath puffed white into the air, quick and shallow, betraying nerves she would never admit.

When she spotted Esther, her posture loosened immediately.

"Esther... you look pale. Are you alright?"

"No," Esther admitted. "But I made my decision."

Lucy blinked, straightening—the night pressed in around them, moonlight sharp enough to cut.

Esther drew a breath that burned her lungs. "I want to go back to the palace."

For a long moment, Lucy only stared at her—not disbelieving, but recalibrating, as if rearranging the world in her head.

"Tonight?" Lucy asked quietly. "You mean... now?"

"Yes," Esther's voice wavered despite her resolve. "I can't keep pretending I don't see what's happening here—the hunger, the people sleeping in the streets with no warmth, the orphanage barely holding together. I can't pretend it isn't my responsibility."

Her throat tightened. "I'm the Princess of Valedara," she said softly. "Even if it means giving up what I want."

The words felt heavier once spoken aloud. Princess. She had worn the title her whole life like a borrowed coat—something that fit well enough until she moved too quickly. Now it settled onto her shoulders with uncomfortable certainty.

This is what Mother felt, Esther thought. Not the crown. Not the ceremony. This moment, standing in the dark, knowing that love did not outweigh responsibility—no matter how much she wished it did.

Fear curled in her stomach, sharp and familiar. Not fear of pain or loss, but of becoming someone she did not fully recognize. Someone who made decisions that hurt the people she loved and called it necessary.

What if I disappear into it? She wondered. *What if there's nothing left of me afterward?*

Her gaze flicked briefly down the empty street, instinct screaming at her to hurry, to finish this before doubt cracked her resolve entirely. She lifted her chin. Even if she was afraid of who she might become, she was more scared of doing nothing.

Lucy's expression flickered between several emotions before settling into something fierce and achingly proud. She stepped forward and took Esther's hands, squeezing hard.

"Esther," she said, voice thick. "I'm proud of you. Truly. But I don't want to watch you disappear into duty until there's nothing left of you."

Esther squeezed back, desperate. "I know. I'm scared of that too."

Lucy swallowed. "Are you certain?"

"Yes," Esther said, her voice cracking. She had to leave now, before doubt clawed its way back in. "If I stay any longer, I won't be able to go at all."

Lucy nodded once. "Then let's get you home."

Relief and grief tangled painfully in Esther's chest.

"I don't trust myself to teleport us. If I hesitate, if I second-guess—this is too important," Esther admitted, rubbing her bare wrist again, eyes dropping. "We need Basil."

Lucy winced. "He's going to lecture us."

"I know."

"And sigh a lot."

"I know."

"But he'll do it."

"I know."

For a brief moment, both girls smiled with just a flicker of their usual selves in the bitter cold. Lucy squeezed her fingers. "Let's go meet our doom then. I haven't even told him I found—"

Her words cut off abruptly, eyes widening as a sound split the night.

Boom.

The ground lurched violently beneath them as a thunderous blast tore through the street. Pressure slammed into Esther's chest, knocking the breath from her lungs. Stone shattered. Dirt and dust erupted upward, swallowing the gate, the moonlight, and the sky.

Esther coughed violently, stumbling back. "Lucy?"

"I'm here!" The dust muffled Lucy's voice. "Esther, stay close—don't breathe too deep—!"

The air crackled, sharp and wrong.

Magic.

A blinding snap of energy tore through the dust.

Zzzrak.

Pain lanced through Esther's body before she could react. Her legs collapsed beneath her, and her vision blurred into streaks of white and black. She felt Lucy's hand grasp for hers—but miss.

Another strike. Another jolt.

Zzzrt.

She hit the ground hard, cheek scraping cold stone. Her thoughts scattered. She reached out blindly, fingers trembling, searching for Lucy.

"Est—" Lucy's voice cut through the haze, frightened, small.

A shadow moved through the dust.

Tall. Deliberate.

The last thing Esther felt was the cold certainty of being watched.

Then the world went black.

Nythir

How to start a rescue mission: stab first, hope for the best.

The explosion ripped the world open. The room shuddered violently; the lantern fell, and dust rained from the ceiling. Nythir jolted upright on instinct—then froze.

Esther's bracelet lay on the pillow beside him.

But Esther was gone.

She had left him on her own two legs. She was the only person he ever dropped his guard around. If anyone had so much as breathed outside that door, he would have noticed.

The knowledge landed like a blade between his ribs.

She had trusted him. Trusted him enough to walk away without waking him, to believe he would understand her silence when he found it.

Nythir pressed his palm hard against his chest, breath coming too fast, too shallow.

He should have woken sooner. Should have known. Should have felt the shift in the air the moment she made her decision.

He had promised himself he would never cage her.

And in keeping that vow, he had left her unguarded.

Guilt coiled hot and sharp beneath his skin. Love had not failed her. He had.

His lungs caved inward. He scrambled out of bed, grabbed the bracelet, and tore into the hallway. Down the stairs. Out the front door.

His mind raced with questions and worry. She wanted him—so why had she left? Why could he not sense her, no matter how far he stretched his wards?

The silence was wrong. Not absence—wrongness.

Nythir had always felt her before he saw her. A warmth at the edge of his awareness. A familiar pull, like gravity remembering its source. Even when she was frightened. Even when she hid.

Now there was nothing.

The emptiness clawed at him, panic blooming cold and fast. He poured more power into the wards, teeth clenched, vision blurring at the edges. Nothing answered.

His magic recoiled, unsettled, as if it too recognized that this was not how things were supposed to be.

The street was chaos—smoke, shouting, running figures lit by flickering spellfire.

"Essie!" he shouted, voice cracking. No answer.

He ran through the streets, sending out his magic to find any lingering spark of hers. The longer her magic did not respond, the more frantic he became.

"Halt!"

He spun, dodging a splice of magic that tore through the air.

A man he did not recognize. And next to him—Sylva.

An acquaintance. Barely. A name from a guild board. Someone Nythir had passed in silence more times than he had spoken to.

But the look Sylva gave him now was lethal.

"He is cloaked in Esther's magic!" the man said, summoning a sword made of wind.

"And... impossible! Queen Estella's magic?"

Nythir sized up the aura knight, aware of the familiar faces—ones that could trick Essie into leaving his side and into their trap.

He grasped his dagger, waiting for them to attack first.

Sylva charged. Steel flashed—dual blades unsheathed, gleaming in the dim light.

"Where is Esther—and Lucy?!" Sylva snarled.

Nythir threw up a shield just in time. Sylva's first strike hit it hard enough to rattle teeth—the next sliced low, followed by a high cut in a perfectly trained rhythm.

"That's what I should be asking you!" Nythir shouted, struggling to hold the barrier.

Sylva continued his assault, each slash chipping away at his shield. Sylva roared, "Tell me where she is!"

"I don't know!"

Sylva froze mid-step, ears twitching.

"You believe that," he growled. "But that doesn't mean you're innocent."

He lunged again.

For a split second—barely long enough to register—Nythir understood. Not the attack. The fear behind it.

Sylva fought like someone protecting something precious, not like someone seeking victory. Every strike was desperate, defensive, fueled by the same terror roaring through Nythir's veins.

Lucy.

The realization did not soften Nythir's movements or slow his blade, but it shifted something sharp and dangerous into something colder.

They were not enemies.

They were mirrors.

Nythir dodged, flipping back with impeccable coordination. His feet barely touched the ground before he launched sideways, dagger drawn in the same motion. Quiet. Efficient. Deadly.

Sylva's blades collided with Nythir's shield, cracking its surface.

"You expect me to ignore the fact that Estella's magic—dead queen magic—is on you?" Sylva spat. "Or that Lucy's trail vanishes at the exact same spot as the princess's?"

"That princess is mine to protect," Nythir shot back, deflecting a slash and countering with a force pulse that shoved Sylva two steps back. "And I've never seen this Lucy person you are so obsessed with."

Sylva's jaw clenched.

"You believe everything you're saying," he said, voice shaking. "Which means someone's playing all of us."

"Then stop trying to kill me!" Nythir shouted.

Sylva attacked harder, blades whirling like a storm. Nythir ducked under a swing, slid beneath Sylva's arm with surprising fluidity, and slashed upward. Their weapons clashed.

Steel sparks. Magic cracks. Panic echoed in every motion.

The stranger—Basil—shouted something, but neither heard him.

This was not just a fight. It was desperation.

Fear.

Love.

And the belief that the other man held the missing pieces.

Then—**Boom!**

A shadow dropped between them. A massive goliath sword slammed into the street, cracking cobblestones apart.

Both men staggered back.

Sable stood with her hand on the hilt, expression flat and unimpressed.

"Okay," she said loudly. "Everyone who wants to continue breathing—stop."

Everyone froze.

"Good," Sable continued. "Luna sent a letter. She also told me to break up any fights. So—" she tapped the cracked ground with her boot, "—mission accomplished."

Footsteps pounded toward them. The older teens from the orphanage arrived first, breathless and holding makeshift weapons—pitchforks, broom handles, kitchen knives.

Behind them came more: refugees—people with torn cloaks and worn boots.

And each of them wore something faintly glowing:

A gold-tinted earring

A ring warm with magic

A bracelet humming softly

Basil's eyes widened.

"Those... those are all Estella's blessings," he whispered. "But why?"

"The Queen saved all of us. In return, we promised to act when our relics awakened."

"How many people did Estella tie into her plan?"

"A lot," Sable said nonchalantly, like she wasn't standing in the middle of a battle zone.

"I was also told to give you this letter from Queen Estella to—someone, I guess. Luna didn't specify."

Nythir and Sylva snatched it at the same time, glaring at each other.

"Let go," Sylva growled, baring his teeth.

"No."

"Enough!" a woman screeched, whacking them in the head with a purse and seizing the letter.

"Irene! I told you to stay inside!" the aura knight shouted, rushing to guard her.

"Not when my children are involved!" she snapped, whacking him again.

Nythir instinctively knew her—the Baroness, feared and respected in equal measure.

She tore the letter open, scanned it, and then shoved it at the aura knight. Sylva read it over his shoulder, then passed it to Nythir.

Dear Basil, Irene, and the man my child loves,
I have done all I could to prepare for this moment. I could not live for my
beloved child, so I beg you: save my girl and my kingdom in my stead.
March to Draewyn Dominion. The others will be there.
I leave the rest to you.

"Nythir!" Lyssara yelled, running through the smoke. "Are you okay? Where's Essie?"

"Why do you look ready to kill someone?" Vorrik asked, hiding behind Lyssara.

"Because we are going to kill someone."

"Who?" Lyssara asked cautiously, nodding to Sable.
"At dawn, we end a kingdom."

39

Esther

How to Identify the Princess: Step one—kidnap both girls. Step two—hope the right one doesn't bite you.

The sharp, chemical bite of ammonia speared up Esther's nose, ripping her from unconsciousness. Her lungs seized as she choked on the pungent sting. The air tasted metallic and wet, thick with mold and old stone.

Esther blinked hard, trying to force clarity. Her head throbbed dully, as if stuffed with cotton and struck with a hammer. Every breath scraped as it entered, shallow and panicked.

The stone beneath her back was damp and unforgiving. Cold seeped into her spine, into her bones, settling with intimate persistence. Somewhere, water dripped steadily, each echoing plink measuring time she did not have.

She cataloged herself instinctively: bruised ribs, burning wrists, no obvious bleeding—Lucy alive.

Magic—

Esther reached inward and met nothing but resistance. The absence made her stomach lurch, like missing a step on a staircase.

Beside her, Lucy gagged violently, the sound bouncing off dripping brick.

"Finally awake?" a sultry voice purred, smooth as velvet stretched over a blade.

Esther forced her heavy head upward. Her vision swam, then sharpened on a breathtaking woman: chocolate-brown hair cascading like polished silk, a tight black dress hugging her figure, fabric gleaming like oil in torchlight.

But it was the grin—sharp, predatory—that made Esther's stomach twist. She recoiled instinctively, but the movement jolted iron against bone.

Her wrists were shackled to the frigid, sweating brick wall; cold seeping into her skin.

Lucy snarled beside her, thrashing like a furious animal. The chains clattered so harshly that Esther's teeth ached. Lucy's wrists were already red and swollen.

"Such crude behavior," the woman laughed. "I am Princess Zaria of Draewyn."

A chill slid down Esther's spine. Her heartbeat stuttered—not for herself, but for Lucy, for Valedara, for every refugee who needed her alive.

She tried to summon magic—just a spark—but the chamber swallowed it whole. The runes carved into the stone hummed, pulling the magic from her like a leech. Esther gasped, as if breathing through cloth while someone pressed against her chest.

The markings crawled along the walls in deliberate patterns, etched deep enough to look ancient—and maintained. Someone had re-cut them recently. The lines glimmered faintly as they drained her magic with methodical hunger.

Esther had seen wards like these once before, in a sealed wing of the Valedaran archives. Designed not to kill, the text had said. Designed to contain.

That knowledge chilled her far more than the chains.

"What do you want with us?" she growled, forcing steel into her voice.

The heavy door groaned open, cold air swirling in. Hinges screamed like something dying, scraping down her spine.

"Your Majesty," Zaria said, bowing. "I present to you the princess of Valedara."

Esther's breath hitched.

The man who entered carried authority like poison—thick, suffocating. His boots thudded with deliberate weight, each strike vibrating through her chains.

"Have you determined which one is the princess?" he asked. His gaze dragged over them like a butcher evaluating cuts of meat.

"Not yet," Zaria replied.

He seized Lucy by the throat so quickly the torches flickered, examining her like livestock.

"Both have brown eyes and blonde hair," he sneered. "One would think a princess would be easier to pick out. But both these girls are painfully mediocre."

"I am not mediocre!" Lucy lunged and bit him—hard enough that Esther heard the crunch.

Pain flared across Esther's chest—not from the slap, but from the fury surging through her. She strained instinctively against her chains, iron biting into her wrists.

Lucy did not cry.

She did not beg.

She bared her teeth and drew blood.

Pride bloomed sharp and dangerous in Esther's heart. Whatever happened next, Lucy would not go quietly. Neither would she.

"You insolent pest!" he roared, striking her. The slap cracked through the chamber, the walls seeming to recoil.

"Your Majesty," Zaria soothed, "leave them to me. I'll send a messenger when I've broken them thoroughly."

"Very well." He rubbed the bite mark and cast one last contemptuous look. "Mediocre."

The door slammed like a tomb, locks sliding into place with brutal finality. Silence settled—dense, icy, absolute.

Zaria remained facing the door, shoulders rising and falling in an irritated sigh, as though the king were the true burden.

Then she turned.

Her wicked grin brightened into something almost theatrically cruel.

"Well," she said, clapping her hands, "now that it's just us... we can have some fun, can't we?"

Esther's pulse thundered. Lucy growled.

"Oh, wonderful spirit," Zaria cooed. "But we won't have to resort to that."

She cracked the door open again, peering out. Sparks hissed from the torches, briefly illuminating her thoughtful frown. Then she shut it gently.

The second it clicked, her entire act disintegrated.

The shift was abrupt, leaving Esther reeling. One moment, Zaria was a blade wrapped in silk. The next, she was frantic, focused—movements precise, nothing to do with cruelty. Her hands shook slightly as she inspected Esther, eyes darting not with hunger, but calculation.

This woman wasn't unstable.

She was compartmentalized.

And that realization was somehow worse.

Monsters were predictable. People like this were not.

She darted to Esther, malice gone as if wiped clean.

"You're not harmed, are you?" she whispered urgently.

"I told them not to be rough with you, but they electrocuted you. I'll send them to the brig later."

Her fingers brushed Esther's jaw, warm and feather-light—checking, not threatening.

"I'm... fine?" Esther murmured, dizzy with confusion.

Lucy kicked uselessly, rattling her chains.

"Stop struggling, you'll hurt yourself!" Zaria scolded. "Calm down."

"Calm down?" Lucy shrieked—until Zaria stuffed a rag in her mouth.

"I'm sorry, but you're giving me a headache, and I need to explain things to Princess Esther."

Princess. The word hit like a stone dropped in Esther's chest.

Zaria turned back to her with surprising tenderness.

"You look just like your mother."

Esther's throat tightened.

"Let me guess—my mother left a message for me with you?"

"You're very astute," Zaria said warmly.

Lucy mumbled furiously through her gag.

"What? No, I didn't give myself away," Esther told her.

"She already knew who I was."

Lucy made a pointed noise.

"Well, I guess I did—but my mom has this whole building-an-army-of-supporters-after-she-died thing—"

Zaria burst into laughter.

"You two are ridiculous. How are you understanding what she says?"

"We've been together a long time," Esther said.

"She basically has twin telepathy—aw, don't get mushy on me, Lucy—fine, I'll ask. She wants to know why we should trust you."

Zaria's expression softened into something heartfelt.

"Simple. Your mother left me with her memory to show you."

She lifted her sleeve and offered her bare wrist.

"This is what she left for you."

A faint gold glow bled beneath her skin—then erupted outward, a tidal wave of light and heat. It slammed into Esther's chest, wrenching a scream from her throat.

Esther's pulse thundered in her ears.

Every instinct screamed at her to pull back, brace herself, run—all useless impulses bound and bleeding against iron and stone. Her magic stirred weakly in response, recognizing the gold glow with aching familiarity.

Mother.

Whatever this was, it wasn't just memory.

It was an inheritance.

The world vanished.

She fell.

40

Esther

How to Carry a Legacy: You begin by burying the seeds your mother died to plant.

Esther's vision drowned in red and gold. Gravity wrenched her downward, her stomach twisting as if she were falling through a moment she'd already lived. Déjà vu pulled at her bones.

She hit cold concrete on her knees. No pain. Just shock.

When her sight steadied, she saw a heavily pregnant woman sitting at a plain table, worry creasing every inch of her face.

"Mother?" Esther whispered.

She stumbled forward, reaching out—but her fingers slipped straight through Estella's shoulder. Through her hair. Through her.

No warmth. No weight. No mother.

The absence hurt more than any wound.

Esther drew her hand back slowly, curling her fingers into a fist as if she could trap the sensation that should have been there. Her chest ached with the effort of breathing, grief pressing down until the world felt narrow and distant.

She had imagined this moment so many times—reunion, explanation, comfort.

Instead, she was a ghost haunting her own mother.

The magic wrapped tighter around her shoulders, unmistakably protective. Estella's presence lingered not in flesh, but in intent.

You're not here to be held, Esther realized. *You're here to be taught.*

Esther wiped her eyes. She refused to miss a single moment. Her mother had left these memories for her.

The memory blossomed.

The transition had no edges. One moment, Esther stood in cold absence—the next, she was submerged in color and sound and living breath. The air felt heavier here, textured with the weight of choice and consequence.

This wasn't a recollection.

It was a place her mother had prepared, layered carefully so Esther could walk on it without breaking.

The realization steadied her. Whatever lay ahead, Estella had not left her unarmed.

Estella sat across from an older man in deep violet robes, one hand resting over her stomach.

"Master Aaron, I don't know what to do," she murmured. "Why do I keep having visions?"

"Unheard of… but not impossible," he muttered.

Esther drifted closer, aching at the tenderness in Estella's movements and at the protective way she touched her belly.

"I've found no records of prophetic magic," Estella said. "No guidance."

"That is because prophecy cannot be learned," Aaron said, shutting a ledger. "It is inherited. And you carry phoenix blood."

Esther felt the truth of it settle into her bones.

Not a spell. Not a discipline.

A lineage.

She glanced down at her own hands—older now, scarred, trembling—and wondered how long her mother had carried this knowledge alone. How many nights Estella had stared into the dark, knowing precisely what she would lose.

She never tried to escape it, Esther realized. *She just prepared me to survive it.*

The thought cracked something open in her chest.

Estella's breath trembled. "I can accept the healing. The fire. The... occasional resurrection accidents. But visions?"

"What do you see?"

A pause. Then—

"My daughter. And that I will not live to raise her."

Esther's breath caught.

Aaron nodded, solemn. "You cannot prevent your death. But you can prepare her."

"How?"

"The visions aren't warnings. They are opportunities. Seeds to plant now so she may thrive later."

The world rippled

Stonehaven reformed around her. Younger. Cleaner. Brighter.

Estella sat on a bench, cradling a baby in her arms. Basil stood guard, sharp and stern, rather than exhausted.

A young succubus girl with starlight hair and twitchy wings bounced beside him.

"Can I hold her?" Luna begged.

"Stop avoiding your lesson," Basil scolded.

Luna poked baby Esther's cheek anyway.

"It's important you learn to hide your talents," Estella said gently. "Power does not always need to be seen."

Esther felt the warmth of the moment, the softness in her mother's voice, the future friendship she never knew existed.

And then it dissolved.

Esther lingered in the warmth even as it faded, heart aching with the ghost of what she had never known. Basil's stern watchfulness. Luna's unfiltered affection. A version of the world where she was... cherished.

They were always there for me, she realized, *even when I didn't remember.*

The knowledge was both comfort and grief intertwined.

This wasn't just her mother's legacy. It was everyone's.

The orphanage appeared—bright, uncrowded, hopeful.

Charon, young and energetic, guided a tiny bandaged girl forward. She supported herself on crutches, pulling a limp leg behind her.

"Lyssara, this is my friend. She's here to help."

Lyssara tripped, and Estella caught her. Golden light flowed from her hands. The limp leg straightened.

Lyssara stared, disbelieving, then burst into tears. "Why?"

Esther's breath hitched as understanding settled fully.

Estella hadn't healed Lyssara because it was strategic.

She had healed her because she was there. Because she could. Because someone was hurting in front of her.

The pattern was suddenly unmistakable.

Not kingdoms first.

People first.

The realization threaded neatly into Esther's own memories—her instinct to stop, to listen, to kneel beside suffering rather than rule above it.

This was the legacy she carried most clearly.

The memory swallowed the answer as it unraveled. Esther understood anyway.

Because she healed everyone she could—knowing she wouldn't be here long enough to keep doing it.

Snow replaced everything.

Teenage Zaria sat bruised and defiant inside a cave.

"You said you can make me queen?" Zaria scoffed. "Why would I trust an enemy queen?"

"Because Draewyn and Valedara need peace," Estella said urgently. "War is coming. I've seen it."

Zaria narrowed her eyes.

"I will give you a runespire infused with my magic. Enough to survive long enough to take the throne."

"And why should I believe you?"

Estella met her glare. "Because I am running out of time. But my daughter... she must live."

Silence stretched thin.

Finally, Zaria took her hand.

Gold erupted between them.

Esther reeled as the power flared not just from its scale—but from the risk.

Estella had gambled everything on a girl who would one day become an enemy—had trusted foresight enough to believe that survival could grow from opposition.

This is what it means to rule, Esther realized. *To make alliances that hurt. To trust people who might betray you.*

The lesson burned deeper than any prophecy.

Power was not certainty.

It was choices with consequences.

And the light didn't burn. It embraced.

The memory bent—and reshaped into something new.

Esther's breath hitched as the scene shifted into a room she recognized only from descriptions: her parents' private study.

Estella sat beside her father. His jaw clenched with worry.

"Arcturus," Estella said softly, "you must arrange a marriage contract between Lupin and Kraggmar's daughter."

Esther's heart stopped at the revelation.

Arcturus frowned. "Estella, why on earth—?"

"Because," she said gently, "we will need Kraggmar's alliance. In one of my visions, war comes to our doorstep. And only Kraggmar stands with us."

"You're certain?"

"I'm certain enough."

She did not mention her death. She hid that truth with shaking resolve.

Esther pressed a hand over her mouth. Lupin was the one promised. Not her. She was never the sacrifice. She was the reason she fought so hard to prevent war. She was loved all this time.

Then—

"Mother! Father!"

A young Lupin burst into the room, terror twisting his face.

"It's Essie—she collapsed—she's not waking up—!"

Arcturus leapt to his feet. "What happened!?"

Lupin sobbed. "The maid—she brought her tea—then she—then Basil—"

The scene snapped into motion.

They ran.

The world blurred until Esther stood in the guest corridor she'd known all her life, but never like this—

Baroness Levon knelt on the floor, cradling a tiny, limp body: six-year-old Esther, unmoving in her lap.

"Please—please wake up," the Baroness begged through tears.

Basil stood nearby, drenched in blood—his own and the maid's. The maid's chest was seared open. Basil's arm hung uselessly.

"I—I stopped her," he rasped. "She—she tried to self-destruct after poisoning the princess. I saved Irene. And Lupin. But—"

His knees buckled.

Arcturus fell beside his daughter with a strangled cry.

Estella went still. The world around her faded as she knelt, staring at the tiny child who wasn't breathing.

"Arcturus," she whispered, voice breaking, "hold her steady."

He obeyed without question—because he already knew what his wife was about to do.

Estella placed both hands over little Esther's chest. Gold began to glow. Then blaze. Then rupture.

Magic tore from her like a flood.

Her phoenix fire. Her healing. Her life.

All pouring into Esther.

Little Esther's chest lit from within as her heart blazed—and crystallized into a glowing runespire.

Esther's adult self staggered, breath punched from her lungs. Her heart... was her mother's sacrifice.

Estella's body slumped. Her magic flickered like dying embers.

Her gaze shifted. Directly toward Esther. Not baby Esther. Not anyone in the past. Her.

Esther felt the gaze land on her like a miracle.

Esther froze.

The weight in the room changed—not magically, but intentionally. This part of the memory had been shaped with care, anchored so that it would hold until this precise moment.

Her mother had known—and known—that one day Esther would stand here—older, broken, afraid—and need to hear these words more than she had ever needed saving.

Esther's knees weakened.

Whatever came next would not be comfort. It would be permission.

"If you're seeing this," Estella whispered, voice echoing across time, "it means I saved you. My dear, beautiful Essie."

Her smile was weak and heartbreaking.

"Live."

And the world shattered into gold.

Esther gasped as the memory dissolved, her heartbeat thrumming with phoenix fire, her mother's sacrifice roaring in her veins.

And when the darkness of the dungeon rushed back in, only one truth remained:

She wasn't born to be saved—she was born to finish what her mother started.

41

ESTHER

How to Bear a Destiny: Let the past carve you open. Let the future stitch you shut.

"Esther!" Lucy cried, cradling Esther's head. "Are you okay?"

"You're out of shackles," Esther whispered, soaking in Lucy's warmth, the familiar scent of lavender clinging to her.

The room felt unreal, like the aftermath of a nightmare that refused to let go. Esther focused on Lucy's arms around her, on the solid truth of her breathing, grounding herself in sensation instead of panic.

The familiar scent cut through the chemical sting still clinging to her senses. Lucy. Alive.

Esther pressed her forehead briefly to Lucy's collarbone, letting herself exist there for a heartbeat longer than was reasonable. She had been alone in that darkness for too long. Whatever came next, she would not face it without anchoring herself first.

"Your friend is feral," Zaria said dryly from the opposite end of the room. Her face was decorated with fresh scratch marks.

Lucy hissed at her, curling protectively around Esther like a wounded wolf. Her wrists were raw, bloody, and one clearly dislocated.

Esther's stomach twisted. Instinctively, her magic reached out—gentle, warm, alive.

"I don't want anyone to sacrifice for my sake," Esther murmured. "Never again."

She sat up slowly, then pushed herself to her feet. Her legs wobbled; nausea rolled through her. But she felt something else too. Something deeper.

Her magic clicked into place. As her mother's spark had finally fit into the last missing groove, she finally felt complete.

The sensation was not overwhelming.

That was what surprised her.

Her magic did not roar or blaze or demand release. It settled, aligning itself with quiet certainty, as if it had been waiting patiently for this exact moment to become whole.

Esther swallowed hard.

This wasn't power borrowed from desperation. This was an inheritance accepted.

Somewhere deep in her chest, something old and aching loosened its grip.

"Why aren't the runes blocking my magic?" Esther asked, placing a trembling hand over one of Zaria's scratches. Golden warmth flowed from her palm.

Zaria didn't flinch. She leaned into the touch, allowing the healing to settle. "Same reason I could use my power," she said simply. "I sabotaged the runes the moment my brother left."

She pointed at the entrance, where the central rune was gouged straight through—split like a broken spine. Esther was impressed by how swiftly she had done it, without being noticed.

"Runes are fickle things," Zaria said, shrugging. "One symbol out of alignment, and the whole array is useless."

"Or explodes," Lucy clicked her tongue, putting herself between Esther and Zaria like a shield.

Zaria smirked. "Exactly."

Esther studied the gouged rune with new eyes. It wasn't sloppy. It was precise. The damage had been done quickly and confidently. By someone who understood exactly how much destruction was necessary and no more. Zaria hadn't panicked. She had planned.

"So," Esther said softly, hugging Lucy from behind. "What's the plan now?"

Zaria didn't hesitate. "You kill my brother. The king of Draewyn."

The room froze.

Esther's breath hitched.

Lucy's snarl vibrated through her ribs.

The torches seemed to flicker, as if recoiling from the weight of it.

Esther took a deep, shaky breath. Her fingers curled into Lucy's shirt.

The words did not echo. They sank. Esther felt them settle into her bones, heavy and immovable. This wasn't a call to arms or a rallying cry. It was an ending—brutal, final, irreversible.

Somewhere in the distance, metal rang against metal.

The war was already moving without her.

For the first time, Esther understood that refusing to choose was itself a choice—one that would cost lives she could never name, faces she would never see.

Her breath shook. This was what destiny actually felt like.

Not glory. Responsibility.

"What do I do?" she asked.

Zaria exhaled like she'd been waiting for that question.

"You let him take you," she said. "He's already on his way. The attack has begun—thanks to the alliances your mother planted. Every faction she ever touched is rising tonight. All of them will storm the castle. All of them will believe they're saving you."

"But they aren't," Esther whispered.

The image unfolded vividly in Esther's mind: a war room thick with smoke and shouting, her presence weaponized against her own people—Valedaran banners hanging limp in enemy hands.

She had always feared being used as leverage. Now she understood the cruel symmetry of it.

If she was to be used, she would decide how.

"No," Zaria agreed. "They're clearing the way for me. For peace. For what your mother wanted."

Her eyes softened. "And when my brother finds you, he'll use you as a hostage. He'll drag you into the war room. He'll gloat. He'll threaten Valedara and extort your kingdom. He'll believe you're helpless."

She stepped closer, holding up a metal band etched in runes.

"This looks like a magic suppressor," Zaria said. "It isn't."

She clicked it around Esther's wrist. Esther's magic hummed, unbothered.

"He needs to believe you're powerless," Zaria explained. "And then, when he takes you to the throne room—when he thinks he's already won—you kill him. Clean. Fast. Decisive. It will frame everything perfectly."

Lucy's voice cracked. "You're asking her to assassinate a king!"

"I'm asking her to stop a tyrant," Zaria said.

Esther's pulse roared in her ears.

My mother died to save her.

She left all these seeds so she could survive. So Valedara could survive.

Her grip on Lucy tightened.

"I'll do it," she whispered.

Lucy's breath caught. "Esther…"

The decision settled with surprising calm. Not relief. Not certainty. Just clarity.

Esther had spent her life bracing for a destiny she never wanted. Now that it stood in front of her—sharp-edged and merciless—she found that she could meet it without flinching.

This wasn't surrender. This was a choice.

Esther turned in her arms. "I'm not doing it because Zaria said so. I'm doing it because my mother saw this war. Because she gave me the chance to end it before it begins."

Lucy cupped her face, trembling. "You always jump straight into danger. It terrifies me every time."

"I'm not just jumping into danger," Esther said. "I'm choosing to protect the future she fought for."

Zaria cleared her throat. "Touching. Unfortunately, you two need to look like you've been tortured."

Lucy's eyes snapped to hers. "Come again?"

"They'll never believe I broke a princess without marks." Zaria gestured to Esther. "And I haven't bruised you at all."

Lucy and Esther looked at each other.

"Oh no," Lucy whispered.

"Oh yes," Zaria said cheerfully.

Lucy groaned. "Esther, I love you, but we're about to hit each other, aren't we?"

Esther winced. "Just a little?"

Lucy's eyes narrowed. "You smirk even once and I'm hitting harder."

"I'm not smir—ow!"

Lucy punched her shoulder.

"You said not to smirk!"

"You did smirk!"

"I smiled!"

"It was smug!"

They shoved each other, slapped weakly, pulled hair, made dramatic yelps—two idiots trying to choreograph believable torture.

Zaria watched, unimpressed. "This is... sad. But effective."

Finally bruised enough to be convincing, Esther and Lucy slumped back against the wall, panting.

The laughter faded slowly, leaving something tender and exposed in its wake. Humor had always been their shield—something they raised instinctively when the world grew too sharp. Even now, even here.

Esther leaned back against the wall, breath unsteady, and wondered if this was how her mother had survived, too.

By laughing just long enough to keep going.

Zaria clasped their shackles shut around their wrists. She paused by the door. "When the screaming starts, be ready."

Then she left.

The room dimmed. Smoke and distant clangs echoed from somewhere above.

Lucy let out a long sigh.

Esther leaned her head against hers. "Lucy? I... I'm sorry."

"For what?"

"For making you my personal maid. For trapping you in the palace with me. For... forcing you into solitude with me."

Lucy blinked, then burst out in disbelieving laughter.

"Trapped? Essie, please. I didn't want to mingle with those cold, cruel nobles. You were the only person in that palace who made me feel safe." She nudged her shoulder. "We weren't alone because of you. We were safe because of you."

Esther's chest tightened. "I love you."

Lucy rolled her eyes, cheeks pink. "Gross. Stop saying sweet things before I cry."

They sat in silence for a moment.

Silence stretched between them—heavy, but not uncomfortable.

Above them, the castle groaned—distant shouts, the faint thunder of movement echoing through stone. The war was no longer an abstract future. It was here.

Esther closed her eyes. If she didn't say this now, she never would.

Then she whispered, "Lucy... there's something I need to tell you."

Lucy tensed. "If you say another stupid thing, I swear I'll bite you."

"No," Esther murmured. "It's about... sex."

Lucy blinked. "...Excuse me?"

"It's not like in the books. It's awkward. And it hurts."

Lucy stared at her. Then gasped.

"You got laid before me!?"

"Lucy—"

"No! Unacceptable!" she raged. "I am kissing someone before I die! I don't care if he smells like cheese and works in the stables—I refuse to let you win in death!"

Esther laughed—a soft, choked, terrified little sound. But it was real. And above them, the first explosion rocked the castle.

42

NYTHIR

HOW TO LEAD AN ARMY: GATHER YOUR LOVED ONES, YOUR ENEMIES, SOME RACCOON-CODED CIVILIANS, AND PRAY.

Dawn had not yet broken, but Nythir stood as if it had. The cold wind scraped across the frozen plains outside Draewyn's ridge, tugging loose strands of hair, carrying the faint metallic smell of awakening magic. The fields were silvered with frost, the sky bruised with the promise of morning, and the earth waited beneath him as though unsure whether it was about to witness glory or disaster.

Nythir felt it settle over him like a mantle he had never asked for. They were watching him. Refugees, guild members, half-trained fighters, civilians clutching whatever weapons they had found—all of them waiting for him to decide what came next. Not because he was the strongest. Not because he was noble.

Because he hadn't broken.

The realization tightened his chest. He had led small groups before. Missions. Raids. Survival. This was different. This was raw faith—and it terrified him more than the enemy ever could.

Behind him gathered... well, not an army. He refused to call them that. Armies had discipline. Formation. Matching equipment. A shared understanding of the word *strategy*. This group had none of those things.

Instead, they had:

Orphans clutching brooms like divine weapons.

Farmers gripping pitchforks with the grim resolve of men who'd spent lifetimes fighting drought.

Women brandishing iron pans with holy conviction.

The Baroness screeching about posture.

Sylva pacing in agitated feline arcs.

Sable staring ahead with the serenity of a corpse.

Basil carving runes into the dirt while looking like he was on the verge of summoning his own grave.

If someone had told Nythir a year ago that he would lead a rescue mission for the woman he loved, accompanied by this... collection of souls, he would have punched the future for insulting him. Now he just braced himself for whatever was about to happen.

Lyssara strolled to his side, braid swinging like a weapon. "Ready to start a war with kitchen utensils?" she asked.

"No," he muttered. "But since when has readiness mattered to anyone here?"

"Never," she agreed with terrifying cheer.

Vorrik proudly held two iron pans together like ceremonial drums. "I am going to dent a king's skull with this."

"That isn't how wars work," Nythir tried, knowing full well it was pointless.

"Neither is our group," Lyssara reminded him.

He had no answer for that.

A low hum vibrated through the frost as Basil stepped away from the massive sigil he'd carved into the hardened earth. The design was beautifully complex—Draewyn circlework intertwined with ancient Valedaran calligraphy, glyphs for movement and protection layered with geometry used during emergency evacuations. Trained mages should have used it, not... this.

Basil straightened. "Everyone step inside. Carefully. Do not cross the—"

The horde surged forward immediately, trampling half the symbols. Someone dragged a pitchfork through a delicate arc. A small child dropped a spoon directly into the circle's core.

Basil made a sound that could only be described as academic heartbreak.

"Please," he begged. "For the love of every deity—do not cross the runic—"

Too late.

The magic was already out of control.

Nythir could feel it vibrating through the ground, uneven and furious, like a heart beating too fast. Basil stood at the center, eyes wild, hands glowing with sigils that refused to remain stable. This wasn't careful spellwork. This was grief given form.

For the first time, Nythir understood that whatever line they had meant not to cross had already been obliterated. There would be no retreat from this.

The Baroness swept forward, radiant with confidence and delusion. "My time to shine."

"Oh gods," Basil whispered.

She opened the golden locket at her throat and tipped Estella's stored blessing into the sigil. The entire field blazed with molten light as every relic and enchanted trinket blessed by Queen Estella awakened in a single breath.

Nythir's teeth buzzed. His vision burned white. The magic surged so violently that the frost cracked beneath their feet.

Vorrik squinted. "Is it supposed to glow this much?"

"No," Basil said.

"No," Sable echoed.

A pulse rolled through the sigil—deep, ancient, alive.

The earth split open.

And a phoenix, enormous and incandescent, tore upward in a column of gold.

Nythir stumbled back. "What—"

The phoenix tilted midair, wings arching like molten scythes, and dove straight at them.

Sylva cursed violently.

Basil tried to run.

Lyssara grabbed Vorrik by the collar. "Not like this!" she shrieked. "Not by a giant flaming chicken!"

The phoenix struck the center of the circle. Fire swallowed everything. Heat. Light. Freefall.

A roar vibrated through Nythir's bones. His stomach dropped. The world spun—

And his feet slammed into solid stone.

He gasped.

They were standing at the front gates of the Draewyn palace. Very alive. Entirely intact. Somehow not ash.

War surged around them immediately—real war, with trained soldiers shouting formation orders, Kraggmar's cavalry sweeping down the ridge in coordinated strikes, Valedaran knights charging with banners held high. Spells cracked through the air, illuminating the courtyard in flashes of violet and gold.

Hovering above the chaos in a skin-tight outfit was Luna. Wings outspread. Tail flicking lazily. Succubus charm radiating from her like perfume.

Half the guards stared at her in slack-jawed devotion.

"Hello, boys," she purred. "Put your weapons down, breathe deeply, and reassess your life choices."

Weapons hit the ground in a chorus of clangs.

Sylva stared. "She is horrifying."

Sable nodded. "She is."

And then the Baroness charged.

She glowed like a fallen star, Estella's blessing turning her into a golden comet. Her purse struck the first guard; he cartwheeled into two others. The glow rippled across the citizens behind her, blessing each movement with impossible protection.

"For Esther! For Lucy! For Valedara!" she hollered, barreling toward the palace.

Basil chased after her, horrified. "Irene! You are not a frontline fighter!"

"I am whatever I want to be!"

Lyssara stood frozen. "I want to be her when I grow up."

"Stay with her," Nythir ordered, drawing his blade. "If she dies, I'm never hearing the end of it."

The mismatched army surged forward, and the real armies faltered at the sight of civilians—not dying, not fleeing, but winning.

A Valedaran knight yelled, "Are those... bakers?"

A Draewyn guard cried, "A woman with a rolling pin just broke my shield!"

Nythir vaulted over a fallen column, silver magic flashing down his arms. A guard lunged; he deflected, countered, and cut through another. His team moved with chaotic precision.

"Lyssara, left!"

She flipped off a statue and kicked a man unconscious.

"Vorrik, stop trying to take their weapons—just hit them!"

"I am hitting them!"

A woman bit a knight's ear.

Lyssara blinked. "She just bit him."

Sylva shrugged. "He deserved it."

Sable cut down three guards in one smooth motion, clearing the path.

They reached the inner palace corridors, and the world shifted.

Draewyn's palace had always been unnerving, even in peacetime. Its architecture favored towering arches and low-burning sconces, shadows stretching long over carved stone. The walls told stories—quite literally. Painted battles and etched victories shimmered faintly as magic pulsed beneath the surface, reacting to the chaos outside.

Every portrait's eyes seemed to follow Nythir. Every step echoed like a judgment. Every breath tightened the knot inside his chest. The palace felt alive in the wrong way.

Every step echoed too long. Every torch burned too steadily, flames unnatural in their stillness. The walls drank sound, swallowing the clatter of boots until it felt as though the building itself was listening.

Nythir reached instinctively for Esther's presence, meeting only the thinnest thread. It flickered weakly at the edge of his awareness, stretched thin and smothered by hostile magic.

Fear cut sharply and immediately through his chest.

She was here. And she was running out of time.

He sprinted faster.

The air changed as they neared the throne room. It grew colder, thinner, tinged with iron and magic—the kind that settled like a weight against the ribs. Nythir felt it before he saw anything.

Esther. Her magic. Faint. Strained. Calling to him like a candle sputtering in the wind.

"Faster," he rasped, and the word scraped raw in his throat.

They rounded one final corner. A pair of heavy obsidian doors loomed, engraved with Draewyn's ancient crest—a wyvern swallowing the sun. The castle's wards pulsed over the doors like veins of light, reacting to the conflict inside.

Nythir didn't slow. He slammed into the doors with silver magic bursting up his arms, forcing them open in a shock of sound—

—and the world narrowed to a pinpoint.

The throne room of Draewyn stretched wide and cold, all sharp edges and polished obsidian. Tall windows filtered dawn light into thin, icy shards. Banners hung from the ceiling—Draewyn's black and crimson sigils, ceremonial and imposing, now torn and fluttering from the battle's vibrations.

The floor had been polished to a mirror sheen ages ago, reflecting the chaos like a second world. The throne itself was carved from blackstone, massive and jagged like a mountain peak ripped from the earth.

But Nythir saw none of it clearly.

The world narrowed to a single, unbearable point.

Esther knelt on the stone like she belonged there—shoulders squared, chin lifted in defiance even as exhaustion carved hollows beneath her eyes. Blood streaked her temple. Her hands were bare. Trembling with no sparks.

Nythir's vision blurred.

He remembered her laughing in the market. Her fingers warm in his. The way she had said his name like it anchored her to the world.

The distance between those moments and this one felt impossible. If he had been seconds later—

He shoved the thought away. Terror eclipsing rage. Not yet. Please, not yet.

A dagger pressed to the delicate line of her throat.

Nythir stopped so abruptly that Lyssara staggered behind him. His lungs strained, refusing to pull in air. Something hot and brutal cracked through his ribs, detonating across his chest.

He had imagined many ways this could have happened. He had feared worse. But nothing—not even the nightmares—prepared him for the sight of her on the ground, forced to kneel as if she were something less than divine.

His body trembled. Not from fear. From the unbearable, rising pressure of everything he had not allowed himself to feel until now.

I failed her. I wasn't fast enough. I should have been here. I should never have let her out of my sight. I can't lose her—stars, I can't—

The Draewyn king jerked Essie closer, blade digging into her skin as a bead of blood welled.

"Ah," he drawled, smirk dripping with cruelty. "The stray dog comes running."

Nythir saw red. Actual red. Magic flared behind his eyes until the world tinted crimson at the edges.

Lyssara sighed loudly as Vorrik whispered, "Oh no..."

Sylva muttered, "He's past reasoning now."

The king tilted Esther's chin with the blade. "Look how desperate you are. All of this... for a troublesome little—"

Something in Nythir snapped like a bowstring stretched too far.

Silver magic exploded up his arms—not controlled, not measured, but raw, feral, instinctive. His hands shook violently, fingers curled as if already around the king's throat.

His voice, when it came, was not loud. It didn't need to be.

"This," he said, each word trembling with rage and something far more fragile beneath it, "is the last mistake you'll ever make."

He stepped forward. Every emotion he'd shoved down for years—fear, guilt, longing, helpless love—rose all at once, choking him. His breath wavered, uneven. The weight of nearly losing her crushed him from the inside.

She could have died. She almost did. He could have arrived to a corpse.

The very thought made his vision blur.

"Essie," he whispered, voice breaking as her name ripped out of him like a prayer and a curse. He hadn't meant to say it aloud. But everything in him was unraveling, and there was no stopping it.

His knees nearly buckled under the realization: He could not do this—he would not survive losing someone he loved.

The Draewyn King pressed the dagger harder.

Esther winced.

Nythir's breath shattered. "Don't hurt her," he said, the plea raw and unprotected. "Please. Don't—"

He was trembling. Not from rage now. From something far more dangerous.

He felt Lyssara tense beside him. Felt Vorrik and Sylva draw weapons. Felt the Baroness readying her purse with lethal intent. Felt Basil's magic coil like a storm behind them.

But all Nythir saw was Essie. Her wide eyes. Her scraped cheek. Her shaking breath. The tiny drop of her blood sliding down the king's blade.

And he knew—If she died now, the world would go silent forever.

The prince of Valedara stumbled into view at the doorway, horror carved so deeply into his expression that she barely recognized him.

Lupin's voice cracked. "Esther—no—"

The Draewyn king dragged her upright by the ropes, blade biting deeper. "Drop your weapons or lose your precious princess."

Esther felt panic ripple through the room like a tremor—the soldiers, the civilians, her friends, her family.

And Nythir—

Nythir stepped forward with magic erupting around him like a star going nova.

"Let. Her. Go."

He didn't shout it. He breathed it—like a prayer breaking apart in his throat. His voice trembled. His hands shook. His eyes—those steady, gentle eyes—were full of terror.

He was unraveling.

For a heartbeat, seeing the fear in him—fear for her—almost broke her resolve.

I can't lose you.

His magic said it. His shaking breath said it. The tremor in his stance said it.

The Draewyn king snarled. "Bow, or she bleeds."

43

Esther

How to End a Kingdom: burn the problem, crown the solution, kiss the boy.

Esther's knees ached where they pressed into the polished blackstone. The cold seeped into her bones, into the bruises blooming along her ribs, into the raw strip of skin beneath the ropes binding her wrists. The dagger's edge dug into the hollow of her throat, steady as a heartbeat, hungry as a threat waiting to become truth.

She kept her breathing slow. Controlled.

If she breathed too fast, she could feel the blade bite deeper.

If she breathed too shallow, she felt her courage slipping like sand.

Inside her chest, however—

Inside her chest lived a storm.

A furious storm that slammed against her ribs, begging to burn its way out. It snarled every time the Draewyn king yanked her hair. It hissed whenever he breathed his cheap-smoke breath down her neck. It screamed every time she felt her own fear trying to rise higher than her resolve.

She couldn't let that storm loose.

Not yet.

Not until—

"Stay still, princess," the king hissed, spittle hitting her cheek. "Your armies should be arriving any moment. Let's hope they value you alive enough."

They would.

She knew they would.

And that was exactly why she couldn't move.

Her magic reached outward like frantic fingers—feeling for the signatures she loved, the ones she trusted.

She felt them.

Nythir's magic first. A pulse of silver so fierce it made her bones ache. It wasn't calm, not anymore—it crashed, wild and desperate, like lightning trying to claw its way across the plains.

Then Lucy's unhinged spark—sharp, reckless, unmistakably Lucy. Basil's was a trembling hum, frantic but determined. Lyssara's was a burning coal, simmering with fury. Vorrik's was a bonfire, crackling with enthusiasm and terrible ideas.

And many others, who she had yet to meet.

Her people.

All of them.

She felt them thundering closer.

Hold on, she told herself. *Just hold on—*

The throne room doors detonated inward.

Stone exploded. Old tapestries shredded in the blast of magical pressure. Guards were flung backwards like children's toys tossed aside.

Dust engulfed the room.

She could barely see—shapes in the haze, silhouettes rushing forward—but she could hear.

"Esther!" Lucy called.

"Nythir—stop—Ny—wait—Nythir!" Basil coughed. "Irene, do *not* go first—Irene—stop—" Basil's voice became more forlorn with each word.

"For Queen Estella!" the Baroness wailed.

"Vorrik, put that man down!" Lyssara shouted.

Esther blinked against the sting of debris as the dust parted just enough to reveal them—her mismatched army, her impossible, ridiculous collection of allies.

Kraggmar orcs barreled through the haze.

Valedaran knights cut down guards at her flanks, led by her father and brother.

The Baroness glowed like a judgmental star, swinging her purse with righteous fury.

Basil ran after her with the energy of a man watching his entire life unravel.

Sable strode forward like the final page of a prophecy no one wanted to read.

Sylva moved low and lethal, tail lashing, eyes glinting.

Lyssara's feral snarl echoed off the walls.

Vorrik swung a halberd backward—backward, why backward?—with catastrophic confidence.

Farmers and refugees stormed behind them, wielding brooms and iron pans like weapons forged for gods.

But leading them—

At the very front—

Was Nythir.

Silver magic coursed up his arms like molten starlight, bright enough to cut through the chaos. His eyes locked onto her with such fierce, unbearable desperation that her breath caught.

He looked like he was breaking.

The Draewyn king jerked her closer, pressing the dagger harder until pain flared and warm blood slid down her neck.

"Stay back!" he roared. "Valedara bows or this girl dies!"

The Valedaran knights froze. Even the orcs hesitated. Even Lucy made a strangled noise of helpless fury.

Her father stumbled into view at the doorway, horror carved so deeply into his expression she barely recognized him.

Lupin's voice cracked. "Esther—no—"

The Draewyn king dragged her upright by the ropes, blade biting deeper. "Drop your weapons or lose your precious princess."

Esther felt the panic ripple through the room like a tremor. The soldiers. The civilians. Her friends. Her family.

And Nythir—

Nythir stepped forward with magic erupting around him like a star going nova.

"Let. Her. Go."

He didn't shout it.

He breathed it—like a prayer breaking apart in his throat.

His voice trembled.

His hands shook.

His eyes—those steady, gentle eyes—were full of terror.

He was unraveling.

And for a heartbeat, seeing the fear in him—fear *for her*—almost broke her resolve.

I can't lose you.

His magic said it.

His shaking breath said it.

The tremor in his stance said it.

The Draewyn king snarled. "Bow, or she bleeds."

Esther closed her eyes.

And the world inside her changed.

She saw flashes behind her eyelids—her mother's handwriting, her mother's voice stitched into memory. She saw the children in the plaza clutching stale bread. The refugees from Kraggmar who whispered thanks as if she'd given them worlds, not crumbs. The burned homes. The dying fields. The people who'd smiled at her with hope that made her chest ache.

If she did nothing—

Draewyn would crush Valedara.

More children would starve.

More homes would burn.

More innocents would die.

And this man—this cruel, power-hungry, small-hearted king—would keep killing until someone stopped him.

Her fear dissolved into something sharper.

She didn't want to kill him.

She didn't want blood on her hands.

She didn't want to become something monstrous.

But—

It's him or my people.

It's him or Lucy and Basil and the Baroness and Lyssara and Vorrik.

It's him or Nythir.

It's him or me.

Her eyes opened.

"No," she whispered.

The word did not tremble.

That surprised her.

Everything around her was chaos—shouting, clashing steel, the roar of magic straining against stone—yet inside, something had gone utterly still. Esther felt the moment settle into place, heavy and irrevocable, like a door closing behind her.

She thought of her mother then. Not the queen. Not the legend.

The woman kneeling in orphanage dirt, hands glowing softly as she healed without asking permission.

People first, Estella had taught her without words.

Esther drew a breath.

And chose.

It wasn't defiance.

It wasn't bravery.

It was a truth she chose.

Her magic bloomed.

Heat surged beneath her skin—gold, molten, ancient. It gathered behind her ribs, swelling like a sun being forged inside her chest. It flooded into her lungs until she could barely breathe without glowing.

She didn't pull her hands free.

She didn't need to.

She exhaled.

Fire.

Golden flames erupted from her palms, her bound wrists, her hair—an inferno blasting outward in a perfect, controlled torrent.

The Draewyn king didn't even have time to scream.

One breath.

One flare of magic.

And he was ash.

His blade clattered to the floor.

His grip collapsed.

His body crumbled like a burnt page.

The silence that followed was absolute.

Not shocked.

Not stunned.

Obedient.

Esther felt the space where the king had stood—a hollow absence where oppressive certainty had once pressed down on every breath. The weight in the room shifted, recalibrating around her presence instead.

Her magic receded slightly, not extinguished, but settled—like fire banked low, waiting.

No one spoke.

No one needed to.

Esther stood alone in the center of the scorch mark, panting, hands still glowing faintly gold. Her throat stung, her heartbeat shook, but she was standing.

She had killed a king.

She didn't regret it.

But it carved something deep inside her.

The room seemed to vibrate with the impossible—fear, awe, a collective breath held.

Her father and brother were statues.

Lucy looked ready to both cry and cheer.

Sylva blinked like he hadn't expected her to go nuclear before breakfast.

The Baroness clutched her pearls, muttering, "My stars."

Basil looked halfway between horrified and proud.

And Nythir—

Nythir stared at her like she had pulled the sun from the sky and held it between her hands.

Something fierce lived in his gaze. Something fragile. Something she wanted to fall into and never climb out of.

The weight of what she'd done settled in her bones.

She had saved them.

All of them.

And she had crossed a line that she could never return from.

A beat passed.

Then—

Lucy burst through the dust like a feral gremlin. She took in the smear of ash, the charred rolling head, and gasped with unrestrained delight.

"That's what you get!" she shrieked, running up to punt the charred head like a soccer ball.

It hit a pillar. Wobbled. Fell.

Lucy threw her arms up. "I *told* you I wasn't dying without kissing a man!"

Sylva froze. "What—"

Lucy grabbed him by the shirt and kissed him like she was conquering a kingdom.

Sylva dropped his daggers. A Kraggmar orc cheered. A Valedaran knight fainted. Even the Baroness merely blinked and whispered, "Well then."

Esther almost laughed.

But she was already looking at him.

Nythir.

He didn't speak.

He didn't move.

He simply opened his arms.

Her breath shattered.

Her duty cracked.

Her composure crumbled.

Her strength flooded out of her in a single heartbeat.

She ran.

Nythir caught her mid-stride, arms wrapping around her with a force that said he had nearly lost her and would never risk it again. She buried her face in his chest, inhaling the scent of smoke and silver magic and home. His hands shook as he lifted her. His breath broke when he pressed his lips to her temple.

He kissed her like he was choosing life.

She kissed him back like she was choosing her future.

"Absolutely not!" King Arcturus shrieked.

"Esther—stop kissing that strange elf!" Lupin howled.

But Esther only kissed him harder.

Because for the first time in her life—

She was choosing her own story.

And no king living or dead could stop her now.

The throne room slowly emptied, chaos bleeding into subdued murmurs as soldiers escorted prisoners out and civilians searched for familiar faces. Lucy was still arguing with Sylva about whether her kiss counted as battlefield valor. The Baroness lectured a guard on posture. Basil looked like he aged ten years in the last twenty minutes.

But Esther barely heard any of it.

Nythir hadn't let go of her.

His grip was not crushing, but desperate—like if he loosened it even slightly, she might vanish again. She felt the tremors in his hands, the hitched breaths he tried to disguise. The way his heartbeat still galloped beneath the thin layer of calm he wore.

She brushed her fingers over the back of his hand. "Nythir," she murmured. "Look at me."

It took a moment.

When he lifted his head, she saw a crack in him—thin, hairline, but devastating. His eyes were red-rimmed, the silver still smoldering under the surface of his skin.

He opened his mouth, closed it, tried again.

"I thought—" His voice broke. He swallowed hard. "Essie, I thought I was going to walk into this room and find—"

His throat closed.

Her own heart squeezed painfully. She touched his cheek.

"You didn't," she whispered. "I'm here."

"That's not—" He shook his head and a single tear slipped free. He didn't even seem to notice it. "That's not enough explanation for what I felt. For what I—" A strangled exhale slipped from him. "I've lost people before. Too many. I know what it feels like when the world goes quiet. And I thought—stars, Essie—I thought the quiet was waiting for me on the other side of that door."

Esther's chest twisted.

She had seen many versions of Nythir—gentle, protective, furious, tender—but she had never seen him like this.

Unmasked.

Unsteady.

Barely holding himself together.

He breathed in through his teeth. "When I saw him holding that dagger to you—when I saw blood—I thought..." His voice crumpled. "I thought I was breaking."

Esther slid her hands up to cup his face fully. "Nythir. You didn't break."

"I did." His breath shuddered. "Inside, I did. But I couldn't— not in front of you—not while he still had you. I had to stay standing. I had to stay angry. Because if I didn't..." He shut his eyes like he was frightened of what he'd see. "I don't know if I would've been able to move at all."

Something inside her softened and shattered all at once.

She pulled him forward until his forehead rested against hers.

"You can break now," she whispered. "You don't have to be strong for me anymore."

His breath caught on a stutter. He bowed his head just slightly, as if his whole body sagged under the weight of relief.

And then, quietly—barely audible—

"Essie, I can't lose you. Not you. Not ever."

"You won't." She wrapped her arms around his shoulders, drawing him closer. "I'm here. I'm alive. I'm not going anywhere."

That was all it took.

His arms tightened around her, burying his face in the crook of her neck. His breath shook in her hair. His shoulders trembled.

Nythir—strong, calm, composed Nythir—finally broke.

Not loudly.

Not dramatically.

Just a silent collapse of fear he had carried alone.

Esther held him, fingers weaving through his hair, breath steady against his cheek. Her magic quieted around him, golden warmth softening the tremors in his chest.

"I've got you," she murmured. "I've got you."

His breath steadied slowly, the shaking easing.

Esther held him without thinking.

Not like someone afraid of losing him — but like someone who would not let go.

His weight sagged against her, grief and terror finally finding release, and Esther realized with a quiet, startled certainty that she was not being protected anymore.

She was the one holding the world together.

The thought did not frighten her.

It steadied her.

When he finally drew back, his eyes were clearer. Exhausted. Raw. But alive.

"Tell me," he whispered, "you're truly all right."

"I am," she promised. "Because you came."

His jaw trembled again, but he breathed out and nodded.

They leaned into each other, forehead to forehead, two survivors holding the pieces of the moment together because they refused to shatter separately.

They hadn't even reached the hall outside the throne room before her father intercepted her.

"Esther," King Arcturus said sharply.

His voice had never sounded like that—like a man standing between awe and terror, not sure which one to bow to.

He waved the others back. Even Lupin, who hesitated but obeyed when Esther gave him a soft, reassuring nod.

The king stared at her in silence.

Not at her face.

At her hands.

Still faintly glowing.

Still warm.

Esther curled her fingers. "Father, I—"

He flinched.

Not from fear of her.

From fear of what her actions meant.

He stepped closer with slow, measured movements, as if approaching something fragile and holy all at once.

"You killed him," he said quietly.

There was no judgment in his tone. Only disbelief. And something heavier.

"I did," she answered, meeting his gaze without apology.

He drew in a slow breath. "I have seen executions. I have seen war. But what you did..." He looked past her at the scorch mark staining the throne room. "That wasn't rage. That wasn't revenge. That was..." His voice crumbled. "That was a queen deciding the future of nations in one heartbeat."

Her throat tightened. "I didn't want to. I had to."

"I know." His voice cracked.

He stepped closer, searching her face for something—guilt, fear, regret. He found none. Only the shaking aftermath of sacrifice.

"Your mother once said," he murmured, "that true rulers are forged in fire. I didn't want that to be true. Not for you. Not for my little girl."

Esther's breath trembled. "Father..."

"She would have been proud." His eyes shone. "And terrified. And in awe. Just as I am."

Her composure wavered. "I don't— I don't know if I'm proud."

"You don't have to be," he said gently. "But you should know this—what you did saved your people. Saved your brother. Saved me. Saved him." His eyes flicked to Nythir, now standing quietly down the hall. "And it saved a future we didn't deserve but desperately needed."

A tear slipped down her cheek.

King Arcturus reached up, slowly, cautiously, and brushed it away with a thumb. His hand cupped her face with trembling reverence.

"I'm sorry," he whispered. "For ever doubting you. For ever underestimating you. For ever being afraid of your power, when it was the only thing that could save us."

Esther leaned into his palm. "I didn't want to be this."

"I know," he said. "But you are. And gods help me..." His voice softened. "I've never been more proud of anything in my life."

Her chest broke open in quiet grief and relief all at once. She hugged him—something she hadn't done since childhood—and he held her tightly, fiercely, like a man who had almost lost the last piece of light in his kingdom.

When she finally stepped back, he kissed her forehead.

"Whatever comes next," he said, "you won't face it alone."

She believed him.

44

Esther

How to Rebuild a Kingdom: yell first, plan later, and hold your boyfriend's hand through the entire political fallout.

The Draewyn conference hall still smelled of burnt velvet and old magic—two scents that clung to stone far longer than blood or fear ever could. Thin curls of incense drifted from sconces carved into the walls, attempting—and failing—to mask the underlying char.

The hall itself was ancient, built into the cliffside with pillars that spiraled upward like twisted trees petrified mid-reach. Runes flowed beneath the stone floor in faint lines of indigo, remnants of Draewyn's spell traditions: truth-binding, council-warding, and an old charm that made raised voices echo three times louder.

Esther suspected she would trigger that one soon. She felt the magic under her feet respond faintly to her presence.

Not flaring.

Not resisting.

Listening.

It was subtle—the kind of awareness only someone newly attuned to power would notice. The runes did not recognize her as queen, but they did not reject her either.

She took that as a warning rather than a welcome.

Draewyn would not kneel easily.

Neither would Valedara.

And somehow, she would have to stand between both.

The long table dominating the center of the hall was carved from volcanic granite, dark and glossy as a stormcloud. The edges bore knotwork symbols that represented Draewyn's older dynasties—unity, vigilance, ruthless order. They felt brittle now, as if relieved to have shed their tyrant.

Looking at them together, Esther felt the strange dissonance of it settle in.

This was not a council shaped by bloodlines or banners.

It was chaos and coincidence and stubborn survival.

People who had chosen to stay when leaving would have found it easier.

She realized, distantly, that this was what scared the old powers most.

Not her magic.

This.

Zaria lounged at the head of the table like it was a throne she'd grown up in. Luna perched across her lap, tail flicking in rhythm with Zaria's breathing, the succubus entirely unbothered by the gravity in the room. Her wings twitched with leftover adrenaline from the battle, casting shadows shaped like mischievous blades across the stone.

Across from them sat King Arcturus, stiff-backed, shoulders tense, his crown askew as though he'd shoved it on in a hurry. His face looked older—creased by a night of terror, relief, and the dawning realization that his daughter had become someone the world would bow to.

Beside him hovered Lupin, pale and twitchy, clearly reliving every moment the Draewyn king's blade had pressed to Esther's throat. His enormous half-orc fiancée stood beside him, wearing her ceremonial armor like it was jewelry. Arietta rested an affectionate hand on Lupin's shoulder; Lupin looked like he might faint from either love or fear.

On Esther's side sat the chaos that had torn through a kingdom and somehow stitched it back together.

Basil, frazzled, ink-stained, and scanning every surface as if checking for lingering curses.

The Baroness, spine straight as a blade, purse on her lap, radiating unspoken violence.

Sylva, trying very hard not to look at Lucy and failing so spectacularly it was almost a talent.

Lucy, basking in the afterglow of battlefield triumph like she had won a kiss—or a war.

Lyssara and Vorrik elbowing each other with the subtlety of stampeding oxen.

Sable, quiet as death, eyes tracking every exit and every heartbeat.

And Nythir.

Nythir sat to her right, hand wrapped around hers like an anchor. His thumb traced slow arcs against her skin, grounding her. He had not let go of her hand since they entered the hall. Not when Basil distributed treaty drafts. Not when the Baroness lectured Sylva about weapon etiquette. Not when King Arcturus cleared his throat and muttered, "Young man, that is—"

"Yes," Nythir said flatly.

"You don't even know what I was going to say," the king said, bewildered.

"Yes," Nythir repeated.

The king sighed.

Esther squeezed his hand once in apology. Nythir squeezed back: *Don't apologize for me.*

Her heart fluttered in her chest before she could stop it.

The room settled in a brittle hush, tension hanging like frost-laden branches waiting to snap.

Zaria stretched lazily. "Shall we begin diplomacy? Or shall we all continue emotionally combusting in a polite circle?"

"I already combusted twice today," the Baroness announced. "My capacity is limited."

Esther inhaled deeply, steadying the storm inside her chest.

"Good," she said. "Because I'm done being polite."

Her father stiffened as if she'd struck him.

The words settled differently than she expected.

Not sharp.

Not reckless.

True.

Esther felt something align inside her — the last lingering fracture between who she had been raised to be and who the world now required her to become.

She wasn't rejecting diplomacy.

She was rejecting silence.

"Esther—"

She stood.

Nythir's fingers tightened around hers, reassuring and fierce at once.

"I love you," she said to her father. "But I am furious with you."

Silence dropped like a falling guillotine.

Arcturus's crown tilted slightly as if even the metal had been shocked. "I know I failed—"

"It's not just about me!" The echo charm carried her voice across the hall, amplifying the quiver beneath her words. "It's about them."

She gestured toward the massive window. Beyond it, the mountains glowed with morning light, shadows pooling at their bases like spilled ink. But what Esther saw wasn't Draewyn's peaks—it was Valedara's alleys and broken market squares.

"Do you know how many children go to sleep cold?" she demanded. "Do you know how many refugees I met who were living off scraps? How many villages burned while we did nothing?"

Her father swallowed hard.

"I received reports—"

"And that is exactly the problem." Esther's voice wavered with heartbreak and fury. "You received numbers. I saw names."

Lupin shifted, looking at the floor.

She zeroed in on him. "Do you know why our alliance with Kraggmar stalled? Why we had no support? Why everything fell apart when raids began?"

Lupin flushed painfully red. "I didn't want to leave you alone."

"Exactly," Esther said. Her voice cracked. "You were so afraid to lose me that you lost them."

Arietta smirked, elbowing him. "I tried to tell you she could take you in a fight."

Lupin wilted.

Some of Esther's anger tilted toward exhaustion rather than flame.

Esther watched Lupin carefully.

He was shaking, not with fear of her but with the dawning realization that protecting someone could also mean failing everyone else.

She softened, just slightly.

This wasn't punishment.

It was trust. The hard kind that demanded growth instead of comfort.

"You love me," she said quietly. "Both of you. But while you guarded me like a fragile ornament, our kingdom starved."

Arcturus bowed his head. "I thought I'd lost you," he whispered. "I couldn't lose you again."

"Father—"

Her voice broke, but she lifted her chin anyway.

"I'm not running from this anymore. I will take the throne. Soon. Not someday. Soon."

Lupin choked on air. "Esther—are you sure—"

"You," she said, pointing at him, "are going to Kraggmar to finalize your marriage."

Arietta beamed. "We leave at dawn."

Lupin swayed like a tree in a storm. "Can we at least wait until the Harvest Festival?"

Esther turned to her father. "And you will help me. Step back as ruler when needed, but not from the work. Not until the kingdom can stand again."

"Whatever you need," he said, voice unsteady.

"Good," she said. "Because I need the truth revealed. And I need Zaria."

Zaria rose gracefully. Luna preened.

"My brother was a tyrant," she said. "But Queen Estella saw it first. She left me her magic. Her warnings. Her faith in her daughter."

Arcturus flinched.

Esther's throat tightened painfully.

"She believed in you," Zaria said softly.

"Then let's rebuild together," Esther said.

Hope rippled through the hall like warm wind breaking through a long winter.

The word *together* lingered.

Esther felt it ripple outward. Not magically. *Socially*. Like a stone dropped into still water, changing the shape of every reflection.

This was the first time she had said it without reservation.

Not *I will fix this.*

Not *follow me.*

Together meant listening and sharing blame. Letting others disagree and stay.

It terrified her.

It felt right.

"Treaties can wait," the Baroness declared. "My future husband will draft them after I confiscate every noble's purse strings."

"I—I truly don't think bloodshed is necessary for—" Basil tried.

"Hush, dear," she said lovingly.

Esther let out a breath she hadn't realized she'd been holding.

Nythir leaned closer, voice low. "You did it."

Esther looked up into blue eyes that held pride, fear, and devotion.

"No," she whispered. "We did."

He smiled, soft as moonlight.

Lucy and Sylva were arguing near the door.

"You can't just stand behind me every time someone approaches with aggressive eye contact," Lucy lectured.

"I wasn't hiding," Sylva said stiffly.

"You used me as cover."

"You have a solid tactical silhouette."

"That is not a compliment!"

"It was intended as one."

Lucy made a strangled noise.

Vorrik jogged past, carrying a ceremonial spear backward. Lyssara chased him, hissing, "Put it down before you impale a diplomat!"

"I am being careful!" Vorrik yelled, nearly stabbing the wall.

Sable glided after them in grim silence. "If either of you causes an incident, I will not hide the bodies."

They quieted immediately.

Zaria and Luna intercepted Nythir as he and Esther stepped into the corridor.

"Well, well," Luna purred, wings fluttering. "Look who's glued to someone."

Nythir didn't flinch. "Not glued. Anchored."

Esther's heart did an unfair leap.

"Aww," Zaria teased, "did you almost lose her?"

Nythir's jaw tightened. Esther squeezed his hand.

"Almost," he said quietly. "And I won't again."

Zaria and Luna exchanged a knowing look but didn't push.

Basil had taken over a side table with treaty drafts, maps, and ink pots. Irene hovered over him, pointing with disciplined fury.

"These headings are crooked."

"They are perfectly aligned."

"They are spiritually crooked."

"That is not a measurable unit."

"It is when I say it is."

Basil exhaled.

Esther watched it all.

The chaos.

The hope.

The strange, mismatched group that would stand beside her in rebuilding a kingdom.

For once, the disorder didn't feel like something to manage.

It felt alive.

Esther realized, with a quiet start, that this was what peace actually looked like. Not silence or stillness. Motion without terror.

She had spent so long believing leadership meant control.

Now she wondered if it meant *trust*.

Her kingdom.

For the first time, it didn't feel like an inheritance or a burden.

It felt like a promise.

When the meetings finally ended and the chaos drifted toward other hallways, Nythir guided Esther to an alcove overlooking Draewyn's cliffs. The wind brushed her hair back, cold and clean, carrying the scent of pine and old frost.

"Breathe," Nythir said, his voice soft.

Esther did.

Her shoulders released.

Her pulse slowed.

"You were brilliant," he murmured.

"I was angry," she said.

"Both can be true." His thumb brushed her cheek. "You're allowed to feel all of it."

She swallowed. "I killed a king."

"You saved a kingdom."

She closed her eyes. "I'm scared of who I'm becoming."

Nythir leaned his forehead against hers. "Then let me be there as you become her."

Her breath shook.

She didn't pull away.

The future pressed close around her, vast and unfinished.

There would be councils that hated her. Nobles who tested her. Decisions that followed her into sleep.

Esther did not feel ready.

And for the first time, she accepted that readiness might not be required.

Tomorrow, they would return to Valedara.

Tomorrow, the kingdom would demand everything from her.

Tonight, she let herself lean into the warmth of the man who had nearly broken when he thought he'd lost her.

Tonight, she would rest.

And she would not spend it alone.

45

Esther

How to Go Home: fix your kingdom, claim your love, and kiss him like he's the future you chose.

Valedara's castle looked different when Esther returned.

Not physically—its towers still cut the sky, its stones still wore centuries of history—but emotionally.

It no longer felt like a cage.

It felt like a responsibility. A promise.

A home she intended to rebuild with her own two hands.

She felt the air shift as she crossed the drawbridge—the faint hum of old magic buried deep in the foundations. Her mother's magic had once threaded through every hall; now it lingered like dust motes waiting for sunlight. The castle wasn't dying, but it was tired. Waiting.

I'll wake you up again, Esther thought.

The thought settled into her chest with quiet certainty.

This place had been built to endure sieges, betrayals, centuries of fear and compromise. But endurance was not the same as care.

Esther brushed her fingers lightly against the stone as she passed, sensing the faint echo of magic deep within the walls—not broken, just neglected. Like a song half-remembered.

She had left this castle as a girl, afraid of being trapped.

She returned as someone who understood that staying could be an act of courage.

The castle guards gawked openly as their small army marched through the gates. Zaria rode beside them on a borrowed horse, Luna perched behind her like they were sewn together.

Esther riding at the head of a glowing, mismatched warband was apparently not something court etiquette classes had prepared them for.

Lucy waved proudly.

Lyssara shouted at guards to *move*, unintimidated by armor or rank.

Vorrik challenged three knights to an arm-wrestling contest before he even got off his horse.

Sylva smoldered handsomely.

Even the royal stables froze at the sight of two massive orcs trying to ask where to put their borrowed war beasts politely.

Watching them all spill through the gates, Esther felt something warm and startling bloom in her chest.

This wasn't an army shaped by doctrine or banners.

It was stubbornness. Loyalty. People who had chosen each other repeatedly when the world offered easier exits.

She wondered if this was what real power looked like—not something inherited, but something gathered slowly, through trust and shared survival.

The old court would never understand this.

She smiled at the thought.

Nythir rode at Esther's side.

Closer than propriety allowed.

Close enough that every shift of their horses brought their knees brushing.

Close enough that her pulse quickened whenever he glanced at her.

He still hadn't let go of her hand. Not once.

Lucy noticed and smirked.

Sylva noticed and *glowered*.

"Don't say it," Lucy whispered sweetly.

"I didn't," Sylva replied. His tail snapped sharply behind him.

"You were thinking it."

"I—"

He pressed his lips together like he'd swallowed a confession.

Lucy beamed like she'd won a duel he didn't know they were having.

We're not done, his glare said.

Try me, her grin answered.

The throne room doors opened, and the court rose to their feet—older nobles trembling, advisors gasping, younger knights muttering confused prayers.

King Arcturu entered first, with a strong, demanding presence.

"My daughter has returned. With allies. With victory. And with the strength Valedara has always needed."

When he stepped back to let her speak, she realized:

He trusts me.

He's proud of me.

He's terrified of losing me again.

The ache hit deep.

The realization carried weight.

Not the brittle trust of obligation or bloodline—but something quieter and more frightening. Trust born of watching her fall, fail, and rise again anyway.

Esther straightened her shoulders.

She could feel the court's eyes on her, measuring, recalibrating.

Let them.

She was done shrinking to fit their expectations.

Esther moved to the center of the dais.

She spoke clearly, firmly, unapologetically: about rebuilding Valedara, about long-neglected citizen needs, about unity with Draewyn, about the oath she was stepping fully into.

Each accusation felt familiar.

Too young. Too emotional. Too dangerous.

Esther recognized them all—echoes of arguments her mother had faced, sharpened by time and fear. The difference now was that Esther could feel the truth of them without being ruled by it.

She did not rush to defend herself.

She listened.

And when she spoke, she did so from certainty rather than defiance.

"She is not fit for the throne!" one noble seethed.

"I am not," Esther agreed, shocking the assembly. "That is why I am allowing my father to continue his reign until I am ready."

A wave rippled through the room—confusion, disagreement, begrudging respect.

Almost all the council nobles had a complaint about Esther being named crown princess. But with each complaint, she responded calmly. Her mother had shared so many memories with her that had prepped her for this.

Esther's mind was flooded with a lifetime of council meetings where her mother argued with nobility and fought for change. Where she carved out a legacy—one Esther was now continuing.

Slowly, no one had any more complaints.

How could they? Esther was glowing.

Not magically—emotionally.

Decisively.

Like a queen.

Through it all, she felt Nythir at her back like a shield, steady as moonlight.

Lucy and Sylva lingered near the steps, whispering furiously.

"They're afraid of her power," Sylva murmured.

"They should be," Lucy said proudly.

"You worry me," Sylva replied.

"You should be flattered."

"I—what?"

Lucy patted his cheek. "Don't think too hard. You'll sprain something."

Sylva's ears flattened, tail snapping indignantly—but beneath it, an amused rumble slid up his throat.

When the council dismissed, when the last formal bow had been made, when the castle finally quieted—

The throne room slowly emptied, leaving only the echo of footsteps and the lingering warmth of victory. Advisors shuffled out in dazed silence, guards bowed awkwardly at the sight of her glowing in her new role, and nobles whispered frantically about "the winds of change" as though she couldn't hear them.

When the last of them vanished down the corridor, King Arcturus exhaled a breath he must have been holding since the day she disappeared.

He stepped toward her, lowering his voice.

"Esther," he said. "You were... extraordinary."

She blinked. "I just spoke the truth."

"No." He shook his head, emotion softening the hard lines in his face. "You spoke like a ruler. Calm when challenged. Steady when provoked. Your mother used to do that. She—"

His voice wavered.

Esther reached for his hand.

He flinched—just slightly, caught off guard—before gripping her fingers tightly. "I was a coward," he murmured. "I didn't know how to raise you without... losing you. When you were taken, I thought the gods were punishing me."

She swallowed. "Father, no—"

"I'm proud of you," he said. "Terrified. But proud."

The words hit harder than she expected.

Esther had faced monsters, kings, and prophecy without flinching—but this almost undid her.

She had wanted this for so long without realizing it.

Not approval.

Understanding.

Nythir stood a respectful distance away, but the moment her shoulders tensed, his stance changed—subtle, protective, ready to intercept any pain.

Arcturus noticed.

His gaze hardened—not threatening, but the unmistakable glare of a father evaluating the man who held his daughter's heart.

"You," the king said, addressing Nythir with the gravitas of thunder. "Elf."

Nythir straightened. "Yes, Your Majesty."

"You kept her alive."

"Yes."

"You would die for her?"

"In a heartbeat."

Esther's breath hitched.

The king studied him with the intensity of someone who'd spent decades weighing threats and allies. Then his posture eased.

"Good," Arcturus said. "Because I nearly had a stroke when you walked in holding hands."

Esther's face turned crimson.

"Father!"

He shrugged. "I'm adjusting. Slowly."

Before Esther could respond, the throne room doors slammed open.

Lupin stormed in like a blizzard with a sword.

Literally *with* a sword.

"Who do I have to fight?" he demanded, scanning the room. "Who touched my sister? Who endangered her? Who even breathed near her with malicious intent? I'll end them."

"Lupin—" Esther sighed.

He gasped dramatically and rushed to her, cupping her face as though checking for invisible injuries.

"Esther, your hair is different. Your aura is different. Your entire soul feels different. What happened? Blink three times if you've been cursed by dark magic."

"I'm fine," she said.

"She's glowing," Nythir murmured, unable to stop the smile tugging at his lips.

Lupin whipped around.

"You." He pointed at Nythir. "Back up. Don't smile at her. Don't breathe on her. Don't—did you hold her hand? You held her hand, didn't you?"

Esther: "Lupin, please."

Lupin slid between them like a human barricade.

"I knew it. He's corrupted you with his elvan allure."

"That's not a thing," Nythir said gently.

"Oh, it is," Lupin snapped. "I read about it in a pamphlet titled *Elves: Should We Be Concerned?*"

Esther pinched the bridge of her nose.

King Arcturus sighed. "Lupin. She's alive. She's safe. And she's choosing her own path."

Lupin deflated slightly... then squared his shoulders again.

"But I reserve the right to duel anyone who breaks her heart."

"Noted," Nythir said. "But unnecessary."

Lupin squinted at him, then—begrudgingly—offered his hand.

"You hurt her," he warned. "I unleash my entire moral support network."

"...Your *what*?" Nythir asked.

"My emotional devastation will haunt you for years."

Esther groaned.

Nythir shook his hand anyway.

And something eased inside her—her family wasn't perfect, but for the first time, it felt like a future she wanted.

After saying goodnight to her father, after Lupin loudly threatened anyone who even *looked* at her wrong, after Lucy dragged Sylva away by his ear, the castle finally stilled.

Quiet.

Breathless.

Soft with the promise of peace.

Nythir stepped toward her, voice low.

The castle had quieted around them, settling into a rare, fragile stillness.

Esther realized she wasn't bracing for the next disaster.

For the first time, she allowed herself to exist in the aftermath. Allowed herself to feel the exhaustion, the joy, the grief, and the relief without trying to organize it into duty.

She turned toward Nythir, already knowing she would follow him anywhere.

"Come with me."

Her heart tripped over itself.

She followed.

They went to her chambers—quiet, dim, moonlight spilling through the window like a blessing.

She closed the door behind them.

Nythir turned toward her, expression unguarded, vulnerable, fierce.

"You nearly died," he said softly.

"So did you," she whispered.

He stepped closer until their breaths touched.

"I don't want to be apart anymore," he said. "Not for a mission. Not for politics. Not for fear. Not for anything."

Esther's heart thudded. "Nythir…"

He reached up, gently brushing a thumb over the faint burn mark on her collarbone. She could have healed it.

He could have healed it.

But she wanted to keep it as a reminder—a scar she would wear with pride.

"You scared me," he said. "Not because you were in danger—though you were—but because I realized something I should've said a long time ago."

She swallowed. "And what's that?"

"That I am in love with you," he murmured. "Utterly. Hopelessly. Permanently. I don't care if you're a fugitive or a queen or the girl who fell on me in the woods. I want you."

Esther felt her heart drop into her stomach and rise into her throat at the same time.

She stepped closer. "Then take me."

His breath hitched.

"Essie—"

She pulled him down into a kiss.

It wasn't frantic like before, Draewyn.

It wasn't desperate, or rushed, or fueled by impending doom.

It was steady.

Warm.

Full of a future, she finally allowed herself.

He kissed her back. Slow at first, then deeper, unhurried with intent. His hands framed her face as though he needed to memorize every inch of her. Esther curled her fingers in his shirt and tugged him closer, until there was no space left to doubt, until she could feel his heartbeat thrum hard and certain against her own.

The world softened around them.

Her body melted into his without thought or fear, instinct guiding her where courage once had been. His mouth traced a reverent path down her jaw, lingering at the corner of her lips as if reluctant to leave them, then lower. He kissed her throat. Across the pulse he'd spent too many nights afraid of losing.

Her gasp broke the quiet.

Nythir shuddered at the sound, a low, helpless breath leaving him as his grip tightened around her waist, grounding and possessive all at once.

"Essie," he murmured, voice rough now, nothing careful left in it.

"Nythir," she breathed back, fingers sliding up to curl at the nape of his neck, holding him there.

He rested his forehead against hers, eyes closed, breath uneven. "Tell me what you want."

She didn't hesitate. "You," she whispered. "Tonight. Tomorrow. Always."

Her hands went to the fastenings of his tunic. He went to the laces of her dress. There was no fumbling, only a shared, silent urgency. The heavy fabric of his tunic whispered to the floor. Her dress followed, a pool of dark blue at their feet. The cool air of the chamber kissed her skin, raising goosebumps, but his gaze was hotter than any fire.

He looked at her, standing in only her thin shift, and the raw hunger in his eyes stole her breath. "You're beautiful," he said, the words a hoarse truth.

His hands settled on her hips, calloused thumbs stroking the delicate skin just above the line of her undergarments. *Every nerve ending there sang.* He lowered his head and kissed the scar on her collarbone, his tongue tracing the mark with a reverence that made her whimper.

He guided her backward toward the bed, his mouth never leaving her skin. He kissed a trail down her sternum, over the swell of her breast through the linen, his hot breath seeping through the fabric. Her head fell back. Her fingers tangled in his dark hair.

"Off," she pleaded, tugging at the fabric of her shift. "Please."

He obliged, pulling the garment up and over her head in one smooth motion. The cool air hit her bare skin, but only for a second before his warmth replaced it. He stared, his gaze drinking her in, and the sheer intensity of his focus was its own kind of touch. Then his mouth found her breast.

Oh, stars.

His lips closed over her nipple, and a sharp, electric pleasure shot straight to the apex of her thighs. He suckled, firm and insistent, while his hand cupped her other breast, kneading, his thumb circling the peak until it was a hard, aching point. She cried out, her hips bucking against nothing, a desperate, empty feeling coiling low in her belly.

He switched sides, lavishing the same attention on her other breast, and her legs trembled. She felt the hard length of him pressed against her thigh, and the knowledge that he was as undone as she was sent a fresh wave of heat through her.

"Nythir," she gasped, her hands scrambling for the waistband of his trousers. He helped her, unfastening them and pushing them down his hips, kicking them away.

Then he was bare against her. Skin to skin. The feel of him, solid and hot and *his*, was almost too much. He was beautiful—all lean muscle and sharp lines and the faint, silvery tracery of old scars that told stories she'd learn later.

He lay her back on the bed, coming over her, bracing his weight on his forearms. He kissed her again, deep and consuming, and she could taste herself on his lips, a salty, intimate tang. His thigh pressed between hers, and she moaned into his mouth, grinding against the hard muscle, seeking friction.

He broke the kiss, his breath ragged against her cheek. "Essie, I need to... I need to feel you."

"Yes," was all she could manage.

He shifted, his hand sliding down her stomach, over the quivering plane of her belly, lower. His fingers brushed through the soft curls, and she jerked. He stroked her, a light, teasing touch that made her whimper.

He slid a finger through her slick folds, circling the sensitive nub at the apex. Her back arched off the bed. *A sharp, perfect shock of pleasure.* He did it again, a little firmer, and her vision swam.

"Please," she begged, not even sure what she was asking for. "Please, Nythir."

He positioned himself at her entrance. He looked into her eyes, his gaze holding hers with an anchor's weight. "Look at me," he whispered.

Then he pushed inside.

It was a slow, inexorable, *blissful* stretch. He was careful, letting her body adjust, but the fullness was overwhelming. She gasped, her nails digging into his shoulders. He was buried to the hilt, and for a moment, they both just stayed there, joined, breathing each other's air, hearts hammering in unison.

He began to move.

A slow, deep withdrawal, then a thrust that rocked her into the mattress. *It was everything.* The friction, the heat, the sheer *rightness* of it. Each stroke lit a new fire inside her. He found a rhythm, deep and steady, each thrust brushing against a spot inside her that made stars burst behind her eyelids.

"Right there," she sobbed, her heels hooking behind his thighs, pulling him deeper. "Don't stop."

He wouldn't. He was relentless. His pace increased, his thrusts growing harder, more urgent. The slap of skin on skin filled the quiet room.

She could feel the tension coiling tighter and tighter inside her, a spring wound to its breaking point. His mouth found hers again in a messy, open-mouthed kiss as he drove into her, over and over.

His hand slipped between their bodies, his fingers finding that aching nub again. A few precise circles was all it took.

The climax shattered her.

It ripped through her with a violence that was pure ecstasy. Her body clamped around him, wave after wave of intense, pulsing pleasure that stole her breath and her sight. She heard her own cry, raw and unfiltered, as she shattered.

Feeling her clench around him, he let out a broken groan, his rhythm faltering. "Essie... I can't..."

He drove into her once, twice more, deep and hard, and then he went rigid above her. A hot flood spilled deep inside her, and he collapsed against her, his face buried in her neck, his whole body shuddering with the force of his release.

They lay tangled, breathless, sweat-slicked. He was still inside her, and she never wanted him to leave. His lips brushed her shoulder, then the scar on her collarbone again.

"Mine," he whispered, the word a vow against her skin.

"Forever," she answered back with a kiss.

46

Esther

How to Harvest: gather grain, gather donations, and gather the horrified expressions of wealthy nobles realizing generosity is now mandatory.

Esther had only three days after her return to usurp the Harvest Ball and Festival completely.

The leaves were browned at the edges. The air was cool—crisp enough to sting her lungs when she stepped onto the balcony. The city below seemed to breathe with her—slower now, but steadier.

Fewer smoke plumes from burned homes.

More lanterns in windows.

More lines outside bakeries—not because there was nothing, but because there was finally something worth lining up for.

The Harvest Festival banners had already begun to appear on the streets. Traditionally, they meant one thing:

A week of feasting for the nobility.

A single night of opulence in the palace ballroom.

And the faint, bitter hope that some scraps would trickle down to the people.

Esther stared at the banners and felt her jaw tighten.

Not this year.

Not anymore.

The council chamber smelled of ink and old arguments.

Esther sat at the head of the table—not on the raised throne, but in a plain chair beside it. Her father had insisted on the throne. She had insisted on the table.

"We have always held the Harvest Ball in the palace," one noble droned, flipping through his notes. "Invitations, performances, a seven-course meal—"

"For nobility," Esther said.

He faltered. "Well. Yes. That is how it is done."

"How it *was* done," Esther corrected.

Murmurs rippled around the table.

King Arcturus sat to her right, watching quietly, letting her speak. Lupin hovered beside Arietta on the other side of the room, trying to look supportive and mostly looking like he wanted to faint.

Esther folded her hands on the table. "This year, the Harvest Festival will be held in the city. In the lower plazas and market streets. No ballroom. No private feast."

Several nobles blanched.

"The people have barely survived raids and famine," she continued, voice firm. "We are rebuilding. We cannot celebrate while pretending they don't exist."

"That's not how this works," a countess said tightly. "The Harvest Ball is a tradition."

"So is ignoring starving children," Esther said. "We're ending at least one of those."

A few councilors drew back as if she'd slapped them.

Her father's mouth twitched—the ghost of a proud smile he quickly hid behind his hand.

Esther continued before they could regroup. "We will use what we already budgeted for the Harvest Ball—but instead of crystal chandeliers, we're funding food, shelter repairs, and winter supplies. The festival will be open to everyone. Free meals at the crown's expense, funded in part by a new initiative."

There it was—the word that would cause trouble.

"Initiative?" one baron repeated suspiciously.

"A Harvest Tithe," Esther said. "Every noble house in good standing with the crown will contribute—food, coin, or materials—proportionate to their estates."

Gasps, sharp as snapping twigs.

"You can't force us to—" someone began.

"You're right," Esther said pleasantly. "I can't force you to care about the people whose labor built your estates and keeps your tables full."

A few lowered their gaze.

She let the silence stretch, then added calmly, "But I *can* decide which families are in good standing with the crown. Which families receive future trade licenses. Which families receive palace contracts and legal protections. Which families receive invitations to coronations, weddings, and state banquets."

Baroness Levon, seated further down the table, smiled slowly like a cat watching a canary walk into a room unescorted.

"So to remain in the crown's favor," Esther finished, "you must demonstrate that you care about more than your own vaults. Publicly. Generously. Consistently."

"That sounds like extortion," grumbled one noble.

"That sounds like accountability," the Baroness said sweetly. "And an excellent opportunity to improve your reputations. Just imagine your names on plaques, darling. *'House So-and-So: Hero of the Hungry.'*"

Several nobles perked up at that.

"House reputations have been strained of late," another muttered. "An association with the rebuilding efforts would help…"

Esther fought the urge to roll her eyes. If they wouldn't move for compassion, she'd drag them by vanity.

Arietta leaned toward Lupin and whispered—not quietly enough—"Your sister is terrifying. I like her."

Lupin made a faint squeaking noise.

King Arcturus cleared his throat. "I support the crown princess in this," he said. "We let things rot for too long. It is time our Harvest Festival reflected what we want this kingdom to be—not what it used to be."

That took the last of the fight out of the room.

Slowly, hesitantly, nobles began to nod.

The Baroness patted her gloves and sat forward. "I will organize the ledgers," she said. "We'll list each house's contribution publicly, of course. It would be a shame if someone forgot and saw their name under *'Absent.'*"

A chill of social terror swept the nobility.

Esther allowed herself a small, satisfied smile.

"Good," she said. "Then let's begin planning the biggest Harvest Festival Valedara has ever seen."

They took over the war room for festival planning.

Lucy pinned color-coded scraps of parchment to a massive map of the city, humming off-key. Sylva stood beside her, arms folded, tail twitching as he watched her plan chaos like a general.

"This plaza for the food stalls," Lucy said, jabbing at the map. "This street for games. The orphanage can run the pie stand. The refugees can sell whatever crafts or skills they have. Oh! And a stage here for performances."

"Performances?" Sylva asked warily.

"Music. Storytelling. Maybe a goat juggling act if Vorrik gets too excited," Lucy said.

Sylva grimaced. "I will not protect the city from goat-based incidents."

"You say that now," she said cheerfully.

Lyssara leaned over the table, tracing patrol routes with a fingertip. "We'll need guards at every entry point. And runners between districts. If someone tries to use the crowd as cover for theft or worse…"

"We'll catch them," Sylva finished, nodding. "I'll set up vantage points."

"If you climb on a roof and glare down at people," Lucy said, "half the city will propose marriage and the other half will assume they're being judged by an angry forest deity."

Sylva opened his mouth, then shut it again, unsure how to argue with that.

Arietta sauntered in, followed by a lumbering Vorrik carrying a crate of festival games.

"We bring Kraggmar traditions," she announced. "Stone-lifting competition. Tug-of-war. Wrestling pit."

"And one event where you chase a greased boar," Vorrik added enthusiastically.

"That's a *Vorrik-specific* creation," Arietta sighed.

"No," Esther said.

He looked offended. "But it's good for community."

"I am drawing the line at greased livestock," she said. "We compromised on the goat."

Lucy perked up. "There's a goat?"

"Later," Esther said quickly.

Basil sat in a corner with four ledgers and six ink pots, muttering to himself as he calculated supply lists.

"We require... twelve additional grain shipments. Expanded soup cauldrons. Reinforced tables. And seven extra healers if we allow arm wrestling near sharp objects."

"We're not allowing sharp objects," Esther said.

Basil flipped a page. "Then four extra healers."

The Baroness glided in like she was arriving at a ball instead of a logistics meeting. She no longer wore the extravagant silks she had once been so proud of—her garments were more practical now, though still brightly colored.

"I have spoken to half the noble houses already," she said. "Most of them are tripping over themselves to be seen as generous. The rest will follow when they realize jewelry donations are going out of fashion and philanthropy is the new trend."

"That was fast," Esther said.

The Baroness smiled. "Fear and fashion are powerful tools, dear. You simply gave me both."

Esther looked around the room.

Her people.

Her chaos.

Her impossible, miraculous second chance to do something real.

For the first time, her magic felt... steady. Heavy in her bones, but not like a burden. Like fuel.

"This isn't just about one festival," she said quietly.

Everyone fell silent.

Esther's gaze dropped to the map. "This is our first promise—that as long as the crown stands, no one in Valedara will be forgotten. Harvest is not just for those who already have plenty. It's for those who almost lost everything."

"Refugees, orphans, the outer villages," Lucy said softly.

Esther nodded. "If the nobles want to stand beside the throne, they stand beside *them*."

Sylva's voice was low. "And if they don't?"

"Then they can enjoy their harvest from far, far away," Esther said. "Without our protection. Or our name."

Basil, of all people, smiled—small and sharp. "I look forward," he said, "to updating the registries."

The day of the Harvest Festival arrived crisp and bright.

Banners fluttered from every balcony, not just the wealthy districts. Everything was hastily thrown together—but beautiful.

The central plaza thrummed with life.

Refugees from burned border villages ran food stalls, serving stews and flatbreads made from recipes no one in Valedara had tasted before. Orphans handed out hot rolls from baskets bigger than they were. Nobles—actual titled nobles—ladled soup side by side with blacksmiths and dockworkers, their silks protected by aprons they clearly didn't know how to tie.

Music drifted on the air—fiddles, drums, a flute someone had rescued from a pawn shop.

Children shrieked with laughter as they bobbed for apples. Vorrik refereed a wrestling pit with more enthusiasm than sense.

"This is chaos," Lupin muttered, standing beside Esther at the edge of the plaza.

"It's beautiful," Esther said.

He glanced at her. "You're really not going to let us hide in the palace this year, are you?"

"Nope."

He sighed. "Arietta volunteered us for the tug-of-war contest."

"Of course she did."

"She says it will 'build goodwill,'" he continued mournfully, "and 'show that my arms are not purely decorative.'"

Esther stifled a laugh. "She loves you."

"I fear that she does," he said gravely—then brightened. "But she also frightens me, so it's balanced."

Esther's gaze swept the crowd again.

There were still gaps—thin faces. People were not yet ready to trust that this wasn't some cruel trick.

But there was also something she hadn't seen in a long time.

Hope.

Lucy bounded up, cheeks flushed, a smear of icing on her nose. "Update: the pie stand is a hit, and Sylva is terrifyingly good at catching people trying to sneak extra portions."

Sylva appeared behind her, arms folded. "We have rules."

"They're hungry," Lucy countered.

"We made more pies," he said. "They can simply get back in line."

"You're being very responsible today," she said thoughtfully. "It's unsettling."

He opened his mouth to argue—then shut it as a small child tugged on his sleeve.

"Excuse me," the beastkin child said, staring up with huge eyes. "Mister fox, sir? There's a man over there who says he donated lots of money, but his wrist smells like lies."

Sylva blinked. Slowly turned. Tracked the direction of the pointing finger.

Across the plaza, a richly dressed lord was bragging to a cluster of onlookers near the public donation chest.

"Ah," Sylva said. "Thank you."

The child beamed and scampered away.

Lucy leaned in. "Go get him."

Sylva's lips curved into a dangerous, pleased line. "With pleasure."

Esther watched him stride across the plaza like a polite storm.

Beside her, the Baroness approached, holding a ledger.

"Report?" Esther asked.

"Most houses contributed generously," the Baroness said. "A few tried to fudge their numbers."

"And?"

"I let Sylva talk to them," she said, "and reminded them their names would be inscribed—accurately—on the public donors' wall outside the palace."

Esther smiled. "And the refugees?"

"Several have already received job offers," the Baroness said. "Some from nobles who once claimed refugees were bad for business." Her eyes sparkled. "Turns out compassion is good for reputation *and* profit. Who knew?"

Esther exhaled slowly.

The plaza glowed in late-afternoon light. Lanterns were being checked and lit. Children sat on the steps, sharing sticky pastries. A group of orphans danced in a circle around Vorrik, who pretended to be slain by a particularly fierce six-year-old with a wooden sword.

This was what she wanted. Not perfection. Not instant miracles. A start.

Someone tugged at her sleeve.

She turned to find an older woman, clothes patched but clean. A little girl peeked from behind her skirts.

"Your Highness," the woman said, voice trembling. "I just wanted to say... thank you. My boys ate until they were full. I don't remember the last time that happened."

Esther's throat closed.

"I should have done it sooner," she said honestly.

The woman shook her head. "You're doing it now. That's more than most."

The little girl stepped forward, clutching something in her fist. "This is for you," she said.

She opened her hand.

In her palm sat a tiny woven bracelet made of bright thread and a single, imperfect bead.

Esther's vision blurred.

She knelt, bringing herself eye level with the girl. "May I wear it?" she asked.

The child nodded fiercely. "Then everyone will know you're our princess too."

Esther tied the bracelet around her wrist with shaking fingers.

"I already was," she whispered. "But now I'll make sure they see it."

As the woman and child disappeared back into the crowd, someone slipped a warm hand into hers.

Nythir.

He smelled like mint and the faint metallic tang of magic.

"You turned a party into a revolution," he murmured.

"I turned a party into what it should have been all along," she said. "It's not enough. Not yet. But it's a start."

He glanced at her wrist—at the little bracelet beside the burn mark on her collarbone he'd kissed so reverently every night.

"It's more than a start," he said. "It's a promise. And you keep your promises, Essie."

She leaned into him, letting herself rest for a moment in the steady line of his body.

"In Stonehaven, we have a saying for nights like this," he added.

"Oh?" she asked. "What is it?"

He smiled. "When the harvest is shared, the winter is kinder."

Her chest loosened. "I like that."

"I like you," he said.

Her cheeks heated. "We are in public."

"We are," he agreed, utterly unbothered.

She laughed.

The sun dipped, lanterns flared, and the city settled into an evening of music and full stomachs.

This Harvest Festival of Valedara would be remembered for years—not as the year the nobility wore the finest silk, but as the first year no one in the capital went to bed hungry while the crown feasted.

Esther squeezed Nythir's hand, feeling the little woven bracelet dig lightly into her skin.

"Next," she said, half to herself, "a wedding."

Nythir's eyes warmed. "I'll be there."

She looked out over her people—her kingdom—bathed in lantern light.

For the first time, the future didn't feel like a distant dream or a looming threat.

It felt like something she was already building, one choice at a time.

She leaned into him, letting the noise of the festival blur into something distant and warm.

Lantern light flickered across his features, softening the edges the world so often tried to sharpen.

Nythir's thumb brushed slowly over the back of her hand, a small, intimate motion that sent awareness skittering through her body far more effectively than any grand gesture could have.

"You did this," he murmured, low enough that only she could hear. "All of it."

"We did," she corrected, though the praise made her pulse quicken.

His gaze dropped to her wrist—to the little woven bracelet nestled beside the marks of battles survived and promises kept. Something dark and tender crossed his expression.

"I like that they claimed you," he said quietly. "That you let them."

Esther tilted her head, studying him. "You sound jealous."

"I am," he admitted readily. "But not in the way that matters."

He stepped closer, just enough that she could feel the heat of him, the steady strength beneath his calm. His hand slid to her waist—not possessive, not demanding—simply there, grounding her.

"This," he said softly, "is what you choose to carry."

Her breath caught.

She reached for him without thinking, fingers curling into the front of his tunic the way they had the night before—sure now, unafraid. He inhaled sharply at the contact, eyes darkening, attention narrowing until the world truly did fall away.

"Careful," he murmured, lips brushing the shell of her ear. "If you keep looking at me like that, I'll forget we're surrounded by half the city."

"Then forget," she whispered.

His answering smile was slow and dangerous.

He kissed her—not hurried, not hidden—just deep enough to make her knees soften, just restrained enough to promise more later. The crowd faded into heat and breath and the solid truth of him against her.

When he pulled back, his forehead rested against hers, their breaths mingling.

"Tonight," he said quietly. "After they've eaten. After the lanterns burn low."

Her pulse leapt.

"Yes."

The word carried everything: exhaustion, hope, want, certainty.

He kissed her once more, gentler this time, as though sealing it.

When they turned back toward the festival, Esther felt different—not lighter, not finished—but complete—claimed in more ways than one.

She squeezed his hand, feeling the future tighten into focus.

One kingdom rebuilding.

One promise kept.

And later—when the city finally slept—a future queen and the man who loved her, alone together, choosing each other again.

47

NYTHIR

How to Prepare to Be King: panic quietly, fail publicly, persevere anyway.

Nythir had faced assassins with less dread than this.

He stared at the parchment in front of him, jaw tight, quill hovering uselessly above the page. The words *Treaty Ratification Procedures* swam slightly, as though they were actively trying to escape his comprehension.

He did not blame them.

"This is a trick," he muttered.

Lyssara, seated far too comfortably across the table, didn't even look up from her tea. "It's a signature."

"It's a weapon," Nythir said flatly. "Why are there three places to initial? Why does one of them require a seal? Why is the seal a phoenix?"

Vorrik leaned back in his chair, boots propped against the wall like a man who had never once worried about governance in his life. "Because kings like cool things."

"I am not cool," Nythir said.

Sylva, perched near the window with a dagger he absolutely did not need indoors, glanced over.

"Lie."

Nythir shot him a look. "I am not."

Sylva's ears flicked. "You want to be."

"I want to survive the week."

That earned a laugh from Vorrik—a loud one. The kind that suggested this was the best entertainment he'd had since the war ended. In the history books, the battle at Draewyn would be written as a groundbreaking war between three nations. In truth, it had been the strangest culmination of individuals ever led by a woman with a purse.

The room they'd trapped him in was a sunlit study tucked away in the quieter wing of the castle. It smelled faintly of old books, wax polish, and impending doom.

Three days.

Three days until the wedding.

Three days until he would stand beside Esther in front of the entire kingdom and promise to be something he had never trained for, never planned for, and never wanted.

Except that she wanted him there.

Except that she chose him.

That was the problem.

The door opened, and Nythir's soul withered a little more.

A court tutor entered, arms laden with books and scrolls, expression kind in the way of someone about to ruin his day.

"Lord Nythir," the man said cheerfully. "Shall we continue?"

Nythir closed his eyes. "Define *continue*."

Two hours later, Nythir was certain his soul had left his body.

He had learned: how to bow correctly (apparently there were *degrees*), which fork to use at a diplomatic table (why were there six?) and that saying the wrong title could technically start a war.

He had also learned that Lyssara found all of this *delightful*.

"Again," she said, watching him attempt a formal greeting. "Slower. You're supposed to look dignified, not like you're bracing for impact."

"I *am* bracing for impact," he hissed. "If I mess this up, Essie will—"

Sylva cleared his throat.

Nythir froze.

Sylva tilted his head slightly. "Fear."

Nythir exhaled. "Yes. Obviously."

"It's loud."

"Can you *not* announce my emotional state to the room?"

"I can," Sylva said mildly. "I am choosing not to."

Vorrik leaned forward, eyes gleaming. "Say the line again."

"No."

"Come on."

"I refuse."

"'It is my honor to—'"

Nythir stood abruptly. "I have killed men for less."

Lyssara smiled sweetly. "You're doing this because you love her."

That stopped him cold.

The room quieted, even Sylva's dagger pausing mid-spin.

Nythir ran a hand through his hair, breath unsteady. "I know."

"She loves you," Lyssara continued gently. "Which means she is trusting you with something terrifying. Not power. *Presence.*"

Vorrik nodded once, uncharacteristically serious. "You don't have to be perfect. You just have to stay."

Nythir swallowed.

That was harder than fighting.

The next lesson involved dancing.

He had foolishly hoped that this would be optional.

The instructor clapped once. "A king must be able to lead his partner."

Nythir stared at the floor. "She leads me."

Lyssara coughed to hide a laugh.

Sylva did *not* hide his.

They placed Nythir in position, corrected his posture, and counted the steps. Left. Right. Turn.

He tripped.

Vorrik applauded.

"Again," Lyssara said.

He tried again.

This time, he didn't trip—but he did spin too fast and nearly collided with a side table.

Sylva caught him by the collar.

"Balance," Sylva said. "Also—panic."

"I am not panicking."

Sylva's ears twitched. "Lie."

Nythir groaned and pressed his forehead briefly to Sylva's shoulder. "I would rather face another army."

"Can arrange," Vorrik offered.

Lyssara shot him a look.

By the time they released him, dusk had crept into the room, casting everything in gold and shadow. Nythir sagged into a chair, exhausted in a way that had nothing to do with physical exertion.

He thought of Essie—probably navigating another council conversation with grace and fire, probably handling ten problems at once without breaking stride.

He would stand beside her.

Even if he shook.

Even if he messed up the bow.

Even if he hated every fork at the table.

"I'll do it," he said quietly.

Lyssara's expression softened. "We know."

"For her," he added. "And for you. And for this ridiculous kingdom."

Vorrik grinned. "That's my future king."

Sylva tilted his head, considering. "Fear has lessened."

Nythir huffed a tired laugh. "Give it time."

As they rose to leave, Nythir glanced back at the abandoned parchment on the table. *Treaty Ratification Procedures* stared back, smug and unreadable.

He squared his shoulders.

Three days.

He could survive three days.

After all, he was marrying the woman he loved.

And that, terrifyingly, felt worth everything.

48

ESTHER

HOW TO GET MARRIED: HOPE FOR A PEACEFUL CEREMONY AND PREPARE FOR CHAOS.

Weeks later, the palace gardens bloomed out of season—like they had forgotten how to obey the calendar.

Roses, lilies, and wildflowers spilled over stone borders in a riot of color. Vines curled up trellises in soft green spirals. Tiny golden motes drifted in the air when the breeze shifted, the last echoes of Estella's magic woven through the soil. If Esther listened closely, she could almost hear her mother humming along with the rustling leaves.

It felt like the garden itself had dressed up for her wedding.

Esther refused extravagance.

"No gold fountains," she told the planners as they hovered nervously around their sketches. "No silk carpets or diamond chandeliers."

Their quills stuttered to a stop.

"What do you want, Your Majesty?" one asked hesitantly.

Esther looked out over the garden, where staff and volunteers hurried about. Orcs argued cheerfully with bakers about oven space. Children chased each other between the hedges. Lanterns were being strung from tree to tree.

"A wedding everyone can attend," she said. "Food for the people. No waste. I want them to feel like they're celebrating with us, not watching from a distance."

Relief and confusion mingled on the planners' faces, but they bowed and hurried away to adjust their plans.

And so they placed long wooden tables instead of gilded ones, with simple lanterns strung overhead. White cloths fluttered in the breeze. Clay cups and mismatched plates lined the surfaces, already waiting for whatever dishes the guests would bring.

Children ran barefoot between the benches.

Farmers brought their best breads and preserves.

Orcs roasted entire boars in pits at the far end of the garden, smoke curling in the air.

Knights tuned their old instruments, testing strings and valves as if their armor had always come with sheet music.

Esther watched it all come together and felt her heart swell almost painfully.

This was not the kind of wedding she had been raised to expect.

It was better.

It was hers.

"Why is there bleating?" she asked aloud.

Lyssara, standing beside her with her arms folded, sighed deeply. "Because Vorrik."

Esther turned.

Vorrik strode into the garden like he was entering a battlefield, proudly carrying a fluffy white goat in his arms. The goat wore a flower crown and what looked suspiciously like tiny leather shoes.

"Vorrik," Esther said slowly. "Why do you have a goat?"

He grinned, tusks flashing. "This is the wedding goat."

The goat bleated, tried to bite his tie, and then twisted to headbutt Lyssara in the hip. The little bells on its shoes jingled with violent enthusiasm.

Lyssara hissed and rubbed her side. "If that creature touches me again, I will turn it into a very festive stew."

"You roast my goat," Vorrik replied gravely, "you roast a family heirloom."

Lucy popped into view from behind a stack of pastry boxes, eyes bright with delight. "Why is it wearing shoes?"

"These are ceremonial hoof covers," Vorrik said, scandalized.

The goat stomped, bells ringing again.

Sylva, standing a few steps away, went rigid.

"No," he said quietly. "Absolutely not. Remove it."

The goat rotated its head, locked eyes with Sylva, and let out a challenging bleat.

Sylva instinctively stepped behind Lucy. "Keep it away from me."

"You are taller," Lucy said, amused. "Why am I your shield?"

"Because you are sturdier in spirit," he muttered.

Lucy's smile turned smug. "I'll accept that."

Esther pressed her fingers against her mouth to hide her laugh. Her nerves hummed under her skin, but the absurdity helped.

The Baroness swept into the garden at that moment, skirts flaring, hair impeccably arranged. She took three elegant steps, caught the edge of a stone, stumbled, flailed, and then straightened as if nothing had happened.

"No one saw that," she announced.

"We all saw that," Lucy said.

The Baroness chose not to hear her. She pushed forward, eyes shining as she looked Esther over.

"Esther, darling, you look radiant—and also vaguely like you might faint," she said. "Excellent. Bridal perfection. Let me see the dress again."

Esther glanced down. Her dress was simple, cream, soft, and light, the fabric flowing when she moved. Golden thread traced phoenix feathers along the hem and bodice, climbing like flames that chose to rise instead of consume.

"It is perfect," the Baroness said firmly. "Understated, symbolic, flattering. Your mother would be proud."

Esther's chest ached in a good, painful way. "I hope so."

The Baroness's expression softened. She reached out and adjusted a loose piece of hair beside Esther's face.

"She would be more than proud," she said. "She would be unbearable about it."

Lucy stepped close and clasped her hands. "I would like to formally report that you are the prettiest person in the garden and I am offended."

"You look beautiful too," Esther said.

"I know," Lucy replied.

A familiar quiet presence drifted in at the fringe of the chaos.

Basil had arrived.

He wore formal robes that still somehow made him look like he should be holding a stack of books. His eyes were sharp, taking in the arrangement of runes in the garden beds and the subtle glow of protective magic around the gathering area.

"Basil," the Baroness said, seizing his sleeve. "Tell me you handled all the magical safeguards. If anyone sets themselves on fire trying to light a lantern, I will simply lie down and never rise again."

"I have layered protections over the entire area," Basil said. "No uncontrolled fire, no stray lightning, no accidental explosive bursts."

Lucy raised a hand. "What about controlled chaos? Asking for a friend."

"If that friend is you," Basil said, "there is no spell strong enough."

Lucy gasped. "Was that... a joke?"

His mouth twitched. "An observation."

Sylva stepped closer, holding a small velvet pouch in his hand.

"Esther," he said. "I brought something for you."

She turned toward him, curious. "You did?"

He opened the pouch and poured a few smooth, pale stones into his palm. They glowed faintly in the sunlight.

"Moonstones," he said. "For clarity. For protection. Us foxes give them at important thresholds. New journeys. New oaths."

Esther's eyes stung. "They are beautiful."

He hesitated, then offered one. "Keep it with you. Just in case Lucy's bad decisions spill over."

"Excuse me," Lucy said. "My decisions are excellent."

"Your results are questionable," Sylva replied.

Lucy elbowed him lightly. "You're being sweet. Don't ruin it."

"I am not being sweet," he said. His tail betrayed him by flicking in a pleased rhythm.

Esther closed her fingers around the stone, feeling its cool weight settle against her palm.

"Thank you," she said softly.

He dipped his head once and stepped back.

For a moment, the noise of the garden faded. Esther looked around at the people bustling through the space—knights stringing lanterns, children sneaking early sweets, orcs arguing lovingly over seasoning, the Baroness lecturing a table arrangement as if it had offended her honor.

This was her life now.

Not the lonely, quiet halls she had once wandered.

Not the frightened, suffocating version of the palace she had grown up in.

Alive. Messy. Loud. Hers.

Her heart raced.

"Lucy," she whispered. "What if I trip? What if I forget my vows? What if I say the wrong thing? What if Nythir changes his mind halfway through the ceremony and just runs into the forest and becomes a hermit or something?"

"Esther," Lucy said, taking her shoulders. "Deep breath. Again. There. Good. One: if you trip, I will also trip so they think it's a performance. Two: your vows are simple and you wrote them. Three: if Nythir runs away, Sylva will track him, Vorrik will tackle him, Lyssara will drag him back, and I will throw cake at him until he repents."

Esther huffed a laugh. "That is not comforting."

"It should be," Lucy said. "You are terrifyingly loved."

From the other side of the garden, a small commotion rose. The ceremonial officiant had arrived and, according to whispers, had already walked into a low-hanging branch, apologized to it, and then tried to bless a squirrel.

The squirrel had not been impressed.

Basil rubbed his temples. "I am beginning to regret agreeing to work with living people."

"You say that every day," the Baroness replied.

"Yes," Basil said. "And I am always correct."

Before Esther could spiral any further, the noise around her shifted. A ripple of awareness passed through the gathered guests. Musicians readied their instruments. Children were shushed. Lanterns burned a little brighter.

Her father was approaching.

King Arcturus walked across the garden in formal robes. They were not heavy with jewels or ostentatious gold. They were well-made and dignified, with phoenix feathers subtly embroidered into the sleeves. His crown sat steady on his head, but his eyes were anything but calm.

They were bright. Wet at the corners.

He stopped in front of her and just looked at her.

For a long, full moment, he did not speak. His gaze traced her face, her dress, the phoenix feathers that matched his. Something in his expression crumpled and rebuilt itself all at once.

"You take after her," he said hoarsely.

"My magic?" Esther asked.

"Your stubbornness," he said. Then he smiled—small and aching. "And your way of making everything look brighter simply by standing in it."

Her throat closed around a rush of feelings she could not name fast enough.

"I always thought," she said quietly, "that you did not want me in the middle of things. That you wanted me hidden away."

"I wanted you safe," he said. "I did not know how to do that without locking you in a box. I was wrong. And when you were gone, I realized that all my careful distance did nothing. I had already lost you, and I had never properly held you."

He reached out and, with a hesitation that hurt to see, cupped her cheek.

"Let me hold you now," he whispered. "At least this once—when it matters like this."

She leaned into his palm and nodded.

"I am proud of you, Esther," he said. "Terrified. But so proud I do not know where to put it."

Tears stung behind her eyes. "I wanted to hear that for so long."

"I wanted to say it for just as long," he admitted. "Your mother handled the soft words. I handled the frightening ones. It seems you learned to do both."

He offered his arm.

"May I walk you to your future?"

She slipped her hand through his arm. "Please."

The garden hushed.

Music began, soft and hopeful.

They stepped forward together.

The aisle was not a narrow strip of red carpet—it was a path between tables, lined with people.

Children holding armfuls of flowers. Elders leaning on canes. Guards standing at attention. Farmers in their best shirts. Orcs who tried to stand still and failed, swaying with the music instead.

As she walked, the sights blurred with her tears. She did not see faces as individual shapes but as one warm, living tapestry. These were the people she had chosen. The people she had almost died for. The people she would keep fighting for.

Her father leaned in just enough for her to hear him.

"You are not walking away from me," he said softly. "You are walking toward everything you deserve. That is all I have ever wanted for you, even when I did a terrible job of showing it."

Esther pressed her forehead briefly against his shoulder.

"Thank you," she whispered. "For staying. For trying. For being here now."

His hand on hers tightened.

Ahead, at the end of the aisle, Nythir waited.

He wore formal clothes of dark fabric and silver accents—understated but impossibly flattering. His hair was neatly tied back, his pointed ears adorned with simple metal cuffs. He looked like a prince by accident, and nothing about him had ever looked more right.

His eyes found hers and widened with wonder, like he was seeing the sunrise for the first time.

Esther's heart felt too big for her ribcage.

When they reached him, King Arcturus exhaled a shaking breath. He took Esther's hand and placed it carefully into Nythir's waiting grip.

"Take care of her," he said.

Nythir's fingers closed around hers, steady and sure. "With everything I am," he replied.

The king nodded once. His chin trembled. He turned and stepped aside, taking his place among the guests.

Esther and Nythir faced each other.

Everything else faded into the background color and sound.

Her hand fit perfectly in his. His thumb brushed the back of her knuckles—a tiny, grounding touch that said he was there, that he was not going anywhere, that this was real.

The officiant spoke, but Esther barely heard the words. Blessings, unity, shared futures, the magic of vows—they washed over her like distant waves.

When it was time, she and Nythir turned their hands so their fingers wove together.

The vows were short. They had written them that way on purpose. Truth did not need many words.

"I choose you," Esther said, her voice clear despite the tightness in her chest. "In duty. In chaos. In fire. In peace. Always."

"I choose you," Nythir answered, his eyes shining. "Even when it terrifies me."

Half the crowd cried.

The other half cheered.

Lupin shouted threats.

Lucy fainted dramatically, dropping backward with perfect theatrical timing. Sylva lunged and caught her before she hit the ground, muttering about fragile humans while staring at her as if she had personally hung every star in the sky.

Lucy peeked one eye open. "Did I fall gracefully?"

"No," he said. "But you fell."

"I will take it," she replied, then sat back up in time for cake.

The officiant said something ceremonial, but neither could pay attention to the words. They only listened when they heard their cue that allowed them to finally kiss.

And when they kissed, the lanterns flickered brighter, warmth swelling through the garden. The phoenix stitching on Esther's dress glimmered like ember-light. The motes of Estella's magic in the air seemed to dance.

Their magic resonated—not exploding, not flaring—but settling into the same quiet hum.

Like two notes that had always belonged to the same chord.

It felt, impossibly, like the kingdom itself approved.

Music flooded the space. People leapt to their feet, clapping and shouting. Children tossed petals. Someone—probably Vorrik—let out a victorious roar. The wedding goat tried to eat a tablecloth.

Later, as the night settled and the stars blinked awake, the long tables were covered in crumbs and empty plates. Lanterns swayed gently overhead. Laughter drifted on the cool air. Someone began a slow song, and couples swayed on the grass.

Nythir lifted Esther into his arms, holding her like she weighed nothing. She looped her arms around his neck and rested her head against his chest, listening to the steady beat beneath his ribs.

They slipped away from the main celebration, heading toward the quieter paths of the palace.

"The best decision I ever made," Esther whispered into the fabric of his coat, "was falling on an elf."

Nythir's arms tightened around her.

"Then I will spend the rest of my life," he murmured into her hair, "making sure you never regret it."

Behind them, the lanterns glowed, the garden bloomed, and the kingdom celebrated.

Ahead of them, the future waited.

EPILOGUE: LUCY

How to Accidentally Become Important: join a guild and get adopted without consent.

The Golden Phoenix Guild had been alive for exactly twelve days, and already Lucy was convinced it would one day kill her.

Not metaphorically.

Actually.

Physically.

Emotionally.

Possibly spiritually.

The office she worked in—her office now—was the size of a ballroom, stacked with maps, missions, magical paperwork (which was somehow worse than regular paperwork), and five separate piles labeled DO NOT TOUCH by Basil.

The new guild headquarters on palace grounds was gorgeous in a "this will absolutely burn down once Vorrik tries to cook" sort of way. Its halls were filled with clashing personalities:

Esther: hyperfocused and glowing with newfound leadership energy.

Nythir: calm, quietly sharpening knives in a way Lucy tried not to overthink.

Lyssara: already threatening to eat the nobles who filed incorrect paperwork.

Vorrik: building bunk beds and yelling motivational compliments.

Sylva: Absolutely not here for Lucy (he insisted).

Also, Sylva: literally here because of Lucy (everyone insisted).

Life was good.

Chaotic, exhausting, and constantly on the verge of an accidental explosion—

But good.

Lucy was halfway through rewriting a recruitment form for the fifth time (why did it need three signatures and a magical blood oath? Who made this? Oh, right—Basil) when a knock rattled the open office door.

Lupin burst in—dramatic, wild-haired, sword in hand as if responding to a national emergency.

"Lucy!" he barked. "You're summoned to the king's office!"

Summoned.

By the king.

Her brain stopped. Her soul briefly left her body for snacks.

"Did I—did I do something?" she asked.

"Yes," Lupin said gravely. "You existed within fifty feet of my father."

"That's illegal?"

"It is now," he muttered. "Because he's in a mood. Come on."

Before she could fully panic, Esther sprinted into the office like a distraught duckling.

"Lucy! I tried to save you!" she wailed, flinging her arms around her.

"Save me from what!?"

"The king," Esther sobbed. "He wouldn't tell us why he summoned you! Nythir thinks it's paperwork manipulation. Basil thinks it's arcane punishment. Vorrik thinks you're finally being offered a duchy—"

"I don't want a duchy!"

"See?" Esther cried. "She doesn't want a duchy! Father!"

From behind her, Sylva appeared silently, which she hated.

"Lucy," he said, tone steady but tail flicking. "If he harms you, I will—"

"Yes?" she asked, hopeful.

"—file a formal complaint."

"...Really?"

"And then kill him," Lupin added.

"That too," Sylva said with a nod.

Esther sniffled loudly. "We'll wait outside the office door like emotional support gremlins."

Lucy inhaled sharply, squared her shoulders, and marched toward the king's study.

She had faced starvation, kidnapping, political warfare, and the Baroness's etiquette critiques—She could handle one king. Probably.

Lucy pushed open the door—

And froze.

Inside stood the Baroness Irene Levon.

In a simple white dress.

Not elegant. Not glamorous. Simple, pure, and soft.

Beside her stood Basil in a beautifully tailored formal suit.

Behind them sat King Arcturus at his desk, looking like life had defeated him roundly and repeatedly.

Lucy blinked.

"...Did I die?" she asked.

"No," King Arcturus said bleakly. "But I might have."

Basil cleared his throat—quiet, dignified, and somehow sounding like an owl swallowing a mouse.

"Lucy," he said. "We have... news."

The Baroness beamed. "We got married!"

Lucy's jaw dropped so fast it nearly cracked against the floor. "You— You what?"

"Married," Basil repeated, adjusting his tie awkwardly. "Just now. By the king. Who is... coping."

King Arcturus groaned softly into his hands.

Lucy pointed at the Baroness. "But— But you— You're in WHITE!"

"I know!" the Baroness said happily. "I look darling."

Lucy pointed at Basil. "And YOU—!"

"Yes," he said with an uncharacteristic smile. "Apparently I do, too."

Lucy stared between them, trying to understand.

"Wh—why am I here?"

"Oh!" Irene clapped. "Because we've adopted you!"

Lucy screamed.

Not loudly.

Not fearfully.

Just a very long, spiraling scream of existential dismay.

King Arcturus winced.

"You're what?" Lucy shouted.

"Your new parents," the Baroness said proudly. "Baroness Irene Levon and Sir Basil Levon—oh stars, that sounds so good."

Basil nodded, looking as though he was analyzing the structural integrity of the moment.

"We thought it appropriate," he added. "Since Irene can not have children—"

Lucy choked. "Oh—Okay—We're just dropping more lore like it's nothing—"

The Baroness nodded graciously. "It's why I never married before. Well, that and I was hopelessly in love with Basil, and he was busy suffering in the archives."

Basil blinked. "Accurate."

King Arcturus looked at Lucy with the dead eyes of a man who had been emotionally overwhelmed for too many consecutive hours.

"So," he said flatly, "by the authority vested in me, et cetera et cetera—Lucy Levon, you are now Baroness of Rosewick."

Lucy's soul re-exited her body.

"I'm a what?" she shrieked.

"Baroness," her new mother repeated proudly.

"Against my will?"

"That's how the best titles happen," the Baroness said.

Lucy pinched the bridge of her nose, inhaling deeply. "But—but what about heirs? Land? Responsibility? Taxes? What if you two have a miracle baby?"

"Oh, sweetheart," Irene said gently. "Even if that were to happen, you are our daughter. And our heir."

Basil added, "We'll be traveling for quite some time during our extended honeymoon. Therefore, you will… manage things."

Lucy felt dizzy.

"I—I can't be a Baroness. I'm barely functional. I've screamed twice today!"

"Yes," Basil agreed. "You will improve."

She staggered backward.

Esther slammed into her the second she exited.

"Lucy! You're alive!"

Lupin leaned dramatically on his sword. "Blink twice if he harmed you."

Sylva stood closest, ears angled forward, tail still.

Lucy stared at the group. Then declared: "I'm a Baroness."

Esther froze.

Lupin screamed.

Sylva blinked very slowly, like trying to confirm reality with his retinas.

Vorrik burst around the corner holding the goat from the wedding. "We celebrate! With goat!"

"No goat," Lucy whispered weakly. "No more goats."

Sylva stepped forward, expression unreadable.

Quietly, privately, he said,

"You're still Lucy."

"Baroness Lucy Levon," she corrected faintly.

A pause.

His tail flicked.

"I liked you better before the title," he said honestly.

She glared. "Well, I didn't ask for it—!"

"I know." He hesitated. "But... I'm glad you're staying with the guild."

Her heart did something unsanctioned.

"...You are?"

"Yes," he said simply. "Very much."

Lucy swallowed.

Then:

"I outrank you now."

Sylva huffed. "Stars help us all."

But he smiled—small and real.

And Lucy, new Baroness of Rosewick, accidental noble, secretary to the Golden Phoenix Guild, and chaos incarnate—Smiled back.

Her new life had begun.

Her story, too.

And she had the very distinct feeling that Sylva was going to be an *extremely complicated* chapter.

About the Author

Dionna lives in a rural town in Western New York, where she writes cozy romantasy filled with heart, hope, and just enough mischief to keep things interesting. Though she released her debut novel at the age of thirty, she has been an author at heart since childhood. She creates stories where chaos and tenderness coexist, and where found family and healing take center stage.

When she is not writing she can be found at home with her multiple pets, possibly watching anime or playing Magic the Gathering with her partner. She will *always* be found with some sort of caffeinated drink in her hand.

www.ingramcontent.com/pod-product-compliance
Lightning Source LLC
LaVergne TN
LVHW041654060526
838201LV00043B/432